"I KNEW YOU WOULD COME TO ME," VANNAH SAID.

"God help me, I tried to resist you, but—" His voice failed him.

Tonight, no man could resist Vannah. The moon bathed her in cool white light, bleaching the paleness of her long, flowing hair even further. A sudden gust of wind caught at her batiste dressing gown with greedy fingers, pulling it away from her while at the same time pressing the nightgown beneath even closer to her slender form, outlining her full breasts.

It was more than a man had a right to bear. Martin felt a surge of desire greater than any he had ever known, and with a groan of surrender, he reached for her. . . .

Ø SIGNET BOOKS
SURRENDER TO LOVE

(0451)

- ☐ **MY BRAZEN HEART by Kathleen Fraser.** She was already love's prisoner, even before the soft velvet and rustling silk fell away to reveal her milk-white flesh. Here was the man she had waited for... He was the one she must possess forever, no matter what the risk...(135164—$3.75)

- ☐ **ENCHANTED NIGHTS by Julia Grice.** Sent to Hawaii as punishment for rejecting two of the most eligible bachelors in Boston, proud and beautiful Celia Griffin found the intoxicating atmosphere was teaching her how to be a woman rather than a lady... especially when she fell under the spell of the most notorious man on the islands—handsome Roman Burnside. (128974—$2.95)

- ☐ **JOURNEY TO DESIRE by Helen Thornton.** Delicate ambers and gold tinted Laurel's silky hair and sparkling eyes. Inflamed by the lovely innocence of this beautiful American flower, the debonair Englishman pursued her eagerly, first with camelias and kisses, then with a wild passion. His sensuous touch dared her to become wanton in his arms. (130480—$3.50)

- ☐ **DEVIL'S DAUGHTER by Catherine Coulter.** She had never dreamed that Kamal, the savage sultan who dared make her a harem slave, would look so like a blond Nordic god.... He was aflame with urgent desire, and he knew he would take by force what he longed to win by love. (141997—$3.95)

Prices slightly higher in Canada

Buy them at your local bookstore or use this convenient coupon for ordering.

NEW AMERICAN LIBRARY,
P.O. Box 999, Bergenfield, New Jersey 07621

Please send me the books I have checked above. I am enclosing $_____ (please add $1.00 to this order to cover postage and handling). Send check or money order—no cash or C.O.D.'s. Prices and numbers are subject to change without notice.

Name_____

Address_____

City_____ State_____ Zip Code_____

Allow 4-6 weeks for delivery.
This offer is subject to withdrawal without notice.

To James Webster Glenn:
Laughter is the best medicine

PUBLISHER'S NOTE

This novel is a work of fiction. Names, characters, places, and incidents either are the product of the author's imagination or are used fictitiously, and any resemblance to actual persons, living or dead, events, or locales is entirely coincidental.

NAL BOOKS ARE AVAILABLE AT QUANTITY DISCOUNTS WHEN USED
TO PROMOTE PRODUCTS OR SERVICES. FOR INFORMATION PLEASE
WRITE TO PREMIUM MARKETING DIVISION, NEW AMERICAN LIBRARY,
1633 BROADWAY, NEW YORK, NEW YORK 10019.

Copyright © 1986 by Leslie O'Grady

All rights reserved

SIGNET TRADEMARK REG. U.S. PAT. OFF. AND FOREIGN COUNTRIES
REGISTERED TRADEMARK—MARCA REGISTRADA
HECHO EN CHICAGO, U.S.A.

SIGNET, SIGNET CLASSIC, MENTOR, PLUME, MERIDIAN AND NAL BOOKS
are published by New American Library,
1633 Broadway, New York, New York 10019

First Printing, April, 1986

1 2 3 4 5 6 7 8 9

PRINTED IN THE UNITED STATES OF AMERICA

Passion's Fortune

LESLIE O'GRADY

A SIGNET BOOK

NEW AMERICAN LIBRARY

Author's Note

Of all the sources consulted about the life and work of Louis Tiffany, two were invaluable; *Louis C. Tiffany: Rebel in Glass* by Robert Koch, and *Tiffany Windows* by Alastair Duncan.

Prologue

New York—1873

SHE HAD ELUDED Gerrold's spies at last.

As she stepped down from the hansom cab and paid the driver, she kept her head down, her face concealed by the voluminous folds of her hood. It was imperative that no one recognize her, for there must be no witnesses to tell where she had gone. She nervously glanced up and down the narrow street and was relieved to find it deserted except for a solitary carriage parked against a high snowbank some distance away.

She shivered and her teeth started chattering, for it was bitterly cold. In a moment of weakness she wished she had worn the luxurious Russian sable cape Gerrold had bought her in St. Petersburg instead of her maid's thin woolen cloak, so harsh and scratchy against her soft, smooth skin, so ineffectual against the numbing cold. But she banished the heretical thought immediately. The fur cape, like her countless Worth gowns and Tiffany jewels, belonged to her former life with Gerrold and had no place in her future. She would come to her lover unencumbered by furs or diamonds, a clean canvas ready to be transformed into his masterpiece. Her hand unconsciously strayed to her midsection. She needed him now more than ever.

She stood there, listening to the cab rattle down the

street toward Seventh Avenue, and she knew her life was about to change forever; there was no turning back now. The die was cast, and she had no regrets, only bright, wonderful dreams and hopes for the future. As she breathed deeply she smelled the unmistakable tang of snow on the air, and when she glanced up at the darkening winter sky, she noticed with some fear that it was the flat, leaden gray that always warned of heavier snows to come. The streets of New York City would become slick and unpassable and all trains would be delayed. She bit her lower lip nervously and beseeched the impending storm to hold off just until she and Alastair made good their escape.

Alastair . . . Whenever she thought of him, she became so overwhelmed by the awesome magnitude of their love that her spirit soared, free and unfettered. Her deep unhappiness ceased to exist, and as soon as he held her in his arms, their hearts beating as one, she would know paradise. She wanted everyone in the world to share her exultation, her blinding joy.

Then she shook herself. What was she doing, standing here daydreaming, when her true love was eagerly waiting for her to come to him? The house was dark and quiet, except for a solitary, lit window guiding her like a beacon to the topmost floor. All other shades were tightly drawn. So his landlady's family was not at home. Trust Alastair to see to it that there would be no witnesses to their flight this evening.

She hurriedly climbed the steep, slippery steps, opened the front door with her own key, and darted inside.

By the time she reached Alastair's studio on the top floor, she was slightly out of breath, and her heart was pounding wildly, more from anticipation than from exertion. She stood there for a moment to compose herself before meeting Alastair and telling him her exciting, wonderful news.

Then she walked up to his door, knocked softly, and opened it with nary a creak. "Alastair?"

The moment she stepped inside and removed her cloak, the hairs on the back of her neck rose in warning, like hackles, and a feeling of dread welled up from the pit of her stomach. Something was wrong. She sensed danger. Instead of being bright, warm, and alive with the reassuring sounds of Alastair softly singing "Oh, Susannah" or muttering to himself as his work progressed, the cavernous studio was shadowy, cold, and quiet. Deathly quiet. Only the pervasive odor of turpentine lingered like overpowering perfume, pungent in her nostrils. But Alastair was not here; otherwise, he would have filled and brightened the room with his presence.

As her eyes traversed the room she saw a lamp glowing in the window facing the street, the light she had seen when she'd disembarked from the cab—the light that made her assume that Alastair was here, waiting for her.

A sudden rustling noise caused her to start, and she realized that she was not alone. There was a man seated in the shadows out of the lamp's range, his back toward her as though he were waiting for someone.

She swallowed hard and threw a nervous glance back at the door. There was still time for her to flee before she was discovered.

Too late. The man stirred. "Ah, there you are, my dear. I've been expecting you."

She recognized the voice at once, and it reverberated through her brain like a death knell. The blood came to a halt in her veins, and she felt the mindless terror of a trapped animal staring up the barrel of a hunter's rifle, awaiting the explosion and oblivion.

"Gerrold. What—what are you doing here?"

He rose, turned, and slowly crossed the room. Her own

sense of guilt made his tall, black-clad figure loom even larger and more terrifying in the weak, flickering lamplight.

Before she could confess or make excuses, Gerrold said, "If you're looking for Mr. McKechnie, I'm afraid he's gone. He said something about receiving a windfall and having to rush off right away to . . ." He hesitated for a moment. "Australia. Yes, that's where he said he was going. To Australia, to start afresh."

Frances suddenly felt giddy and light-headed. Australia. The end of the world.

Gerrold walked over to an easel, cocked his head to the side, and studied the unfinished painting of a tranquil Long Island beach at daybreak. Then he grimaced. "It would appear that his paintings weren't selling very well here in New York, and he thought the Australians might be less discriminating. Too bad. Such a handsome, charming fellow, but if this is any indication of his work, he is sorely lacking in talent, I'm afraid." Then he turned back toward her. "As I was saying, he regretted not being able to get word to you sooner, but his stroke of good fortune was so very sudden and unexpected. I'm sure you understand."

"Yes. Yes, I do."

Now Gerrold's gaze was cold and critical as he examined her plain attire, and since it was far from his expectations and demands of perfection, he pursed his lips in disapproval. "Ah, now I know why you're dressed as a parlormaid. McKechnie said he was supposed to paint you as a peasant girl by candlelight; that's why he wanted you to come to his studio at such a late hour. I take it that's why you're here, Frances, and not at home?"

For a moment Frances stared at him in puzzlement. What was all this nonsense about her being painted by candlelight? And then she understood all too well. He was giving her the chance—her one and only chance, if she knew Gerrold—to redeem herself. If she renounced Alastair and pretended that they had never been lovers, Gerrold would be free to pretend that his wife had never been unfaithful to him. They could go on with their lives as though nothing had happened. The choice was hers. She could either live a lie or lose her home, her respectability, and the protection of Gerrold's name.

Frances cleared her throat, the decision made. "Yes, Gerrold, that is why I came here this evening. Mr. McKechnie was going to paint me by candlelight as a surprise for you. I—" The lies caught in her throat, and for a moment she thought she would choke on them. Then she rallied valiantly, and when she spoke, her voice was clear and decisive. "I wish Mr. McKechnie had told me sooner of his plans. It's too cold to venture out for no reason at all." No reason at all, now or forever.

Gerrold smiled, satisfied. "I quite agree. I would suggest that we go home. The carriage is parked just down the street. I take it you didn't notice?"

When he turned his back and started walking toward the rear of the studio, Frances searched the room with desperate, hungry eyes, drinking in the smallest detail from the threadbare Turkish carpet to Alastair's wooden palette stained with more colors than God ever imagined. She burned such images into her mind and heart, for she still loved Alastair despite his betrayal, and she knew she would have to live on such memories for the rest of her life.

All she had to do was stare up at the skylight, now rendered opaque by its blanket of snow, and a picture leapt vividly to mind, of a different room bathed in bright, golden light that gilded everything it touched. She saw herself and Alastair sitting close to each other at the rickety table near the window, a gypsy lovers' feast of bread and cheese spread out before them as they endlessly talked and laughed and planned. Oh, what plans they had made! His wide blue eyes would lovingly trace the contours of her face as he told her repeatedly how very beautiful she was, and his fingers would idly caress a golden curl, then stray down to her cheek. Her cheek of ivory velvet, he called it. Their feast barely touched, he would rise, extend his hand, and lead her over to the bed hidden behind an old Japanese folding screen at the other side of the room.

There he would undress her slowly, reverentially caressing each patch of bare flesh with his lips and fingertips before proceeding to the next. First came her neck as he unbuttoned her gown, then her shoulders after he pushed the fabric out of his way. Finally, when her skin was warm and eyes glowing with anticipation, her lover would peel open the bodice of her dress so that her breasts were bared to him, and he would make tender love to her until her senses sang and she became intoxicated with the most wondrous pleasure imaginable.

Frances blinked, and the golden vision vanished as quickly as a dream upon waking, leaving only cold and darkness in its place. She would never know such complete ecstasy again. Alastair was gone forever. She would face that fact and be strong, but when she thought of spending the rest of her life enduring Gerrold's rough, crude advances and his obscene demands, she was frightened, for she knew that there would be no escape this time. Ever. He would see to that. She squeezed her eyes shut and prayed for courage.

Frances heard Gerrold's slow, measured footsteps behind her, and suddenly she felt something heavy and soft fall across her hunched shoulders. When she looked down, she saw that Gerrold had brought her sable cape. Had he been so very sure of Alastair then? Had he been so very sure of her?

"I always know what's best for you, my dear," he whispered, his breath hot and unpleasant against her ear.

She suppressed a shudder and drew the fur collar closer

around her face, seeking warmth and comfort, but there was none to be had.

Alastair! His name was a silent cry of anguish and despair wrenched from the very depths of her soul.

Gerrold offered her his arm, but Frances pretended not to notice the gesture and hurried out of the studio ahead of him. However, he quickly caught up with her, possessively drew her arm through his, and they left together without another word, having only the silence in common. When they stepped outside into the cold, he hailed their driver, and Frances watched the familiar carriage turn slowly in the street and draw inexorably toward them, looking for all the world like a Black Maria coming to haul her off to prison to serve her life sentence.

At that moment the smoldering fires of rebellion flared afresh, and Frances was on the verge of confronting Gerrold and telling him that she was leaving him. But even as she entertained the thought she knew herself well enough to know that she lacked the courage to take such a drastic measure. The unknown was just too frightening, and as she reminded herself over and over, she had the child to consider now, not just herself.

She felt something cold and wet against her cheek, and when she looked up at the low pewter sky, she noticed that it had started to snow again, thousands of large white flakes lazily drifting down, one after another. They clung to her eyelashes and melted on her lips, tasting surprisingly salty like tears, while many settled on the dark fur of her cape. The flakes were falling faster and faster now, gaining momentum as they quickly filled and obliterated the hansom tracks crisscrossing the street. Now no one would know that she had ever been here at all. But it didn't matter, she thought numbly. Nothing mattered anymore.

The carriage took them home.

Chapter One

Newport—1884

"SAVANNAH WEBB, YOU COME back here right this instant, or, I'm warning you, there'll be the devil to pay!"

Vannah clapped her hands tightly over her ears to shut out her governess's angry, imperious command to return to the schoolroom and instead ran even faster down the long, winding upstairs corridor, her footsteps keeping time with her pounding heart. Breathless at last, she stopped, dropped her hands, and listened carefully. All she heard was her own ragged breathing, so she knew she had eluded her pursuer at last. She was safe for the time being, but she desperately needed a hiding place where Blackie couldn't find her.

Darting around another corner, Vannah nearly collided with a young housemaid burdened with a stack of fresh linens, but the woman managed to quickly veer aside with a good-humored chuckle and a startled, "By all the saints, Miss Savannah, you look as though Satan himself is chasin' you! Where are you off to in such a hurry?"

The child stopped just long enough to reply, "I'm running away from Blackie—I mean Miss Blackwell—my governess. Please don't tell her I came this way, Kathleen."

"Don't you fret, child. If I see the woman, I'll send her hurryin' off in the opposite direction."

"Thank you." And the child sped off.

Even though Vannah was safe for now, it would only be

a matter of time before Blackie discovered the deception, so she rushed down the servants' stairs and out the back door into the warm, glorious July sun—and freedom.

She started to cross the estate's many acres of lush green lawn, her long, coltish legs increasing their stride, causing her tawny braid to fly out behind her and bob against her back. Then she scanned the sunken gardens for any sign of groundsmen, but there were no witnesses to her flight, for if any of the servants told Blackie that they had seen her come this way, it would only be a matter of minutes before the governess deduced her whereabouts. Then she would deliver one of her stern lectures on obedience, march Vannah back to the house like some prisoner of war, and later send her to bed without her supper for the third night in a row. But if Vannah succeeded, she might have the entire morning to herself, long, leisurely hours in which to do what she pleased instead of those tedious mathematics lessons. Even the thought of her eventual capture couldn't put a damper on her high spirits as she reached the grove of stately copper beeches at the farthest end of the estate.

Running faster now, she ignored the raucous protests of jays and crows overhead and didn't stop until she reached her playhouse, Petit Clairvaux.

When she opened the front door of the gray stone building and went inside, Vannah ignored the four elaborately furnished downstairs rooms and instead trotted right upstairs to her favorite room, the studio. It was a spacious, sunny room, though quite austere with plain white painted walls and floor and no furniture other than a small child's desk over in one corner. But Vannah didn't care, for this was her refuge from the bewildering adult world with its unfair rules and unreasonable demands, a place where she could be alone and be herself, not what someone else expected her to be.

Her footsteps echoing loudly through the empty room,

she went to the desk and took out a large sheet of plain white paper and a box of worn colored chalks. Then she dragged a chair over to one of the windows where the light was bright and strong. Satisfied, her gaze went to the row of built-in cupboards lining the opposite wall. These were stuffed almost to overflowing with expensive dolls and other toys, but Vannah seldom played with them, except for one very special one. She crossed the room, opened a cupboard door, and peered inside.

"Good morning, Mademoiselle Fanchette," she said.

Bonjour, Vannah.

Fanchette, the largest and prettiest of the many French dolls, boasted jointed limbs and pale gold human hair exactly like Vannah's. And she was not merely a toy, she was the child's most trusted playmate and confidante, privy to her most secret thoughts.

Vannah stared into the bright blue glass eyes, and whispered, "I have been most disobedient to Miss Blackwell, Fanchette."

I know. You've been insufferable to your poor governess for some time now, and she has been kindness itself to you. Doesn't she make sure you wear the prettiest dresses, like that blue one you have on? Doesn't she listen to your prayers every night? Why, even at this very moment she probably knows just where you are, yet she's letting you have some time to yourself.

Vannah hung her head in shame, then lifted the doll tenderly in her arms and carried it back to her chair. She seated Fanchette on the windowsill and smoothed out her long, wide skirt of ivory Alençon lace.

"Yesterday Blackie punished me by sending me to bed without my supper," she confessed, "and Sapphira made boiled soft-shell crabs especially for me too."

Punishment is not supposed to be pleasant. But you're fortunate. She could have punished you by forbidding you to ride your pony or draw. You know how grown-ups are. They take away what you love best.

Vannah nodded in agreement, braced her elbows against the arms of her chair, and cupped her small, round chin in the palm of one hand. "You're right, of course, Fanchette. I must be nicer to Blackie in the future, starting today. I know she cares about me, and I hurt her deeply when I don't listen to her. I don't know what I would do if she ever forbade me to draw." Then she sighed and sat back in her chair. "Do you know what she said to me today? She said that for the past year I've been a little tyrant, refusing to do my lessons and throwing fits whenever I don't get my own way. She said I'm eleven years old, not a baby, and if I don't stop being so hateful and rebellious, none of the servants will like me anymore."

Well, she's right. And if you continue to misbehave, perhaps she'll even accept a new position with another family and leave. And then you'll get a new governess, someone strict and horrid, who won't let you do anything.

"I know that. I'm becoming a spoiled little monster, but I don't know why. I'd hate for Blackie to leave." Vannah sighed wistfully and tossed her long braid back over her shoulder. "I've been so, so naughty."

I think that's because you're lonely, Vannah. You want someone besides Miss Blackwell to pay attention to you.

"I am not lonely, Fanchette!" Vannah cried indignantly.

Oh, I think you are.

Vannah hesitated, then murmured, "You're probably right, as always. I know I have no friends, except for you and Blackie. Mother is always too sick to be my friend, and besides, I am only allowed to see her when she's having one of her good days. And I hardly ever see Father, except when he's rushing off somewhere."

Vannah stared out the window at a little brown sparrow valiantly trying to build a small nest of twigs and string in a high branch of a nearby tree. Her father was more of a stranger to her than her mother, and Vannah was a little afraid of him. Whenever he looked her way, his pale blue eyes were as cold as a snowstorm in January, and instead of speaking in a normal tone of voice, he always barked or growled at her, making her cringe inside.

Gerrold Webb never requested to see her before tea and never made any surprise visits to the schoolroom to ask how her studies were progressing or to listen to her recite her multiplication tables. The only time Vannah ever saw her father at length was on her birthday, when he always presented her with a doll, year after year, as though he couldn't think of anything else a little girl would rather have. And, of course, there was the Christmas Day ritual, when Vannah would be seated with great ceremony on the parlor floor beside a towering spruce tree the servants had spent all day decorating, and her father would hand her box after box to open. If her eyes widened and she squealed in delight at the contents, he beamed down at her with one of his rare smiles, but if her response wasn't to his satisfaction, his face hardened into stone. Vannah was always careful to make him smile on Christmas Day.

When she asked Blackie why she never saw her father, the governess looked guarded and blank in the way grownups did when they wanted to keep something from a child. All she would say was, "Your father is a very wealthy, very important man, my dear. He's always very busy making lots of money so you will have beautiful clothes and enough to eat, not like many children in this world who go unclothed and hungry. You should be thankful that your father provides you with everything you could possibly want."

But he didn't give her what she wanted most.

What is the matter? Why do you look so sad?

Hot, treacherous tears suddenly burned Vannah's eyes,

and she hurried to wipe them away with the back of her hand before the doll caught her crying. She grew sullen and muttered, "I don't want to talk to you anymore."

Then she reached for her paper and chalk and began sketching the doll with rapid, furious strokes. Mademoiselle Fanchette wisely did not pry and said no more.

Gerrold Webb had just finished reading a most disturbing letter when he happened to glance up and see the woman approaching him across the green expanse of lawn. He knew immediately that she was one of the servants, for only they would be wearing stiff black bombazine on such a warm summer morning, but damned if he knew which one. There were dozens of such women in his employ, and he only remembered the names of the pretty ones.

As she drew closer in her long, purposeful stride that he found repulsively mannish, Gerrold finally recognized the intruder as his daughter's governess, a woman by the name of Black-something or Welles-something. He felt suddenly irritated that she was approaching him so boldly while he was sitting on his lawn, enjoying the panoramic view of the Atlantic Ocean practically at his very doorstep. She should have put in a request through his secretary to see him, and they would then meet at Gerrold's convenience, not hers. He was the master, and that was the way he wanted things done in his household. Well, he would soon put this upstart in her place.

The woman was close enough for him to discern her features, and his worst suspicions were confirmed as he assessed her with the skill of a true connoisseur of women. She was exactly the type he was never attracted to: short, squat, and with a plain, uninteresting face he wouldn't have looked twice at if she passed him in the street. No, he thought with an inward chuckle, this one would not be luring him away from the abundant charms of the spirited young actress he had sequestered away aboard his yacht, the *Savannah*, now anchored in Newport Harbor.

"Mr. Webb," the governess began in an irritating nasal voice as she stood before him with a nervous smile, "I realize that this is an intrusion—"

"Yes, you are intruding, Miss, er . . . ?"

She blushed. "Blackwell. I am—"

"My daughter's governess. Yes, I know. If you have something to say to me concerning my daughter's studies, just make an appointment with my secretary and we shall discuss it at some future time."

The governess clasped her hands primly before her and stood her ground as obstinately as a mule. "What I have to say to you about Savannah is of the utmost importance, Mr. Webb, and cannot wait."

Gerrold gave her a black look that sent most servants slinking away in fear for their positions. But this one was not easily intimidated.

"Please forgive me, sir, for speaking so boldly," she said without a trace of repentance in her voice. "I don't mean to interrupt you, but I'm sure you put your daughter's welfare above all else, Mr. Webb."

She was clever all right, and he grudgingly admired her spirit. He smiled. "By 'all else' do you mean a pleasant morning, basking in the sun and admiring this splendid ocean view, Miss Blackwell? Yes, I do put my daughter's welfare before such trifling pleasures." Before the governess could say anything else, he indicated a white wicker chair across from him, forcing her to look directly into the sun, at a distinct disadvantage. "Sit down, Miss Blackwell, and tell me what is so urgent about my daughter that you just had to see me?"

Miss Blackwell quickly seated herself on the edge of the chair and smoothed her skirt nervously. "Mr. Webb, during this past year Savannah has become an impossible child—wild, uncontrollable, and rebellious."

He felt irritated with her again. "Is that all you interrupted me for, Miss Blackwell? To tell me that my daughter is uncontrollable? Discipline is your responsibility. That is what I pay you for, most generously, I might add. If you cannot discipline a mere child . . ." He let his words and the threat they carried hang in mid-sentence.

Usually his sarcasm reduced women to tears but not this one. She squinted and shaded her eyes resolutely with one hand so she could look directly at him. "Mr. Webb, in the five years that I have been Savannah's governess, I have done my duties to the best of my ability. She can speak fluent French and a little German, play the piano rather well, dance gracefully, and conduct herself as befitting a young lady of her station. Until recently she has been a paragon—a delightful child—and I've enjoyed teaching her. I feel I supply more than adequate discipline. Whenever she misbehaves, I send her to bed without her supper." Now the poor woman's face actually fell, and she looked most troubled. "I fear I may have to resort to forbidding her to draw if—"

"Draw?" Gerrold sat up straight and scowled. "Did you say my daughter draws, Miss Blackwell?"

"Why, yes, sir. Your Savannah is quite an accomplished little artist for her age. You should see some of her watercolor sketches. I think she has genuine talent."

Gerrold's thoughts flew back nearly a decade, opening painful old wounds he had thought long since healed. What had been the name of that artist fellow Frances had fancied herself in love with? McKechnie, Alastair McKechnie. It was a name he would never forget. After Gerrold had discovered their innocent flirtation he had had no difficulty breaking it up by buying the greedy fellow off with an outrageous sum of money and an incentive to emigrate to Australia.

After that humiliating episode Gerrold had never allowed anyone in his family to sit for his portrait, not himself, not his daughter, and certainly not his susceptible wife.

"Mr. Webb?" The governess's grating voice broke through his reverie, forcing him to listen to her again.

"Yes, Miss Blackwell? As you were saying . . ."

"As I was saying, sir, I won't be around for much longer to care for Savannah." She actually blushed and simpered like a young girl. "You see, I am to be married next month, so I also came to give you notice that I will be leaving your employ at the end of this month. I'm afraid Savannah will have to learn to get used to someone else."

Gerrold pursed his lips in annoyance. How dare she inconvenience him at a time like this? "Well, Miss Blackwell, I certainly can't expect you to forgo your own wedding just to take care of my daughter, now can I?"

"No, sir, you can't."

"Never fear, we'll plod along somehow without you."

If he was trying to make her feel guilty enough to change her mind and stay, he didn't succeed. All the governess said was, "I am sure you will, sir."

"And thank you for bringing the matter of my daughter's disobedience to my attention."

"You're welcome, sir."

"Oh, and one last matter, Miss Blackwell . . ."

"Yes, Mr. Webb?"

"I want you to collect every one of whatever it is my daughter draws with and burn them." He ignored the woman's startled gasp of horror and her bulging eyes. "I don't wish her to draw, paint, or even have art lessons of any kind, is that clearly understood?"

"But, Mr. Webb—"

He held up his hand to silence her. "I have made up my mind, Miss Blackwell. Savannah will grow up to be a fine lady one day, and she has responsibilities to me and to her family to make a good marriage with some suitable young man of my choosing. I believe that art lessons encourage a girl to be dreamy and lead to a hysterical romantic imagination. They fill her head with all sorts of unrealistic notions that I find totally repugnant. If she's allowed to continue, the next thing I know, she'll be talking gibberish about foregoing marriage to become an artist, starving and freezing in some Parisian garret." Gerrold Webb glared at her. "I'll not tolerate it, Miss Blackwell." Then he smiled smugly. "And, besides, if my daughter has been as disobedient as you have claimed, then this shall be her punishment. Most fitting, don't you think?"

The governess's gaunt cheeks had turned a deep shade of red, and she sputtered when she spoke. "But—but, sir, all young ladies learn to draw and paint. It's considered a desirable accomplishment that enhances femininity. I know your daughter very well, and I am confident that Savannah would never entertain any unconventional thoughts." Her tone became pleading. "Please, Mr. Webb. Don't do this to her. It would break her heart."

Gerrold felt an angry flush spring into his own cheeks. "I don't give a damn what anyone else does or thinks, Miss Blackwell! If I say my daughter shall never draw again, then my daughter shall never draw again, and that is that! Do I make myself clear?"

"Yes, sir!" She bit off each word angrily and sat up, defiance etched in her straight back and scowling face.

"And if I ever discover that you have not carried out my orders, Miss Blackwell, you shall be leaving my employ sooner than you expected. And that bridegroom of yours will never find employment again."

Now the woman turned as white as her chair, and

Gerrold finally saw fear in her eyes, for she knew he was wealthy and powerful enough to carry out such a threat. "I will see to it immediately, Mr. Webb," she said in a subdued voice, conquered at last.

"See that you do. Good day to you, Miss Blackwell."

She rose, turned, and started to walk away without another word.

"Oh, Miss Blackwell . . ."

She stopped and looked back at him. "Yes, Mr. Webb?"

"I said, good day to you."

The governess hesitated for just one second, then capitulated. "Good day to you, Mr. Webb."

When she was not quite out of earshot, Gerrold muttered, "So much for uppity servants." Then he laced his fingers together, leaned back in his comfortable chair, and stared out at the blue-green sea, letting the roar of the breakers soothe him as they rolled in and crashed against the rocks, sending a fine white spray shooting high into the air. He had more important matters to worry about than finding a new governess for his headstrong daughter. Actually, if Frances were a real wife to him, she would be hiring a new governess. It was a mother's responsibility, after all.

Suddenly Gerrold recalled the letter he had folded and stuffed into his pocket, and an alternate plan sprang to mind. He smiled slowly as he retrieved the correspondence and read it once more. Of course! It was the perfect solution for all concerned but especially for himself. He pocketed the letter and went to pay a call on his invalid wife.

Frances occupied a small suite of rooms upstairs in the southwest wing that commanded a vast view of the Atlantic Ocean from the adjoining upstairs terrace. But she never went out on the terrace. She always stayed inside, preferring her rooms because they were cozy, but Gerrold privately felt that she saw them as a rabbit warren, someplace dark and safe to hide from reality. The moment they arrived in Newport for the summer at the end of June, a trembling, exhausted Frances had to be carried up to her rooms and never came out until it was time to make the nerve-racking train journey back to New York City in September.

As soon as he knocked on her bedroom door and was admitted by his wife's nurse, Gerrold's nostrils were assailed by the sickroom stench of medicines and warm, stale air, and he had to fight the impulse to gag and put his handkerchief to his nose. Heavy crimson drapes had been drawn against the windows, as though the light of this fine summer day were poison, and confining its occupant to a cocoon of darkness. For a moment Gerrold was blinded and had to blink several times until his eyes became accustomed to the absence of light.

He could see his wife's carved mahogany bed, wide enough for only a solitary occupant, and a small table littered with dozens of brown glass bottles and jars of various tonics, restoratives, and elixirs that never seemed to do anything to make her better. Frances was lying in bed, propped up against several frilly, embroidered pillows, a heavy blanket tucked around her even in this hot weather, for she was forever cold. She was so thin and frail, she looked as though she'd shatter into a thousand pieces like broken glass if anyone so much as raised his voice to her.

Gerrold approached the bed as quietly as if he were in church. "How are you today, my dearest heart?" he asked in a hushed voice.

She turned her head toward him with great effort, and he recoiled when he saw the change in her, even since his last rare visit. There were deep hollows indenting her pale cheeks and purple smudges beneath her sapphire eyes, once so coquettish and vibrant, but now dull and lifeless, as though some inner fire had long been extinguished. Her long golden hair, which Gerrold had once loved to stroke and sift through his fingers, had become dried out and brittle, losing its silken texture despite the best efforts of Frances's maid to keep it presentable. Frances had been breathtakingly beautiful once, the envy of every woman and the desire of every man in New York City.

She tried to smile, and he feared that her parchment-thin skin would crack from the strain. "I'm not well, I'm afraid. I awoke this morning with a strange, tingly feeling in my limbs. I could barely lift my head from the pillow. Nurse Ferris said . . ."

While his wife continued to describe her latest malady in a weak and whispery voice that Gerrold had to strain to hear, his thoughts flew back in time to the beautiful young woman who had captivated his heart, before childbirth had plunged her into round after unending round of incurable illness.

Frances Adams had come from a fine, though impoverished, Connecticut family, but her lack of a dowry had been of no concern to Gerrold. A proud, young aristocrat from Georgia, he had enough money for the both of them, his father having made a fortune selling blankets to the Confederate Army during the Civil War, and enterprising Gerrold having tripled it by speculation on Wall Street. Fortunately, with his many and successful business interests, Gerrold didn't need to marry for money as so many had. What he had been seeking, once he decided to conquer these barbarian Yankees, was a beautiful young woman of superior birth and breeding who would give him an entrée into exclusive New York society as well as many strong sons to carry on the proud Webb name. And he thought that he had found her in the beautiful, gentle Frances Adams that night at the Claytons' cotillion.

She was enchanting, vivacious, and captivating, the perfect wife for an ambitious man. And the fact that every other eligible bachelor in the room wanted her only made Gerrold Webb even more determined to win her. He proposed to her a week later and she accepted.

Gerrold had had such dreams for them in those early halcyon days of his marriage, and he certainly could not be faulted as a perfect, doting husband. Hadn't he taken Frances to Europe for a six-month honeymoon, showering her with expensive gowns from Worth in Paris and buying their splendid four-story brownstone on Thirty-third Street for a wedding present? What more could a woman want?

And she repaid him by carrying on a silly, meaningless flirtation with a miserable, worthless artist. Gerrold would never forgive her for that. Never.

As he watched her lying there, prattling on and on about her current illness, Gerrold felt a seething resentment toward her. Frances should have been like the other beautiful women his friends had married, concerned with pleasing him and advancing the Webbs socially. But the stark reality was Frances lying here in darkness, hiding away as one afraid of life, her world narrowly circumscribed by a collection of brown glass medicine bottles and her own fears.

Suddenly his patience reached the breaking point. He longed to reach over and shake his helpless wife like a rag doll, then fling open the drapes and force her to look upon the sunshine. But he restrained himself and instead reached into his breast pocket, removing the letter and smoothing the wrinkles from its surface as he spoke.

"I received a letter from your sister this morning," he said.

Frances's eyes suddenly brightened with a glimmer of interest. "Constance?"

"Yes. She's in New York, staying at our town house."

"Constance? Here? In America? Why didn't she write to tell us she was coming?"

"It seems she's in some difficulty."

Frances's voice grew louder. "Difficulty?"

Did the woman have to echo his every word as though she were a simpleton? Gerrold fought to control his rising temper. "Yes. Bad news, I'm afraid. It appears that her husband went to Ireland to inspect his estate there and— now I want you to be very, very brave, my dear—he was shot and killed by one of his disgruntled tenants."

Frances gasped, turned gray, and her bony hand flew to her mouth as though to stifle a scream. She was shaking so badly for one terrifying moment that Gerrold thought she was going to have some type of seizure.

"Travers is—is . . . dead?" she gasped.

Gerrold nodded gravely.

"Oh, dear God! How horrible! My poor, poor Constance must be beside herself with grief." Then Frances sat up with great effort. "But what is she doing here? I'm sure Travers left her well cared for with his estate in England and the one in Ireland now. England's been Constance's home for ten years now, and I'm surprised that she isn't staying there." Her brow was furrowed with worry. "Something must be wrong, Gerrold."

Gerrold nodded. "According to your sister's letter, Travers died before he could change his will and provide for her. Everything went to his children from his previous marriage, and Constance was cut out without a cent. She goes on to tell how her stepchildren quite vindictively refused to even allow her to live in the dower house on their father's estate. You'll remember how she always said they hated her for taking their mother's place." He paused. "They literally forced her to leave England."

Frances fell back with a low moan of misery. "So Constance is here because she has no place else to go."

"That would appear to be the reason. I've decided to leave for New York in a few days and learn how we can help her," he said. The very thought of a leisurely yacht trip with his attentive, obliging guest made a thin film of sweat rise on Gerrold's brow.

Now Frances moistened her lips nervously. "You—you will allow my sister to stay with us whatever the reason, won't you, Gerrold? You won't send her away."

He smiled reassuringly and patted her hot, dry hand. "You know me better than that, my dear. Constance is a member of our family and welcome to stay with us for as long as she likes."

Frances looked relieved. "You are too kind, Gerrold, too kind."

He was silent for a moment, stroking his mustache as he thought carefully about what he was going to say next, then decided that it was best to say nothing more to Frances about his other plans for her sister. Any other arrangements that were made between Constance and Gerrold would be between themselves. The less Frances knew, the better.

Kissing his wife's limp, unresponsive hand, Gerrold smiled, bowed, and wished her good day. He thought he heard an imperceptible sigh of relief as he left her to her darkness and solitude.

When Vannah was told of her father's cruel, unreasonable decree that she never be allowed to draw again, she flew into hysterics, screaming, sobbing, and beating the floor of her playhouse studio with both fists and feet. But she stopped the moment Miss Blackwell suggested that Vannah, herself, should try asking her father nicely if she could be allowed to continue her drawing. If Vannah also showed him some of her best sketches, he just might change his mind.

Two days later Vannah was granted an audience with her father.

Despite the fact that Miss Blackwell had made her look so angelic in her prettiest pink muslin dress, then brushed her waist-length hair until it was silky and glossy, Vannah felt as though she were going to her own execution. She could almost hear her knees knocking together; her palms were damp and sticky and her stomach was filled with a thousand butterflies all fluttering to escape.

When she reached the door of her father's dark and gloomy study, she knocked timidly, opened it, and went inside.

Vannah noticed right away that she and her father were not alone. Another man stood near the high windows off to her left, his back toward her. From what she could see, he was taller than her father and broad-shouldered, with crisply curling chestnut hair that appeared reddish-brown in the shaft of strong sunlight streaming in from the windows. When he turned around and looked directly at her, Vannah stared and blushed furiously, for he was the most handsome man she had ever seen.

She smiled shyly at him, but he merely nodded curtly in return and turned back to the window, obviously finding the gardens and ocean more worthy of his notice than a mere child.

"Savannah!" her father said, his voice barking out at her, startling her and making her jump. "You wanted to see me."

"Yes, Father," she replied, sounding like a meek, squeaking mouse. She had thought that their audience was going to be private, and the presence of the rude, surly stranger was making her feel self-conscious and reticent.

"Speak up, child, and don't hang back. I'm not going to bite you, now am I?"

Before Vannah could reply, the stranger spoke up in a deep, resonant voice with a pronounced English accent. "I can see that I'm intruding. If you'll excuse me, Webb, I'll—"

"Don't be absurd, Ash," Vannah's father said with a scowl and an impatient wave of his hand that made his guest's dark, flaring brows come together in a scowl. "I'm sure whatever matter my daughter has to discuss with me won't take long, so stay right where you are." Vannah's look of chagrin was lost on him, for he said to her, "Come over here and give your papa a kiss."

Vannah rounded the long oak desk obediently and walked over to his chair. Her father inclined his head slightly so that she could touch her lips to his cheek, which was very smooth and smelled pleasantly spicy. He did not smile or reach out to hug her as she wished he would.

When he straightened, he said to his guest in an offhand manner, "Oh, by the way, Ash, this is my daughter, Savannah, named after my birthplace."

Vannah waited a second for her father to introduce the man called Ash to her, but when he didn't, Vannah decided to take matters into her own hands. She faced their guest and made her prettiest curtsy, just as Blackie had taught her. "I am very pleased to make your acquaintance, Mr. Ash."

He smiled at her in an amused, patronizing way that made Vannah wish she hadn't bothered, but then he surprised her by stepping forward and bowing. "My name is Martin Ash, and I must say the pleasure is all mine, Miss Webb."

Vannah had to tilt her head back to look up at him, he was so tall. She noticed that he had most unusual eyes of a deep emerald hue that smoldered with the intensity of green fire as they seemed to look right through her. His thorough scrutiny made Vannah feel uncomfortably hot all over with a queer wrenching in the pit of her stomach that had nothing whatsoever to do with butterflies.

Suddenly her father broke the spell by saying brusquely, "Well, let's not dawdle, shall we? Sit down, Savannah. You, too, Ash." When both were seated, he folded his hands and added, "Now, Savannah, just why did you want to see me?"

As if a daughter should need a particular reason to see her own father.

"I understand that I no longer will be allowed to draw, Father," she said, exactly as she and Blackie had rehearsed.

"Yes, that is correct, Savannah."

"I am here to ask"—no, Blackie had told her to say *beg*—"to beg you to reconsider, Father."

Even though Vannah kept her eyes straight ahead, trained on her father, she was keenly aware of the man sitting so close to her that she could have brushed his arm with her own if she so much as wriggled in her seat.

Vannah risked a glance out of the corner of her eye and found herself momentarily distracted. Up close Martin Ash was even better-looking than she first supposed, with a broad forehead, long straight nose, and sharp cheekbones that made his face lean and strong. Vannah thought his mouth odd, however, for the upper lip was so thin as to be almost nonexistent, while the lower lip was full.

Her father's heavy brows were coming together in a scowl, making him look even more fierce and displeased. "And why should I reconsider?"

Vannah reluctantly tore her eyes away from Martin Ash's face, swallowed hard, and rose to timidly place sketches of Clairvaux, her pony, and a watercolor portrait of her mother on the desk before her father.

"I would like you to reconsider because I am very skilled at drawing, as you can see from these sketches I have done. Besides," Vannah added in what she hoped was a persuasive voice, "I do enjoy it so, Father, and am asking—begging—you to allow me to continue."

Then she returned to her seat to await a final decision that she knew would be irreversible. The butterflies attacked her stomach in full force.

He picked up the drawings and glanced at them briefly while wrinkling his nose as though he had just avoided stepping in a pile of horse droppings in the street. Then he tossed her work aside with a grimace. "I can't agree with you, Savannah. These drawings aren't very good at all, compared to others I've seen drawn by young ladies your age. I barely recognized Clairvaux, let alone your pony, and as for that being a drawing of your mother . . ." He shook his head.

Vannah heard a great roaring in her ears, and she sucked in her breath sharply to make the sound go away. Beside her, Martin Ash was staring out into space, obviously bored by the proceedings and oblivious to her agony.

Her father continued with, "I don't know why that governess of yours has been encouraging you, since you obviously have no talent." Now he rose and went to the window behind the desk. "I am sorry to have to be so blunt with you. I know the truth can often be quite painful, but it can shape your character and make you stronger if you learn to accept it."

As she listened to her father she fought to control herself at all costs, for she sensed that it would please him if she broke down and cried. So Vannah said nothing, her cheeks burning in deep mortification. She could see Martin Ash staring at her, though she could not tell what was going through his mind at that moment. He probably thought the drawings were as bad as her father claimed. Vannah hated her father even more for thinking so little of her feelings that he could allow another person to witness her humiliation. She bit down hard on her lower lip until she tasted salt.

Suddenly her father said, "Take a look at these drawings, Ash. Let's hear what you think."

Vannah was out of her chair and halfway across the room before her father realized what was happening. She heard him shout her name imperiously and demand that she come back, but she was already out the door, and running back to her playhouse to tell Mademoiselle Fanchette that she wanted to die.

Later, when she had cried so much that her eyes were red and swollen and her head throbbed from the force of her emotions, Vannah decided to return to the main house and report her miserable failure to Blackie. She trudged down the stairs and had just entered the foyer when there came a soft, persistent tapping on the front door.

It had to be Blackie, here to comfort her.

As Vannah swung the door open she said, "Your plan didn't work, Miss Blackwell. Father—"

She stopped short the moment she saw that the caller was not her governess.

"Oh, it's you, Mr. Ash. . . . What do you want?"

He towered in the doorway, his broad form blocking the light as he looked down at her without smiling. "I hope I'm not disturbing you, Miss Webb, but there is something I must say to you. One of the maids told me that you might be here."

Vannah thrust out her chin belligerently. "And what is it you have to say to me, Mr. Ash? That my drawings really are as bad as my father claimed?"

Suddenly he broke out in a wide grin that displayed white, even teeth, making him look more human and much less forbidding. "My, aren't we the prickly one?"

"I am always prickly when people are rude to me just because I am a child."

Martin Ash quickly composed his face along more serious lines, but the glimmer of amusement refused to leave his eyes. "And you thought I was rude to you back there in your father's study?"

She lowered her gaze to the ground and nodded.

"Then I do apologize," he said, his voice soft and sincere. "You must forgive me if I appeared rude. I didn't mean to be." And he extended his hand.

"I shall accept your apology, Mr. Ash," Vannah muttered. When his hand took hers in a firm grip, she was quite unprepared for the jolt that shot through her at his touch. Disconcerted, Vannah jerked her hand away and covered the abruptness of her gesture by saying, "Come. We can talk inside if you like."

Martin Ash had to bend his head in order to clear the front door, and he was such a large man that he seemed to fill the foyer. As he followed her into the playhouse's drawing room with quiet, fluid grace, Vannah could see him staring appreciatively at the rosewood wainscoting, the marble fireplace, and the mahogany furniture.

"Why, this is even larger than the cottages on my family's estate in England," he said in wonder, shaking his head. "A family of six or more could live in here quite comfortably, you know."

Vannah nodded as she seated herself in a damask-covered wing chair and indicated the divan for her guest. "There's even a kitchen with a stove that works in case my governess and I decide to take our meals here."

"Rather elaborate, don't you think, for—"

"For a mere child?" Vannah said, finishing for him. "I suppose it is. When Clairvaux was being built, my father had the architect design this playhouse just for me. It's exactly like the main house, except it doesn't have as many rooms, of course." She looked wistful. "I would have preferred something smaller, but no one ever asked me what I wanted."

"You're a very fortunate young lady, Miss Webb."

"In some respects, Mr. Ash," she replied. When the young man's eyes widened and his brows rose, Vannah added, "Did I say something odd? You looked at me quite strangely just then."

Martin Ash just shook his head as he seated himself. "No, it's just that you constantly startle me, Miss Webb. I must confess that I've never met a child quite like you."

Vannah felt her cheeks grow hot at his compliment, and she didn't know quite what to say in response.

He broke the embarrassed silence for her. "What I came to tell you, Miss Webb, is that I thought your drawings were excellent. If you hadn't rushed off the way you did, you would have heard me tell your father as much."

Vannah's mouth dropped, and she just stared at him. "What—what did you say, Mr. Ash?"

"I said I thought your drawings were excellent."

Still, she could not believe him, for her father's cruel and thoughtless criticisms had badly eroded her self-confidence. "Do you really think so, Mr. Ash?"

"Yes. Yes, I do." Then he smiled again, and Vannah wondered how she ever could have thought this charming man rude and surly. "I am certainly no artist, but I think I know an excellent drawing when I see one. Not only were yours technically excellent, they revealed a great deal of yourself in them as well." When he saw the doubt creeping back into her eyes, he added gently, "You can be sure that I would not lie about something that is obviously so important to you."

Vannah was a shrewd, perceptive child who could always tell when adults were lying, and she knew that this man was not lying to her now. She felt herself awash in a warm glow of pride. "Thank you, Mr. Ash. You couldn't have given me a better gift if you'd given me a—a bracelet of rubies and diamonds!"

Martin Ash threw back his head and laughed, a deep, mirthful sound that seemed to well up from the bottom of his shoes and take possession of him. "Good. I'm glad I could be of service to someone." Then he grew serious once again, this handsome man with his quicksilver moods. "Your father told me why he doesn't wish you to draw again, and while I disagree with him, I'm afraid I couldn't make him change his mind. He's adamant that you never be allowed to draw."

Vannah thought her eyes were going to pop out of her head. "You—you tried to make him change his mind?"

He nodded nonchalantly. "I'm afraid I made him very angry with me, for I suspect he's not accustomed to having his authority challenged, but he did ask for my opinion and I had to speak my mind. To keep silent would have been an unpardonable act of cowardice."

Once again Vannah saw Martin Ash in an entirely different light, and she realized once again how gravely she had misjudged him. "Thank you for championing me, Mr. Ash."

During the awkward silence that ensued, Vannah found herself staring down at the young man's large, powerful hands with square, blunt fingers, like a common laborer's. Yet Martin Ash was obviously as much a gentleman as her own father. Vannah found this contradiction intriguing.

Suddenly Martin Ash reached into his waistcoat pocket, took out an engraved shiny gold watch, and said, "Well, I'm afraid it's almost time for me to leave, so—"

"You're leaving?" Vannah demanded, panicking. She desperately wanted him to stay, for she liked him and wanted to know everything there was to know about this man with the courage to stand up to her powerful father.

"But you mustn't go yet. You've only just arrived at Clairvaux."

He rose now and smiled regretfully. "I only stopped in Newport briefly to call upon your Aunt Constance, whom I thought had already arrived here from England. But it seems she hasn't, so I must be on my way."

Vannah walked him to the door, then stopped and said plaintively, "Will I ever see you again, Mr. Ash?"

He smiled. "Oh, you haven't seen the last of me, I can assure you."

Then he bowed, but before he could turn away, Vannah grasped his hand impulsively and kissed the back of it, the hairs that grew there surprisingly soft against her lips. "I'll never forget what you did for me, Mr. Ash," she swore. "Never."

Without giving him time to reply, she wheeled around and darted back into the playhouse, racing up the stairs two at a time, not stopping until she reached her studio. Breathing hard, she rushed over to the window and hid behind a curtain.

Below her, Martin Ash was walking slowly away, the dappled sunlight playing off his dark hair and the cloth of his black frock coat. When he came to the end of the flagstone path, he turned to look back at Petit Clairvaux. His brow was furrowed as though something puzzled him. For an instant Vannah felt his narrowed eyes bore into hers, then he turned and strode off without so much as a fleeting good-bye wave.

For a long time after Martin Ash had gone, Vannah sat by the window, her thoughts filled with the brooding, handsome stranger who had taken the time to befriend her and turn her defeat into victory by offering her a few heartfelt words of encouragement. Then she rose, ran out of the playhouse, and went skipping down the flagstone path back to Clairvaux.

Chapter Two

CONSTANCE TRAVERS GLARED at the clock on the mantel for the fifth time in as many minutes.

Gerrold should have arrived hours ago. Where is he? she thought as she fanned herself furiously, finding precious little relief in the quick, hot gusts of air blowing against her face.

Lord, New York City was like a furnace in the summer! Constance's long-sleeved, high-collared faille dress, with its several petticoats and braided wire bustle, made her feel as though she were being baked in an oven. It would be such a relief to leave this stifling, malodorous city for the fresh air of Newport.

That is, if Gerrold came to take her away.

The last time Constance had seen her brother-in-law was seven years ago when she and her late husband had come to the United States to spend the summer with the Webbs in then-fashionable Saratoga. From the moment the Travers's boat docked and Constance caught Gerrold's eye in an undulating sea of nameless faces, she knew that he now wanted her as much as she had always wanted him. Later, when he implied that he would be most receptive to a discreet dalliance with her, she resisted and coyly feigned ignorance of his intentions, not because she had any scruples about sleeping with her own sister's husband but because she wanted to make Gerrold pay for spurning her to marry Frances all those years ago.

Now Constance was in desperate need of a favor from him and regretted her hastiness to have her petty vengeance.

She crossed the drawing room in short, nervous steps, peered out from behind a curtain, and looked up and down the street for any sign of him. She started when she saw a grand carriage drawn by four matching bay horses pull up in front of the town house. Gerrold had finally arrived. Her heart seemed to fly to her throat, and she hurried back to the mirror over the fireplace for one last quick appraisal, for she knew full well that her future depended upon how she favorably impressed her brother-in-law.

Constance wished that Gerrold's first look at her after all this time could be with her dressed in something other than deepest mourning—a modish ball gown perhaps, to reveal her full white breasts—or a day dress of periwinkle blue that would enhance the unusual smoky blue-gray color of her eyes. She was definitely not one of those women who wore black well. At first she feared that all this unrelieved black lace and plain material made her look too dreary and old, but with her hollow cheeks and ivory skin she was relieved to find herself looking rather fragile and helpless. She chuckled, for she was neither. Not anymore.

After tucking a stray wisp of golden-brown hair into place, she rushed back to the window in time to see Gerrold alight from his carriage.

He was still as handsome as that first night she had ever seen him, when he stood framed in the doorway of Minnie Clayton's ballroom and surveyed the crème de la crème of New York debutantes as though he were a Turkish potentate about to choose one for his harem. And right from that moment she fell headlong in love and prayed that he would choose her. She had been devastated when he chose Frances, but then, all the men chose her sister in those days.

As Constance studied Gerrold now she was glad to see that he was still as imposing and distinguished as ever, wearing wealth and power as casually as he wore his finely tailored linen suit. She had to draw back quickly from the window, lest he catch her staring, so she had no chance to glimpse his face. She didn't need to. It had haunted her enough over the years.

The moment she heard the door bell ring and the butler's hurried footsteps in the hall, Constance smoothed her skirt, breathed deeply to calm her nerves, and blotted the moisture from her upper lip one last time with her handkerchief. She did not want to look as though she had been eagerly awaiting his arrival, so she hurried over to the fireplace and pretended to study a rare Sèvres vase on the mantel. Her back would be toward the door when Gerrold entered, if she calculated it just right, but she made sure that he would see her face reflected in the mirror.

There were muffled voices and footsteps in the foyer, then a familiar voice said, "Constance?"

She turned with a broad smile. "Gerrold!"

His corresponding smile made her quiver as he strode across the room toward her. "You have no idea how wonderful it is to see you again after all these years."

She took a step forward and gracefully extended her hand, delighted to see that he hadn't changed very much at all. Gerrold's fair hair had darkened to a deep gold, and he now wore a dapper mustache, but his blue eyes were still as clear and bold as she remembered, and right now they were flicking over her with a rapaciousness that pleased and satisfied her. So he still found her attractive.

Before she could say another word, he took her hand

and kissed it in the European manner. "I was so sorry to hear of Travers's death. You have my deepest condolences."

"Thank you, Gerrold," she murmured as she withdrew her hand from his warm, disconcerting grasp and tried to look sufficiently bereaved. "It was a great blow to us all. He just went over to Ireland to inspect his estate. None of us ever dreamed he wouldn't return." She dabbed at her eyes with her handkerchief for effect, then took a deep breath to collect herself. "Do forgive me, Gerrold. I must apologize for arriving so unexpectedly on your doorstep like some destitute waif. If Mother and Father were still alive, I would have gone back to them in New Haven, but . . ."

"You needn't explain, Constance. You know my home is always open to you. You are family, remember?" He had the most charming drawl, smooth and lilting, not hard and clipped like British speech. "We Southerners always take care of our own."

"You don't know how relieved that makes me feel! I must confess that I wasn't quite sure how you would react to my sudden appearance, but I had no one else to turn to."

"I'm glad you did. But do forgive me for being such a poor host. Won't you sit down?"

When Constance was seated beside him on the horsehair sofa, Gerrold had a better opportunity to study her. He was startled and delighted to discover that she hadn't aged at all. Constance's smooth, pale skin was unlined, except around the eyes, and she could still boast the slender figure of a sixteen-year-old girl. Just listening to her low, breathy voice sent a shiver skittering down Gerrold's spine, and he could imagine her whispering exciting words of love to him in the darkness.

The very nearness of her, the soft scent of her perfume, like a field of flowers just after a summer storm, brought a responsive tightening in his loins. He held his breath and fought against the dizziness of his rising desire.

"Has Parkins been taking good care of you?" he asked. Anything to take his mind off her.

"Your butler? Yes, he has. Any other man would have been astounded to find a strange woman standing on his doorstep with several trunks by her side, but not the magnificent Parkins. In fact, all of your servants have made me feel right at home."

Gerrold smiled in approval. "I would have their hides if they did any less, and they know it. We've been summering in Newport, so most of the staff is there. Only a few of the servants remain behind here in New York."

Constance sighed. "Perhaps I should have gone directly to Newport."

"If you had, you would have seen an English neighbor of yours," Gerrold said.

Constance raised her finely arched brows in puzzlement. "An English neighbor of mine . . . Now who could that be?"

"The Honorable Martin Ash."

She smiled with pleasure. "Martin! Whatever is he doing here in America?"

Gerrold told her how the young Englishman had been en route to Washington on business for his father when he decided to stop in Newport to call on Constance. "He didn't realize that you had gone to New York instead."

"Martin is a most charming and delightful young man," Constance said. That was all Gerrold needed to know about Martin Ash for now.

"You think so? I found him a trifle cold and standoffish."

"Oh, he can be that too." Before Gerrold could say another word, Constance changed the subject. "And how are Frances and Savannah?"

Gerrold's face lost its enthusiasm at the mention of his

wife's name, and he looked away. "Frances hasn't changed. She still has those nameless illnesses the doctors have no cure for, and she still won't leave her rooms except to travel between New York and Newport. Even that short trip is too much for her.

"And as for my daughter, I don't concern myself overmuch with her. I leave her upbringing to her governesses. It would be different if she were a boy, of course." He smiled again. "Now I want to hear all about you, Constance."

So she spent the next half hour telling him all about her late husband and her vindictive stepchildren.

When she finished, she leaned forward and looked over at Gerrold in appeal. "You and Frances were my last hope."

Now he rose, his face expressionless, and for one terrible moment Constance thought that he was going to refuse to take her in. It would be just like him, she thought bitterly as she watched him pace around the room to have his revenge for all the times she had refused his advances during her stay at Saratoga.

"As I said, Constance, you know you are always welcome in my house. In fact, I want you to stay with us because you can help me with a problem that was recently brought to my attention." He stopped and looked at her. "On the day I received your letter, Savannah's governess gave me her notice. The woman has the audacity to abandon my daughter to get married, so there will be no one to look after Savannah."

So that was what he had in mind, Constance thought spitefully. She who had known a life of privilege and ease as a countess, a member of the British aristocracy, was to be humiliated by being relegated to the lowly position of governess in her own sister's home.

Just as she was on the verge of rising and telling her

esteemed brother-in-law just what she thought of his offer, Gerrold's next words brought her up short.

"You would be doing me a great favor by hiring a new governess."

Constance gave an inward sigh of relief. "But won't Frances want to do that herself?"

"With Frances so very ill, she hasn't been able to do anything for quite some time. She hasn't been able to oversee the household or serve as my hostess." He sighed and sat down beside her again. "You're worldly, having lived in Europe and all. I don't need to tell you that a man's entire career often depends upon his wife. Please don't take offense. I know Frances is your sister, but I'm afraid that she has hindered, rather than helped, my rise."

Now there was a hopeful, pleading look in his eyes that she had never seen there before, for Gerrold Webb was a proud man who hated to beg or ask for favors. "I need a chatelaine for my houses, someone to manage the servants and plan dinners and balls that will help me to advance socially. Frances just can't do these things, but you could."

It was not a request but an order.

Then he smiled. "Even if you don't, you're still welcome to stay with us for as long as you like." Before Constance could reply, he sighed. "Now, I'm not suggesting that you take your sister's place. You know I love Frances as I love life itself, but there are just some things I need that my wife can't provide."

And because Constance was so worldly, she suspected that her handsome, virile brother-in-law was referring to certain other duties his invalid wife couldn't perform, those of the marriage bed. Constance knew that her gentle sister had always viewed lovemaking with fear and revulsion, a viewpoint Constance had shared until the lusty Travers introduced her to the infinite delights of carnal love. Now she could be said to enjoy such pleasures too much.

When Constance looked into Gerrold's eyes and saw the desire burning in their depths, she knew at that moment that he was offering her far more than a role as keeper of his kingdom. There would come a time when he would want her for his mistress as well. She would finally have the man she had always wanted. The price would be high, but she was willing to pay it.

"I would be delighted to serve as your hostess, Gerrold," she said with a coquettish smile, "and I promise not to disappoint you."

He grinned as his gaze raked her up and down once again. "Oh, I'm quite sure you won't disappoint me, Constance. Quite sure."

Two days later Constance and Gerrold were in Newport, Rhode Island, taking a sunset stroll across Clairvaux's wide, gently sloping lawn, which faced the vast, unsettled sea.

Constance remembered the Newport of years ago as a sleepy seaside refuge for wealthy Southerners who came north, seeking to escape the debilitating summer heat of their own states. But then it was rediscovered as a resort by those with newfound wealth, such as the Belmonts, Kips, and Rhinelanders, who began building the magnificent mansions that lined Bellevue Avenue. Now anyone with money or social pretensions wanted a summer home here.

She inhaled deeply, filling her lungs with the tangy scent of brine, so clean and bracing after the foul, fetid air of New York City. The same breeze whipping up whitecaps in the distance tugged at her skirts and threatened to tear her hat right off her head, so she had to anchor the straw bonnet with one hand. Below her, where the cliff rose straight up from a narrow strip of shore, waves crashed relentlessly against rocks strewn with red-and-brown seaweed, and overhead, a flock of sea gulls soared and swooped down, snatching an evening meal of fish right from the sea, then careening back up into the vivid blue-and-orange sky. Constance found their mournful cries perversely cheerful and welcoming.

She turned to survey Clairvaux, the three-story forty-room mansion her brother-in-law modestly referred to as his "cottage," and the majesty of it took her breath away. Patterned after a French château Gerrold had once visited near Paris, the mansion was all warm gray stone with a steep mansard roof set with overlapping slate tiles and many tall chimneys. This evening the fiery setting sun was like Midas, turning Clairvaux into gold with one deft touch.

How appropriate, Constance thought, that Gerrold Webb should live in a house of gold, even if it was an illusion of a few minutes' duration.

When they reached the flagstone terrace enclosed on three sides by the main house and its two wings, Gerrold glanced up at his wife's rooms and said tightly, "How was your meeting with Frances this morning?"

Constance suddenly felt sad at the thought of her sister. "I was appalled at the change in her. Frances was always so beautiful, so vivacious, but now . . . she's like some pathetic ghost, so wan and faded. Is lying in her bed all day and talking incessantly about her illness all she does?"

"Not always," Gerrold replied, his voice edged with rancor as he stared grimly ahead. "Sometimes she has what her nurse calls her good days." He shook his head and muttered, "Good days . . . what a farce. All she does is get out of bed, get dressed, and sit in a chaise for a few minutes while Savannah visits with her."

Constance patted his arm sympathetically as they walked away from the house. "I am so very, very sorry, Gerrold. It must be very difficult for you."

His head jerked around, and those blue eyes were boring into hers with a searing intensity. "It is, Constance. Very difficult. Almost impossible to endure, in fact."

Constance returned his bold look and didn't let her gaze falter. "Well, I'm here now, Gerrold." That's all she said, without coyness, and by his slow smile, she knew that he understood precisely what she was offering.

Then he started talking about how his wife seldom saw her own child, and Constance felt a fresh surge of pity for her sister, but at the same time, she scorned her for her weakness in succumbing to the seduction of illness. In their youth Frances had always been the stronger of the two while Constance was quiet and introspective, content to remain in her vivacious sister's shadow. Now their situations were reversed.

Constance glanced over at the man by her side and decided that Frances didn't deserve a husband like Gerrold Webb, so strong, so vital, so difficult to manage. He needed a sharp, clever woman who would regard him as a constant challenge. Gerrold needed a woman like Constance.

When they passed yet another marble urn decorated with cupids and overflowing with ivy, Gerrold said, "I thought your meeting with Savannah went well. Very well indeed."

How could Gerrold be so blind? she wondered. Hadn't he noticed the way Savannah's eyes narrowed in blatant hostility, like a cornered fox cub, the moment they rested on the aunt she hadn't seen since she was four years old? And when that governess nudged Savannah forward to be reintroduced, hadn't Gerrold even noticed the way she hung back, a mulish, distrustful expression on her face? No, all Gerrold did was beam and bark out orders. "Curtsy to your Aunt Constance, Savannah" and "Now give your aunt a hug, Savannah." The moment Constance felt that skinny body stiffen in her arms and quickly draw away, she knew that her niece considered her an enemy, a usurper. The child sensed why Constance was here, and understandably she resented it.

Still, Constance's heart had gone out to her at once, for there was an air of deep loneliness and misery about the child that shouldn't have been there in one so very young. She was too pretty. Although still a little gawky and unsure, with spindly legs and a child's moon face, Savannah was going to be a beauty someday, of that Constance was certain.

She was confident that she could win over the child eventually. It was just a matter of finding the right pathway to her heart, that was all. And Constance was a master at that.

Savannah was moping in her bedroom where Blackie had sent her to bed without her supper for saying such bad things about her Aunt Constance. But she didn't care. From the first moment she had set eyes on her, Vannah had developed a fierce dislike and mistrust of her aunt and had said as much to her governess, who had quickly punished her. At least she had Mademoiselle Fanchette for company.

Vannah sighed, flung herself on the bed, and looked over at her doll, which was propped up in a rocking chair. "I hate being a little girl, Fanchette. I hate having to do everything grown-ups tell me to."

Someday you'll be all grown-up yourself and able to do exactly what you want.

That thought comforted Vannah, and she smiled for the first time since her aunt's arrival.

"Well, at least I won't have to take Blackie's orders anymore. She told me she's getting married and leaving Clairvaux forever. I'll probably never see her again. I'm glad, glad, glad!" But the catch in her voice belied her brave words.

Fanchette watched out of wide glass eyes but said nothing.

Restless, Vannah rose and went to a window, but what she saw agitated her even more.

"Look at this, Fanchette," she muttered between clenched teeth. "There's Father walking with Aunt Constance."

Vannah grudgingly admitted that her father and aunt made a handsome couple. Aunt Constance, all dressed in black because she was in mourning for her murdered husband, contrasted sharply with Vannah's father, wearing a light, cream-colored linen suit, perfect for the cool evening of a New England summer. Father was just a head taller than Aunt Constance, making him appear to be strong and protective of her as he slowed his long stride to accommodate hers, and she leaned forward to say something to him. That disturbed Vannah because it looked as though they were sharing secrets.

"That should be my mother down there," she said to her doll, "not Aunt Constance."

But your mother is very sick, Vannah. She can't go for walks with your father.

"They think I am stupid just because I am a child, Fanchette. They think I don't know why she has come here."

She is here to take your mother's place.

"I know that." Vannah scowled, and wished that one of the ancient copper beeches would come crashing down on Aunt Constance. Then she would never have to worry about her aunt again.

Vannah could tolerate it no longer, so she rose, hugged her doll hard, and went back to her bed. "I am not going to let her take my mother's place, Fanchette. I may have to be nice to her, but she will never make me like her. Never. You'll see."

* * *

Although Vannah vowed never to accept Aunt Constance, the servants had no other choice. In the three weeks that had passed since Constance's arrival at Clairvaux, she established herself with ironhanded efficiency, making all of the servants realize quite quickly that a new mistress was in command now. Those who didn't were told to find employment elsewhere.

One morning Constance sought Gerrold in his study to discuss the impending dismissal of a surly footman. The moment she walked into the room, she sensed that something was about to happen.

As she approached Gerrold's desk she noticed that he made no attempt to rise, just leaned back in his chair and gazed at her with frank concentration, rather like an expectant jungle cat sizing up its prey. Constance felt his eyes dart over her as she drew ever closer, and she could tell that he was wondering what her body looked like unclothed. Her breathing quickened and she looked for a telltale response, but no matter how badly she wanted him, she knew he must be allowed to make the first move. Gerrold Webb was not one of those men who were excited by a woman who took the initiative. She watched and waited.

Now he rose. "Constance . . . you look especially lovely today. I'm so glad you decided to pack away those ugly black dresses and come out of mourning. That shade of blue is much more suitable."

She thanked him, wondering if she should bring up the matter of the footman.

Without warning Gerrold rounded the desk, grasped her hand, and brought it to his lips. The sensation of his warm mouth against her sensitive palm sent hot shivers of delight racing through her. She could feel the first wave of excitement bring a schoolgirl's blush to her cheeks as Gerrold's hard blue eyes suddenly softened with desire. She became acutely aware of him as her slumbering senses awoke of their own volition. Her nostrils were filled with the spicy scent of his shaving soap, the starch in his collar, and his own subtle, unmistakably male scent.

Now Gerrold was undoing the tiny pearl buttons at the end of her sleeve, his nimble fingers making short work of them. Constance could feel his hot breath against her fingers, then the tickle of his mustache as his mouth wandered slowly down her wrist. When Gerrold began caressing her throbbing pulse with the pointed tip of his tongue, a delicious erotic shudder racked her body.

"Gerrold, please . . ." She had intended it as a rebuff, but somehow her protest sounded more like an assent, and she swayed toward him, yearning for him to take her into his arms at last.

"Do you want me, Constance?" Now his warm tongue was trailing in slow, enticing circles up her inner arm, deliberately tasting her. He stopped and growled, "Say you want me, Constance! Say it!"

"Gerrold, I have always wanted you!"

As soon as those words were spoken, as soon as the barriers of politeness and convention were down, the very air in the room seemed to crackle and dance with unbearable tension. Nothing else mattered except their raging passion.

They moved simultaneously, their bodies colliding in their urgency to embrace. Constance locked her arms around Gerrold's neck so her pliant body could mold itself to his, and his arms supported her waist and back, one knee parting her legs through her skirt as he gathered her to him. Both could feel the other's rapidly rising heat through the layers of clothing that separated and restrained them.

There was nothing gentle about Gerrold's first kiss. His

lips came down swiftly and hard on hers, his probing tongue forcing entry so he could possess her mouth, startling and delighting her. And she surprised him in turn by matching his passion, forcing him to retreat while she claimed his mouth with a deep, intimate kiss of her own.

He pulled away, breathless, and laughed, a low grumble that vibrated through the room. "What a woman you are, Constance! At last I've met my match."

She accepted the compliment as her due and smiled, running her fingertips down his mustache, savoring the rough, yet silky, texture of it. "When you love me, you shall forget all the other women you've ever known."

Her words inflamed him just as she intended. "Is that a promise? Now, we'll just have to see if your boast has any substance to it, won't we? But I must warn you that I am no gentle lover. If the prospect frightens you—"

"I am so very weary of gentle lovers, Gerrold."

He smiled, a roguish twist of the lips. "We are well matched, then." Then he stepped away from her and surveyed the room. "I want to take you here . . . now."

A sudden gust of wind scattered some papers off the desk, and Constance's eyes widened in unease. "But what about the servants? Aren't you afraid that one of them will walk in on us?"

Without a word Gerrold strode across the room, locked the doors, and returned to her side. "No one will dare interrupt us."

When they finished undressing and stood naked before each other, Gerrold took Constance's hand and led her over to a patch of sunlight on the floor. As he pulled her down on top of him and began to love her, he said things to her, not gentle murmurings of love and adoration but crude, gritty words that made Constance blush yet paradoxically aroused her in a way no other man had ever done before. As Gerrold had promised, he was no gentle lover.

Constance tried not to let her responses rise above a whimper, lest a gardener passing by an open window hear her, but she couldn't control herself. Gerrold was just too skillful and relentless with both hands and questing tongue. She felt as though she were being broken on a rack of pleasure.

"Please, Gerrold." She groaned, her clutching fingers entwined in his flaxen hair.

He lifted his head from her breasts just long enough to say, "No, my dear, not yet."

Despite her frantic entreaties, he kept bringing her just to the peak of ecstasy again and again, tantalizing her until she could bear it no longer and screamed, begging him to put an end to her exquisite torment.

Suddenly there came a loud, intruding knock on the study door, shattering the mood.

Constance froze, but the knowledge that someone was standing just outside in the hallway, listening, drove Gerrold into a frenzy of passion. He ignored Constance's pleas and loved her like a wild man until she lost all control and cried out, a wild-animal sound of satisfaction and ecstasy.

The knocking stopped just as Gerrold reached the pinnacle of his own excitement. His bellow of triumph echoed through the silent room as he shuddered, then lay still, covering Constance's body with his own. Only then did he whisper soft, sweet endearments to her.

Finally Constance sighed and stretched out like a lithe, contented cat, savoring the rough carpet beneath her back and the warm sun caressing her breasts and thighs as intimately as Gerrold had just moments ago. Her body would be bruised and sore tomorrow, testaments to Gerrold's unbridled passion, but she didn't care. He had turned her into a creature of pure sensation, but now that her body had appeased its hunger, her intellect began to intrude.

She realized that she had just made love to her sister's husband.

She decided then and there that she would make restitution and ease her own conscience by devoting herself to Savannah and raising her the way Frances would have, were she able.

But when Gerrold reached for her yet again, she went willingly into his arms with soft whimpers of surrender and deep need. She would deal with her conscience later.

Vannah stared across the breakfast table at Aunt Constance and wished that the woman would just leave her alone.

It had all started about a month after Aunt Constance's arrival, when she insisted that her niece have breakfast with her every morning. If it wasn't all foggy and gray outside, as soon as Vannah arrived at around eight o'clock, her aunt would open the French doors that led out onto her private terrace, and she and Vannah would sit at a table outside where they could enjoy a view of the ocean in the path of a cool morning breeze. Vannah would eat her porridge and sip her cocoa in silence while her aunt drank several cups of black Chinese tea and nibbled on sweet strawberries that were grown year-round in the Clairvaux hothouses. She talked incessantly of England, France, and other places she had visited.

Usually Vannah didn't converse much in return, but this morning her aunt finally hit upon a topic of conversation that piqued Vannah's interest.

Aunt Constance said, "Did you meet Mr. Ash when he was here?"

"Yes," Vannah replied, taking a piece of toast from its

silver caddy. "He mentioned that he had come here to see you but that you hadn't yet arrived."

Aunt Constance seemed surprised to find her niece talking after days of silence. "I've known him for years. His family and my husband's family are neighbors in Sussex."

"He seemed like a very nice young man. How old is he?"

"Twenty-one or thereabouts." Aunt Constance went on with "I find Martin too serious and melancholy for such a young man, but then, I suppose it's because he's so frustrated."

"Frustrated? What does that mean?"

"It means that he can't have something he wants very badly."

Vannah's curiosity was aroused, but she said nothing, hoping her aunt would continue of her own volition.

"You see, Vannah, Martin has to face the prospect that one day the only life he has ever known will be taken away from him and he will be forced to make his own way in the world."

"I don't understand," Vannah said, frowning.

Aunt Constance was silent while she sipped her tea. "Martin has an older brother named Avery. Someday he will inherit everything—the title, the fortune, the family estate—and Martin will get nothing."

Vannah felt her cheeks burn with righteous indignation. "But that's not very fair!"

"Life is often unfair, Vannah," she said gently. Then Aunt Constance got a faraway look in her eyes, and when she spoke, it was as though she were talking to herself. "It really isn't fair. Martin is so handsome, so compelling, and poor Avery is just a dried-up old stick."

"But what will Mr. Ash do?" Vannah wanted to know.

Her aunt shrugged. "Do what all younger sons of English peers do, I suppose. Join the army or the navy or the church." Her lips twitched at the corners, as though she were smiling at some secret joke. "No, not the church." Then she collected herself with a shake of her head. "You must remember that even those who are most deserving often don't get what they want in life."

With that sobering pronouncement to think about, Vannah turned her attention back to the rest of her porridge.

Later, as was their custom now, they went riding down Bellevue Avenue, past other grand houses, and stopped in Newport to patronize the shops, never leaving until Aunt Constance bought a new toy or book for her niece.

But Vannah always felt guilty. She knew she could be loyal only to her Aunt Constance or her mother, not both.

Then, one foggy morning, Vannah's new governess appeared at Constance's door and told her that Vannah was complaining of a stomachache and could not come to breakfast.

When Constance did go to Vannah's room to check on her, she found her niece looking very pale and drawn, sitting up in bed and playing listlessly with the pairs of wooden animals in her Noah's Ark.

"Your governess told me that you have a stomachache, Vannah," Constance said softly. She sat down on the edge of the bed and brushed a few stray wisps of hair off the girl's forehead in a maternal gesture.

Vannah nodded and looked so woebegone that Constance's heart went out to her. "Well, there will be no lessons for you today, but hopefully you'll be up and around tomorrow. I'll be expecting you for breakfast as usual."

The next morning it wasn't Vannah who appeared at the door but the governess once again, who reported that Vannah now complained of feeling hot and cold all over.

Constance felt sudden panic as she rang for her maid

and ordered the governess to send someone for a doctor immediately.

The doctor, a fatherly man with fuzzy gray hair that seemed to grow every which way, came to Clairvaux immediately for the only child of such a wealthy man as Gerrold Webb. Constance was anxiously by his side while he examined Vannah and punctuated every prod with a soft "Hmmm." Finally he rose, sighed, and said grimly, "May I have a word with you privately, Lady Travers?"

Oh, my God! thought Constance in alarm. The child is deathly ill. She swallowed hard. "Yes, of course, Dr. Halls. We can talk in my sitting room."

When they were alone, the doctor turned to Constance with a stern expression. "Madam, I have been a physician for twenty years, and I think I can tell when a child is pretending to be sick."

"Pretending?" Constance stared at him, her eyes wide with shock. "Vannah is pretending?"

He nodded curtly and stuck his thumbs into his vest pockets. "There's nothing wrong with that child. She's as healthy as the proverbial horse."

Constance had to sit down. "But why would she do such a thing?"

"Children fake illness for a variety of reasons, madam. Some do it to get attention while others try to escape from something unpleasant."

Like the unwanted company of her aunt.

Constance knotted her fingers together. "I realize that I am new to Clairvaux, Doctor, but Vannah seemed to be enjoying herself so much these last few weeks. She seemed to be accepting me."

"Perhaps she has learned to emulate her mother," Dr. Halls said tartly, with surprising candor.

Constance blushed, for she suspected that he was right. "Well, thank you, Dr. Halls. I regret having to summon you here for no reason, and I thank you once again for coming so promptly."

He smiled his warm, fatherly smile. "It's better to be safe than sorry, now isn't it? Feel free to call me at any time, Lady Travers, should the need arise."

When the doctor left, Constance opened the French doors and stepped out onto her terrace, but even the tranquil ocean view couldn't calm her this morning. Vannah had certainly pulled the wool over her eyes. Constance had actually believed that Vannah enjoyed their breakfasts together and their outings to Newport. Oh, she would have her moods, but that was to be expected. Now that she thought about it, Constance had never seen Vannah smile at her with genuine warmth and affection. Oh, she would smile when something pleased her, but never directly at Constance. When she looked at her aunt, there was always mistrust in those huge eyes.

The child was clever and devious, just like her mother. She knew that if she openly defied her aunt, her father would step in and punish her severely, but if she rebelled obliquely by feigning illness, no one could accuse her of being disrespectful.

Well, Constance decided with a tight pursing of her lips, she had only just begun to fight for her niece's affections, and Vannah's former governess, Miss Blackwell, was going to help her.

She rang for her maid and told her to pack their bags because they were going on a short trip to Providence and would be away for several days.

Vannah was having a history lesson when the summons came from Aunt Constance, but the governess excused her.

Several minutes later Vannah stood before the door to her aunt's sitting room and knocked softly. Suddenly the door flew open, as though her aunt had been standing on the other side, her hand on the knob, just waiting for Vannah.

"Come in, Vannah, dear, come in," Aunt Constance said breathlessly. "I have a surprise for you, one I think you'll like."

When Vannah said nothing, Constance took her hand and led her over to a drum table where a large box stood. Vannah noticed that her aunt was very animated today, her cheeks flushed, and her smoky eyes sparkling with excitement, as though she had some secret she just couldn't wait to share.

Now she lifted the box, turned around, and announced, "This is for you."

Vannah just stared at the package in puzzlement and suspicion. What had her aunt bought for her now in her attempt to buy Vannah's loyalty?

"Well?" Aunt Constance demanded impatiently. "Aren't you the least bit curious to see what's inside? I went all the way to Providence for it."

"I have enough dolls already, thank you," Vannah mumbled.

Her aunt took a step forward, her voice soft and cajoling. "Oh, it's something you'll like much, much better than another doll, of that I can assure you." She smiled again. "Come. Take it. See what's inside."

Now Vannah's curiosity was getting the best of her. What could be the harm in looking in Aunt Constance's stupid old box? She took the package and dropped down to the floor.

When the lid was off and Vannah saw what was inside, her eyes widened, and her gasp of astonishment filled the room.

"Aunt Constance . . ." she murmured in delight, dipping into the box repeatedly to pull out fine handmade papers in various sizes and textures; brushes with soft sable bristles; cakes of watercolor paint in every shade Vannah had ever seen; sticks of soft charcoal, chalk, and pencils for sketching. She felt as though she had happened upon a buried treasure and was overwhelmed by its riches.

As she watched her niece's face light up with a joy Constance had never seen there before, she said a silent prayer of thanks to Miss Blackwell for showing her the pathway to Vannah's heart.

"Miss Blackwell—I mean, Mrs. Jewett—told me how much you loved to draw," she said.

Vannah looked up at her. "Father has changed his mind, then? I am to be allowed to draw and paint, after all? I must be dreaming, Aunt Constance!"

Without warning all the pleasure drained out of her aunt's face to be replaced by uneasiness and guilt. Her gaze slid away. "No, Vannah, your father hasn't changed his mind about that."

Vannah felt very irritated and wished that her aunt would just speak plainly. "Well, if Father hasn't changed his mind, why did you buy these things for me? It seems rather silly to buy something that will never be used."

And suddenly Vannah understood all too well.

She stood up and turned away, spurning the very treasure she yearned for.

"Vannah, what's the matter?" Aunt Constance pleaded. "Don't you like your surprise? Is there something wrong with it?"

Vannah whirled around, rage and dislike making her face hot. "If Miss Blackwell told you how much I love to draw, she also must have told you that Father has forbidden me to do it. Are you trying to make him hate me? Is that why you're doing this?"

"Vannah!" Constance cried. "I'm hurt that you could even think such a thing of me! I bought this gift for you because Miss Blackwell told me you wanted to draw." The woman looked pained, as though a great struggle were being waged inside her mind. "Do you want to draw, Vannah?" she asked.

Vannah swallowed hard and stared at her aunt for what seemed like hours. She suspected that Aunt Constance had another reason for giving her the art supplies, but she couldn't quite determine what it was. Vannah knew adults lied to children, telling them one thing when they meant another, yet whatever her aunt's reasons, she was still offering Vannah the chance to do what she loved best. She looked at the implements scattered around the floor and nodded.

"Well, then, you shall," Aunt Constance said with relief. "But it must be our secret. Only you and I will know about it, and you mustn't tell anyone else. No one."

Now Aunt Constance put her hands on Vannah's shoulders, forcing her to look up at her. Gone was the sweet, lighthearted tone of voice her aunt usually used, to be replaced by one of gravity that Vannah found a little frightening and upsetting. "Listen to me very, very carefully, Vannah. I know you are a clever, intelligent little girl, so I know you'll understand what I'm about to say. Your father thinks you shouldn't draw, but I disagree with him. According to Miss Blackwell—excuse me, Mrs. Jewett now—you have a great deal of artistic talent, and I think it should be developed. However, both you and I know all too well that your father's wishes must be obeyed because he is your father and the master of this house."

Vannah stared at her without speaking, sensing the enormity of what her aunt was about to say.

Aunt Constance moistened her lips nervously. "I cannot impress upon you how very dangerous this undertaking will be. If your father finds out, he will send me away from this house in disgrace. I would have no money and no place to go. I would never be allowed to see you or my sister ever again, and I would probably starve." Or worse, she thought grimly to herself.

Vannah felt the gooseflesh rise on her skin. She had never before defied her father, and the prospect was daunting. "Just what is it we're going to do, Aunt Constance?"

Constance took a deep breath. "On the way back from Providence I devised a plan that just might work. I am going to tell your governess that you are to spend several hours a day in my rooms learning proper deportment and the social graces. We'll lock the door and won't open it for anyone. During that time you may draw or paint. I'm afraid that you're going to be very restricted in your subject matter, but you mustn't draw outside of these rooms. Do you understand?"

Vannah nodded, trying to contain her growing excitement.

Her aunt added, "None of these items are to leave this room, either, and you must never draw in your own rooms or even in the playhouse. Otherwise, someone is sure to see and report it to your father. Then all will be lost."

She then went over to a carved oak chest at the foot of her bed, knelt down, and unlocked it with a key. "I'm going to store your supplies in here. Only I have the key, so our secret will be safe."

"What happens when I need more supplies?" Vannah asked.

"Miss—Mrs. Jewett has agreed to buy them for you in Providence and send them to me secretly."

As she watched her aunt rise, Vannah realized just how great a gift was being offered to her and at what cost. Suddenly she felt such an outpouring of warmth and affection for her Aunt Constance that it melted the icy crust of mistrust that had encased Vannah's emotions for so long. She no longer felt so hopelessly alone and friendless.

"I'm taking a great risk for you, Vannah," Aunt Constance warned her gravely. "I hope you realize that and appreciate it. No one—not your governess, not any of the servants, not even your own mother—can know what you do when you come here for your deportment lessons. Are you grown-up enough to keep such a secret, even when you think you'll burst if you don't tell someone?"

As Vannah nodded, she also realized that her aunt was placing her future in Vannah's hands. If she went to her father and reported that his wife's sister was encouraging his child to disobey, Aunt Constance would be sent away in disgrace, and Vannah would be free of her forever.

But now that they shared this bond of trust and caring, Vannah would guard their secret with her life.

Yet she couldn't resist asking, "You would do this for me, Aunt Constance?"

"Yes, Vannah, I would."

"Why?"

Because taking such a great risk for you eases my guilty conscience, she thought. But she said, "I just want to see you happy, that's all."

And all she wants in return, Vannah realized, is for me to like her.

Without hesitation she suddenly ran over to her aunt and threw her arms around her, clutching her as though she would never let her go. "Oh, thank you, Aunt Constance, thank you so much. You'll never regret doing this for me. Never. I promise."

"I hope so, Vannah" was all she said, but even Vannah caught the doubt in her voice.

Chapter Three

Newport—1885

BY THE TIME THE WEBBS returned to Newport the following summer, Constance and Vannah were well versed in deception.

Every day, after having breakfast with Aunt Constance, Vannah would begin her "deportment" lessons. The doors were locked against curious servants, and Vannah decided whether to sketch in pencil, ink, or watercolor that morning. The subject matter available to her was limited to the contents of her aunt's suite or her own imagination. When she tired of painting seascapes or flowers, she sketched her Aunt Constance.

Usually she worked quietly and undisturbed. Occasionally a sudden knock on the door would send Vannah scurrying to hide pencils and paper beneath the sofa or bed, and when the door was opened, all the intruder would see was Vannah walking across the room with a large, heavy book balanced precariously on top of her head, ostensibly to improve her posture.

When Vannah's lessons were through for the day, she washed out her brushes and pans in the washroom's marble basin, then hid her work and the supplies in her aunt's chest.

Vannah had never been so content or happy. The earlier animosity she had felt toward her aunt vanished the moment they became co-conspirators. There was a perceptible change in the young daughter of the house, and others were beginning to notice.

Frances Webb awoke feeling better than she had in years. Her head wasn't pounding relentlessly, and her stomach didn't feel queasy. Best of all, the crippling, unrelenting lassitude, the oppressive feeling that she was weighted down with heavy, invisible stones had vanished. She smiled. She was going to have one of her good days for the first time in months.

She threw aside the top sheet and sat on the edge of the bed, waiting for the dizziness to conquer her and drive her back. Nothing. Frances smiled again. Out of habit she reached toward the bottles on her nightstand, then stopped herself. She told herself that she would not be needing her medicines this morning. Her hand fell back.

Frances breathed slowly and deeply, stood up, and waited, then she took a few tentative steps. When she didn't sway or collapse on the floor, she grew confident enough to cross the room to the window and managed to draw open the heavy damask curtain by throwing her weight against it.

As the dazzling sunlight came pouring into the dark, shadowed room, Frances was momentarily blinded by the flash and had to close her eyes against the sudden, intense pain.

Gradually she was able to peer through slitted lids then, as her eyes became accustomed to the bright, unfamiliar light, she was able to open them all the way. The sight that greeted her was well worth the effort.

She had almost forgotten how glorious a summer's day could be. Above, the sky was a delicate robin's-egg blue, unsullied by a single cloud, and below her window stretched the endless emerald lawn of Clairvaux. Beyond that was the sea, its blue-green surface shimmering and sparkling in the sun like a dowager's diamond parure.

Frances turned away from the window, reveling in her newfound strength. She strode around the room boldly now, flinging back the curtains, letting the sunlight come pouring in like liquid gold, banishing the sickness and the darkness, until her own bedroom was alien to her. That done, she laughed and held a bedpost for support, but except for feeling slightly out of breath from her exertions, the dizziness and lassitude hadn't returned.

That was how Nurse Ferris found her.

She stopped in her tracks, surveyed the sickroom through wide, astonished eyes, and almost dropped the breakfast tray she carried.

"Mrs. Webb! Whatever are you doing out of bed?"

Frances looked guilty, and her fingers fluttered near her mouth contritely. "Oh, please don't be so angry with me, Edna. I was just feeling so wonderful this morning that I had to get up and see the sun."

The nurse stared at her wordlessly. Judging from the wild glint in Mrs. Webb's eyes and the high color in her face, her charge was overexcited and on the verge of hysteria. But the accomplished Nurse Ferris knew just how to handle Mrs. Webb.

"That's all well and good," she said firmly, setting down the breakfast tray with its bowl of oatmeal and pot of tea, "but you know that your constitution is much too delicate for such outbursts of enthusiasm. I must insist that you get back into bed this instant."

Suddenly Frances didn't want to go back to bed. Rebellion flared deep inside her breast, and she longed to raise her voice to the domineering Nurse Ferris and tell her that she, Frances Webb, mistress of Clairvaux, did not want to return to bed. But, just as quickly as it rose, the flame of rebellion died. She didn't have the strength to keep it burning with the required intensity.

Frances sighed in resignation and allowed the stern

Nurse Ferris to lead her back to bed. "But I am feeling better, Edna, really."

"Well, we'll just see how you feel after you've eaten your breakfast." She pulled the sheet back over Frances, then set her patient's tray before her.

"But I am having one of my good days, Edna," Frances said while the nurse poured her tea. "I will want to see my daughter later."

"Fine, Mrs. Webb. You eat your breakfast and I'll get Miss Savannah." And the nurse left the room.

When she returned minutes later, she said, "I'm afraid your daughter is having her deportment lessons now and cannot be disturbed, Mrs. Webb."

Frances felt a brief flash of disappointment, followed by annoyance. "Nurse Ferris, I don't ask to see my daughter every day, and when I am having one of my few good days, I do expect a visit from her, deportment lessons or no deportment lessons, whatever they may be!" The outburst left her drained, and she fell back against her pillows, gasping.

The nurse started, surprised at this sudden display of temper in her usually placid patient. But she reasserted herself at once. "Now, Mrs. Webb, you mustn't excite yourself. I'll go back to Mrs. Travers and tell her that the lessons must be interrupted."

When she was alone again, Frances sighed. In spite of the illnesses that ravaged her body, her mind had remained sharp and perceptive. Frances sensed things. She had noticed the changes taking place in the Webb household; major, alarming changes that had started with the arrival of her sister from England last summer. Constance had taken over most of those duties that Frances had once performed before her illness.

Constance was the true mistress of Clairvaux now, and Frances was torn between feeling gratitude and resentment.

"But at least I still have my daughter," she said to herself in triumph. "Constance may take away everything else, but she can't take my daughter away from me."

Then Nurse Ferris returned to say that Savannah would join her shortly, and Frances rang for her maid to dress her.

Once dressed in a silk dressing gown of a warm rose hue, her wool challis shawl draped over her shoulders to guard against a chill, Frances went to her sitting room to await her daughter. No sooner had she reclined on the chaise longue when there came a soft knock on the door and her maid admitted Savannah.

"Savannah, my angel . . ." she murmured, smiling as she extended her thin arms.

Vannah tried her best to appear pleased, but in reality she was not. Her mother's request to see her this morning meant that Vannah was going to be deprived of an entire hour of precious drawing time today. She had whined and begged Aunt Constance not to let her go, but her aunt insisted that she must make the sacrifice. Vannah finally had no choice but to capitulate. She tried to remember her aunt's warnings to be pleasant as she crossed the room to be enfolded in her mother's waiting embrace.

"Good morning, Mama," she said, kissing her mother's hot, dry cheek. She smelled musty and unpleasant, not sweet like Aunt Constance.

When Vannah stood back, Frances looked her over eagerly, for she hadn't been well enough to see her own child for the last four months.

"My, Savannah, how you've grown!" The child's round face had more definition, with cheekbones appearing and the beginnings of a softly rounded bosom straining against the bodice of her dress. "I won't be able to call you my little girl any longer."

Vannah blushed and smiled in pleasure, for she had

been all too aware of the sudden, mysterious changes taking place in her body, and she was glad that her mother noticed, even if no one else did.

"How are you, Mama?" she asked.

"Just fine," Frances replied, hugging her to her flat, bony chest. "I haven't felt this good in a long, long time."

When released, Vannah seated herself in the small chair at the head of the chaise and waited for her mother to continue speaking.

Frances stared at Savannah, puzzled by her standoffish behavior. Usually the child was so bright and effusive when admitted to her mother's presence, but today, Savannah just sat there, swinging her legs back and forth, kicking at the rungs of her chair, her eyes darting nervously around the room. She seemed impatient and, Frances thought with alarm, acting like she really didn't want to be with her mother today.

When the silence threatened to make her cry, Frances smiled bravely and said, "Do you still ride that little white pony of yours?"

"Yes, Mama." Vannah knew she should have tried to make conversation, but she couldn't stop thinking of the sketch of Aunt Constance waiting to be completed. It was the best Vannah had ever done.

Frances waited, and when nothing more was forthcoming, she cleared her throat and tried again. "You're growing so fast, pretty soon you'll be too big to ride a pony. I'll have to talk with your father about buying you a real horse. Would you like that?"

"You needn't trouble yourself, Mama. Aunt Constance has already spoken to Papa about getting me my own horse."

"I see. And how are your French lessons progressing?"

"Very well, Mama. And Stephania says I'm doing well also."

"Stephania?" Frances said in alarm, her fingers fluttering nervously around her mouth. "Who is this Stephania?"

Vannah gave her mother a look of impatience. "Why, my Italian tutor, of course. Stephania Lucci comes from the town every afternoon to give me Italian lessons."

"I didn't know you were receiving instruction in that language."

Vannah smiled. "Aunt Constance thought it would be necessary if I ever visited Italy one day."

"Oh, and I suppose your aunt has made all the arrangements for you to go there soon?"

Oblivious to the jealousy and heavy sarcasm in her mother's voice, Vannah said, "Aunt Constance did say that we might visit Europe soon."

Frances placed her fingertips to her forehead, where a headache was beginning to form. Vannah, looking for any opportunity to extricate herself from her mother's presence, saw the gesture.

"Mama, are you sure you're well enough to visit?"

"I'm afraid my headache is returning, that's all." She closed her eyes with a sigh, wrapped her shawl more closely around her to ward off the sudden chill that enveloped her, and rested her head back against the chaise.

"If you're not feeling well now, perhaps I had better leave," Vannah said hopefully, rising.

Hearing the unmistakable eagerness in her daughter's voice made Frances feel as though a dagger had been thrust deep into her heart, but she smiled bravely. "Yes, perhaps that would be best, my angel."

Vannah rose and kissed her mother again, not realizing that relief was written plainly on her face. "I hope you will be feeling better again soon, Mama." Then she turned and forced herself to leave the sitting room at a sedate walk rather than a run. Once the door was closed behind her, however, Vannah broke loose and went racing down the hall, back to Aunt Constance and her unfinished drawing.

Frances heard her daughter's hurried footsteps through the closed door. Her heart was numb with shock and disappointment as she realized that Savannah had resented visiting her today and obviously couldn't wait to flee back to her aunt.

Life in the Webb household was passing Frances by. She might as well be dead for all her family cared.

Suddenly two great tears of hopelessness fell from her eyes, and her headache began to grow. As she began sobbing, her head throbbed even harder, growing in intensity. Frances rose and staggered blindly across the room, trying to reach her bedchamber before the lassitude robbed her limbs of strength once again. She managed to reach her bed before her legs failed to support her weight, and she collapsed with a grateful sigh. She was so tired. She had to rest.

Then she reached for the bottles on the nightstand.

Constance rarely had a thought to spare for her invalid sister these days. In three days' time she would be giving a lavish, spectacular ball, her first since becoming Gerrold's hostess, and most of her waking hours and even her dreams for the past month had been consumed by plans and strategies that would have put the Battle of Waterloo to shame. Gerrold was depending on her to make it the social event of this Newport season, and she simply refused to fail, for her future depended on it.

Constance's conquest of exclusive New York society had been subtle and well planned. Last fall, when she returned to the city with the family and the social season began right after the Madison Square Garden Horse Show, she didn't even attempt to take society by storm. Rather she began quietly and modestly. She didn't try to outshine the other women with expensive Parisian gowns and a king's ransom worth of jewels or surge to the forefront through lavish entertainments that were bound to make the leading hostesses resentful or envious, for she needed their goodwill and support if she was to succeed.

Instead Constance had Gerrold approach various business acquaintances and persuade these influential men to have their wives invite the Webbs to small supper parties or musical evenings. When these ladies realized that Lady Travers was a member of the British aristocracy by marriage and a charming guest as well, the invitations began pouring in.

Soon Constance responded by issuing invitations to intimate dinners of her own, and she brought a French chef over from Paris and paid him an exorbitant wage just to make sure that her guests dined like royalty when they came to Gerrold Webb's home. Within months Constance's invitations were among the most sought after in New York, and those that had once slighted Gerrold Webb now vied for the honor of receiving him and his lovely sister-in-law in their homes.

But Constance had yet to give her first ball, the ultimate test of her popularity and her ability to attract the best people.

Vannah sat cross-legged on the floor, held the silver hand mirror up to her face, and scowled at her reflection. "Aunt Constance, do you think I'm ugly?"

Constance, who was seated on the divan and checking over the menu for the ball, glanced at her niece, surprised to see that she was not drawing or painting today. "Of course not, Vannah! Wherever did you get the idea that you were ugly?"

Vannah continued to stare at herself, searching for flaws.

"When we went bathing at Bailey's Beach yesterday, that Andrew Pritchard threw sand at me and called me ugly."

"Is he that horrid little boy with the red hair, freckles, and pug nose?"

"That's the one."

"He's not exactly handsome, himself, now is he?" Constance set down her list and went over to Vannah. "Oh, I don't think he meant it, Vannah."

A troubled, hurt face looked up at her. "Well, if he didn't mean it, why did he even say it?"

"Because horrid little boys often say things they don't mean." And so do grown men, she added wryly to herself, but Vannah had plenty of time to learn that on her own. "Actually he probably threw sand at you to call attention to himself and make you notice him."

Vannah made a face of disbelief. "Really?"

"Yes, really. In fact, he probably likes you but is too afraid to come right out and say it."

"Ugh!" Vannah cried. "Andrew Pritchard . . . He's so homely, I wouldn't want him to like me. And besides, he smells like frogs."

Then she and Aunt Constance laughed.

Vannah stared at herself in the mirror again. "Do you think I'm pretty, Aunt Constance?"

"Of course I do. Look at your hair. It's a lovely shade of pale gold that looks just like sunlight. And look at your eyes, how large and blue they are. They dominate your face. Someday, when you're all grown-up, you are going to bewitch men with your beauty."

Vannah's eyes widened in surprise. "Like a witch in a fairy tale?"

"Yes, but a good witch. Your beauty will cast a spell over men and they will seek you out. They will all vie for your hand like Sir Lancelot vying for Queen Guinevere."

Vannah flushed with pleasure and turned to the mirror

again, trying to see in herself what her Aunt Constance saw, and searched for some signs of that beauty that would one day bewitch men. But all she could see were eyes too large and round for her small face and a long, thin nose with a high bridge. She was disappointed.

"Many fine, handsome gentlemen will want to go riding with you in Central Park or skating in the winter. There will be still others who will want to call on you, and one special man you will marry."

"Will I fall in love?" Vannah had been thinking of that most elusive of emotions a great deal lately.

"Perhaps," Aunt Constance replied. She did not have the heart to tell her niece that when she did marry, it would be to a man of her father's choosing, to consolidate two great fortunes or advance the Webb family socially. Love would have nothing to do with it.

"It's all very bewildering, Aunt Constance."

"Wait until you grow up, Vannah, and then you'll understand."

She sighed. "Why is it taking so long?"

"It just does, that's all. But, don't worry. You'll be grown-up and a fine lady before you know it, and then you'll wish you were young again." Constance found herself repeating words her own mother had said to her so long ago.

"No, I won't. I'll be glad I'm grown-up. I won't ever want to be little again."

Suddenly Vannah looked expectantly at her aunt and blurted out, "Can I go to the ball?"

"I hate to disappoint you, but balls are only for grown-ups. You know that." Seeing her niece's crestfallen look, Constance added, "You're twelve years old now, Vannah, and you still have some growing up to do."

"And then I'll be able to go to balls and have handsome gentlemen give me favors?"

"Yes, Vannah, I promise. Now, aren't you going to draw at all today?"

Vannah got out her papers and pencils and quietly began sketching a vase of flowers on the table near the window, but her mind was filled with visions of the Sir Lancelot, who would one day vie for her hand.

After her lessons were over for the day Vannah decided to escape to her playhouse and go roller skating around the upstairs studio. As she came running down the marble staircase into the main hall, she noticed that a new painting had been hung near the entrance. She stopped and stared.

The painting, in a wide frame of ornate gold leaf, was twice as tall as Vannah. A knight, mounted on a sedate white steed with an arched neck and flowing mane, was dressed in polished armor that reflected the sun, and he carried a huge broadsword with an engraved hilt. The name "Sir Lancelot" was inscribed on a small brass plate bolted into the bottom of the frame.

As Vannah drew closer to examine the painting she gasped in surprise. Sir Lancelot looked exactly like Martin Ash.

She realized at once that her imagination was playing tricks on her, for there was only a slight physical resemblance between the two. Rather, the artist had captured certain qualities in his knight that Martin Ash also possessed. Both Martin and Sir Lancelot had faces that were strong, yet gentle, and they shared determined mouths. But while Lancelot's eyes mirrored all his inner righteousness and goodness, Martin's were enigmatic and revealed nothing to the casual observer. How well Vannah remembered those smoldering green eyes and everything else about him.

As she stared up at the portrait a strange feeling came

over her, a tingling that started at the tip of her toes and worked its way up to the top of her head. She wanted to climb right into the painting and extend her hand to Sir Lancelot—or was it Martin Ash? She could envision him taking his foot out of the stirrup so she could place hers into it, then effortlessly hoisting her up behind him. Vannah actually felt the icy coldness of his armor as she wrapped her arms around his waist and the heat of his body beneath it, rising to warm her. He turned his head to look deep down into her eyes and said that she was the most beautiful woman he had ever seen. She had bewitched him, cast a spell over him, and he was going to carry her off to his castle, the towers of which were shrouded in clouds of mist and faintly visible beyond the treetops. When Vannah closed her eyes, she heard the thunder of his horse's hooves, felt the animal rock beneath her with long, powerful strides. The wind was soft against her cheeks as it blew through her hair, and overhead, birds were singing beautiful, unearthly melodies.

"Miss Savannah, are you all right?"

The dream vanished, and Vannah was back standing in the hall, staring at the painting of Sir Lancelot. She turned to find the maid Kathleen looking at her, as though she were a banshee come to life.

"I'm fine, Kathleen," she replied, then ran out the door toward her playhouse where she could dream undisturbed.

Constance stood before her full-length cheval glass, checking her appearance one last time before going downstairs. She smiled in satisfaction. Worth had certainly outdone himself with this gown of shimmering sea-foam green mousseline de soie that fit her lush, womanly figure to perfection.

Then she walked over to her jewelry case and decided to

wear the dramatic waist-length rope of lustrous graduated pearls her late husband had given her.

Suddenly there came an impatient knock at the door. Constance called out, "Come in," as she attempted to adjust the pearls around her neck.

She turned around to find Gerrold standing there, looking distinguished and elegant in his evening attire. She felt his critical gaze rove over her, from her elaborate upswept coiffeur down to the short train of her gown. When Constance saw disappointment in the depths of his eyes, her own pleasure quickly died and she swallowed hard.

"Gerrold, what is wrong? Don't you like my gown?" she asked nervously. "I'll change into something else if you prefer."

Without replying he walked into the room and studied her again.

"You look . . ." He hesitated, and she held her breath, waiting for his pronouncement. "Beautiful, as always."

She let her breath out slowly so he wouldn't see how relieved she was, then smiled radiantly.

"Except," he added, contemptuously flicking at her pearls, "for these."

Suddenly he reached into his breast pocket and removed a thin leather case. "I don't want to see those pearls around your neck tonight. You're going to wear these instead." And he thrust the box into her hands.

When Constance lifted the lid, her eyes widened. Lying on a bed of white satin was a necklace of gold set with two large square-cut emeralds and a dozen diamonds that blazed up at her.

"Gerrold! I—I don't know what to say. They're lovely."

He was already behind her, unclasping the offending pearls with practiced ease. "I consulted with Worth's about the color of the gown you were planning to wear tonight, then I went to Tiffany's to find something suitable. They suggested these."

Constance held the necklace in place and stared at herself in the mirror while Gerrold secured the clasp. The jewels were modest in comparison to those Constance knew the other women would be wearing tonight, but they were perfect, just the sort of jewels a wealthy man would select for his sister-in-law to show his appreciation for her serving as his hostess. Anything more expensive or elaborate would be more suited to a wife, and that would certainly cause tongues to wag tonight. The world might speculate about Constance's true position in the Webb household, but her life must always appear to be the very picture of propriety and decorum. Gerrold and Constance both saw to that. They would not let something as simple as the value of a necklace betray their illicit liaison to a world that was ruled by appearances.

But Constance was most satisfied with her necklace. It was a handsome start.

"Thank you," she said softly, slipping her arms around his neck and kissing him once more. "You are a generous man, Gerrold."

He smiled. "You'll find I'm most generous to those who please me."

"And I fully intend to go on pleasing you, Gerrold, for as long as you let me."

When they broke away, he ran his fingertips down the smooth curve of her cheek. "And I have another surprise for you as well."

Constance thought of the floor-length sable coat she had so vocally admired this winter. "Whatever it is, Gerrold, you shouldn't have. You have been too generous to me already."

He smiled. "My surprise is not a something but a someone." When Constance looked puzzled, he said, "Your friend, Martin Ash, will be attending our ball tonight. He arrived while you were dressing."

Constance stepped back in surprise. "Martin? Here? Whatever is he doing in Newport?"

"I understand that his business in Washington is completed and he's on his way back to England. He decided to stop to see you before he left."

Constance tried to hide her excitement. "It will be wonderful to see him again."

"Yes, I thought you'd be pleased. But come, my dear. Let's go downstairs. Our first guests should be arriving shortly."

Constance hesitated. "Gerrold, before we do that, there is something I must tell you."

"Yes, what is it?"

Constance took a deep breath and braced herself for an explosion. "Mrs. Caroline Astor declined our invitation. She will not be attending our ball tonight."

Gerrold's eyes turned glacial, his face a dark, furious red, but all he said was, "I suspected as much. After all, we weren't invited to her annual ball this January, so I had assumed that we are not yet among the chosen ones."

Constance had long suspected that Gerrold would kill, if only he could get away with it, for an invitation to Mrs. Astor's annual ball. They were the most coveted invitations in New York society, for the ballroom in her Thirty-fourth Street brownstone was large enough to accommodate only four hundred guests, thus restricting the number that could be invited and increasing the event's exclusivity.

She placed a comforting hand on his arm. "At least Alva Vanderbilt has taken you up."

Gerrold chuckled to hide his bitter disappointment. "Thank heavens! Otherwise we would be social outcasts. Well, I don't give a damn about Mrs. Caroline Astor. I fully intend to enjoy my own ball. Come, let's go, shall we?"

As Constance placed her hand in the crook of his arm she knew that for all Gerrold's indifference to the social whims of that Astor woman, her acceptance mattered a great deal to him.

Constance resolved to try harder.

Vannah knelt before the open window as a cool summer breeze stirred the sheer curtains and blew the sweet scents of flowers, freshly cut grass, and the sea into her bedroom. She had been kneeling here, her arms resting against the windowsill, ever since her governess had put her to bed an hour ago, and she sighed in impatience.

Finally her vigil was rewarded.

"They're coming, Fanchette!" Vannah leaned forward eagerly, straining to see the first carriage move through the wrought-iron double gates and down the long drive that was visible from the bedroom window.

A full moon had risen over the copper beeches, casting a cool, silvery glow over the grounds of Clairvaux, illuminating the landscape nearly to the intensity of daylight. The moonlight was so bright, Vannah could even discern the horses' markings and the drivers' livery as they approached the house.

Why aren't you at the ball?

"Because I am not old enough," Vannah replied, mesmerized as another carriage, then another and another, fell in behind the first one in a seemingly endless procession.

Well, even if you can't go to the ball, you could watch from the top of the stairs. Surely that is permissible.

Vannah pulled herself away from the window to turn and look at her doll seated in a chair and barely visible in the darkened bedroom. "Do you think I should?"

What would be the harm of it?

"If Aunt Constance catches me, she'll be furious."

Your aunt is going to be too busy with her guests to notice you.

Vannah stared at Fanchette, her brow furrowed in concentration as she debated what to do. True, she was supposed to be in bed for the night, but if she were quiet and careful to stay out of sight, surely no one could possibly object to her observing the festivities. She rose and padded noiselessly out of her bedroom.

Vannah hurried down familiar corridors, feeling her way along the wall in the darkness. As she grew closer and closer to the main hall, the sounds of people talking grew louder and louder, underscored by the faint strains of music floating up from the ballroom. Vannah could feel excitement in the air as she tiptoed up to the banister that ran along the width of the upstairs gallery before sweeping down the staircase.

She dropped down, silent and unobserved, and peered out from between the pink marble rungs that supported the banister. Below her, the entry hall was filled with people milling around, and Vannah had never seen such finery in her life. The women looked ravishing in their gowns of white, pale blue, pink, and green, all with trains that swept the floor behind them as they glided around. They blazed with colorful rubies, emeralds, and diamonds that caught the light and sparkled fitfully like the sea at midday. In contrast, the men all looked alike and seemed rather drab in their black evening attire.

Beyond the crush of people Aunt Constance and her father were standing before the portrait of Sir Lancelot to greet the guests still filing in. Vannah thought her aunt looked like a fairy princess in a gown of pale green, her smile radiant and unceasing as she tirelessly greeted guest after guest. Even Vannah's father actually looked pleasant tonight, his stern features softened by a warm smile.

Vannah noticed that every once in a while her aunt would glance up at her father, and he would smile down at Constance in return. It was as though they were passing secret, unspoken messages between them, and she wondered what they were saying with their eyes.

Minutes passed, and still the people kept coming in an endless wave. As Vannah sat there quietly, so careful to avoid drawing attention to herself, the late hour, the heat, the low buzz of conversation, and the hum of the music all conspired to have a hypnotic effect on her. Before she knew what was happening, her eyelids began to grow heavy and droop. She stifled a yawn, feeling very drowsy. Soon her head lolled against the marble rungs and she dozed.

Much later Vannah rallied and awoke with a start. The foyer was now empty and in semidarkness. All was quiet. She couldn't even hear any more voices or music coming from the ballroom.

As Vannah started to rise and return to her room, a sudden movement by Sir Lancelot's portrait caught her attention and made her hesitate. She blinked and rubbed her eyes. At first her sleepy, half-waking, half-dreaming state toyed with her imagination, making her think that the knight in the portrait had come to life and stepped down to join the ranks of mortal revelers. But the illusion was a fleeting one. This Lancelot wore elegant evening clothes like all the other men here this evening, not a gleaming suit of armor. She pressed her face between the rungs for a closer look. All she could see from the top of the stairs was that the man was tall and had curly chestnut hair. And then she knew.

"Mr. Ash!"

Then, as if he had heard her whisper of shock, he glanced up, caught her watching, and smiled slightly. Just one look from eyes that she knew to be that haunting green caused her breath to catch in her throat. Vannah felt a warm glow spread through her, a delicious tingling that crept from her toes to the very top of her head. She could not tear her eyes away, though she knew it was impolite to stare at someone the way she was staring at Martin Ash.

Suddenly her heart began racing when she saw Martin Ash come trotting with effortless grace up the marble steps. In his hand was a long, narrow box wrapped in blue paper. Vannah knew it contained one of the favors, an ivory and painted paper fan a gentleman was supposed to give to the lady he wished to dance the first dance with.

As the young man reached the top step Vannah suddenly wished that she were wearing more clothing than her thin night shift. Standing there with the soft batiste clinging to her budding breasts and slender hips, she realized instinctively that it was unseemly to allow any man to see her in such a state of undress, even a friend like Martin Ash. She was too innocent to know exactly why, only that she shouldn't.

"Good evening, Mr. Ash," she said, swallowing hard and wondering why her knees suddenly felt like rubber, forcing her to grasp the cold marble banister for support.

He granted her one of his rare smiles. "So you do remember me, after all. I'm flattered."

"I remember you." How could she ever forget the man who had championed her against her powerful father, the man who had given her tattered self-confidence back to her? "You tried to persuade my father to allow me to draw."

"And did I?"

Vannah was tempted to tell him the truth, then she remembered that Aunt Constance had sworn her to secrecy. She reluctantly shook her head.

His face fell. "I'm so very sorry." And she could tell that he meant it.

They stood there awkwardly, Vannah tongue-tied as she stared at the floor. She could feel Martin Ash's eyes on her, but she realized with a sinking heart that he was not sending her any secret, unspoken messages.

He cleared his throat and held out the box to her. "Since you couldn't come to the ball, I wanted you to have this."

And he handed Vannah the favor he was supposed to give to the lady he wanted the first dance with.

His eyes, she noticed as she took the box and stared up at him in awe, were quite kind in his serious face. She knew she should have thanked him, but her tongue seemed stuck to the roof of her mouth and the words wouldn't come. So she turned and dashed like a shy, startled fawn down the darkened corridor.

When Vannah reached the safety of her room, she stood there leaning against the closed door for what seemed like hours, the box pressed against her pounding heart. She looked at Fanchette, but the doll would not speak and just sat there in its dress of Alençon lace, its glass eyes staring out into space. Suddenly her treasured confidante seemed like nothing more than a porcelain head, glass eyes, and bisque body, a toy like any other. Somehow she knew that Fanchette would never speak again. Martin Ash had done something disturbing to Vannah tonight, something that he wasn't even aware of. But Vannah knew how he had changed her and in what way.

Finally she walked away from the door toward the window where the moonlight was still streaming in. She demolished the box's wrapping paper and lifted the lid. Vannah stared at the painted fan in wonder, slowly opening and closing the ivory sticks like she had seen her aunt do so many times. It was the kind of gift a man gave to a woman, and Martin Ash had given it to her. When she was old enough to carry a fan, she would carry no other.

She climbed into bed where she dreamed of a gallant chestnut-haired knight with smoldering green eyes.

The eastern sky was flushed a delicate rose-pink, and the top of the sun was just beginning to rise out of the tranquil sea when the last of the diehard revelers wearily climbed into their waiting carriages and started for home.

It was dawn and the ball was over. The last melodic strains of "Home Sweet Home" had long since died, and the terrace stood empty, save for dozens of small round tables littered with plates and glasses left over from the early-morning breakfast of eggs, sausages, and more champagne.

Constance and Gerrold came strolling arm in arm across the terrace, speaking in low, tired voices, neither of them noticing the silent, solitary figure watching them from the shelter of the grape arbor near the gardens. Gerrold looked around, and when he was satisfied that no one was looking, he grabbed Constance, pressing her back against his arm so she could not escape the violent passion of his embrace. Then his hands were all over her, patting, stroking, tugging. Both were so preoccupied with each other that neither of them heard a small smothered cry of anguish.

Frances, who had managed to stay awake half the night by the sheer force of her determination, turned and slipped unseen into the house and up to her rooms. She had seen and understood too much tonight, and all she wanted now was to forget.

Martin Ash stayed at Clairvaux for only three short days, and despite Vannah's best efforts, she only saw him twice during that period. Not only did her father monopolize the young man's company, he decreed that Vannah should be kept out of the adults' way, so she was restricted to her governess's company.

Vannah was heartbroken, especially when she learned from Aunt Constance that Martin Ash's father had died, his brother inheriting everything, and that Martin was returning to England to enlist in the British army.

Vannah wasn't to see him again for three long years.

Chapter Four

Newport—1888

THREE FIGURES STROLLED on the lawn between the mansion and the sea.

"So tell us, Ash, why did you resign your army commission? Couldn't take the blood and guts, eh?"

Martin Ash shielded his eyes against the glare of the bright sun with his large hand and stared out to sea at the white sail of a small boat dipping and rising erratically in the distance. He needed those few seconds to fortify himself against Gerrold Webb's incessant jibes and his intimations that the young Englishman was somehow less of a man because he had failed to make a success of the military career he was ill suited for and had hated in the first place.

Ash's smile was a little forced and his eyes as cold and hard as green bottle glass. "The fighting and the dying didn't bother me overmuch. The enemy is the enemy, and one must do one's duty, after all. But to answer your question, Webb, I resigned my commission because my commanding officers were all bloody fools, pompous asses the lot of them, who thought rank and wealth necessarily conferred intelligence and the ability to lead."

In fact, Ash added to himself, they were all exactly like you.

The implication flew right over Webb's head, for he said, "Don't blame you a bit, Ash. Never could abide taking orders myself," but Constance, strolling by his side, had to suppress a smile and avert her face lest she burst out laughing.

"Still," Webb went on, "it's a pity you have to be cut out of your inheritance by an accident of birth. Just because your brother had the good luck to be born a couple of years ahead of you, he gets it all. I'll wager there's no love lost between you, eh?"

"I bear him no animosity," Ash said with a shrug, and meant it. "Avery has always been fair to me. He's even offered me a home at Ashwood for as long as I choose to stay there, but he'll be getting married soon, and I feel I would just be underfoot. If I were the eldest, I would inherit. It's just the way our system has run for centuries, that's all, and one accepts it."

"Seems like a mighty poor system to me," Gerrold Webb muttered as they continued their stroll past the greenhouses and stables that could accommodate forty horses. "Here in America our children aren't fettered by such an antiquated system of primogeniture. Our sons and daughters are free to inherit equally. And if one of them turns out to be a gambler or a drunkard, then he can be neatly cut out of the will before he has a chance to squander it all. You can't do that in England, now can you?"

"No, one can't if an estate is entailed," Ash admitted.

Constance, growing tired of all this talk of inheritances and estates, smoothly intervened with, "Now that you're out of the army, Martin, what will you do?"

"What I'm going to say may surprise you." Then he hesitated, looking from Gerrold to Constance, who was especially fresh and lovely in a dress of pale yellow silk. "I have decided to seek my fortune in America, since you have already touted the many opportunities in this great land of yours, Webb. I'm en route to Wyoming to run a cattle ranch for a syndicate of British investors."

Gerrold stopped in his tracks while Constance's eyes widened, and she uttered a soft exclamation of dismay.

Webb extended his hand. "A peer of the realm punching cattle in Wyoming . . . I admire you, Ash. That takes courage, and I wish you all the luck."

Ash grasped the proffered hand and smiled. "And I'm sure I'll need every bit of luck I possess. I hear it's a harsh life, but a rewarding one if I succeed." He didn't even allow himself the luxury of thinking of another failure.

Constance didn't smile, and her smoky eyes were filled with doubt. "But, Martin, it's so—so different than the life you're used to."

He shook his head. "In some ways, perhaps, but I know something about running an estate, so I doubt that a ranch can be much different, and my experience in the army has taught me how to lead those who work for me."

"But I've heard that the winters are especially cold and brutal, and there are such terrible dangers there. Outlaws, red Indians . . ." Constance shuddered delicately.

Martin shrugged. "I'll wager they can't be any more dangerous or fearsome than the tribesmen of Africa where I served with my regiment."

"Well," Constance said, her eyes suspiciously bright, "I'm glad you at least came to Newport to spend some time with us before starting out on this new venture of yours."

Actually Constance was always Martin's only reason for stopping in Newport in the past and his only reason for coming there now. He had never quite overcome his love for her, a love she had always insisted was infatuation, nothing more. Because they had been neighbors in England, it had been so easy for him to pursue her, a woman nearly twelve years his senior, a woman married to a longtime family friend, a woman he could never hope to possess.

When she finally made him understand that she treasured him as a friend, nothing more, that she loved her husband and would not be unfaithful to him, Martin almost went mad from the agony of her rejection. And when Travers was murdered and Constance was being savaged by her stepchildren, Martin's hopes that she would turn to him and accept his suit were cruelly dashed. He was too young, she insisted, and she could not possibly marry him. Friendship was all he could ever expect. She promised that he would feel differently in time and that the acute pain would eventually vanish.

She had been right, of course, this gentle, wise woman with the beguiling smoky eyes and soft, husky voice. Time and a wide variety of other women had healed his wounds, and he did come to love her as a good friend.

As he watched her stroll by Webb's side her ivory-handled sunshade protecting her fair complexion from the hot July sun, Martin wondered if she was her brother-in-law's mistress. The very thought made a muscle twitch in his hard jaw. He disliked Gerrold Webb. Granted, his host was shrewd and clever when it came to making money, but he was pompous, overbearing, and vulgar, despite the exquisite, tasteful possessions surrounding him. Martin doubted that Gerrold Webb was letting Constance live with him out of the goodness of his heart, for the man had probably never put another person's welfare before his own in his entire life.

He thought of Webb's daughter and wondered if her

father had ever relented on his heartless decree that the child never be allowed to draw again.

"And how is your daughter, Webb?" Martin asked.

"I really don't concern myself with her," was the indifferent reply. "Now, if she were a boy, it'd be a different matter entirely. But a girl is her mother's responsibility or, in this case," he added with a warm glance in Constance's direction, "her aunt's."

Constance flicked Webb a brief look of disappointment, then she turned to Martin with her brightest smile. "Savannah is just fine, Martin. She's fifteen years old now, not a little girl any longer. I think you'll see a great change in her."

This dismayed Martin, for he had liked Savannah just as she was, natural and unspoiled, not twisted by all the opulence that surrounded her.

"She's less shy than she once was," Constance went on, "with more poise and self-assurance. And she has many friends now. It's so important for a girl to make friends."

As they approached Vannah's playhouse Constance said, "You'll soon have the opportunity to judge for yourself. Here's Vannah now."

As Martin watched, Vannah came walking down the flagstone path, her brow furrowed as though lost in thought, unaware that she was being observed.

Martin was astounded at the change in her since the night of the ball, when he had caught her barefooted and in her nightgown, watching secretly from the top of the stairs, her wistful eyes filled with yearning. Now she came up to his shoulder, and her skinny child's body had filled out into soft curves like a woman's. Even though she was so very young, her oval face with its high cheekbones and fine nose hinted at the beauty she would one day be.

My God, she is exquisite! he said to himself. Not only was Vannah physically beautiful, there was a goodness and gentleness about her as well. And he sensed that lingering just beneath that protective surface of childhood innocence lay a passionate nature just waiting to be released.

Then she looked up and their eyes met.

Vannah stopped short and just stared. She had dreamed of Martin Ash so often during the last three years, she couldn't believe he was standing right here before her.

Her eyes devoured every detail of Martin's appearance. He was just as tall as she remembered, though thinner, and the African sun had streaked his chestnut hair with reddish glints and added a few new lines to his face. The rugged bronze glow of his skin contrasting so sharply with the startling whiteness of his linen suit made his eyes appear an even deeper shade of green.

Those compelling eyes that had haunted Vannah's waking thoughts and nighttime dreams now seemed to smolder and darken as his gaze held hers. Yet they were also just as guarded as ever. Vannah felt her chest constrict painfully.

"Where are your manners, Savannah?" her father barked. "Aren't you going to greet our guest?"

His words jolted her out of her reverie. Vannah smiled, stepped forward, and extended her hand. "How do you do, Mr. Ash? It's such a pleasure to see you again."

A ghost of a smile played about his mouth as he took her hand and smiled over it. "The pleasure is all mine, Miss Webb."

The pressure of his strong fingers as they held hers for the briefest of moments was enough to bring the color flooding to Vannah's pale cheeks.

She tried to appear poised and grown-up as she said, "And how long do you intend to stay with us in Newport this time?"

"Oh, for several weeks, or until your father and aunt tire of my company," he replied.

"And then Martin's off to Wyoming," Aunt Constance supplied. "Our fine Englishman has decided to try his hand at cattle ranching."

Vannah felt her spirits plummet, and she looked up at Martin in alarm. She had read all about the Wild West in *Frank Leslie's Illustrated Magazine*, and she knew that it was no place for Martin Ash to be. She had hoped he had come to stay here for a good long time, not go traipsing off to some wild, untamed land with outlaws and cattle rustlers lurking around every bend. That left her with so little time.

"How—how interesting," Vannah said, trying to keep the disappointment out of her voice. "I didn't know Englishmen knew anything about ranching."

"I don't," he replied, "but I'm quite adept at learning."

Several weeks . . . Vannah had so little time to convince Martin Ash that she was grown-up at long last and that she loved him.

Three weeks later Vannah sat in the schoolroom, unable to concentrate on her history lesson.

She had done everything she could think of to make Martin Ash fall in love with her, but nothing was working.

No doubt he thought she was too young.

Too young . . . too young . . . too young . . . How Vannah hated those words! So she had tried to appear older to impress Martin with her maturity. When Aunt Constance refused to let her put her hair up or wear dresses that trailed the ground, Vannah dazzled Martin with her fluency in French and German and her skill at the piano. He was always quiet but attentive and seemed to enjoy her company for walks or rides. Yet he never once looked at her the way her father always looked at Aunt Constance, sending those silent, mysterious messages with his eyes.

Vannah sighed in frustration. Martin saw her as a little girl, not a young woman ready for love.

When Vannah's lessons were over for the day, she was feeling so dejected, she decided to go riding by herself. In four more days Martin would be leaving Clairvaux for his ranch in Wyoming, and then she would never see him again.

As she entered the stable yard, her boots tapping against the cobblestones, she saw that her father and Martin were already there. Vannah felt curiously warm and light-headed as she stared at Martin in rapt adoration.

She had never really noticed men before. Oh, she noticed if they were short or tall, handsome or ugly, dark-haired or fair, but that was about all. With Martin, however, Vannah observed that his black riding jacket fit his broad shoulders to perfection while the tan breeches and glossy black boots accentuated thighs and calves that were well shaped and pleasing. The tight kidskin gloves he wore made his large hands look strong and capable.

Today her father was letting Martin ride his spirited chestnut stallion, Pegasus, an honor not conferred on many, for it took a highly skilled rider to control the volatile animal.

As Vannah stood off to the side and watched Martin vault easily into the saddle, her heartbeat began to quicken with excitement. He looked superb as he found his seat and gathered the reins in one hand, patting Pegasus's gleaming, arched neck with the other to soothe the mettlesome stallion, who was making the cobblestones ring as he pawed the ground with iron-shod hooves. Martin was like some mythical centaur at one with his horse, the very picture of power, control, and grace. He was Lancelot. Vannah yearned to have him extend his hand to her and pull her up in back of him for the wildest ride of her life.

Please, Martin, she silently begged. Notice me.

He smiled down at her. "Savannah, have you seen your Aunt Constance's new mare, Duchess?" He nodded to a corner of the stable yard where a sleek, liver-colored horse was tethered to an iron ring set in the stone wall.

"She's beautiful," Vannah replied, "and she looks fast."

"She is," her father said, drawing alongside Pegasus on a rawboned bay, "and she's not for children, so don't try to talk your aunt into letting you ride her. You'd be thrown for sure."

Then, without another word, the two men started to ride out of the yard.

Vannah watched them trot their horses as soon as they were onto smooth earth, then she crossed the stable yard to her aunt's new horse. While large for a mare, Duchess appeared docile enough and even nuzzled Vannah's extended palm. "I don't see what all the fuss is about," Vannah crooned, stroking the mare's cheek. "You seem gentle enough."

And then Vannah had an idea of how she could impress Martin Ash once and for all.

Minutes later Vannah was trotting off on Duchess, having convinced one of the newly hired undergrooms that she was allowed to ride any horse in the stables. The mare was certainly taller than Vannah's own horse and her stride was longer, but Vannah felt no fear. She had something to prove, and she was going to do it.

As Vannah rode Duchess around the greenhouses she was beginning to think that her father's warnings about the mare were groundless. While a bit frisky, the horse was obedient and responded at once to the slightest pull on the reins or the touch of a heel. Vannah found her confidence soaring.

Now she could see her father and Martin racing their horses along the cliff's edge. Fleet-footed Pegasus was well out in front, his mane and tail streaming out behind him, while Martin leaned forward, so much a part of his mount that Vannah believed both horse and rider could leap right off the cliff's edge, fly over the ocean, and off into the clouds, just like his mythological namesake. She stopped Duchess just to watch and admire.

When the men slowed down, Vannah touched her heel to the mare and rode toward them. As soon as her father saw her his face darkened ominously, and the scowl between his eyes deepened.

"Savannah!" he snapped. "Get off that horse this instant! Didn't I tell you not to ride her? She's too dangerous for a child to ride."

Vannah felt her cheeks burn, but she refused to let herself be humiliated in front of Martin Ash again.

"But I am not a child, Father!" she retorted. "I am an excellent rider, and I'll prove that I can handle Duchess."

And before her father could say another word, Vannah turned the mare's head, leaned forward, and gave her a kick that sent her cantering toward a high hurdle that had been set up for the men. As she pounded toward the jump Vannah heard someone shout her name behind her, but she ignored the warning, for the jump commanded all her concentration.

Suddenly, as the rail fence loomed up before her, it looked so high and formidable that for one second Vannah was overcome by doubt. That second's hesitation was all her mount needed. Sensing her rider's uncertainty, Duchess faltered, lost her momentum, and shied away from the fence just when she should have been gathering herself to clear it. Vannah, poised for the jump, found herself propelled forward even as her horse veered to the right and seemed to disappear from beneath her. Then she was sailing through the air and over the fence.

The ground came rushing up to meet her, and the

world exploded in pain and a shower of brightly colored stars before going completely black.

Martin Ash was out of the saddle and by her side even before Pegasus slid to a halt on his haunches, his forelegs off the ground.

Not far behind him a livid Gerrold Webb was shouting, "Why in the name of God did that little fool try to ride that mare after I expressly forbade her to? And whatever possessed her to try to take that jump? Didn't she realize it was too high for her? Damn fool of a child!"

Martin ignored the other man's rantings as he knelt down beside the form lying so very still on the grass, one shoulder twisted beneath her. He yanked off his gloves, praying that Vannah was still alive as he carefully and gently rolled her on her back, examining her head and eyes. Lord, her face was so very ashen, but at least she was breathing. Martin stripped off his jacket, folded it, and gently placed it beneath Vannah's head like a pillow.

"Thank God her neck's not broken and she doesn't seem to have any head injuries," he said to the glowering Webb as he efficiently probed her limp arms and legs.

"This wouldn't have happened if the little fool had obeyed me," Webb muttered, slapping his riding crop against his boot in annoyance.

Martin stared up at him in disbelief, then exploded. "Is that all you can think of? Your daughter—your only child—might have been killed!"

Webb was stunned into silence but only for a second. "If she had been a boy, she would have had more sense. I'll go back to the stables and send someone for a doctor."

And he strode off, still muttering under his breath about his fool of a daughter.

"Vannah?" Martin murmured, carefully slipping his arm beneath her narrow shoulders so he could cradle her in his arms, and he noticed that her left shoulder was swollen and probably dislocated. He prayed fervently that that was all that was wrong with her.

"Wake up now. Tell me you're all right." When she groaned softly in response, he stroked her white cheek with his fingertips. "That's it. That's my girl. Come on. Open your eyes. Please."

Enveloped in blessed blackness, Vannah heard the voice from a long way off, relentlessly urging her to come back into the light. She tried to fight it and remain in the comforting darkness, but she couldn't. Her eyelids fluttered. Vannah blinked dazedly and found herself looking up into Martin Ash's strained and fearful face.

"M—Martin?" She could feel the hard muscles of his arm supporting her so capably, and she wished she could stay this way forever. Vannah closed her eyes with a soft sigh, content just to listen to the steady beating of his heart beneath her head.

Although just as furious with her as her father, Martin forced himself to remain calm, for the last thing she needed was to have someone shouting at her. "Yes, Vannah, I'm here. Your horse shied at the jump and you were thrown. I want you to tell me if anything is broken. Do you feel any pain?"

Vannah squeezed her eyes shut and gasped as a white-hot pain shot through her at the slightest movement. "My—my shoulder," she muttered between clenched teeth. "I think it's broken."

Martin smiled reassuringly. "I suspect that you've just dislocated it." Then he grew somber again. "You'd probably feel better if it were set right now. Do you want me to try?"

Vannah looked up at him and nodded, for she would trust Martin with her life.

"This may hurt like hell," he said, warning her as he laid her back against his jacket and stood looking down at her.

"I'm not a baby," Vannah retorted contemptuously, bringing another smile to Martin's lips.

"I think you're the bravest young lady I've ever met," he said as he braced his booted foot against Vannah's armpit and took her hand.

Despite the pain, Martin's words of praise brought a warm flush of pleasure to Vannah's cheeks, lulling her into unsuspecting compliance.

Without warning Martin jerked her arm, and Vannah howled as she felt the dislocated joint being wrenched back into place with an excruciating jolt of pain and a sickening click. Vannah felt her stomach heave, and when Martin released her hand, she rolled over onto her knees, retching violently onto the grass.

"Dear God, I'm so sorry I had to hurt you," Martin said, dropping on one knee beside her.

Vannah shuddered helplessly as one spasm after another racked her body, but through it all she was conscious of Martin's hand gently rubbing her back, his deep voice soothing. And when it was over, he wiped Vannah's mouth with his handkerchief and constructed a sling for her arm out of his cravat.

"You were very brave," he said as he knotted it around her neck and slipped her arm into the makeshift sling.

Vannah felt her cheeks turn pink again at his praise. "My shoulder does feel better." She looked at Duchess, standing there quietly, and she knew what she had to do. "I want to get back on my horse; otherwise, I shall lose my confidence and never ride again."

From his own falls in the hunting field Martin knew that she spoke the truth, and though reluctant to let her do it, Martin found his respect for her courage growing.

He said, "As much as I admire your courage, Vannah, I can't allow you to remount Duchess. She is too spirited for—"

"A child to ride?" she retorted hotly, forgetting the subsiding pain in her shoulder. "Well, Martin Ash, I'll have you know that I am an excellent rider, in spite of what my father says. And I was handling Duchess very well, I'll have you know, and if I hadn't lost my nerve at the last minute, she would have flown over that jump in grand style."

Without waiting for him to say anything she strode over to where Duchess stood, patted the mare on the neck, and reassured her that the fall had not been her fault. Then Vannah turned and said, "Well, Mr. Ash, aren't you going to help me mount?"

She looked so haughty, so determined, he realized the utter futility of arguing with her. He grasped her around the waist and lifted her into the sidesaddle effortlessly, for she was as light as a piece of paper.

"If you could just lead Duchess around for me," she said through stiff white lips, "I would be most grateful."

Martin grasped Duchess's bridle and began leading her around, all the while keeping an eye on her rider. When Vannah began to sway in the saddle, he brought the mare to a halt.

"You're getting down right this instant," he growled, his eyes flashing in a mixture of anger and concern as he reached up for her.

Vannah swayed, and Martin drew her to him to steady her. She leaned against him, her cheek pressed to his chest, and she could hear the steady, reassuring rhythm of his heart beating, feel the solidity and strength of his arm around her. She decided that she could endure anything as long as Martin would hold her this way forever.

The embrace lasted only a second, then Martin was setting her away from him. "Come," he said, slipping his arm around her waist. "Let's get you back to the house."

When Dr. Halls arrived, he examined Vannah thoroughly and admonished her never to take a hurdle without a horse again. After the doctor left, her father gave her a stern lecture on disobedience and told her that she would not be allowed to go riding for a week after her shoulder was healed.

But Vannah didn't care. She had proved to Martin Ash that she was not a child.

They were calling her. She could hear the footman's cry of, "Miss Sa-va-a-a-nah!" lingering on the air before an incoming wave came pounding down on the rocks with a resounding crash that drowned out his words. As the beckoning voice grew closer and closer Vannah froze, not daring to make a sound lest her hiding place be discovered. She knew there was scant chance of that, for her perch between the rocks on the beach could not be seen from the cliff above because of the large, overhanging boulder that shielded her. The only way Vannah could be seen was by someone strolling up the beach.

Soon the footman wandered off to seek her elsewhere, and she was alone, save for the wind, sea, and rocks. Not even a solitary sea gull drifted across the horizon today, and she was glad.

When Vannah was satisfied that she wouldn't be disturbed, she reached into the voluminous pocket of her cloak and took out a small sketch pad, a bottle of India ink, and a pen, then proceeded to sketch.

Ever since she had embarked on the secret art lessons, Vannah had never drawn outside of her aunt's rooms. The chance of discovery was just too great a risk. But today she had to. Vannah was sure she was safe here because she could see someone coming down the beach before they saw her, and she would have ample time to hide her paper and ink between one of the many deep crevices that existed between the rocks. No one would know what she had been doing unless she wanted them to.

Martin Ash was leaving today, and she couldn't bear to say good-bye. So she decided to hide where no one could find her. And she had to draw to keep from thinking about him.

Vannah frowned in concentration as she sketched, the scratching of the pen's nib sounding louder to her than the roar of the ocean. She sketched swiftly, skillfully, pausing only long enough to brush away strands of hair a belligerent breeze blew across her face, or the tears that suddenly scalded her eyes.

He's leaving and I shall never see him again. And I never told him how much I love him, she thought to herself.

Her drawing complete, she replaced the stopper, wiped the pen's nib clean with a handkerchief, and placed both in her pocket.

Vannah stared down at her handiwork through teary eyes, then slipped it beneath the cover of her sketch pad. It was all she would have to remember him by. She hugged the pad to her and huddled against the warm rock. She had never felt so miserable or alone, so desolate. She felt like dying.

Finally, when her cloak was damp and she could cry no more, she happened to glance down the beach. In the distance a tall, familiar figure was walking toward her. At any moment he would see her and know where she was hiding. Vannah knew that she could clamber up the rocks and elude him easily, but she didn't. She just sat where she was and waited for Martin Ash to come to her.

He didn't see her until he was halfway down the beach. She was wearing a drab brown cloak the color of rocks and seaweed, but her golden hair blazed in the early-afternoon sun, guiding him. Seated on her throne of rock, Vannah looked like Neptune's daughter with dolphins and sea creatures at her command.

As Martin approached her hiding place he almost turned and left her to her solitude, for this was going to be one of the hardest partings he had ever endured. He knew that, and he wasn't looking forward to it.

"Vannah," he said with a smile, "everyone has been looking all over Clairvaux for you."

She wouldn't look at him, just hugged something to her breast and murmured, "I—I know. I didn't want them to find me. I wanted to be alone."

"And you would have let me leave without saying goodbye to you?"

Now she did look at him, and he saw that she had been crying.

"I hate good-byes," she said in a curiously adult voice.

"So do I," he said gently, "but sometimes they must be said."

When Vannah remained silent, Martin searched his mind for something to say. He picked up a smooth, round pebble, turned, and flung it out to sea to give himself time to collect his thoughts.

Then he turned back to her. "What is that you're holding?"

"A sketch pad," she replied, almost defiantly.

He stared at her in astonishment, then he broke into a wide grin. "So you have been drawing all this time, in spite of your father's decree. I'm pleased to hear it."

This time a brief smile lit up her sad little face. "Aunt Constance has been helping me." And, while Martin listened, Vannah told him all about her so-called deportment lessons and what transpired every day behind locked doors.

Suddenly her face clouded, and the joy of conspiracy was replaced by fear. "But no one knows I draw. No one, not even my friends. My father would be furious if he ever found out. I know you won't tell him, will you?"

"You know I would never betray you, Vannah."

"I know," she replied, and looked away.

A strained silence fell between them, filled only by the constant roar of the sea. Finally Martin said, "May I see what you've drawn?"

Vannah panicked. If he saw what she had just drawn from deep within her heart, he would know at once how she felt about him. But perhaps it would be for the best. If she couldn't bring herself to tell him her deepest feelings, perhaps she should let her work speak for her.

She handed him the sketch pad.

When Martin lifted the cover and saw what she had drawn, he was so overcome that for a moment he was speechless. Finally he said, "Vannah, I don't know what to say. This is by far the finest sketch anyone has ever done of me. I once sat for my portrait when I was just about your age, but even that painting was not as fine as this sketch." He smiled and in a light, teasing tone said, "My only criticism is that you've made me far too handsome and far too noble."

"I did it from memory," Vannah replied, wiping her wet cheeks with her fingers. "You may keep it if you like. Just make certain that my father never sees it."

"Thank you," he replied, carefully folding the small sketch and placing it in his breast pocket. "I shall treasure it always."

Martin squinted and stared out at the horizon. "I think it's almost time for me to leave. Won't you come and bid me farewell?"

Vannah could contain herself no longer. Even though she squeezed her eyes shut, the tears flowed, anyway. She shook her head fiercely, her heart breaking.

Suddenly she sensed that Martin had clambered up on

the rocks and was sitting beside her. "Vannah, what's wrong?" he asked softly. "Why are you crying?"

"Because—because I don't want you to go," she sobbed, her shoulders shaking. "I'll miss you so much."

"And I'll miss you, Vannah, very much. But I have to go. This is something I have to do."

"Why?" she demanded. "Why can't you just stay at Clairvaux forever?"

"Because I can't. I couldn't just live off your father's hospitality forever. You know that. A man has to make his own way in the world. Some, like my older brother, have an inheritance, and others, like your father, have made themselves a fortune. I'm trying to find a place where I fit in. You're not a child, Vannah. Surely you understand that."

"But couldn't you seek your fortune in New York instead of Wyoming? That's the end of the earth!"

Martin shook his head as he reached out and gently stroked her hair, so soft and silken against his fingers. "I'm afraid not."

Vannah reached over and grasped his hand. "Then take me with you, Martin! You must know how much I love you." She looked over at his face with earnest, pleading eyes.

Martin was so startled by her confession, he pulled away more abruptly than he intended and jumped down from the rock. The sudden warmth of her touch and the unexpected response it had evoked in him played havoc with his emotions. He couldn't admit to himself that he had been attracted to Vannah during these last few weeks. She was just an innocent child, after all, and he was a grown man of twenty-five who should have known better than to encourage her infatuation.

And now she had to test the limits of his self-control by confessing that she was in love with him. Martin ground his teeth together and strengthened his resolve, knowing that he had to resist the look in her wistful eyes or he would be damned.

"Vannah, I know you think you love me—"

"I do love you, Martin, with all my heart."

"No, you only think you do. You're just infatuated with me, Vannah. There is a difference, and someday when you're older, you'll realize just what that difference is."

Now her blue eyes flashed as she jumped down from her throne of rock to stand beside him. But her fury died and was replaced by tears of helplessness again. "I am so very tired of being told that I am a child. Tired!"

"I know, Vannah, I know. I felt the same way when I was growing up. My older brother was always allowed to do things I wasn't, and no matter how old I grew, he was always older than I and always allowed privileges. It seemed as though I'd never become a man."

He smiled at her. "But one day soon you will be an adult, and then you'll understand what I'm saying."

"But I don't want to wait, Martin. I want to go with you to Wyoming, and later, when I'm all grown-up, we can marry."

He was touched by the innocence of her offer. "I can't take you with me, Vannah," he said raggedly. "It's not right!"

"But why not?"

He tried not to think of her shiny golden hair being blown by the breeze or the look of innocent desire deep in those eyes. Perhaps one day . . .

Martin picked up another pebble and tossed it into the hungry sea. "Ask your Aunt Constance. She'll tell you why."

"Is it because you don't love me?" Vannah persisted.

Martin ran his hand through his hair, his mind racing

to extricate himself from this delicate situation without hurting this vulnerable girl any more than was necessary.

"I do love you, Vannah, but only as a dear friend or a brother. I don't love you as a man loves a woman, as your father loves your mother."

Vannah's face fell, and she flinched as if he had struck her.

At her crestfallen expression Martin added, "I'm sorry. I don't want to hurt you, but I'm afraid I can't say I love you when I don't. That would be dishonest."

He prayed fervently that one day the blinders of childhood would be lifted from her eyes and she would understand what was now so painful for her to accept.

"I—I thought you were like the Sir Lancelot in the portrait, and one day you would come for me and take me away."

The guileless words so touched his heart that he wanted to take her in his arms and just hold her, but he restrained himself, for he knew that this gesture of comfort would be misinterpreted.

"That's a pretty fantasy, Vannah," he said, "but it's a child's fantasy. A lovely dream, not reality. I am only a man, not a knight in shining armor. I'm far from the perfect vision you have made me out to be, far from the man you have drawn. I know how much you hate to hear this, but I'm afraid I must repeat myself. Someday, when you are older, you will understand and thank me."

Then Martin turned and started walking away before his resolve failed him. "Good-bye, Vannah," he said, heading down the beach at a brisk walk.

Through her tears Vannah watched him slowly negotiate the rocky beach and climb the narrow path that led up to the cliff's edge. When he reached the top, he stopped and stood there for a moment, looking down at her. Then he raised one arm in a final salute.

Vannah did not wave back but stared out to sea as the tears coursed unchecked down her face. When she looked up at the cliff's edge again, Martin Ash was gone, taking a part of herself with him.

Chapter Five

VANNAH CUPPED HER chin in her palm and stared dejectedly out the window at the building next door. Over a month had passed since her family had returned to New York in their private railroad car, and over two months had crawled by since that July afternoon when she'd seen Martin Ash for the last time.

Just the very thought of that tall figure striding toward her across the sands caused a lump to form in her throat and tears to spring unbidden to her eyes. Vannah swallowed hard, took a deep breath, and turned her attention back to the half-finished watercolor sketch she had been working on all morning. But today, as in all the preceding days, Vannah found scant pleasure or pride in her work. There had been a time when watching some object come alive with a few deft, well-placed brush strokes would amaze and gratify her, making her marvel at her own skill and talent. Now that satisfaction had disappeared with Martin Ash.

She sighed again as she moistened the sable brush and stroked it across the cake of blue paint. Would the terrible ache inside ever go away? she wondered. She had always heard adults say that time healed all wounds, but the anguish of losing Martin Ash just seemed to grow more intense with each passing day, and by next month she would surely go mad from her loss.

Constance, seated across the room in a chintz-covered wing chair, looked up from the copy of *The Adventures of Huckleberry Finn* she was reading. She had long suspected that Martin Ash was the cause of Vannah's bout of listlessness and dejection. The only explanation Constance could think of was that Vannah fancied herself in love with Martin and he had rejected her. She knew Martin well enough to know that he must have let Vannah down very gently, but even so, the entire experience had obviously devastated her niece. Constance shook her head sadly at the heartbreak of first love.

She wanted to take Vannah in her arms, hug her tightly, and reassure her that everything was going to be all right, but she knew that Vannah wouldn't welcome such an intrusion into her private misery.

Constance rose, walked over to Vannah's chair, and stared down at her rendition of a chipped crockery pitcher and bowl of red apples. She smiled in delight. "Why, Vannah, that's absolutely beautiful! Those apples look so real, I could just reach in, pluck one out, and eat it."

For the first time in weeks Vannah felt satisfaction at her accomplishments. "Thank you. It is rather good, if I do say so myself."

"Good? You're much too modest. It's excellent. You have genuine talent, my girl, genuine talent. And I'll never regret our secret 'deportment lessons.' "

"Neither will I. I must tell you, though, that there have been many times when I've almost told some of my friends."

Constance felt herself go tense. "But you haven't, have you?"

Vannah shook her head. "I made you a promise and I've kept it. I haven't breathed a word to anyone."

Constance closed her eyes and gave a little sigh of relief.

Now Vannah looked up. "There's something else I've been meaning to ask you for some time now, Aunt Constance."

"Yes, Vannah, what is it?"

"Do you think I could have some oil paints and canvas? If I'm to be a real artist someday, I really should learn to master oil paints. All of the great artists did oil paintings."

Constance smiled ruefully. "I suspect that their fathers didn't forbid them to draw at all." Seeing Vannah's crestfallen look, she said, "The smell of oil and turpentine would give our secret away. You know that. I'm afraid you'll just have to content yourself with your watercolors, Vannah. I'm sure there are many artists who worked only in that medium."

She sighed. "I know I should be satisfied with just being able to draw at all."

"Be thankful for small favors."

Suddenly Constance glanced at the enameled clock on the mantel, noticed that it was almost eleven o'clock, and started. "Oh, my goodness! I'd almost forgotten. The stained glass window your father commissioned from Mr. Tiffany is going to be unveiled today. Let's go downstairs and watch, shall we?"

"Mr. Tiffany . . ." Vannah murmured, swishing her brush in clear water, then packing away her supplies. "He's the man who refurbished our house in New York, isn't he?"

"Yes," Constance replied, going to a mirror and making sure not a hair was out of place. "McKim, Mead, and White did the architectural changes, but Mr. Tiffany was responsible for the interior design."

Vannah had gotten the surprise of her life when they returned to the city in September and she walked through the front door of the brownstone. She thought she had wandered into another house by mistake. Gone was the familiar plain dark foyer with its long table against one wall and the giant apidastra plant in the corner. In its place was an Arabian Nights fantasy with brilliant mosaic windows and exotic hanging lamps made of gleaming brass and suspended by chains.

And, except for the family's bedrooms on the third floor, the rest of the house had undergone a similar transformation. The staid, stuffy parlor now boasted delicate Japanese wallpapers and a magnificent fireplace edged with handmade tiles, and the woodwork in the library was carved with an exotic blend of Viking and Celtic designs. Several rooms on the second floor had had their walls torn down to create a ballroom where none had existed before.

During the summer the Webbs had been at Newport, their town house had been gutted and redesigned by Louis Comfort Tiffany, one of New York's society's most sought-after designers.

"I love our new house," Vannah said as she followed her aunt out of the suite, "but why did Father have it redone? I thought it looked nice the way it was."

Actually Constance knew that the refurbished brownstone was a sop to Gerrold's wounded pride. For some time now he had been enviously eyeing all of the mansions springing up along Fifth Avenue. He hadn't minded Alexander Stewart's white marble building just one block away, because that had been there before Gerrold bought the brownstone and moved into the neighborhood. But when William Henry Vanderbilt, the commodore's eldest son, built his twin brownstone mansions between Fifty-first and Fifty-second Streets, Gerrold sensed a trend in the making like a spaniel scenting ducks. He always had to be first at anything.

His suspicions were confirmed when William Kissam Vanderbilt, William Henry's second son, erected a traffic-stopping François I château at the corner of Fifty-second Street, and this was followed by a red, pressed-brick Fontainebleau for Cornelius II.

Gerrold felt he belonged there right alongside the likes of the Vanderbilts, but after spending four million dollars to erect Clairvaux in Newport, he simply could not afford to build a similar structure on Fifth Avenue, no matter how badly he wanted to. It was said that a man had to be worth at least fifty million dollars to afford such a grand city palace, and Gerrold's fortune fell short of that standard by about ten million. And, oh, how it rankled!

So he had to satisfy his need with a socially acceptable alternative. If he couldn't have a new mansion in the city, he could at least have his present house gutted and redecorated by either the Herter Brothers or Louis Comfort Tiffany. Gerrold preferred Tiffany's style because it was considered more "artistic" and therefore uncommon, so the son of the city's most famous jeweler was given the commission.

But Constance couldn't reveal this to Vannah, so all she said was, "Oh, I suspect your father just wanted a change, my dear."

Vannah seemed to accept that, for she said nothing as she followed her aunt downstairs to the parlor.

When they entered the room, Vannah was most surprised to see her mother present today, reclining on a chaise. Her father was also there, talking to a pleasant-looking man with a reddish-brown beard, and both stopped the moment Aunt Constance came into the room.

"Ah, there you are, Constance, just in time for the

unveiling," Gerrold said. "Come, you must meet Mr. Tiffany."

When Vannah saw that she wasn't going to be introduced to their august guest, she walked over to her mother, who was reclining on the chaise, her paisley shawl wrapped around her thin shoulders even though the parlor was warm.

"I'm glad to see you're well enough to come downstairs, Mama," she said with a smile.

Her mother looked as though she were going to cry. "Actually, I am not well, my angel, not well at all. I awoke this morning feeling very tired, but your father insisted that I come downstairs for a few minutes. I don't know why."

Suddenly Constance broke away from the two men to come stand near the chaise, and Gerrold addressed them. "I wanted you three to be the first to see the stained glass window that I have commissioned from Mr. Tiffany, and which was just installed this morning."

Now Vannah could see the crimson velvet drape hanging to the right of the fireplace, and she wondered if it was covering the window.

Gerrold beamed at Constance. "I think you'll be pleased. Mr. Tiffany . . . ?"

Their guest reached for the drape and tugged at one corner. As the material fell away, he quietly announced, "The Adams Sisters."

No one was quite prepared for what followed. Frances burst into tears. Constance just stared in awe. Vannah moved toward the window as if in a trance.

"Why, it's like a painting made of glass," she murmured, transfixed.

The scene consisted of two women on a terrace with the sea in the background. Since the faces were painted with the skill of a portraiturist, it was obvious that the one reclining on a chaise was Vannah's mother and the other leaning against a balustrade was Aunt Constance. Vibrant morning glories in varying shades of blue glass edged the window on one side.

Vannah had never seen anything like it. True, the Gothic ballroom at Clairvaux contained several stained glass windows, but nothing to match the beauty and intensity of this. Although every element in the window was outlined in black leading, the glass didn't have the flat, one-dimensional quality of most of the stained glass windows Vannah had seen. This glass contained subtleties of shading similar to those she achieved with her watercolors.

She sensed someone standing behind her and heard a low, pleasant voice say, "This window began its life as a painting, did you know that?"

Vannah turned to look up into the sparkling blue eyes of Mr. Tiffany himself. She shook her head.

"Either myself or one of my designers first makes a watercolor sketch of the window. You must be familiar with watercolors, Miss Webb."

Vannah almost nodded, then caught herself just in time. "No, Mr. Tiffany," she said, and thought she heard a sigh of relief from her Aunt Constance.

Mr. Tiffany raised his brows in surprise. "I thought all young gentlewomen learned to draw and paint."

"Not I."

"A pity. Several of my best designers are women. In fact, a woman worked on this very window."

Vannah's father stepped forward, and judging by the deep scowl between his brows, he was most displeased with the direction this conversation was taking.

"Obviously a woman of great artistic talent," he said, placing his hands on Vannah's shoulders to emphasize that she was not included among their ranks. Then he turned to his wife. "So, what do you think of your portrait, my dear? Wasn't it clever of me to think of having it done in glass, instead of just a painting?"

But Frances said nothing; just kept staring at the window while great tears streamed down her cheeks.

Her husband was plainly embarrassed and chagrined by her less than enthusiastic reaction to his tribute. "Now, now, my dearest heart, why the tears? I thought you would be pleased by my surprise." Then he added over his shoulder to Mr. Tiffany, "You must excuse my wife. She has been ill for some time and is prone to these sudden moods. Constance, help me to get her back upstairs. You must excuse us for a moment, Tiffany."

Gerrold gathered his wife in his arms while Constance followed him out of the parlor, leaving Vannah alone with Mr. Tiffany.

She turned to him, excitement shining in her eyes. "Why are some parts of the window painted, like the faces and hands, and others, like the flowers, just pieces of glass?"

He smiled down at her. "What do you think, Miss Webb?"

She frowned up at the window, studying it. "I suppose it is because features are too small and delicately shaded to wrap the leading around."

Mr. Tiffany nodded in approval. "The artist wants to outline as much of an object's form as possible with leading—they're called cames, by the way." He gestured as he spoke, following the shape of one of the women with his fingertip. "But I strive to shade with the glass itself. Occasionally that's impossible, so I must resort to paint."

"It's fascinating," Vannah murmured. "Aunt Constance's gown seems to be billowing in a breeze, as though it were made of cloth instead of glass. How marvelous it must be to be able to create something so beautiful."

She was so transfixed by the window that she failed to

notice Mr. Tiffany studying her with equal intensity. Finally he said, "I sense in you a kindred spirit, Miss Webb."

Vannah felt her cheeks grow hot. "What—what do you mean, Mr. Tiffany?"

"I can tell that you appreciate art and beauty."

"I like to think I do, but I am no artist, like you, Mr. Tiffany."

"A pity," he replied.

"And you say a woman designed this?"

He nodded. "And another woman cut the glass pieces."

A woman just like me, Vannah thought.

"It's the most beautiful thing I've ever seen," she declared. "I like it so much better than a painting."

"Well, if you think so, you must come to visit my house someday and see my studio."

"I would like that," Vannah said.

And then her father returned and drew Mr. Tiffany off somewhere, leaving Vannah alone in the parlor.

She stared up at the stained glass window in wonder, her imagination fired by the skill and artistry necessary to create such a work. She thought of her own watercolors, just pretty pictures on paper, and she suddenly felt a vague restlessness and dissatisfaction. But to paint a picture that was transformed into glass—now that was something to be proud of.

At that moment Vannah knew what she wanted to do with her life as surely as if she had turned the page of a book and saw the answer written there in letters as bold and black as leading.

"I want to design stained glass windows for Mr. Tiffany." When she realized that she had spoken aloud, she looked around the parlor guiltily, lest someone overhear her. No one was there to witness her declaration.

I don't know how, but I will find a way, she promised

herself. No one must ever know about my dream. No one. Not even Aunt Constance.

Vannah's desire to design windows became her secret obsession. Whenever she did a watercolor sketch, she tried to envision how it would look translated into glass. Often she would hold it up to a window to get the full effect of light shining through it, illuminating it from behind. Yet she realized that there was much she needed to know before such a dream became reality, and she had to acquire that knowledge without arousing anyone's suspicions, especially her father's.

She decided that would best be accomplished by learning all about Mr. Tiffany and his work.

Luckily for Vannah, Mr. Tiffany's second wife—his first having died of a lung disease—was very active in several of the same charities as Aunt Constance, and the two women became friends. This gave Aunt Constance the perfect excuse to call on the Tiffanys, and Vannah never missed an opportunity to accompany her to the Tiffany house, a rambling Romanesque chateau of reddish-brown stone that stood on Madison Avenue and Seventy-second Street.

Right from the first time she walked into the sprawling top-floor studio, Vannah was entranced and excited by the room's richness and imagination. Above the main entrance to the studio was an organ loft filled to overflowing with flowers and huge Oriental vases, and once inside, attention was immediately claimed by the unusual brick-and-concrete fireplace that dominated the center of the room. It was hollowed out on four sides so that the studio could be lighted from every direction. The sloping roof was set with great windows of greenish-yellow glass that softly filtered the sunlight. Everywhere Vannah looked, she saw something to delight her: rugs and animal pelts, hanging lamps in rich tones of copper and bronze, paintings, wicker furniture, vases, bowls, and iridescent glass everywhere, all precious possessions lovingly displayed without a feeling of clutter.

As the months passed, Vannah gleaned much information about Mr. Tiffany and his work, if not from the man himself, than from his wife or daughter. She knew that he was the son of New York's best-known jeweler but that he had wanted to become an artist rather than following in his father's footsteps. He had formed his own interior design company called Louis Comfort Tiffany and Associated Artists and had become so successful that he was hired to redecorate Mark Twain's house in neighboring Connecticut and invited to perform the same magic on the White House for President Arthur.

Constance didn't give a second thought to her niece's sudden preoccupation with the Tiffanys. On the contrary, she was relieved to see Vannah taking an interest in something other than moping about and pining for Martin Ash. By accompanying Aunt Constance on such calls, Vannah was developing the social skills she would later need to secure her rightful place in society.

As long as Vannah was allowed to visit the Tiffanys and nurture her secret dream of one day designing stained glass windows, she went along with her aunt's plans for her social development. She expanded her circle of friends to include people her father thought of as socially acceptable and became a popular, much-sought-after addition to any gathering of young people.

By the time she was sixteen, she received several proposals of marriage, all of which she promptly disregarded.

Then came Vannah's seventeenth birthday and a shattering of her innocence forever.

"More flowers, Miss Savannah. Lovely white orchids, they are."

"Just put them with the others, Maeve," Vannah replied, taking the card to read who was responsible for this latest tribute on her seventeenth birthday.

"Just listen to you, miss," the maid said with good-natured familiarity. "This is the twentieth bouquet of flowers you've received today, and all you can say is, 'Just put them with the others, Maeve.' A bit offhand about our throng of admirers, aren't we?"

Vannah shook her head when she read the name Andrew Pritchard scrawled on the card, then she glanced up at her maid. "Oh, I don't mean to be, Maeve. It's just that . . ." She shrugged helplessly.

Maeve understood at once, and her face softened in sympathy. "It's just that none of these gentlemen is special enough to you."

Vannah nodded. "Exactly. A bouquet of daisies gathered from a field would mean more to me than all the roses or orchids in the world if I loved the man who gave them to me."

"I can understand that, miss." Maeve set the bouquet down near a vase containing three dozen red roses, curtsied to Savannah, and left.

When she was alone, Vannah stared at all the bouquets filling the tables in her private sitting room and sighed dismally. How different she would feel if one of them was from Martin Ash.

She hadn't stopped thinking of him during the two years that had passed since the day he left Clairvaux. Even though Vannah had met many personable young men since then, brothers and cousins and friends of her friends, young men like the ones who had sent her lavish floral tributes on her seventeenth birthday, none of them could stir her emotions the way Martin Ash had. They were all handsome enough, but their callow faces lacked mystery and their personalities lacked depth. She couldn't imagine allowing one of them to kiss her.

Vannah walked over to her full-length cheval glass to look at herself with a critical eye. She was always so astonished at what her reflection revealed, for even though many told her she was beautiful, she had only just recently begun to accept their pronouncements. But Aunt Constance's prediction had come true.

She had grown tall and straight, with a regal carriage befitting a princess. Vannah often wished that her narrow, boyish hips were rounder, but she was more than satisfied with her splendid bosom, as were all the young men who stared at it when they thought she wasn't looking. Her neck was long and swanlike, her face a perfect oval. An aspiring poet among her admirers once wrote an ode to the symmetry of her wide blue eyes, straight nose, and full, rosy lips. Crowned with a mass of thick, glossy hair that fell nearly to her waist, Vannah was an acknowledged beauty.

She only wished that the man of her dreams were here to appreciate it.

Now, as Vannah looked around at the many birthday gifts she had received, she remembered that there were still one or two details concerning her party that she had to discuss with Aunt Constance, so she turned on her heel and went to find her.

Vannah knocked several times on her aunt's sitting room door, but no one answered, so she opened it and went inside. The room was empty. Vannah was just about to leave when she was brought up short by a strange noise emanating from her aunt's bedchamber. It sounded like a low moan of distress.

Later Vannah knew that she should have announced her presence by calling out, but there was an odd quality about the sound that both puzzled her and aroused her curiosity. So she remained silent and cautiously tiptoed toward the dressing room that connected the sitting room to the bedchamber.

The dressing room door was ajar. Vannah hesitated, but when she heard another moan, louder and lingering this time, she pushed the door open and slipped quickly into the small, dark room, taking care not to reveal her presence by bumping into anything. She moved quietly toward the other door that connected this room with the bedchamber. It, too, was open just a crack. Burning with curiosity, Vannah went up to it and peered inside.

What she saw was so unexpected and shocking, she had to press her knuckles to her mouth to stifle a gasp.

Two naked people were on the bed, Aunt Constance and the man beneath her, only the top of his golden head and muscular shoulders visible to Vannah from her hiding place. Aunt Constance appeared to be straddling him, her unpinned golden-brown hair tumbling wildly down past her white shoulders, her head thrown back in abandon. Then she began to move, a slow, rocking motion that caused her heavy breasts to swing back and forth.

As Vannah watched, her breathing shallow and her cheeks burning in mortification, she knew that she should flee before she saw too much, but somehow the forbidden act she was witnessing both repulsed and fascinated her. She knew her aunt was making love to someone. She and her friends had often speculated about the act in detail and what it entailed, but nothing had quite prepared Vannah for what she was witnessing now.

Part of her wanted to preserve her innocence by tearing herself away, while another part of her burned to know more about such forbidden secrets. That part of her won.

She stared, wide-eyed, as her aunt began moving faster now, eyes closed and lips parted to emit low growls. She sounded like she was enduring great pain, but the expression on her face was one of sheer rapture. A thin film of sweat glazed her alabaster skin, and damp tendrils of hair stuck to her face.

When the man groaned and reached up to squeeze Aunt Constance's breasts, Vannah finally glimpsed his face and had the shock of her life.

Father!

Vannah screamed the word at the top of her lungs, but when the couple on the bed didn't stop what they were doing to stare at her, Vannah knew the scream had existed only in her own mind. The shock suddenly gave her leaden legs life, and she backed away from the door slowly, for she dreaded to think what her punishment would be if she were discovered eavesdropping on this particular intimate scene.

Somehow she managed to escape from Aunt Constance's chambers undetected and stagger back to her own rooms where she locked the door behind her with trembling fingers and tried to assess rationally what she had just witnessed.

Aunt Constance and Vannah's own father were lovers. Even though she had witnessed their coupling with her own eyes, she couldn't accept it. Her own father . . .

Vannah went around the room, pulling bouquets from their vases until her arms were full, then she went into her washroom and unceremoniously dumped them all together into the marble bathtub where she wouldn't have to look at them again.

Then she sat herself down in a chair, drew her knees up to her chest, and curled herself up in a tight little ball. Then she wept—whether for her aunt's betrayal or her own lost innocence, she couldn't tell.

"What's wrong, Vannah?" Constance demanded several weeks later.

"Nothing."

Constance pursed her lips in annoyance as she stared down at her niece making silly, insignificant doodles instead of a picture. "I'm sorry, Vannah, I know you too well to believe that. Ever since you came down with that mysterious illness the day of your birthday party, you haven't been the same. You don't want to go on outings with your friends anymore, and you haven't visited the Tiffanys in several weeks."

Constance picked up the drawing Vannah was working on, looked at it, then threw it down contemptuously. "You haven't even been applying yourself to your artwork. Please don't keep secrets from me, Vannah. Won't you tell me what's wrong?"

Now, and many times before, Vannah wanted to blurt out, "You're nothing but a whore, Aunt Constance! I saw you coupling with my father when you thought no one was watching. My poor sick mother doesn't even suspect that her own sister is her husband's mistress."

But she couldn't. In spite of everything, Vannah couldn't bring herself to hate her aunt. The woman had done so much for her since joining the family six years ago. Vannah hated herself for being disloyal to her mother, but she couldn't see what purpose it would serve to tell her aunt what secret she had accidentally discovered on her seventeenth birthday.

Yet she couldn't stand to remain in the same house with her father and aunt. She had to get away, at least for a little while, to think matters through.

She looked over at her Aunt Constance. "What do you think about my going away, Aunt Constance?"

Constance started. "Go away? What on earth do you mean, Vannah?" Surely her niece wasn't asking to be sent to Martin Ash in Wyoming!

"I want to go to a finishing school in Europe," she

announced. Vannah had been thinking of this idea ever since Louis Tiffany returned from a trip to Europe and related wondrous tales of all the artistic activity going on there.

"But why?" Constance wanted to know. "You'll be eighteen next year and ready for your coming-out ball."

"That's a year away," Vannah pointed out. "Besides, I think it would be very good for me. You've always taught me that travel broadens one. Just think of all the wonderful opportunities I would have to meet girls from different countries, perfect my French and German, learn something about another culture."

Constance was still not convinced that these were Vannah's true reasons for wanting to go to finishing school, but she wisely held her tongue. "As a matter of fact, your father broached the subject with me just the other day. He was wondering how you might like going abroad for a year, away from your family, and I discouraged him."

Actually Gerrold's reasons for sending his daughter to Europe were a far cry from Vannah's. He was hoping she would make important connections that would enable her father to secure a European nobleman for his son-in-law.

"Well, if Father approves, Aunt Constance, then I think I should go. It would only be for a year. I'd be home in plenty of time for my coming-out ball."

"You do know that you wouldn't be able to draw or paint during that time," Constance warned.

Vannah smiled for the first time in days. "But I draw so well now, I really don't think that a year will make a difference."

"Well, if you really think you want to go . . ."

"I do, Aunt Constance."

"Won't you miss all of your friends and a summer in Newport?"

"Yes, but it will only be for a year. The experience will be worth it."

Aunt Constance sighed in resignation. "Very well. I shall speak to your father right away. I know a particularly fine boarding school on the outskirts of Paris. . . ."

In a month's time Vannah was boarding a ship on her way to France.

Chapter Six

New York City—1891

"WHERE IN THE DEVIL IS SHE?" Gerrold grumbled, craning his neck to peer over the bobbing heads of all the other people crowding the landing stage. "The passengers have all disembarked, and I don't see Savannah anywhere. Are you certain she said she would be arriving today?"

By his side, Constance frowned in consternation as a man in a garish green checkered suit and brown bowler hat jostled rudely against her before elbowing his way through the crowds.

"I'm certain," she replied, scanning a wave of unfamiliar faces. "Vannah's cable said she would be arriving Tuesday, June third, at eleven o'clock on the *Teutonic*. She's got to be here somewhere, Gerrold. She can't have gotten lost on an ocean liner of all things."

"Hmph. Perhaps she never got on the ship at all and is still somewhere in France," Gerrold muttered. "Or perhaps she got on the wrong one."

Suddenly, off to the side, a familiar voice scoffed, "Credit me with a little more sense than that, Father," and both Constance and Gerrold whirled around to come face-to-face with Vannah herself.

"I don't know whether to be insulted or flattered that neither of you recognized me," she went on nonchalantly as she opened her amber-handle silk parasol to shade her delicate complexion from the June sun. "I've been waving at you frantically ever since I started down the gangplank, but both of you just kept on looking right past me as I fought my way through this throng. Tell me, have I really changed that much in one year's time?"

"Vannah!" Constance cried, then regarded her niece in astonishment. "Changed! No wonder we didn't recognize you. You've become quite the elegant Parisienne, my dear, quite the lady of fashion."

And so she had. Vannah wore a smart ivory traveling ensemble that bore Worth's indelible stamp. The gown itself was simple in style, but the bishop's mantle worn over it was studded with jet cabochons and had a dramatic yoke of jetted passementerie, with a rain fringe of still more jet that swung gently with Vannah's every move. Her fair hair was upswept in the latest style beneath a small, saucy hat of ivory fabric set with two white aigrette plumes that made her look even taller and more regal.

My little Vannah looks like a princess, an American princess, Constance thought, her eyes suddenly misting with unexpected tears.

"Enough of our staring," Constance said gruffly, then drew her niece to her for a crushing hug. "Welcome home, my dear. Lord, how I have missed you!"

When Constance finally released Vannah, Gerrold stepped forward to give his daughter a perfunctory peck on the cheek. "Well it's about time," he growled. "We've been waiting here in the hot sun for hours."

Savannah's blue eyes flashed as she bristled at his tone. "Well, Father, I can hardly be held responsible for the navigation of the ship, now can I?"

Gerrold was so taken aback by his daughter's retort that for a moment he was stunned speechless. Then he scowled and found his voice. "So that's what you've learned during your year abroad, how to talk back to your own father. Well, young lady—"

"Gerrold, please," Constance said, smoothly intervening as always. "Surely this can wait until we're home and Vannah is settled. I'm sure she's exhausted, and she still has to endure customs yet."

Gerrold looked around at the erstwhile crowd that had thinned out considerably since their arrival. "Well, once we get you through customs, we'll be on our way home. The carriage is waiting right over there."

Vannah chuckled as she recalled her twenty steamer trunks piled high on the dock. "Well, I hope you've brought along two wagons to cart all of my luggage back with us. I'm afraid I bought out Worth's while I was in Paris. I fear you are going to disown me when you receive my outrageous clothing bills, Father."

"Nonsense," Gerrold said as he offered one arm to Constance and the other to Vannah. "A man wants his daughter to be a credit to him, and she can't do that if she goes around looking like a dowd, now can she?"

When they finally went through customs and were walking back to the Webb carriage, Vannah grew suddenly pensive. "How is Mother?"

"The same," her father replied with the usual cold indifference he displayed when speaking of his invalid wife.

"I'm afraid so, dear," Constance said more gently at Vannah's disappointed look. "She still has her good days, but they are more and more infrequent. I try to visit her as much as possible, but most of the time she is too ill to have callers."

"Did she miss me at all while I was away?" Vannah asked as her father handed her into the carriage.

"But of course!" Constance replied. "Nurse Ferris told me she spoke of you often."

When the three of them were seated, Constance seemed eager to talk about something else. "Well, we have so much to catch up on. I don't know where to begin. Vannah, how did you find Paris and Miss Fitzmaurice's school?"

Successfully distracted, Vannah smiled, lighting up her face and animating her sapphire eyes. "It was wonderful, Aunt Constance, simply wonderful. I must confess that I fell in love with that city at once, even Monsieur Eiffel's tower that all of the Parisians hate. I must tell you about the most amusing thing that happened to me the very first day I was there. . . ."

While Vannah told her story of being mistaken for the daughter of a Russian diplomat and nearly abducted by a pair of wild-looking Cossacks, her father quietly and objectively studied her, truly taking an interest in her for the first time in his life.

He assessed her coldly and dispassionately, as though she were one of his priceless possessions rather than his own flesh and blood. In several weeks Vannah would be having her coming-out ball on her birthday, and then the world would know that Gerrold Webb's only daughter was ready for marriage. He wondered how much she would fetch in the marriage market, and he smiled in anticipation. Gerrold hadn't yet decided if he would seek another large fortune to merge with his own or marry Vannah off to someone of higher social standing than the Webbs. Perhaps a French prince or an English duke in the family might prove to be an advantageous connection.

Gerrold frowned slightly. He would have to think long and carefully about marrying off his daughter to some foreigner. He knew that such transatlantic marriages of Old World aristocracy and New World money had been going on for decades now, but he had met far too many impoverished, fortune-hunting English dukes lately, all with their rapacious eyes on plentiful American dollars to repair their decaying estates and support their hereditary way of life. Something inherent in Gerrold Webb's democratic nature balked at bailing out an effete aristocrat who hadn't done an honest day's work in his life. On the other hand, perhaps the prestige of a title would be well worth a million or two just to see the envious looks when he spoke of his daughter the duchess or his daughter the princess.

And his Savannah was certainly beautiful enough to grace any royal throne. Who would have imagined that such a shy, gawky child would mature into a beautiful, vivacious young woman?

Well, in any case, Vannah's marriage would be a business transaction, but as in all his business transactions, Gerrold Webb would make sure that he got comparable value for his dollar.

"Father," Vannah said with a bemused smile from her corner of the carriage, "why are you staring at me as though I've suddenly grown two heads?"

She caught him by surprise, and he fought to recover himself. "I'm just so overwhelmed at the change in you, that's all. A man's got a right to stare at his beautiful daughter, hasn't he?"

Vannah's silvery laugh of pleasure filled the carriage. "Well, what did you expect? I'm not a child anymore."

Her niece's statement of the obvious caused sentimental tears to flood Constance's eyes, and she busied herself looking out the carriage window so no one else would notice. Constance had achieved what she set out to do:

raise her invalid sister's daughter as if she were her own. And in all modesty she thought she had done an admirable job of it. She had finally made restitution for taking her sister's husband, at least in her own mind.

"Aunt Constance?" Vannah was leaning toward her, concern written plainly on her face. "Are you all right?"

Constance fumbled for her lace-edged handkerchief and dabbed at the corners of her eyes. "Just waxing a little sentimental, my dear. It's not so very long ago, you know, that you were just a little slip of a thing in short dresses and one long braid. And now here you are, all grown-up and so very beautiful."

Vannah smiled sympathetically and patted her aunt's hand. She tried to find the right words that would bring Aunt Constance comfort, but there were none to be had. She had grown up. She wasn't that little slip of a girl any longer. And she was beginning to formulate definite ideas about what she wanted to do with her life, though she realized that this wasn't the time or the place to discuss them. There would be plenty of time to shock her aunt and father later.

Instead she laughed and said, "Well, let's not get all teary, shall we? I'm home now." She looked from her aunt to her father. "Well, what has been happening in my absence?"

So Constance began talking, and by the time the carriage pulled up before the Thirty-fourth Street brownstone, Vannah felt as though she had never left New York.

When she walked through the front door, Vannah was surprised and touched to find that Parkins, the butler, had assembled the entire household staff in the foyer to greet her. After a short, eloquent speech of welcome, he handed her a small silver salver covered with cards from more than a dozen young gentlemen who had called already. He also informed her that flowers had been arriving all morning as well, but those had already been taken to her rooms. She thanked him, then informed her father and aunt that she wanted a leisurely hot bath and a chance to rest before she went to see her mother.

Once she was nearly submerged in her green marble bath, the warm, moss-scented water lapping gently against her shoulders as her head rested against the tub's rim, Vannah turned her thoughts to her eye-opening year in Paris.

It had been the most exciting year of her life—revealing, shocking, broadening, liberating—and she looked upon its end with genuine regret. She knew and understood so much more now, about herself, her parents, her Aunt Constance, and life itself that she might never have known if she hadn't experienced Paris in its infinite variety.

And it was all because of a vibrant young French noblewoman named Lysette de Mornay.

Vannah chuckled as she lifted one long, shapely leg out of the water and lathered it with scented glycerine soap. "Father, if you had any idea that I was to room with such a bad influence as Lysette, you would have pulled me out of Miss Fitzmaurice's so fast . . ." She chuckled again.

Lysette had been so intriguing because she was the only girl of Vannah's own age she had ever met who had had a real flesh-and-blood lover. Lysette had actually done what Vannah and her friends only speculated about.

Vannah reclined in the tub, letting the soothing water buoy her as she watched the steam rise gently from its surface. And Lysette had been so, so eager to share her knowledge with the curious, inexperienced American.

"My dear, dear, Van-nah," she would say, laughing, "you American girls know so little about men, so little about *amour*. But Lysette is going to change all that. Lysette is going to tell you everything she knows, which is considerable."

And she did, every night under the cover of darkness, when the lights were out and the hall matron's footsteps had died away, her rounds finally over. From Lysette's conversations Vannah soon learned that she and her friends had barely scratched the surface concerning physical love between a man and a woman. Some of the more intimate details of that mysterious act deeply shocked Vannah at first, but Lysette assured her that her reaction was common for sheltered, virginal Americans with no experience of men. Lysette also assured her that such feelings would pass.

"But, Van-nah," she would say with a sigh and a shrug, "why are you so afraid of what is so pleasurable? Believe Lysette when she says that once you have known a man, all the silly fears—poof!—they disappear like smoke. And then you laugh and wonder how you could have been so . . . *stupide*. Finally you come to enjoy it so much that you don't want your lover to leave your bed. I can see the doubt in your eyes, but *oui*, it is true. One day you shall see for yourself."

Still, despite such reassurances, Vannah was skeptical.

As she climbed out of the tub and wrapped herself in a soft, fluffy pink towel, Vannah sighed. She had much to thank Lysette for, not only for her patient and detailed explanations of *amour*, but also for insight into why her father and her aunt had defied convention to become lovers.

"How could my own father do such a thing to his own wife, my mother?" she had complained to her newfound friend.

Lysette had taken Vannah's hands in her own and squeezed them. "Ah, my *pauvre* Van-nah," she crooned like a wiser older sister. "There is still so much you have to understand about the men and their ways." And then she explained that a young, virile man such as Vannah's father couldn't be expected to abstain from that which was so vital to his sex and lead a life of abstinence, like a monk.

"But he's breaking his marriage vows!" Vannah protested. "He promised to be faithful to my mother in sickness and in health."

Lysette gave one of her fatalistic Gallic shrugs. "Do not judge your father too harshly, Van-nah. He is only a frail human, subject to weaknesses of the flesh. To me he sounds most kind, to spare your *pauvre maman* the rigors of his virility. And what about your aunt? She lost her beloved husband, no? She must have been lonely herself. They were just two lonely people who needed each other, Van-nah, and I think you should try to find it in your heart to understand and forgive. We Frenchmen are so much more tolerant of these matters. You could learn much from us."

As the months wore on Vannah was able to come to terms with the fact that her father and aunt were lovers, and by the time she was scheduled to leave for New York, she decided that she would forget she had ever seen them together.

Now, as she finished drying herself, slipped into her long silk dressing gown, and left the bathroom for her bedroom, Vannah recalled other memorable aspects of her year in Paris. In spite of the fact that the young ladies of Miss Fitzmaurice's were heavily chaperoned wherever they went, Vannah had never enjoyed such freedom in her life, and she never missed an opportunity to attend a walking tour of the Louvre, visit a cathedral to see its stained glass windows, or stop to discuss technique with an artist painting some colorful scene of Parisian life.

For although she had promised Aunt Constance that she would never draw or paint while she was in Paris, Vannah had not agreed to forget about art entirely. In fact, she talked and thought of nothing else.

Vannah let down her hair, crimped into curly tendrils from the steam of her bath, then frowned as she seated herself at her vanity table and began brushing her golden mane with long, sure strokes. With a long, drawn-out sigh Vannah rang for her maid to help her dress. She could postpone the inevitable no longer, no matter how much she dreaded it. It was time she called upon her mother.

Frances stopped writing, cocked her head to the side like a curious bird, and listened. Nothing. She must have imagined that she heard the door to her sitting room open, but she couldn't be too cautious these days. Nurse Ferris walked as noiselessly as a cat and could creep up on her unawares.

She continued writing several more lines, blotted the paper dry, folded it, and hurriedly inserted the letter into an envelope. Then she concealed it in the wide pocket of her dressing gown so Nurse Ferris wouldn't see it.

Vannah was due home from Europe today. Vannah would help her. She could trust her own daughter to deliver her letter. It was crucial to her plan.

Frances smiled as she rose from her rosewood writing desk and crossed the room. She had been so clever this past year, so very clever. No one, not Constance, not Gerrold, not even Nurse Ferris, who saw her every day, knew that she was finally on the verge of conquering her illness. And she didn't want any of them to know. Not just yet.

She clenched her hands into fists until her knuckles turned white and her nails dug into her palms. She had almost lost her will to live on the night of that ball at Clairvaux so many years ago, when she had seen her husband take her own sister in his arms and kiss her with more tenderness than he had ever shown to Frances. After that night she had sought both solace and escape in her medicines and in the dark recesses of her own mind.

But when Savannah had left for Paris last year, something inside of Frances had been shaken to the core. She would not have an ally to protect her against Gerrold if her own daughter were away. It was then that Frances decided that she would have to get well again. It was then that she came up with her plan.

The sound of her sitting-room door opening sent Frances rushing back to her bed, and not a moment too soon.

"Mrs. Webb," Edna Ferris said from the doorway, "your daughter has returned from Paris and wishes to see you if you are having one of your good days."

Frances smiled wanly. "Savannah! Of course I want to see her, Edna. Please help me to my chaise longue, then go and get my daughter. Don't dawdle now. I'm most anxious to see her. It's been a long, long time, you know."

The nurse did as she was told, and while she was off fetching Savannah, Frances reclined on the chaise and arranged her shawl around her shoulders. She glanced at herself nervously in her hand mirror. Did she look presentable?

Then there came a knock at the door, and when Frances replied, "Come in," Savannah walked in.

"Good afternoon, Mother. How are you?" she said with a warm smile. "I trust you've been well during my absence."

Frances's eyes widened, and the mirror slipped from her nerveless fingers to clatter on the floor. "Alastair!" she gasped, recoiling in shock against the chaise's bolster.

"Mother, what's wrong?" Vannah demanded as she hurried across the room to her mother's side. "Are you all right? You look terribly pale, as though you've just seen a ghost."

Vannah set down the boxes she carried, then knelt by the chaise. She took her mother's cold hands between her own. "Is that any way to greet your daughter after she's been abroad for a whole year?" she teased.

Frances pulled her hands away, and her fingers fluttered nervously near her mouth. "No, of course it isn't. You just startled me a bit, that's all." She reached over and hugged her fiercely. "My dear, dear angel. You don't know how very much I've missed you and longed for your return."

Vannah smiled. "And it's good to be home now, Mother. Tell me. How have you been?"

But Frances was too distracted to keep her mind on Vannah's questions. Was it merely her imagination or had Vannah suddenly grown to resemble her father even more during the last year she was away? Frances stared at her daughter hard, searching for any hint of a resemblance, any at all. No, she hadn't imagined it. Vannah had Alastair's eyes, so large and of such a dark blue shade that no one could ever mistake them for Gerrold's eyes at all, for his were pale and expressionless, like a lizard's. And Vannah's lips were exactly like Alastair's, perfectly proportioned, with a soft fullness to the lower lip. Then Frances looked down at her daughter's hands, and her heart skipped a panic-stricken beat. Savannah's hands had the long, tapered fingers of an artist, just like her father's, just like Alastair's.

Alastair, Alastair, Alastair . . .

"Mother, say something to me, please! You frighten me so when your mind wanders."

Frances was jolted out of her nightmare by fingers digging into her shoulders as Savannah grasped her and shook her. When her eyes focused, she found herself staring into her daughter's desperate, worried face.

"I'm all right," she insisted, shrugging off Savannah's hands and pulling her shawl around her more closely, for the room had suddenly felt chilly again. "You needn't shake me as though I were a naughty child or a madwoman. I'm only sick, not mad."

"I'm sorry, Mother. I didn't mean to upset you. It's just that you weren't answering my questions and you had the oddest look on your face."

"I'm fine," Frances insisted, "just fine. Now, my angel, I want you to sit right next to me and tell me everything that happened to you while you were in Paris. Gerrold and I went there on our wedding trip, but that was many, many years ago, and I would imagine the city has changed so much since then."

Her appearance of normalcy seemed to allay her daughter's fears, for Savannah smiled with obvious relief and seated herself in her usual chair near her mother's chaise. Frances made a great pretense of listening to Savannah's stories about life at Miss Fitzmaurice's and the pleasures of Paris, but in reality she was thinking of Gerrold.

Frances felt a real fear growing deep in her breast. Surely Gerrold had noticed the resemblance by this time. Surely he had discovered her secret by now. Surely he had realized that his wife had betrayed him and given birth to another man's child.

Frances knew she had to protect the innocent, unsuspecting Savannah from Gerrold's wrath should he ever discover the truth. But how? Then she recalled the letter in the pocket of her dressing gown.

"Would you do me a very great favor, my angel?" Frances asked abruptly, interrupting Savannah.

"Why, of course, Mother."

Frances took the letter out of her pocket and thrust it into her daughter's hands. "Would you take this letter to Madame Denise, my dressmaker? I am in need of some new dressing gowns, and I would like her to come to the house for a fitting, seeing as how I cannot go to her shop."

Savannah looked as though she were on the verge of

saying something, then changed her mind. Her voice had a flat, resigned tone as she said, "Of course, Mother. Whatever you wish."

"And please don't tell your Aunt Constance. She has so much on her mind with running the house, I don't want to bother her with something so trivial."

"I won't, Mother. Tell me, how are you and Aunt Constance getting along? Does she visit you often?"

"Occasionally, when I am having one of my good days." Frances smiled. "We have such pleasant little chats over tea. We talk endlessly of our childhood in Connecticut, and of our own dear Mama and Papa, God rest their souls. We talk about all our former beaux and speculate about whatever happened to them, and we recall dances we went to as young girls." It was so much easier to relive the past with Constance. It kept Frances from thinking of the present and the future.

"I'm glad," Savannah said, and looked relieved again. Then she rose. "I bought a few things for you in Paris, Mother. I hope you like them."

Frances was genuinely touched. "Oh, my angel! How very thoughtful of you to remember your old mother!"

"I won't have you talking about yourself that way, Mother. You're not old," Savannah said, handing her a large box wrapped in light blue paper and tied with a dark blue ribbon.

Frances was as surprised and delighted as a child on Christmas morning when she opened the boxes to reveal a peach silk kimono, a large bottle of Guerlain perfume, and a leather-bound copy of *A Tale of Two Cities*. The smaller boxes contained handkerchiefs, colored stockings, and ivory hair combs.

As Frances looked down at the gifts scattered around her and murmured her thanks, she felt her eyes fill with sentimental tears. Alastair had always been just as thoughtful, buying her little gifts that she could never bring home, lest a suspicious Gerrold question her about where they came from. But Alastair's daughter had inherited that same generosity of spirit, and that pleased Frances.

"Mother, what's this?" Vannah asked softly, draping her arm around her mother's thin shoulders. "Why are you crying? I thought you'd be happy to have me home."

"I am, my angel, I am. I'm just a little tired and overwrought. I'm not supposed to have this much excitement in one day, you know. It's bad for my constitution, as Nurse Ferris always reminds me."

"Well, I'll leave you, then, and let you get a little rest," Vannah said, rising. Then she leaned over and kissed her mother's hot, dry cheek. "I'll come again whenever you're able to have visitors, Mother."

"Thank you." She watched her daughter cross the room, and when she got to the door, Frances stopped her with, "Savannah?"

Vannah turned. "Yes?"

"Don't forget to deliver my note to Madame Denise."

"Don't worry, Mother, I won't. I'll bring it to her the first thing tomorrow morning."

"And don't tell anyone. It's very important that you not tell anyone that you're doing this for me."

"You have nothing to worry about. I promise that I won't tell a soul."

"Thank you. I knew I could count on you."

Once Vannah was out in the corridor she leaned heavily against the closed doors to compose herself after her emotionally draining visit with her mother. Tears of pity and sorrow stung her eyes, but she took a deep breath to keep them from falling. All during her year abroad she had prayed that matters would be different when she returned, that her mother would finally conquer her illness and that the Webbs would be a family at last.

But now, she realized as she stood wiping her tear-stained cheeks, it had been a futile exercise in wishful thinking. Her mother was never going to get better. It was time Vannah faced the truth she had been avoiding all these years. Aunt Constance was more of a mother to her than her own mother had ever been.

Vannah walked down the corridor, tapping her mother's letter to Madame Denise against her palm. When she reached her room, she found her maid waiting to tell her that several of her friends were waiting downstairs to welcome her home.

The following morning Vannah told her aunt exactly what she wanted to do with her life.

Constance stared at her niece across the breakfast table and set her teacup down carefully, lest she spill its contents.

"You want to do *what?*"

Vannah smiled. "I said, I want to design stained glass windows for Mr. Tiffany."

Constance nervously toyed with a topaz hanging from her neck as she tried to gather her wits about her. "I must say, Vannah, that this has come as something of a shock to me."

Vannah's eyes widened, and she looked unruffled. "I don't see why, Aunt Constance. You've always known how much drawing and painting mean to me."

Yes, Constance said to herself, but I never dreamed you would actually want to use your talents to become an artist.

She cleared her throat. "You mean to say that you want to go to work every day, like a common shop girl?"

Now Vannah sat back in her chair and wore her mulish expression. "It's not the same, Aunt Constance. I would be using my God-given talent to create something beautiful. Surely you can't object to that."

Constance restrained herself from telling her enthusiastic niece that her father was sure to have many objections to this scheme of hers. The thought of his daughter working at anything would enrage Gerrold more than anything ever could, and Constance knew it. She had to contrive some way to keep Vannah from broaching the subject with her father.

Constance said, "Will you do me a favor, Vannah?"

"What, Aunt Constance?" Vannah asked suspiciously.

"Don't mention this to your father just yet." When Vannah looked like she was about to protest, Constance rushed on with, "If you tell him you want to design windows, he'll know that we have been disobeying him all these years. He will know that I've helped you to draw behind his back, and he will be furious with me. You are only eighteen and have yet to experience your first season. Give yourself some time. Enjoy yourself. Then, when you're twenty-one, if you still want to design windows, we shall approach your father together and tell him what we've been doing. But I need time, Vannah, time to think of a way to break this to your father without jeopardizing his high regard for me. Will you do that for me?"

She could tell by the mutinous expression on Vannah's face that she did not think it fair at all. "I can assure you that if you go to your father right now, he will not be at all receptive to your desires, Vannah," Constance said. "But if you were of age and seemed to know your own mind—"

"Twenty-one!" Vannah wailed. "But that's three years away! I want to design windows now."

"Please don't argue with me, Vannah! The time will pass very quickly."

Vannah looked skeptical, but she gave a resigned sigh. "All right, Aunt Constance. If you think it's best, I shall wait until I'm older before telling Father of my plans. But don't think that I shall forget them."

Constance breathed a sigh of relief. Actually she had no intention of ever telling Gerrold about Vannah's drawing or her desire to design stained glass windows. Much could happen in three years' time. Vannah could be swept off her feet by some dashing young man and all thoughts of designing stained glass windows forgotten.

She was staking her future on the likelihood of that happening.

One week after Vannah's return Gerrold Webb had just finished lunch and was working in his study when Parkins interrupted him to hand him a long white envelope.

"This was just delivered by messenger, sir," Parkins said. "The lad said that his employer expected a reply this afternoon."

"A bit presumptuous of him, don't you think? I reply in my own good time," Gerrold said, taking the envelope. "Thank you, Parkins. That will be all."

When he was alone again, he stared at the envelope that bore no return address, just his name scrawled across the front in tipsy black lettering. He was of half a mind to toss the thing aside with his other papers and open it when he was good and ready, but his curiosity got the best of him, and he slit the flap with his silver letter opener.

When he read what was inside, Gerrold Webb uttered a rare thanks to God that he had opened it immediately.

"The bastard," he muttered, flinging the letter as far across his desk as he could so as not to be contaminated by it. "How in Heaven's name did he find out?" Then he leaned back in his leather swivel chair and uttered every oath and imprecation that came to mind. When his diatribe was finished, he buried his pale face in his shaking hands and tried to think of a way to extricate himself from a potentially scandalous situation.

But this time there was no way out. He was beaten and

he knew it. Now it was his turn to pay, like so many others before him. He wondered how much blood money the colonel would exact from him.

Gerrold rose, read the letter again, then folded it and slipped it into his pocket. He opened his safe, took out an outrageous sum of money, then ordered his carriage brought around.

Ten minutes later Gerrold was standing in the noisy outer editorial offices of *Town Topics, the Journal of Society*. He glanced around in distaste at the worn red plush carpeting and shabby desks and was of half a mind to turn on his heel and thumb his nose at Colonel William d'Alton Mann and his blackmailing publication. But he clenched his teeth resolutely and restrained himself. He couldn't afford to be so arrogant with Mann. He had too much to lose. This was one time he was just going to have to accept defeat and lose gracefully.

Without looking up from the paper he was editing, a young man seated at the desk to Gerrold's left asked, "What are you here for?"

"I'm here to see Colonel Mann," Gerrold replied coldly, eyeing the two large black cats crouched on the windowsill and watching the man out of slitted, accusatory eyes.

The young man jerked his thumb toward the rear of the editorial room.

Gerrold glared at him, then strode toward the private office of his blackmailer. When he came to the closed door, he grew so furious that he almost went barging in, then he recalled tales of the loaded pistol the colonel kept in his top drawer and the heavy walking stick protruding from out of the wire wastebasket just within reach. Gerrold took a deep breath to bring his soaring temper under control. He knew that the colonel must be placated at all costs.

He knocked, heard a voice bid him enter, then walked

inside, coming face-to-face with Colonel William d'Alton Mann, inventor, entrepreneur, and unscrupulous society blackmailer.

That such a malicious man should resemble Saint Nicholas, beloved bearer of gifts to children at Christmas, was especially repugnant to Gerrold, but that was part of the colonel's charm. Who could believe that this hearty, jovial fellow with sparkling, blue-gray eyes, red, bulbous nose, and snow-white hair and beard could print such scandalous tidbits about the wealthy in his weekly society newspaper?

"I see you got my letter, Webb," he said with a smile and a wheezing chuckle. "And you came promptly too. I like promptness in a man."

"This isn't a social call, Mann," Gerrold said in frosty tones. "In your letter you stated that you had an item about me that was scheduled for publication this week. I would like to see it."

"Of course, Webb. I have it right here." And he handed his caller a piece of paper that had been sitting right before him on his desk as if in anticipation of Webb's arrival.

As Gerrold read, he could feel all color drain from his face and the sweat rise on his brow.

The paragraph said: "A prominent resident of Thirty-fourth Street has become hopelessly entangled in a web of his own making. It seems that this august member of Society has been succumbing to the charms of his own sister-in-law. How convenient that the lady lives under the same roof."

Although the paragraph mentioned no names, as was the colonel's custom to avoid being sued for libel, Gerrold knew full well that half of New York could easily decipher his identity from the few well-placed, obvious clues the cagey colonel had planted throughout the article. Gerrold was the only resident of Thirty-fourth Street that he knew

"It's been a pleasure doing business with you, Webb. A real pleasure. And if we can ever do business in the future, you can be sure that you'll be hearing from me again."

"You can be damned sure I'll see that you never get the opportunity."

As he left, Gerrold heard a faint, "We shall see, Webb, we shall see."

Chapter Seven

"WHAT CAN BE KEEPING my daughter?" Gerrold growled as he paced the foyer. "Don't tell me Savannah is going to be late for her own coming-out ball!"

Constance placed a reassuring hand on his arm. "I'm sure she'll be right down, Gerrold. Her maid had just finished threading the chain of diamonds through her hair when I last looked in on her."

Gerrold beamed at his own cleverness when he thought of the unique gift he had given his daughter for her coming-out ball. Instead of buying a common tiara he had Tiffany's jewelers set the stones into a thin gold chain as long as Savannah was tall. When threaded through her hair, the sparkling diamonds would look like a scattering of stars beneath the lights of the ballroom's three chandeliers.

Suddenly a voice from the top of the stairs said, "I'm not late, am I?" And Gerrold and Constance looked up to see Vannah standing there.

"Oh, Gerrold . . ." Constance murmured in awe.

In her Worth gown of white mousseline de soie encrusted with thousands of tiny seed pearls, Vannah was indeed a vision to behold. Placing one gloved hand on the banister, she expertly gathered her train in the other and gracefully descended the staircase.

"How do I look?" she asked worriedly, opening her painted ivory fan with a snap.

"You'll be the most beautiful lady here tonight, my darling," Constance said, touching her cheek to Vannah's.

Gerrold stroked his mustache and beamed proudly. "You certainly are a credit to me, daughter."

"Thank you, Father," Vannah said politely, though in truth her father's comment did not please her. Why couldn't he ever appreciate her for herself alone, not as a reflection on himself?

Then she turned to her aunt. "Where are we going to stand to receive our guests?"

Constance walked over to the long table bearing an elaborate floral arrangement of three dozen white-and-purple orchids. "We'll stand right here. The light above is soft and flattering."

"An excellent choice, sister," came a strong, clear voice from the top of the stairs.

Vannah, Constance, and Gerrold looked up simultaneously to see none other than Frances start to descend the staircase, one hand lightly guiding her way down the banister, the other holding up the skirt of her wine-colored taffeta gown so she wouldn't stumble and trip over it.

"Mother!" Vannah gasped as her fan fell from her hand and clattered to the floor.

Constance could only stare, but Gerrold's face was an angry mask as he started up the stairs, two at a time. When he reached his wife's side, he put his hand on her arm as if to restrain her, but she deliberately shrugged him off and sailed right past him.

"What are you doing out of your rooms, dearest heart?" he asked between clenched teeth, fighting to keep his temper under control. "You are not a well woman, Frances. You know very well that you should be in bed, resting and conserving your strength."

"Oh, but I'm much, much better, Gerrold," she replied with a smile. "In fact, I haven't felt this good in years." When she reached the foot of the stairs, she looked at her daughter and sister with an amused twinkle in her eyes. "Don't you like my little surprise? Madame Denise made this dress especially for my daughter's debut."

So that's why she wanted me not to tell anyone about her secret letter to Madame Denise, Vannah thought to herself.

As her father retrieved her fan Vannah said, "Mother, please. Father is right. You had better go back to bed."

"Savannah, my angel, do you really think I would let anything keep me away from my own daughter's coming-out ball?" Frances asked.

"Frances—" Constance began.

"It's only fitting that a mother stand by her daughter's side to receive their guests, is it not?"

"Not when that mother has been an invalid for the past seventeen years," Gerrold retorted, reaching for her. "Come along, Frances, and don't make a scene. I'm going to escort you back to your room right now and have Nurse Ferris give you something to calm your nerves and help you sleep."

"No!" she cried vehemently, her eyes rolling wildly as she jerked her arm out of his grasp. "I will not go back to my rooms. I am well, I have a new gown for the occasion, and I am going to attend my daughter's ball. And no one is going to stop me!"

"We shall just see about that," Gerrold muttered, a threatening gleam lighting his eyes.

Vannah stepped forward. "Father, please. Let Mother stay. If she doesn't feel well, she can always go back to her rooms. But if she's feeling as well as she claims, what could be the harm in letting her attend the ball tonight?"

"I'm surprised at you, Savannah," her father snapped. "You know that too much excitement isn't good for your mother, and here you are encouraging her to push herself to the point of a nervous collapse!"

Vannah felt her cheeks burn with long-suppressed defiance. "She is my mother, and I think her place is by my side tonight."

Before her father could make a stinging retort, the door bell rang and the unobtrusive Parkins stepped out of the shadows to answer it.

"Oh, dear, our first guests," Constance said in alarm, fingering her emerald necklace nervously. Ever the peacemaker, she added, "Gerrold, let's not let our guests witness this family dispute, shall we? I agree with Vannah. Why not let Frances receive our guests? As Vannah pointed out, if it's too much for her, she can always go back to her rooms."

The last thing Gerrold wanted was for any of his guests to catch him squabbling with Frances, so he quickly capitulated. "You're right, Constance. This is no time to argue." Then he turned to his wife, but his tone was cold and menacing. "All right, Frances. You may stay."

Her smile was radiant. "Thank you, Gerrold. You have made me very happy."

But she had made him very unhappy with this surprise appearance of hers, and as Gerrold took his place beside his wife and daughter, he resolved that Frances was never going to spring any more such surprises on him again.

Constance pasted a smile on her face and resolutely kept it there as the fourth wave of guests surged toward her.

While she recalled names and faces with practiced ease and chatted amiably with everyone, her thoughts couldn't be farther from the upcoming Newport season or the latest charity ball being held at the Metropolitan Opera House.

All she could think of was how Frances had ruined her own daughter's coming-out ball.

Oh, there was no doubt in anyone's mind that her sister had certainly caused the sensation of the year. Old friends who hadn't seen her in nearly two decades were exclaiming over her miraculous recovery and how wonderful she looked. In fact, Frances was the chief topic of conversation tonight instead of Vannah.

This was to have been Savannah's night, and it had been stolen from her by her own mother.

I hope you're satisfied, Frances, Constance thought bitterly to herself. You've spoiled everything.

Constance stopped chatting long enough to risk a glance at her niece. And Savannah looked so lovely, too, with her beautiful gown and her hair looking as though it were dusted with stars. If she felt overshadowed by her mother, she certainly didn't show it. In fact she seemed content to let her mother bask in the limelight tonight. Under the circumstances Constance didn't think she would have been so generous or forgiving.

Suddenly she felt a hand on her elbow and turned to find Gerrold by her side.

"Look who has just arrived," he murmured excitedly, nodding toward the door.

Constance gasped, catching his excitement. "Caroline Astor! She must have just returned from Europe."

"Just in time for Vannah's coming-out ball," Gerrold said.

As Constance watched Mrs. Astor move with stately grace toward her hostess, she found it difficult to believe that this dumpy little woman with the dark wig and thick lips had ruled New York society with an implacable iron hand for so many years. Tales of her absolute authority were legendary. Constance had heard stories about how, twenty years ago, Mrs. Astor had determined that it took three generations for a man to shake off the stigma of "new money" and to become a gentleman. Her own family, of course, met the criteria, but others, like the Vanderbilts and Webbs, were only the second generation and did not qualify to be admitted to Mrs. Astor's august ranks and were therefore deemed socially unacceptable.

Gerrold had been trying to win her favor for years, without success. Until tonight. Constance wondered why the formidable grande dame had suddenly relented. Perhaps the rumors that her influence was on the wane were true.

Now, as Mrs. Astor chatted with Frances and Vannah, Constance had her first really good look at the woman. She wore a Worth gown of white satin with a green velvet bodice and green train, and she dripped diamonds. Diamond stars were set in her wig, and diamonds winked all the way down her back, where she had reversed a necklace to achieve such an effect. Privately Constance thought it a trifle tasteless and overdone, but she just smiled graciously and welcomed Mrs. Astor to their home when the lady next came to her.

When Mrs. Astor moved on to the ballroom, Gerrold grasped Constance's hand so tightly, she winced. "At long last!" he crowed.

Constance smiled at him and returned the pressure of his fingers. "I'm so happy for you, Gerrold."

"I don't know how you did it, Constance, but thank you," he said, looking down at her, his pale eyes warm and glowing with unspoken promises. Gerrold brought her hand up to his lips and kissed it, not caring who witnessed the gesture or even if it appeared in the next issue of *Town*

Topics. Then he gave her a long, level look of intimacy. "I'll show you my appreciation later, my dear."

Constance felt her pulse quicken in anticipation as she returned to the task of greeting their guests. Gerrold was always so appreciative of her, so tangible in his rewards. She sighed in contentment.

When was the line going to end? Vannah wondered.

She felt as though her face were going to crack any minute from constantly smiling, and her hand had been grasped and crushed so many times by various Vanderbilts and Goulds that her fingers were beginning to go numb. Vannah couldn't wait to join her friends already in the ballroom.

Finally, to Vannah's relief, it was over. The last guest was accounted for, and Parkins was closing the doors. From a hidden alcove Aunt Constance brought out the three dozen bouquets Vannah had received just that morning from admiring gentlemen and helped arrange the flowers and their trailing satin ribbons in Vannah's arms, for custom required her to carry them into the ballroom as an accolade to her popularity and beauty.

When both arms were ladened with the fragrant flowers, Vannah was ready. Her mother brushed away a tear, Aunt Constance smiled reassuringly, and her father beamed proudly, though the presence of Caroline Astor had more to do with his triumphant expression than his daughter.

Then they all walked into the ballroom together.

As Vannah sat on one of many of the small gilt chairs lining the ballroom, she was glad that she'd had the foresight to leave several dances blank on her dance card so she could rest now and then. She was hot and out of breath. The intricate quadrille she had spent weeks practicing for had taken two hours to complete, and her feet were beginning to ache, especially after that last rousing polka.

Suddenly the dance ended, and Vannah found herself surrounded by handsome young men, all vying for her attention like dogs fighting over a bone. As she chatted with one about horses and another about the unseasonably warm weather, Vannah waited for the excitement and the breathlessness to grip her that she had always felt in Martin Ash's company, but nothing happened. Even though she was conversing with these young men, she wasn't really involved with them. She felt as though she were off in a corner somewhere, watching herself play the flirtatious debutante.

What is wrong with me? she wondered. Here I am with some of the handsomest, wealthiest, and most eligible men in New York at my feet, and I feel nothing for any one of them. Nothing!

The next hour passed in a blur of color and sound. Vannah danced several dances with several equally bland gentlemen whose faces she could barely remember, much less their conversation, and then it was time for dinner, which was being held in the formal dining room.

It was after dinner, when all the guests flocked back to the ballroom for more dancing, that tragedy struck.

As another young gentleman took Vannah in his arms and swung her onto the dance floor in a gliding waltz, she was astonished to see that even her own mother was dancing tonight.

Vannah tried to keep her attention focused on her partner, who was boring her to death with his plans to enter his family's brokerage firm, but she was too busy keeping an eye on her mother, who looked decidedly pale as she went whirling by.

And then the unthinkable happened.

As Vannah watched in mute horror her mother faltered, swayed, then collapsed to the floor like a rag doll.

"Mother!" Vannah screamed, tearing herself out of her partner's arms to run to Frances's side, where she lay in a crumpled heap of wine silk.

The dancers all stopped and stared. The music jerked to a halt. Conversation ceased as Vannah turned her mother over and gently cradled her in her arms.

"What happened?" her father barked as he suddenly seemed to come out of nowhere to kneel by his daughter's side.

"I don't know," Vannah wailed, tears of helplessness streaming down her cheeks. "She seemed all right. She was dancing and then she just collapsed."

"I'll carry her back to her room," her father said, putting one arm beneath his wife's knees and another around her shoulders. "She never should have attempted to come downstairs tonight. I warned her that it would be too strenuous, but she wouldn't listen. And as for you, young lady . . . you just had to encourage her, didn't you? Well, I hope you're satisfied now."

Constance pushed her way through the crowd to peer worriedly at them. "Oh, my God, Gerrold! What happened?"

When Vannah told her, she turned quite pale. "Will my sister be all right?"

Gerrold hoisted the limp, lifeless figure into his arms as though she weighed no more than a cat. "I really don't know. Constance, there must be a doctor here somewhere. Why don't you try to find him, then circulate among our guests and attempt to salvage what's left of the evening?"

"I'm coming with you, Father," Vannah said.

"Suit yourself" was his curt reply as he strode out of the ballroom with his unconscious wife in his arms.

* * *

Vannah hovered over her mother while Nurse Ferris undressed her and put her to bed, then she waited with her father until the doctor arrived. Minutes later he came out of Frances's bedchamber and reassured Gerrold and Vannah that Mrs. Webb was only suffering from exhaustion and nervous collapse, and would recover with enough bed rest.

Satisfied that her mother wasn't dying, Vannah told her father that she thought it would be best if she returned to their guests, and he agreed.

As she made her way alone down the quiet, dimly lit corridors at the rear of the house, Vannah felt a deep, unshakable sense of melancholy grip her. She had been looking forward to her coming-out ball for such a long time, but now that she was in the midst of it, she was disappointed.

She had been half hoping to meet another Sir Lancelot tonight, someone exactly like Martin Ash, someone exciting, mysterious, compelling, a man who could make her breathless and shivery with one lingering glance. But she hadn't. Every man she had met tonight was as bland and unpalatable as the porridge she used to eat for breakfast as a child.

"Perhaps Sir Lancelot just doesn't exist," she muttered dismally to herself.

After walking down a flight of stairs to the first floor and rounding a corner, Vannah suddenly stopped short. The door to her father's study was open, and a light was shining from inside the room. Vannah frowned. This section of the house was deserted because all of the guests were in the ballroom, and as far as Vannah knew, her father was still upstairs tending to his wife.

Who was in Gerrold Webb's study?

Taking a deep breath, Vannah moved slowly and stealthily down the corridor, taking great care that the train on her gown didn't rustle and give her away. When she came to the open doorway, she peered inside.

The only light shining in the dark study was the small lamp on her father's desk, and even that didn't give a clear picture of the man standing there, hurriedly rifling through some papers he had spread on the desk top beneath the lamp's small circle of light.

Someone had broken into her father's study and was reading his private papers.

Vannah felt her cheeks grow hot with anger and indignation, and without a thought for her personal safety, she recklessly stepped into the doorway and reached up to turn on the electric light. As brightness illuminated the room the intruder started guiltily and stared at her in alarm, but before he could make any attempt to flee, Vannah strode farther into the room and blocked his escape.

"Just who are you," she demanded imperiously, "and what are you doing here in my father's private study?"

The intruder was the oddest-looking man Vannah had ever seen, and she realized at once that he hadn't gone through the receiving line; otherwise, she would have remembered him. He was taller than she by a head, and so very thin that a good strong wind could have blown him over. Although he wore formal evening attire like every other man here tonight, it didn't suit him somehow, for his long black hair and scraggly beard looked as though they had never known a barber's shears. He was strangely out of place, like a burly dockworker wearing a woman's evening gown.

"I asked you who you are and what you are doing here!" Vannah said sharply, raising her voice and taking a brave step forward.

"You'll learn the answer to that all in good time, Miss Webb," the intruder said, rounding the desk quickly to stare back at her.

Even though the man's face was hidden behind that bushy, unkempt beard, Vannah could tell that he was not at all good-looking, for he had a prominent aquiline nose and deep-set eyes that seemed hidden beneath flaring, shaggy brows. As he jammed his hands into his pockets and regarded her with nerve-racking boldness, Vannah felt as though she were being scrutinized by some menacing bird of prey seeking to make her his dinner.

"I'll tell you who you are," she said haughtily, resenting the fact that he didn't appear to be afraid of her at all. "You're a common thief who broke into my father's study to steal money."

His eyes twinkled, and he appeared to be laughing at her. "I am not a common thief, and I did not come here to steal money."

"I don't believe you," Vannah retorted. "No one enters this study without my father's permission."

While keeping one wary eye on the man, who seemed to be more amused than fearful, she rounded the desk on the other side and cried out in triumph when she saw several drawers still open with papers in disarray, as though someone had just been searching through them.

"So, it was my father's personal papers you were after!"

"My, princess, you're a veritable police detective, aren't you?"

Vannah glowered at him and, without another word, turned and started for the door so she could summon help.

"We'll just see how cocky you are when my father gets through with you, thief."

She almost reached it when she felt a restraining hand close about her shoulder, strong fingers digging into her flesh.

"Not so fast, princess."

Vannah gasped at the odious familiarity of the man as she whirled around to confront him, but all he did was grasp her wrists tightly before she even realized what was happening. She found herself staring into eyes as black and bottomless as onyx, and for the first time since coming into the room, Vannah felt the first stirrings of fear grip her.

She was alone with a dangerous criminal, with no one to come to her rescue if she screamed.

"Let go of me!" she cried, trying to pull away, but she was helpless against the relentless hold he had on her.

Her captor only grinned, a flash of white teeth glimpsed through that thicket of beard. "Even a cat may look upon a king, or in this case, a beast may look upon a beauty."

Vannah mustered all of her remaining dignity, stopped struggling, and regarded him with cool contempt and much hauteur. "I said let me go."

He narrowed his eyes and his gaze never wavered. "I'm sure you expect everyone to jump the moment you give the order, princess. Well, I'm not one of your servants. I don't obey any man, or woman for that matter. I shall hold you this way for as long as I please."

"Fine. The longer you remain here, thief, the greater your chances of being caught."

He threw back his head and laughed scornfully, then abruptly dropped Vannah's wrists. But before she could bolt for the study door, he moved fast and was there ahead of her, closing and locking it before she could escape. Then he leaned back against the door, crossed his arms over his narrow chest, and raptly studied her again.

"So you think I'm a thief, eh?" His voice was surprisingly cultured and well modulated for such a scruffy specimen, not at all what Vannah expected.

"What else would you call someone caught rifling through someone else's desk?"

"But it's rather like the pot calling the kettle black, isn't it?"

Vannah frowned. "What do you mean?"

"Your father, Gerrold Webb, is the biggest thief of all."

White-hot anger shot through her. "That's a lie! My father is not a thief."

The intruder gave her a pitying look. "Oh, he isn't?"

"No, he's not! What gives you the right to make such false accusations?"

The man was breathing heavily through his nose, as if to compose himself. "I have every right, princess. How do you think he pays for this fashionable brownstone and his fake French château in Newport? How do you think he pays for those fine jewels you wear and that Worth gown? I'll tell you how."

The man stepped toward her now, his black eyes shining with some inner fire of fanatacism. "He makes it off the sweat of poor working men and women. He makes it through bribes and corruption of government officials. He lies and cheats and swindles the American public, then laughs in their faces when the law looks the other way."

"You're lying," Vannah insisted, stamping her foot in vexation. "My father would never do any of those things you accuse him of."

He shook his head pityingly. "Oh, but he has, and his father before him. It runs in the family. Don't you even know how your own grandfather made his fortune during the Civil War? He made it by selling blankets to the Confederacy. He was paid top dollar to supply thick, warm woolen blankets, but what he provided were nothing more than cheap, thin cotton ones that couldn't keep a flea warm in the summer, never mind a man facing the cold and sleet and snow of winter. And he put those handsome profits right back into his own pockets. And what about the poor foot soldier trying to get a decent night's sleep before he went into battle and possibly to his own death the next day?" The intruder shrugged. "Your grandfather stole it from him."

"You're lying. My grandfather did no such thing."

"Oh, but he did, princess. True, he wasn't as corrupt as that swine J. Pierpont Morgan, reselling defective rifles back to the U.S. government, but he was still a thief." Suddenly the man's voice softened, becoming almost gentle and kind. "I don't know why I'm even wasting my breath telling you all this. It is, after all, in your own best interests to disbelieve me, now isn't it?"

"What do you mean?"

"It's your father's ill-gotten gains that keep you in fine jewels and Worth gowns, now isn't it?" His voice changed again, becoming harsh and mocking. "Poor, shallow, naive princess. Don't you realize that you're nothing more than a beautiful possession to your father and men like him? You're nothing more than a walking, talking shop window for their wealth. You're a pawn to be married off to the highest bidder."

Vannah could think of no suitable retort, for she had been entertaining the same unthinkable, heretical thoughts herself. She turned her back to the man by the door and said, "Get out while you still have the chance. Leave me alone."

He walked so silently, she wasn't even aware that he was standing behind her until he spoke in that soft, hypnotic voice of his.

"Do you ever think, princess, do you ever feel? Have you ever wondered what it's like out there, outside this gilded cage of yours, or are you content to remain ignorant while others do your thinking for you?"

She turned slowly, and her arm just avoided brushing against him. Vannah's face was only inches from his own, so close that she could see her own furious, indignant face reflected in the fathomless depths of his black eyes.

"You may think you know me, but you don't, thief. One should never judge a book by its cover," she said slowly and deliberately. "Perhaps I might surprise you."

For once the intruder seemed at a loss for words. He just stared at Vannah without smiling, his eyes boring into hers. Then he grinned. "Perhaps you might at that."

With an insolent wink that made Vannah gasp in rage, he strode out of the study, down the corridor, and disappeared.

She waited until the hurried sound of his footsteps faded before she collected her father's papers and put them back into the drawers as best she could, tidied up the desk, and returned to her guests.

For two days after her coming-out ball Vannah found herself plagued by thoughts of the brash, bold intruder and his implausible accusations against her father. If she had been any one of her friends, Vannah would have dismissed the strange, strident man without a second thought. But because she was so sensitive and perceptive, his hurtful words continued to prey on her.

Was she really just a mindless, beautiful shell without a thought in her pretty little head? She knew she was not. The intruder had judged her on her jewels and her Worth gown, just as she had judged him by his wild, unkempt appearance and the strange circumstances of their meeting.

Against her better judgment she found herself thinking of him often. Vannah had never been so intrigued by a man since meeting Martin Ash, yet she knew virtually nothing about him. She didn't even know his name. Perhaps he was one of those anarchists she had heard so many Parisians speak of with fear and loathing, seeking to bring about the downfall of the established social order through violence and redistributing all wealth to the masses.

PASSION'S FORTUNE 163

"A dangerous man, Vannah," she warned herself. And exciting.

And then came the day when she learned the identity of her disturbing intruder.

Several days after the ball Vannah was in her sitting room reading when one of the maids entered, handed her a bulky envelope, and said it had come in the morning mail. When the maid left, Vannah opened the package and was surprised to find a folded newspaper inside with a note that read, "Thank you for your assistance (see page three)—Paul Demarest," clipped to the front page. Frowning with curiosity, Vannah noticed that the paper was called *The Bugle—The Battle Cry of the Working Man*.

When Vannah turned to page three as instructed, the headline leapt right out at her: THE WEALTHY STRUT WHILE THE POOR STARVE.

She began reading.

> While this city's countless homeless are sleeping in doorways, alleys, and gutters, foraging in garbage for a mere crust of bread to fill their empty bellies, the well-fed wealthy were congregating at the Thirty-fourth Street home of Gerrold Webb to celebrate the coming of age of his daughter, Savannah, well known in certain circles for her beauty and not much else.

Vannah gasped in indignation but continued to read.

> This reporter has never seen such waste and extravagance in his entire life. Miss Webb's gown is reported to have cost one thousand dollars in Paris. One thousand dollars, readers! That is more money than most of us will make in two years through decent, honest labor, earned by the sweat of our brows rather than corruption. And just think what a

price such a gown would fetch at a pawnshop where poor mothers pawn their most cherished possessions to help feed their children.

The cost of the floral decorations alone must have made a sizable dent in Gerrold Webb's overflowing coffers. Your reporter stopped counting the *gloire de Paris* roses at two thousand. Are *The Bugle*'s loyal readers aware that these lovely blooms cost one dollar apiece, enough to feed a family of four for several days? I won't mention all the orchids I saw, except to inform you that these flowers are even more rare and expensive than the roses. Rumor has it that they were shipped up from warmer southern climes by barge just to beautify the house for Miss Webb's ball. And what happened to them afterward? Your reporter suspects that they were all thrown out with the trash for some poor urchin to eat.

And speaking of eating, your reporter could go on and on about the sumptuous dinner catered by Pinard and served on plates made out of real gold, but that seems a sin when so many in this city would welcome a scrap of meat served on newspaper. But perhaps when they go to bed with their starving, grumbling bellies, they can be cheered and comforted by the thought of the lovely Miss Webb in her Worth gown, with enough diamonds scattered in her hair to fill the night sky with stars. Your reporter wishes he had but one of Miss Webb's diamonds to feed this city's hungry and shelter the homeless.

When she finished reading, Vannah just sat there, trembling and white-faced, her eyes glazed as she stared out into space. Finally she flung the paper down and rose to her feet. There were a few things she had to say to this Mr. Paul Demarest.

* * *

An hour later Vannah arrived at the shabby East Side editorial offices of *The Bugle* and climbed up four flights of creaking stairs. The moment she entered the large, airless room that smelled strongly of ink, coffee, and sweat, the sound of typewriters pounding away suddenly dwindled and ceased, and she felt a dozen male eyes upon her. But Vannah, quite accustomed to being stared at, ignored them and just raised her proud chin a notch higher as she walked over to the closest desk and inquired where she might find Paul Demarest.

For a moment the bleary-eyed man just stared at her as though he had never seen a woman in his life, then muttered, "He's back there. Last desk on the right."

Vannah thanked him, then started down the long aisle between two rows of desks. She felt for all the world like she was running a gauntlet, but she kept her eyes straight ahead, neither looking right nor left, for she had sighted her prey sitting just where the other man had said he would be.

She would have recognized her intruder anywhere with his uncombed mane of black hair and his bushy beard. As she drew closer she could see that his suit was rumpled and creased as though he had slept in it, and his beard sprinkled with crumbs from his breakfast. Vannah wrinkled her nose in distaste.

He was hunched over his desk, a pencil in hand, seemingly intent upon a piece of paper he held in his other hand, so he didn't see Vannah come in until she had marched right up to his desk. When he glanced up and saw her, his eyes widened in surprise and he remembered his manners enough to jump to his feet, hastily brushing the crumbs from his beard while he rose.

"Miss Webb, I—" he began, obviously caught off-guard and quite flustered.

Vannah smiled coldly, relishing his discomfort even if it was only momentary. "Mr. Demarest, I believe? I just stopped by today to tell you how very much I enjoyed your article about my coming-out ball. I especially enjoyed the part about how our noble reporter would feed and clothe the hungry if he had but one of the diamonds I wore in my hair."

She reached into her handbag, removed something, and held her outstretched arm over Demarest's desk. Then she slowly released what she held, letting the long gold chain set with diamonds sift down onto the man's desk where it formed a gleaming and glittering mound of gold and diamonds.

Vannah glared at him out of blazing eyes. "Well, Mr. Demarest, now you have not one of my diamonds but all of them. I know you won't be satisfied until you have taken away everything my father owns, but I'm afraid my small contribution will have to do."

When Vannah turned to go, Demarest said, "I can't accept them, Miss Webb," through clenched teeth.

She whirled around, her brows arched in surprise. "What, Mr. Demarest? Do you mean to tell me that our fine, idealistic reporter is refusing an opportunity to feed the hungry and house the homeless? If you could save the world with just one of my diamonds, just think what you could do with all of them!"

"Go home, Miss Webb," he growled, jamming his hands into his pockets. "I don't know why you came here or what you intended to prove. Did you want to impress me with what a kind and generous woman you are? If so, you have failed miserably. You only succeeded in making yourself look quite the fool."

Vannah felt irrational tears sting her eyes. "I may be a foolish woman, Mr. Demarest, but at least I do not pretend to be something I'm not. You present yourself to your readers as the great crusading idealist, willing and ready to change the world for the price of a diamond, yet when it is offered to you, you refuse it. It is you who are the fool, sir, not I."

And without another word Vannah scooped up her diamonds, whirled on her heel, and went gliding out of *The Bugle*'s offices.

Paul Demarest was still standing, staring at her straight back, even after Vannah disappeared through the office door in a cloud of pale pink muslin. He snapped out of his reverie only when he realized that his co-workers had all fallen silent and were watching him.

"Don't any of you have work to do?" he growled, then dropped down at his desk and continued editing the copy at hand.

At least he tried to. Savannah Webb's perfume— French, no doubt, and obscenely expensive, he thought in disgust—lingered so tantalizingly in the warm, stale air of the office. Her scent was mossy and subtle, not at all sweet, and as it teased his nostrils, he thought of her lovely face with its flawless complexion and sparkling eyes.

A beautiful face, nothing more, he reminded himself savagely, a mask to fool and trap the unwary. And like all beautiful women, she expected life to be easy for her just because she was beautiful. She was shallow, flighty, vain, selfish, without substance or scruples. . . .

Much as he longed to believe the worst of her, something nagged at him.

If she were all of those things, wouldn't she just have ignored his article? But his stinging words had moved her enough to come down to *The Bugle*'s offices and offer her diamonds to the poor. Perhaps he had misjudged her, after all. Perhaps she had already surprised him.

"You're getting soft, Demarest," he muttered to himself, crossing out an offending sentence. "The lady **is** just what she seems, nothing more."

But why couldn't he get her out of his mind?

Chapter Eight

AUTUMN CAME EARLY to New York City that year.

As Vannah rode her new bay mare through Central Park, she noticed that most of the trees had started to turn already, and their once green leaves were now vivid shades of gold, orange, scarlet, and rust. A sudden gust of wind, brisk and chilly for early October, scattered dried brown leaves beneath her horse's hooves with a soft rustling noise that caused Vannah to shiver in anticipation of winter.

Suddenly Vannah heard someone calling her name.

She looked around and noticed a tall man in a tattered, loose-fitting black coat standing beside an old, rickety bicycle, his hand upraised to catch her attention. At first glance he didn't look at all familiar, so Vannah stared straight ahead and kept her horse at a slow, sedate walk, for she never spoke to strangers.

But when the man wheeled his bicycle closer, looked up at her, and said, "Miss Webb?" she recognized him right away, and her soaring temper made the cool autumn day seem as hot as summer.

"Why, if it isn't Mr. Demarest," she said, without stopping her horse. "I beg your pardon. I almost didn't recognize you without your beard and the food stains on your clothing."

When she looked down at Mr. Demarest, trying valiantly to keep up with her horse, she was dismayed to see him smiling, more amused than daunted by her cutting words.

"Scathing comments about my personal appearance will always fail to wound me, Miss Webb," he said.

Vannah had to grudgingly admit that he really wasn't that bad-looking without his scraggly beard to make him look as old as Abraham Lincoln and twice as forbidding. One even came to ignore his huge beak of a nose after a while.

She sighed. "What is it you want, Mr. Demarest?"

The black hawk's eyes bored into hers. "Would you mind dismounting and walking a bit with me, Miss Webb? You have no idea how formidable you look perched up there like an Amazon."

Vannah felt righteous indignation flow through her. "I will not, Mr. Demarest!" Now she did stop her horse to address him. "After that vituperative article you wrote about me, sir, and the abominable way you treated me when I came to your offices, I have nothing whatsoever to discuss with you." He opened his mouth to say something, but before he could get a word out, Vannah added, "I suggest that you get yourself out of my horse's way. She is a true aristocrat. She hates bicyclists and newspaper reporters."

And as if to prove her words, Vannah's bay mare flattened her ears against her head and began dancing in place, ready to kick out with iron-shod hooves and strike Paul Demarest down. Vannah never saw a man move so fast in all her life. Demarest jumped back, his face white with fear as he dragged his bicycle along with him, all the while keeping his wary eye on the horse's dancing back legs, which could lash out at any minute.

When he was out of harm's way, he cried indignantly, "I saw you. You made your horse do that!"

Vannah's silvery laugh caused heads to turn and stare. "How perceptive of you, Mr. Demarest! But take heart. I could have had her trample you if I had really wanted to hurt you."

And Vannah touched her heel to her horse's side and went trotting off down the street for home.

Little did she realize that she had not seen the last of the persistent Paul Demarest.

Several days after so boldly accosting Vannah in Central Park, Paul Demarest called upon her at home. Seething with anger at the man's impertinence, Vannah told Parkins to tell Mr. Demarest that she would never be at home to him no matter when he called. When that failed, he tried sending letters, but Vannah obstinately returned every single one of them, unopened, to *The Bugle*'s offices. He once succeeded in getting her to the telephone by pretending to be Louis Comfort Tiffany, but when Vannah discovered his true identity, she hung up on him.

And then Demarest started following her.

Sometimes Vannah would happen to glance out the parlor window and see him standing across the street from her house, his hands jammed into his coat pockets, his cheeks ruddy from the unseasonably cold air. She felt sorry for him but not enough to invite him in to warm himself.

Vannah became quite adept at evading him throughout most of October. The man did have to work at his dubious profession, so she didn't see him that often, but sometimes he would surprise her by turning up in the oddest places at unexpected times. One afternoon she saw him try to fight his way toward her through a crowd of shoppers in Macy's, and one evening she spotted his face among a throng of onlookers as she and her family were leaving the Metropolitan Opera House.

Then he dropped out of sight.

When several weeks passed with no sign of the persistent Mr. Demarest, Vannah began to feel safe again. And that was her undoing.

The second Tuesday in November dawned bright and clear, though bitterly cold, and Vannah felt the need for a little artistic exposure, so she decided it would be a perfect day to visit the Metropolitan Museum of Art. Even her father had no objections to her cultivating an interest in art, as long as she didn't draw herself, so Vannah used every opportunity to study paintings whenever she could.

Vannah usually took a maid with her to keep from being accosted by men who weren't gentlemen, but today she really wanted to wander through the museum alone. Besides, she wondered as she stepped into the carriage and gave the driver directions, how dangerous could a crowded museum be?

She was soon to find out.

The moment she arrived, Vannah went to the gallery of the Old Masters and strolled through it, marveling at the works of Van Dyck, Gainsborough, and Turner, knowing that she would sell her soul to possess even one tenth of their artistic genius. Then she noticed that an art student had set up her easel before Rosa Bonheur's *Horse Fair* and was in the process of copying the painting.

As Vannah stood quietly behind the girl, watching her paint, she could barely contain the envy that welled up inside her every time she saw one of these students copying a painting. How wonderful it must have been to attend a real art school and to be able to paint like this in broad daylight, before dozens of people! Vannah would have given anything to trade places with this girl, copying a painting in the Metropolitan Museum, letting the world know that she was an artist.

She was about to engage her in conversation when a voice behind her said, "She is rather good, isn't she, princess?"

Vannah recognized the voice at once, and a shiver of revulsion crawled up her spine. "Mr. Demarest," she said in her best voice of ice without turning her head to look at him.

"Do you paint, Miss Webb?" he asked conversationally.

"Alas, I don't, Mr. Demarest," she replied, still keeping her eyes straight ahead. "I'm sure that surprises you. After all, don't all young women of wealth and social position idle away their useless lives painting pretty pictures?"

Now Vannah did turn to look at her tormentor, purposely adjusting the wide Russian sable collar trimming her *velours du nord* jacket to call attention to its luxuriousness and warmth. She instantly regretted the mean-spirited gesture when she saw Mr. Demarest's sorry state.

The man looked as though he had followed her on foot all the way from Thirty-fourth Street to the museum near East Eighty-second Street, for he was shivering uncontrollably, even in the warm building. The tops of his ears were red, for he wore no hat on such a cold day, and Vannah suspected that his hands, jammed into the pockets of his tattered black coat, were also bare and just as red. Although Demarest's face looked pinched and cold, his wide-set eyes of onyx were as warm and bright as coals.

"You are a most elusive young woman, princess," he said.

"Why do you persist in following me, Mr. Demarest?" she inquired in exasperation, lifting her stubborn chin a notch and meeting his steady look with a haughty appraisal of her own. "You know we have nothing to say to each other."

"Oh, but we do, Miss Webb," he said, trying valiantly to keep his teeth from chattering.

Vannah felt the blood rush to her cheeks. "Oh, very well, Mr. Demarest. I am heartily sick of this little game of cat-and-mouse, so will you please say whatever it is you feel compelled to say to me and then leave me alone?"

The man seemed relieved and even managed a slight smile through stiff white lips. "Is there somewhere we can talk in private?"

"I believe there is a small lunchroom not far from here. You look as though you are in dire need of a hot cup of coffee, Mr. Demarest."

"My, my . . . do I detect a note of tender concern for my welfare in that cold, cruel voice of yours, princess?"

"My motives are purely selfish, as you would expect. I just don't want you perishing of cold at my feet; that is the extent of my tender concern for your welfare."

As they left the warmth of the museum for the frigid, blustery outdoors, Paul Demarest folded his arms across his chest and began shivering again. Vannah studied him contemptuously.

"Wherever did you buy that coat, Mr. Demarest? From some ragpicker?" she said. "But then, I suppose an idealistic, crusading journalist never concerns himself with life's creature comforts like the rest of us poor mortals. Or is it because your newspaper doesn't pay you a decent enough wage to be able to afford a good, warm winter coat?"

He looked at her, his dark eyes narrowing. "That's a low blow, princess, even for you."

Vannah just smiled benignly as she held out her large sable muff to him. "Too poor to afford a pair of gloves as well, Mr. Demarest? Then take this. I think you are more in need of it than I."

Her goading finally succeeded in touching a raw nerve. Demarest stopped, his eyes flashing with anger and contempt. "You spoiled little bitch! I don't know what made me think that you were different from the others of your ilk. I don't know why I bothered to try to see you for the past month, just to apologize to you for that article I wrote. In your case, Miss Webb, the book's blank cover does indeed reveal what's inside. Nothing!"

And he turned on his heel and started to storm off.

Much to Vannah's surprise and chagrin, tears suddenly sprang to her eyes. Her conscience got the best of her, and she found herself hiking up her long, heavy skirt with one hand and running down the street after him. "Mr. Demarest, please wait!" But he ignored her and kept on walking, increasing his stride. Finally she managed to catch up to him and stop him by grabbing his arm.

When he whirled around to face her, his flaring brows scowling in anger, she said, "It is I who should apologize to you. That was a rude and insensitive thing for me to say to you back there, and I am thoroughly ashamed of myself." Vannah had to look away from his unrelenting eyes. "But you see, the things you said about me in that article hurt me very deeply, and when someone hurts me, I tend to want to hurt them back. It's one of my many faults, I'm afraid," she added.

"It's a common human reaction to want to strike back," he agreed. "But did you really have to make your horse try to kick me that day in Central Park?"

Vannah felt herself blush in mortification until Paul Demarest burst out laughing. Suddenly she was laughing with him, sharing the humor of the situation, until another spasm of shivering overtook him.

"There's the lunchroom," Vannah said. "Let's get out of the cold, shall we?"

Mercifully the noontime patrons of the small lunchroom had all returned to their offices, so Vannah and Demarest were able to secure a table in a quiet, out-of-the-way corner where they could talk without having to shout over the din of a hundred voices speaking in unison.

While her companion went to order coffee and hot chocolate, Vannah had time to think about the odd situation she had put herself in. Here she was, Gerrold Webb's daughter, sitting—unchaperoned—in a public lunchroom with a man she barely knew, a socially unacceptable man who would never be received by her father, a man whose philosophy was dedicated to the destruction of her own way of life.

"Vannah Webb, you must be out of your mind," she muttered to herself as she watched Demarest walk across the scuffed, bare wood floor with a thick white china mug in each hand.

He set a steaming mug of hot chocolate down before her, then seated himself across from her and proceeded to wrap his hands around his mug of coffee, letting the hot cup warm them before bringing it to his lips and sipping the scalding liquid gingerly. She noticed that his hands were raw, chapped, and ink-stained, with large, bony knuckles and clean, but ragged, fingernails.

They drank in silence for a few minutes, Vannah studying him surreptitiously by the thin wintry light coming in from the north window. Paul Demarest's thick black hair was neater than she remembered, though tousled from the wind and still long enough at the back to almost touch his collar. Without his offensive beard he looked much younger than she had first supposed, perhaps even as young as twenty-four. But it was his eyes that intrigued her.

Unlike Martin Ash's eyes, always so veiled and guarded, Paul Demarest's were candid and revealing. Too candid and revealing, Vannah decided, for they were regarding her now with blatant masculine interest. And to her surprise and chagrin she found herself liking it.

When he had drunk half his coffee, he ran his hand through his hair, mussing it further. "I brought you here to apologize to you, Miss Webb, and apologize I will. But you must understand something." He leaned forward, hands clutching his coffee mug more for support than for warmth this time. "I will not apologize for the substance of my article. I believe that exorbitant wealth shared by a few is one of the greatest social evils of our times when there are so many who do without in this great land of ours."

Vannah felt herself bristling at his tone. "You are attacking my family and my friends' families, Mr. Demarest. You cannot expect me to sit idly by and listen to you malign them." She started to rise.

When he reached out and placed a restraining hand lightly on her arm, Vannah tried to jerk away from the familiarity of his touch and the feelings it aroused, but she couldn't. Luckily he didn't seem to notice the effect he was having on her.

"There I go again. I should have guessed that your familial loyalties run deep," he said with a rueful smile. "Please don't run away from me again, princess, for I, too, have grown tired of our little game. Can't we tolerate each other's differing opinions? Isn't that what democracy is all about?"

Vannah smiled slowly and eased herself back into her chair. "I'm sure we can have a civilized conversation, Mr. Demarest."

He grinned in approval, and the warmth of his smile went all the way up to his eyes. "Thank you, Miss Webb." Then he was silent, as if to collect his thoughts. "But I do apologize for saying what I did about you. You were right. I did judge by appearances and I misjudged you. I realized it that day you came marching into *The Bugle*'s offices and tried to give me your diamonds."

Vannah's gaze fell to her mug, and she ran her finger

along its handle. "It was a sincere offer, Mr. Demarest. I wasn't just being dramatic. I wanted you to take them, sell them, and help the poor you were writing about. You can still have them if you like."

Demarest smiled at her naïveté and continued. "At the time I suspected your motives. Later I realized that most society women would have just ignored my article and gone about their shallow lives." He leaned forward again, his eyes glowing with fervor. "But you cared, Miss Webb. My words touched you even as they wounded you. You at least tried to make amends for the sins of your class."

Now Vannah stared at him through narrowed eyes. "Mr. Demarest, I think you may have misjudged me in another direction. You speak as though you have found a new convert to your philosophy, but nothing could be further from the truth. Just because I would have given you my diamonds doesn't mean that I'll help you to destroy my family's way of life. I make no apologies for being wealthy. I do hope you understand that."

Paul Demarest relinquished his coffee mug long enough to fold his arms across the table and lean toward her. "And you misjudge me, Miss Webb. True, I see myself as an idealistic crusader against injustice, but journalism and politics are not my whole life." He added gently and with something akin to embarrassment, "I am a man too."

And he looked at Vannah in a way that had nothing whatsoever to do with idealism or politics.

Vannah's sharp intake of breath betrayed her, and she quickly looked away to hide her emotions, suddenly disconcerted by the baffling man seated across from her.

What is happening to me? she asked herself wildly as she stared out the window and tried to compose herself. I love Martin Ash. I'm not supposed to feel this way about another man, especially a dangerous man like Paul Demarest.

But when she hazarded a glance at him and found him staring at her as one transfixed, she could deny the attraction no longer. Vannah watched helplessly as his burning onyx eyes took in the rakish sable hat that contrasted so becomingly with her fair hair, then slowly roved down across her cheekbones and chin before finding their way back up to her eyes and meeting her gaze unflinchingly.

She felt as though he had reached over and traced the contours of her face with his fingertips, so powerful was that look. Vannah felt suddenly giddy, the way she usually felt from drinking champagne too quickly.

If Paul Demarest was aware of the inner turmoil stirring within her, he gave no sign. All he said was, "I hope you don't bear me any grudges for those things I said to you the night you surprised me in your father's study. I wasn't invited to your party. I wanted to take a look at your father's private papers to see if I could find proof of his unethical business practices."

"You ask a lot, Mr. Demarest," Vannah said.

He grinned disarmingly. "That is true. But I'm willing to forgive you for making your horse try to kick me that day in the park, and that is asking quite a lot of me. I dislike horses. Disgusting creatures."

Vannah couldn't help smiling. "I suppose we are even, then. Perhaps we can be friends after all."

He studied her in silence for a minute before saying, "Do you think we can, Miss Webb? We are, after all, not at all alike. In fact, I can't think of two people who are more different. I'm uncouth, opinionated, stubborn, and you're beautiful—"

"Opinionated, stubborn . . ." Vannah finished for him with a smile. Then she shrugged. "I like to think I have an open mind. As long as I don't try to change you, and you don't try to change me, perhaps we can become friends.

But if that's not possible, at least we have stopped being enemies."

Now she looked out the window again and noticed that the light had changed. "I'm afraid I have tarried too long, Mr. Demarest. My poor coachman is probably still parked outside of the Metropolitan Museum, wondering where I have gotten to. I really must be going." Then Vannah rose and said, "Thank you for the hot chocolate."

He was on his feet in an instant. "Thank you for agreeing to speak with me, Miss Webb." Suddenly he looked as awkward as a schoolboy, this sharp, cynical man who had always behaved with the supreme confidence of one who knows his cause to be right and just. "When—when can I see you again?"

"You want to see me again?" she asked, her voice rising in surprise and ill-concealed pleasure.

"Yes. Yes, I would. Very much. Soon."

For a moment Vannah just stood there in silence. She knew that the sensible thing to do would be to make her apologies and reject him gently but firmly, by telling him that they could never meet again. Yet she wasn't feeling the least bit sensible about Paul Demarest.

There was only one man who had ever stirred her emotions so deeply, and that was Martin Ash. But he thought her a child. Standing before her was a man who saw her as a woman.

She was feeling all shivery inside again. There was a very real attraction between them that couldn't be denied, despite the disparity in their backgrounds. Vannah had sensed it from the moment she had so cruelly taunted him about being poor and offered him her sable muff. And then when they had shared coffee and hot chocolate together . . .

She tugged on her black kidskin gloves to hide the

shaking in her hands, then moistened her dry lips. "The Metropolitan Museum, next Tuesday, at the same time?"

Vannah held her breath, waiting for his answer.

He looked both relieved and pleased. "That will be fine. Let me walk you to your carriage."

They left the lunchroom and fought the strong, brisk wind all the way back to the museum, where Vannah's carriage was still parked, the driver waiting patiently with his horses for her return. He didn't blink an eye when he saw her walking toward him on the arm of a strange man but just nodded to her.

When Demarest opened the carriage door for her, Vannah noticed that his shoulders were shaking again from the cold, so she said, "I insist that you ride with me. My driver will take you back to your offices if you wish."

"You needn't go out of your way. I'll take a cab," he replied stiffly, his pride getting the better of him.

Vannah smiled mischievously. "Are you afraid that you'll be compromising your high principles if you ride in Gerrold Webb's carriage, Mr. Demarest?"

"Well, as long as none of my friends see me . . ." he muttered, looking around.

After assisting her he joined her, and the carriage eased itself out into traffic and headed downtown.

After only a few clandestine meetings with Paul Demarest, Vannah knew she was in love. He argued with her, bullied her, challenged her, while she in turn teased him constantly, forcing Paul to laugh at himself.

She was determined to go on seeing him, and with the complicity of a few close friends who agreed to provide her with alibis whenever necessary, Vannah was able to leave the house several times a week without anyone suspecting.

November slid into December with surprising swiftness,

and Vannah felt a contentment she hadn't known since those halcyon days in Newport with Martin Ash.

When Christmas came, she restrained her impulsive, generous nature when it came to choosing a gift for Paul from Macy's. There were so many things she wanted to buy for him, but she settled on a pair of fine calfskin gloves and a warm woolen scarf. He gave her a tortoiseshell comb for her hair that must have cost him a week's wages.

On New Year's Day, a time when all gentlemen went calling on as many of their friends as they could and the women stayed home to receive such callers, Paul both startled and delighted Vannah when he walked in the door and paid his respects to Aunt Constance and Vannah as if he didn't know them. Vannah had a difficult time controlling herself when he bowed to her and wished her a Happy New Year. Aunt Constance was polite as always and seemed to dismiss him as one of the many strangers who used the Dutch tradition of the New Year's open house as an excuse to get a free meal. Only Vannah noticed the sparkle of mirth in Paul's dark eyes and the suppressed smile whenever he caught her eye.

Vannah felt as though she were walking on air. She didn't notice the way Aunt Constance was watching her from across the room, her eyes narrowing in suspicion, then widening in comprehension as they moved from Vannah to the man with the black eyes and back to Vannah.

Since Vannah was so reluctant to meet an unmarried gentleman in his apartment, she and Paul often met at the home of one of his married journalist friends for propriety's sake, so there would be someone to chaperon them.

One day in early January, when the mistress of the house discreetly disappeared into the kitchen so they could be alone, Paul suddenly took something from behind the sofa and hid it behind his back.

"I have something for you," he said. "Guess what it is."

At first Vannah almost protested that he shouldn't have, for Paul had so little money to spend on himself, let alone her. But she held her tongue, for if there was one thing she had learned about Paul Demarest, it was that he was a proud, pigheaded man and might take offense if she refused his gift.

"Two thousand *gloire de Paris* roses," she guessed with a teasing smile.

"Hidden behind my back? No, try again."

"A ride on the elevated railway?"

"Will you please be serious, princess? This is something I'm positive no man has ever given you before."

Vannah clasped her hands together in childish glee. "A talking raven! Oh, Paul, thank you! I've wanted one ever since I read that Edgar Allan Poe poem. I'll name him Nevermore."

Now Paul was on the verge of losing his temper with her. "No, my sweet, silly princess, it's not a talking raven." He thrust out what he'd been hiding behind his back.

"Books?" Vannah's eyes widened as she took the books and pamphlets and read several of the titles aloud. "John Stuart Mill, *The Subjection of Women* . . . *A Climb in the Rocky Mountains* by Isabella Bird Bishop?" She smiled in delight. "You mean to tell me that a woman has climbed the Rocky Mountains? I never knew that!"

"There's much you don't know about the accomplishments of your own sex," he said sternly. "And it's high time you learned."

As Vannah stared down at his gifts she was so moved, she felt her eyes suddenly mist over with tears. "You're right, Paul. No man has ever given me such a wonderful gift before. That's because most men see me as a beautiful object to be adorned and displayed. They don't think I even have a mind, so why give me something that will make me think?"

"What have I been telling you? I know you have a fine mind," he said with quiet intensity and confidence, "and I know you can use it."

"Thank you, Paul, for having such faith in me," Vannah said, going to him and giving him a kiss on the cheek.

When she stepped back, he was looking at her with such fire in his eyes that Vannah thought her bones would melt. Then, with a slow, patient gesture he reached up to cup one cheek in his palm. He held it there until he was sure that Vannah wasn't going to pull away, then he lowered his head to touch his lips to her own.

The soft, chaste pressure lasted for the briefest of moments, and when it was over, Vannah gave him a lazy, teasing smile, quite unaware of the seductiveness of her voice and expression. "Is that the very best you can do, Mr. Demarest?"

"Oh, no, princess," Paul replied softly, "that is not the best I can do at all."

With a shake of his head he pulled her into his arms with such force that it took Vannah's breath away. Paul may have been thin, but his body was wiry and strong against her own, and Vannah found her arms sliding instinctively around his waist as she closed her eyes and turned her head to receive his kiss.

His mouth came down hard on hers for the second time, and Vannah felt as though she were flying. She whimpered as she leaned toward him, responding with an eagerness and ferocity of feeling that surprised her.

She managed to tear herself away to stare deeply into his eyes, now glittering with the fire of desire, and she came to a decision.

"I want you, Paul," she said, her voice husky. "I want us to become lovers."

He gasped for breath like a drowning man. "Are you sure, princess? You know I've never wanted to make you do something you might later regret."

Vannah gave him a trembling smile. "Oh, I won't regret it, Paul."

He nodded toward the kitchen. "Shall we leave our benevolent watchdog and go to my apartment?"

Vannah glanced at a clock on the mantel and her face fell. "If I don't return home soon, Aunt Constance is sure to begin asking questions. How about tomorrow?"

Paul nodded reluctantly. "The last thing I want is to make your family suspicious. We'll meet tomorrow, then."

Vannah smiled and kissed him again, then took her reading material and left.

She was just walking through the door when Parkins appeared out of nowhere and said, "Mr. Webb wishes to see you in his study immediately, Miss Savannah."

After she thanked the butler and hid her books, she went to the study.

"Father, you wanted to see me?"

He said nothing in response, just leaned back in his swivel chair and watched her out of narrowed eyes that looked as cold as this blustery January afternoon. Vannah could tell that something was very wrong. She felt her stomach begin to churn, the way it had when she was eleven years old and begging her father to change his mind and allow her to draw.

She seated herself in one of the leather chairs across from him and waited expectantly for the explosion.

"Did you really think you could get away with it?" was all he said.

"Get away with what?" Vannah asked, wondering what she had done now.

Her father tipped his chair forward, placed both hands on his desk, and leaned closer to her. "Don't lie to me, Savannah. Don't play the innocent. I'm referring to your shameful, sneaky little assignations with one Paul Demarest."

Vannah felt the blood rush from her face, and for one terrifying moment she thought she was going to faint. With superhuman effort she took a deep breath and controlled herself. "How—how did you know?" she asked in a trembling voice.

Her father made a hissing sound of disgust and rose to stand behind his desk. "Do you think I'm stupid, Savannah? Do you think I don't know what's going on in my own house?" His voice was loud and furious enough to reverberate through the room. "Did you really think that you would be able to—to cavort around this city without someone noticing you, daughter? I can't tell you how many of my friends have told me of seeing you and some young man they didn't know strolling through the Metropolitan Museum, usually on a Tuesday."

Vannah felt her cheeks redden.

"And did you really think I wouldn't question my coachman when I began to have these suspicions that you were seeing an unsuitable young man behind my back?"

Now Vannah rose defiantly, her anger matching her father's. "I'll have you know that even though Paul Demarest may be poor, and therefore unsuitable in your eyes, he's worth twenty Vanderbilts!"

At first her father seemed stunned that she would contradict him so vehemently, then he scowled, the cleft deepening between his brows. "He is the lowliest trash, Savannah, not even good enough to sweep horse dung off the street in front of our house let alone associate with us. Paul Demarest is—"

"No! I won't have you disparaging him, Father!" she cried. "How can you say such terrible things about him when you don't even know him?"

"I know he's the same filthy swine who writes for that so-called newspaper. That's all I need to know about such rabble."

Vannah shook her head. "He's intelligent, Father, and kind and gentle. He—"

Before Vannah could continue, her father looked as though he had had a shocking revelation, rounded his desk in three strides, and grasped her by the shoulders. "Have you allowed him to take liberties with your person, Savannah?" he bellowed into her face until she recoiled "Have you slept with him? Are you lovers? Answer me, damn it!"

"No!" Vannah cried, hot tears of shame falling from her eyes. "Paul has always been a perfect gentleman. He's never even tried to kiss me," she purposely lied, even as she recalled her own passionate response to him just half an hour ago.

Her father looked relieved and his hands fell away. "Thank God for that. Thank God I wasn't too late."

Vannah moved away from him, whimpering softly as she rubbed the places where her father's bruising, punishing fingers had bitten into her soft flesh. But it was too late for her. She and Paul would never become lovers tomorrow or ever.

"But I wish we had been lovers," she said defiantly.

An uncontrollable rage consumed Gerrold like brushfire, and before he could stop himself, he raised his hand and smartly slapped his daughter across the face with his open palm. The crack seemed to echo like a gunshot through the hushed study. He watched Savannah's head jerk to the side, and the terror and fear fill her startled eyes as she tried to scramble away out of his reach, her burning red cheek cradled in her hand.

"Never," he said with great restraint, wagging his finger at her. "Never speak to your father that way again, Savannah."

But if he thought that she was still a child, to be cowed by his authority or threats of physical punishment, Gerrold Webb was mistaken.

In the few seconds that had passed since her father struck her, Vanna realized that she had lost Paul forever. She had nothing left to lose now, and she fought back in anger and frustration.

"No, Father, I won't keep silent. You can slap me in the face as much as you like or take a switch to me, but I will not keep silent if I think you are wrong. And you are wrong about Paul Demarest. Wrong!" Now she rose to her full height and let her hand fall from her sore, burning cheek. "And you can't stop me from seeing Paul, either. You can lock me in my room and feed me bread and water, but it won't make any difference. You can't watch me day and night. I'll find a way to be with him, sooner or later."

"Don't you see what this man has done to you?" he asked. "He's taught you defiance and instilled in you a lack of respect for your own father, qualities that no decent gentleman would encourage in a lady. But then, he's not a gentleman, is he? He's just a—"

"He's more of a gentleman than many men I know," she retorted. "And you're wrong, Father. All Paul has taught me is that respect has to be earned."

Gerrold glared at her but managed to hold his tongue. He sighed regretfully and returned to his desk. "So I take it that nothing I have to say will make you change your mind about seeing this Demarest fellow?"

"No, Father."

"My foolish, headstrong daughter," he murmured sorrowfully. He took no pleasure in besting such a weak opponent, especially his own daughter. "Well, Savannah, if that's the way you feel about it, then you leave me no other alternative."

She regarded him suspiciously. "What do you mean, Father?"

He leaned across his desk again, his pale, merciless eyes chilling her to the core as he stared at her. "The time for niceties is past, daughter," he said calmly. "If you are going to persist in defying me, then we're going to play this little game according to my rules."

Vannah felt her blood run cold at the ominous sound to her father's words.

He picked up some papers from his desk and appeared to study them, but Vannah had a feeling that he already knew what they contained. He said, "I have had some of my associates investigate this Demarest fellow and his family." He ignored his daughter's outraged gasp and went on with, "His father is a teacher of history at Columbia College, I believe, and his only sister is married to a man who works for a coal mining company. He has two older brothers who are out in California." Now Gerrold Webb did look at his daughter. "You may not be aware of this, Savannah, but I am a generous contributor to Columbia College. I always have been. I don't think the college would be too pleased if I were to suddenly withdraw my support, do you?"

Vannah's mouth went dry, and her smarting cheek stopped hurting. "What are you saying, Father?"

"I'm saying that if you don't agree to stop seeing Demarest, his father will lose his position at Columbia College and never find another. I will personally see to it. Then his brother-in-law will lose his job with the coal mining company—since I am on its board of directors as well— and never work again. Do I make myself clearly understood, Savannah?"

Vannah thought of Paul, who often spoke so proudly of his family, especially his father. "You wouldn't! You couldn't be that cruel."

He just looked at her wordlessly, but his eyes told her that he would have no scruples about carrying out such a threat.

Vannah knew that it would be useless to throw herself at his feet and beg for mercy, that any entreaties would fall upon deaf ears. So, though her heart was breaking and her eyes were filled with tears, she faced her father with courage and fortitude.

"I never wanted to believe him, but now I see that Paul was right about you. You're a cold, ruthless man, Father, who has doubtlessly lied, swindled, and bribed to acquire your fortune. My own father." Vannah shook her head sadly and turned to leave.

Gerrold was unmoved. "You shall have to think of some way to break off with him, Savannah. I leave that to your discretion."

"Don't worry, Father," she said bitterly. "I'll think of something."

"Don't judge me too harshly, Savannah. Someday you'll understand that I had to be cruel for your own good. Someday you'll realize that you and Demarest would never have suited each other. You're a princess and he's a peasant. He's—"

But he was abruptly cut off by the sound of the door closing after her, and then Gerrold Webb was alone. He felt no remorse for what he had done, for he knew that he was right, as usual. Well, he did regret the fact that Savannah had disappointed him. She was turning out just like her mother, infatuated with unsuitable men. Perhaps it ran in Frances's family, like some inherited disease.

At least he had caught it just in time—for Savannah's sake as well as his own.

* * *

When Vannah reached the welcome solitude of her own room, she flung herself on her bed and let the tears flow unchecked. Her heart-rending sobs shook her shoulders and filled the room, and she clutched and clawed at the bed's coverlet in her frustration.

Finally, when it seemed that she had cried her eyes dry and no more tears would fall, she rose and went to her sitting room. She would never be allowed to see Paul again. They would never stroll through the museum together, never drink hot chocolate and coffee in a lunchroom, never argue good-naturedly and laugh. She would never see his onyx eyes light up with pleasure at the sight of her, never hear his voice soften and grow gentle when he spoke her name. She would never feel his kisses upon her mouth again, never know what it would be like to give herself to him completely.

She cared too much for Paul to let her father destroy his family. No, she had to accept the fact that their relationship was doomed and she was helpless to prevent it, no matter how much it tore at her inside.

With a heavy heart she went to her writing desk and wrote the hardest letter of her life.

The following morning Paul came immediately in response to her note, as she knew he would.

Paul looked around the parlor, his gaze lingering on the Tiffany window. "I never thought I'd see the day when I was actually invited to Gerrold Webb's house," he muttered. Then, after taking her hands in his, he added, "I must say that I'm quite shocked by your summons. I thought we agreed to meet at my apartment today."

Seeing him standing there so expectantly, his hair tousled by the wind and his cheeks ruddy, Vannah almost lost all of her resolve. But when she thought of the terrible fate awaiting Paul's family, she summoned up a hidden reserve of strength to do what she had to do.

"There's something I must say to you, Paul," she said stiffly, without smiling, as she pulled her hands away.

"Oh, this sounds serious," he said with a teasing smile. "Don't tell me you're in the family way after just two kisses, because I—"

"Paul, will you just please stop it!" Vannah shouted.

"Vannah, what's wrong?" he demanded, his light mood gone.

She took a deep breath and gripped the back of the divan as hard as she could, for more courage. "I don't know quite how to say this to you. . . . I don't ever want to see you again."

Vannah forced herself to look at him, though the misery that flooded his eyes made her look away. "I'm—I'm sorry. I know it's woefully inadequate, but what else can I say?"

"Why?" he asked quietly.

Vannah wished that he would shout at her and shake her, anything but that quiet uttering of that solitary word. But his shock was too great and his grief too deep for anger.

"Isn't that rather obvious to you? Because we're so unlike, of course," she replied in carefully rehearsed tones. "I'm wealthy and you're as poor as a churchmouse. You couldn't even afford a pair of gloves to keep your hands warm in the winter. You were right about me all along, Paul. I am shallow. I admit it. I love each and every one of my thousand-dollar Worth gowns and my jewels. It was novel and exciting to keep company with someone so far beneath me, but now that novelty has worn off and it's time to say good-bye."

"Vannah!" he cried in bewilderment. "What you're saying is not true!"

"Oh, but it is, Paul. Every word of it."

His eyes narrowed in suspicion. "Do you take me for a fool? Just yesterday you were ready to go to bed with me, and now you expect me to believe that you feel nothing for me? That you can turn your emotions off and on like tap water?"

"It was the first time a man has ever kissed me." Vannah shrugged lamely. "I got carried away, that's all."

Paul shook his head. "No. I still don't believe you. This is not the woman I know talking. It's some cruel, heartless stranger reciting carefully rehearsed lines."

He walked up to her, his black eyes bright. "What is your real reason for telling me that you never want to see me again? Has your father found out about us? Is he forcing you to break it off with me?"

Now came the crucial part. She shook her head and made herself giggle like a practiced flirt. "Poor Paul. You're just like every other man who can't accept it when a woman tells him that she no longer desires his company. My father had nothing to do with this, as much as you don't want to believe that. I merely have tired of you and am more interested in some other gentlemen of my own social standing. It's quite simple, really."

"Has he threatened you? Has he threatened to harm me in some way?" His face lit up with sudden comprehension. "That's the reason for this farce, isn't it?"

Vannah averted her face so he wouldn't guess the truth. "Don't be absurd. My father hasn't threatened anyone. You just refuse to believe the truth."

"Vannah!" Her name was a cry of anguish and need. "Don't do this to me . . . to us!"

"Oh, Paul . . . you are beginning to bore me." Vannah raised her hand to delicately smother a yawn. "Must you always be so melodramatic?"

He reached for her and tried to take her into his arms, but she skillfully darted just out of reach.

"If you lay one hand on me, Mr. Demarest," she warned, "I shall scream this house down. I mean it!"

He stiffened, and his hands fell to his sides. When he looked at her, his eyes were filled with a mixture of confusion, disbelief, and loathing.

"Very well," he said curtly, biting off each word. "If that's the way you want it . . ."

"I do, Paul. It would be best if you left now."

"It will be my pleasure," he muttered savagely.

But before he left, he pulled the gloves she had given him out of his coat pocket and flung them back at her. Because Vannah was so startled, she didn't move away in time, and they smacked her squarely in the chest, then fell to the floor with a thud. Without so much as a backward glance Paul Demarest walked out of her life forever.

Vannah waited until she heard the front door slam shut before she dissolved into tears and collapsed on the divan.

That April, *The Bugle* lost one of its best reporters when Paul Demarest unexpectedly resigned and announced that he was traveling to California to be with his brothers and seek a new life there. Soon circulation dropped alarmingly, and *The Bugle* went bankrupt. If Gerrold Webb and his friends had anything to do with the paper's demise, they kept it to themselves.

Chapter Nine

Newport—1893

THE SUMMER SUN HAD SET long ago, cooling Newport and bathing it in the warm, lingering glow of twilight. Fashionable Bellevue Avenue, which had once been nothing more than a dusty lane leading out of town, was so quiet and so nearly deserted now, it was difficult to believe that just an hour ago the two-laned thoroughfare had been alive with the sounds of spinning carriage wheels, clopping hooves, tooting horns, and cracking whips. Every type of equipage imaginable—elegant barouches, landaus, victorias, dogcarts, tandems, and four-in-hands—drawn by splendid, high-stepping horses in brass-fitted harnesses were driven up and down the three-mile stretch by smartly liveried coachmen during the daily ritual of the sunset promenade.

It was a time for the wealthy, elite summer residents of Newport to don their finery and pay homage to one another, a time to see and be seen by their equals and envied by those who had neither the wit nor the fortune needed to join their exalted ranks.

Now all of the fashionables had returned to their replicas of English manor houses and French châteaux, leaving only a solitary rented carriage to make its way at a leisurely pace down the avenue.

Inside, Martin Ash watched the lamps being lit in the downstairs windows of simple wooden houses and elegant mansions alike, in preparation for the darkness soon to fall. He found the scene welcoming, comforting, somehow civilized.

There had been a time when he had hated Newport, finding many of its inhabitants pretentious and ostentatious, everyone vying with each other to build the biggest mansion, stock their huge stables with the finest horseflesh, and give the most lavish ball without any consideration for taste.

However, now Martin grudgingly appreciated the summer colony's beauty and grace. And he hungered for beauty.

Oh, he thought with a knowing smile, Katherine would hate it with a passion. She, who couldn't tell a Chopin polonaise from a Beethoven sonata but knew the names of every prairie wildflower, would dismiss these people as too "fancy-dancy" with their two-hundred-fifty-foot yachts, private railroad cars, and forty-room "summer cottages."

Ash sighed as he ran his fingertips gingerly down the straight, puckered scar that sliced beneath his right cheekbone. That had been the problem. Katherine belonged to the mountains and the ranges of Wyoming, but Martin Ash did not and never would.

He quickly put her out of his mind. That part of his life was over and best forgotten.

When he felt his carriage slow down and turn, Ash knew that he had reached the wide wrought-iron gates of Clairvaux at last. He wondered if the Webbs would be surprised to see him, since he hadn't sent them either telegram or letter to announce his arrival.

But as the carriage rumbled through the gates Martin Ash was blissfully unaware that a surprise of a different sort awaited him at Clairvaux tonight.

* * *

Vannah slowly paced around her room, feeling unusually despondent tonight. Another ball. How many had she attended since her debut two years ago? Two hundred? Four hundred? She had stopped counting long ago, so she supposed it didn't make any difference. They were all alike. The same vapid young men bored her on the dance floor; the same dull conversations lulled her to sleep during dinner.

When Vannah wasn't attending the balls and dinners Aunt Constance gave, she was accompanying her father and aunt to similar functions at Beechwood, Roselawn, or any number of houses with similar grandiose names. Her beauty made her in demand for the many amateur theatricals and *tableaux vivants* someone was always staging for an evening's entertainment, but at least these amusements were mildly diverting.

During the day she would forgo such popular Newport pastimes as playing tennis at the casino and watching polo matches and restrict herself to bathing at Bailey's Beach or riding. Then, later, her father insisted that she participate in the sunset promenade with him and Aunt Constance in the coach-and-four, though she would have preferred to stay home and draw.

"Paul was right. What a useless, empty life I lead," she muttered, suddenly feeling very sorry for herself.

Paul . . . How her heart still ached for him, even after all this time!

Vannah knew exactly why she was feeling so moody. She lived in mortal fear that any day now her father would take her aside and tell her that her marriage was all arranged. She knew that several men had already expressed an interest in her, but her father had so far refused them all. Vannah wondered what he was waiting for. After all, she had been "out" for two years already.

Feeling suddenly restless, Vannah decided to clear her

head by going for a walk in the garden before the guests started arriving. She tugged on her long white gloves, took the ivory fan from her chest of drawers, and started downstairs.

Walking down Clairvaux's long upstairs corridors, she found herself looking forward to a quiet evening stroll, with the air redolent of damp earth, freshly mown grass, and a tangy sea breeze blowing in from the ocean. The ocean in the evening, with the moonlight dancing off its surface like a million tiny mirrors, always calmed her.

Perhaps there she could forget about Paul, at least for a little while.

Martin was standing in the foyer, waiting for the butler to announce him to Gerrold Webb, when he looked up to find an ethereal vision spun from gold and light standing at the head of the stairs.

He stared at her, momentarily dumbfounded by her radiance. And then he recognized her.

"It can't be," he muttered. "Savannah?"

Until the man spoke her name Vannah hadn't realized that there was someone standing in the dimly lit foyer. But as she glided down the stairs in a faint rustle of silk, she could discern a tall man near the portrait of Sir Lancelot.

At first she thought he was one of the gardeners, dressed as he was in a shapeless jacket, a chambray shirt open at the neck, and a pair of dusty denim dungarees worn over well-scuffed boots. He held a wide-brimmed hat in his hand, though the sun had set long ago.

Just as Vannah was on the verge of advising him to use the servants' entrance, something familiar about the man stayed her tongue. Frowning in puzzlement, she crossed the foyer with light, quick steps and got the surprise of her life.

"Martin?" she cried, her voice rising in disbelief. "Martin Ash?"

He stepped forward. "Little Savannah Webb, all grown-up at last and so very beautiful."

There had once been a time when Vannah would have expired of sheer delight to hear Martin utter those very same words, but now they sounded false and hollow to her ears, like all the other pretty, meaningless compliments she had received from so many other men.

"Thank you," she said politely, and proceeded to scrutinize him curiously.

Except for a long scar running diagonally across one cheek, Martin had changed very little in six years. He was still devilishly handsome, with his sun-weathered skin and those devastating green eyes that had haunted Vannah's dreams down through the years. And now that she was a grown woman with some experience of men, she could at last identify what it was about him that had attracted her right from the start: his unabashed masculinity. There was an aura of raw power about Martin Ash, an air of masterfulness and control.

Vannah waited hopefully for the breathless, weak-kneed response she always experienced when she thought of Martin in the past. She wanted to melt in his arms, feel his lips on her own, smooth and warm, but she felt nothing. And she knew the reason why.

When she was a child, she thought herself in love with Martin. Paradoxically, now that she was a grown woman, she could recognize her feelings for what they really were—infatuation, as he had insisted all along. Paul Demarest had taught her the true meaning of love.

"Oh, Martin . . . however did you get that scar?" Vannah asked when she realized that she had been staring too long. Then she flushed in embarrassment. "That was very rude of me and I apologize. Do forgive me for asking."

"There is nothing to forgive," he said with a wide grin. Then he reached up and ran his fingertips down the scar's length. "I received this souvenir one day when I was out tracking down some men who had been stealing my cattle. They hid behind some rocks and ambushed me, leaving me for dead. Fortunately they weren't very thorough. The bullet only grazed me, and they didn't bother to make sure I was dead." And, fortunately, Katherine had found him and saved his life, but he didn't tell Savannah that.

Vannah shivered, causing the crystal beads on her gown to jump and twinkle. "How—how barbaric! But it does give you a rakish air, rather like a buccaneer."

"So I've been told."

"Please excuse my atrocious manners. Of course you'll be staying here with us, so I'll have a room made ready and your baggage taken upstairs."

"The butler has already gone to announce me to your father."

Before Vannah could say another word, Gerrold Webb's voice came booming at them from the downstairs corridor. "Well, look at what the wind just blew in. Martin Ash! It's been a long time."

"Webb," Martin said as they shook hands. "I trust you'll forgive me for arriving unannounced like this. I suppose I should have stopped somewhere to send a telegram."

"Oh, with twenty bedchambers in this cottage, I'm sure we can find somewhere to put you."

Now Aunt Constance came hurrying down the staircase.

"Martin!" she cried in disbelief and delight. "My word, this is a pleasant surprise! I thought you had disappeared off the face of the earth. You can't imagine how pleased I was when Gerrold told me that you were here."

Constance stood on tiptoe and kissed him with the familiarity of an old friend, first on one cheek, then on the other. Next she stood back and scowled at him. "My dear boy, let me look at you. You're so thin! And wherever did you get that scar?"

Before their guest could reply, Gerrold was interrupting with, "Now, now, Constance, there will be plenty of time for that later. I'm sure Ash is weary after traveling such a great distance and would like a little time to dine and refresh himself before joining us and our guests in the ballroom."

Martin gave an apologetic smile. "Will you forgive me, Constance, for taking my leave of you so soon after my arrival? But I must confess that I am a bit worn-out and more than a bit famished."

She patted him on the arm. "Of course, Martin. We'll have Parkins show you to your room and bring you a tray." Constance shook her head in amazement. "It is wonderful to see you again, old friend. We have much to talk about."

Once Martin would have hated her calling him her "old friend," but now it didn't seem to matter.

Suddenly Parkins appeared out of nowhere, and Gerrold told him to show their guest to the Green Room. Then Vannah, her aunt, and her father returned to the ballroom.

An hour later Martin was standing on the sidelines, watching a hundred dancers dash around the floor in a high-spirited galop. He had almost forgotten what it was like to stand in a cavernous ballroom banked with thousands of fragrant, colorful roses and softly illuminated by hundreds of candles burning in sparkling crystal chandeliers overhead. His eyes feasted on the perfumed, bejeweled women, all beautiful in their pastel silk gowns. For the past six years he had been deprived of elegance, beauty, and refinement, and he hadn't quite realized until this very moment just now how much he had missed seeing the sparkle of diamonds at a woman's throat, the rich patina of well-rubbed mahogany and rosewood furniture in a room, the power and emotion evoked by a great work of art hanging on a wall.

He thought of his simple log ranch-house in Wyoming, well built and functional with about as much grace and style as a shoebox, each room small and square. Oh, Katherine had tried her best to make it a home, but she was a pragmatic rancher's daughter with simple tastes who couldn't understand why anyone would pay hard-earned gold to buy a Turkish carpet from some foreign country when she could braid one out of rags that would keep the dirt off the floor just as well. But then, she had never really understood him or his hunger for beauty and civilized comforts. He knew that his "fancy-dancy" European ways had always mystified her right up until the day he left.

Martin sighed. He harbored no hard feelings against Wyoming. The ranching life might not have made him wealthy, but it had been good for him in other ways. It had been a hard life, and only the strongest survived, giving a man a sense of self-reliance and a measure of his true worth. But, as he had explained to Katherine, fate had intervened, sending his life moving in a different direction now, and it was time to move on. She could either move with him or remain behind with all that was familiar. He had known what her choice would be.

He was momentarily distracted by the sight of Savannah Webb mingling with her guests, saying a few words to some, conversing longer with others. But beneath her polite smiles, her surface poise, and self-assurance Martin sensed that there was something amiss.

He crossed the ballroom toward her.

Savannah knew the exact moment Martin entered the ballroom.

Conversation ceased for several seconds as women turned to stare appreciatively at the handsome, dark-haired man with that air of wildness lurking just beneath his civilized demeanor. The men regarded him speculatively, sizing him up as a possible ally or rival.

As Martin sauntered across the ballroom he seemed totally oblivious to the effect he was having on everyone present. Then he was standing before Vannah, asking her for the next dance.

The moment Martin led her out onto the dance floor and took her in his arms, Vannah knew that she had been a fool to think she could remain oblivious to him, no matter how much she still loved Paul. Yet she strengthened her determination to do just that. She would ignore the persistent pressure of his hand on her waist and that look of unconcealed admiration in his intense green eyes.

When Vannah could tolerate it no longer, she tried conversation. "So, will you be our guest for very long, or must you run right back to your ranch?"

"Actually I'm on my way back to England," he replied. His face suddenly set in somber lines, and his smile died. "I received word some months ago that my brother, his wife, and their three-year-old son were drowned when their gondola capsized on a holiday in Venice."

"Oh, no!" Vannah murmured. "How dreadful. I am so, so sorry."

Martin inclined his head in acknowledgment. "Now that my brother and his heir are both gone, I am next in line to become the Marquis of Fleet." He grimaced. "I never dreamed I would inherit, and especially not under such tragic and painful circumstances, but perhaps that is where my destiny lies."

"What do you mean?"

Martin smiled ruefully. "All of my life I've lived in my older brother's shadow, never really finding my place in the world. I wasn't suited to military life, and I didn't make my fortune ranching, so perhaps I'll find what I've been looking for back in England."

"But what about your ranch?"

"I've informed the syndicate that my responsibilities now lie elsewhere, and they've sent someone else in my place. I will not be returning to Wyoming." Or Katherine.

Vannah looked up at him in puzzlement. "Now that you're a marquis, whatever am I to call you? Milord? Your Lordship?"

He grinned. "Martin will do nicely."

Vannah smiled briefly, then she got a faraway look in her eyes that troubled Martin. He was vain enough to think that most women enjoyed his company, and Vannah's lack of interest was beginning to annoy him, especially when he was trying so hard to charm her.

"It's a bit stifling in here, don't you think?" he asked. "Why don't we go out on the terrace?"

Vannah nodded listlessly, so he steered her out of the crush of dancers, secured two glasses of champagne from a passing footman, and followed her through the French doors.

They strolled toward the farthest end of the flagstone terrace, sipping their champagne in silence.

"It's a beautiful night," Vannah murmured, setting her glass down and leaning against the balustrade while she looked out over the lawn toward the calm, untroubled sea.

The moon was only a slivered crescent tonight, but Martin could still see Vannah clearly from the lights in the ballroom beyond.

He did not waste time on surface pleasantries and meaningless chitchat. "What's wrong, Vannah?" he said.

"Wrong?" She stiffened, suddenly wary, and would not look at him. "Why, nothing. Nothing at all."

"Oh, but there is." He backed against the cold stone railing and carefully set his glass down. "I noticed it the moment I saw you, that deep sadness in your eyes. And when we were dancing, it was as though I were dancing with a sleepwalker. What has happened to you?"

"Nothing!" And she turned as if to flee.

Martin reached out and caught her hand. "Please, Vannah, don't run away from me. I thought we were friends."

She stared at him in confusion, and he could tell that she didn't know what to say.

"You can trust me, you know. I won't eat you."

That coaxed a smile out of her, and finally, with a little sigh of resignation, Vannah said, "Two years ago I fell in love with a man my father deemed unsuitable. He forced us to part."

The queer catch in her voice caught Martin's attention, and when he looked at her, he saw the tears sparkling against her lashes and the trembling of her lower lip as she fought to control herself.

Without thinking he grasped her arms and drew her against him. "Oh, Vannah, I am so, so sorry," he murmured into her soft, perfumed hair as he held her tightly.

At first Vannah tried to resist, for no man had held her since that afternoon she and Paul had shared their one and only embrace. But Martin's arms around her felt so solid and comforting, his whispers so reassuring, she felt all of her pent-up emotions suddenly come pouring out, and she began sobbing softly against his shoulder.

"That's it," he crooned.

When Vannah's tears finally subsided and she felt as though a great weight had been lifted from her shoulders, she stepped back and dabbed at her eyes with the handkerchief that materialized out of nowhere.

"I—I'm sorry," she stammered. "I—I don't know what came over me. I just miss Paul so much!"

And while Martin listened, Vannah told him all about the radical journalist she still loved and how her father had threatened to destroy his family if Vannah didn't agree to break off with him.

When she was through, Martin said, "It will be better one day, I promise. You'll fall in love again, and—"

"Paul Demarest was the love of my life," Vannah snapped, jerking away from him, her eyes flashing cold, silver fire. Then her lip curled contemptuously as she looked back toward the ballroom where many of the young men who sought her favor went waltzing in a blur past the closed French doors.

"Do you think I could bring myself to marry one of those callow fools after I have known a man like Paul Demarest?"

"I didn't mean to anger you," Martin said.

Vannah looked at him long and hard for a moment, then her face softened and she smiled. "I apologize for snapping at you, Martin. But no one will ever take Paul's place in my heart or my life."

"He must have been a special man to win your love."

"Oh, he may have been homely—he used to call the two of us Beauty and the Beast," Vannah replied, "but he was as handsome as Adonis to me. And do you know what I loved best about him?"

Martin wasn't sure he could stand to hear Vannah discussing another man in such glowing terms, but he said, "What?"

"He treated me like a person with a mind of her own, not some lovely ornament to hang on his arm and his every word. Do you know what he gave me once?"

Martin thought of what he would have given her and replied, "A single white rosebud."

Vannah's brows rose in surprise, for she had expected him to say, "Diamonds and furs," like any other man.

"No," she replied. "Books!"

Now it was Martin's turn to look surprised. "Did he

now? What were their titles?" When Vannah told him, he nodded approvingly. "Very good. Did I ever tell you that I plan to start my own publishing firm when I return to England? Why do you look so astonished, Vannah? Do you think that just because I've been a soldier and a rancher I disdain intellectual pursuits?"

She blushed, for she had been thinking exactly that. "I—I just never took you for a bookworm, Martin."

"Oh, don't let this handsome face fool you," he said with a self-deprecating grin. "I am a man of many diverse interests. Didn't I once tell you that you had artistic talent?"

Vannah smiled at the memory. "How could I ever forget? You defended me to my father."

But somehow Martin's efforts on her behalf all those years ago did not impress her as much as what Paul had done for her.

Martin sensed this at once and frowned in annoyance. There were other men besides Paul Demarest who appreciated intelligence as well as beauty in a woman, and he counted himself among their ranks. But Vannah was so blinded by love, she refused to see it.

He folded his arms across his chest. "If you were so much in love, why didn't you marry?"

Vannah's face fell, and she looked heartsick as she explained why she and her one true love weren't together.

Martin sipped his champagne as he listened patiently, then scowled. "It seems that Demarest was a little too quick to believe you, don't you think? If I wanted a woman, I would fight to the death for her."

Vannah bristled indignantly. "I was very convincing."

"I see."

She turned away, suddenly furious with him without quite knowing why. "I'm going inside. It's become very chilly out here."

Without another word Martin escorted her back to the ballroom.

During the days that followed, Martin started to feel less like a rancher and more like himself, and it was all because of Savannah.

Oh, politeness demanded that he spend a certain amount of time with his host, who, once he learned that Martin was now the Marquis of Fleet, persisted in addressing him as simply "Fleet." Gerrold dragged him off to the Reading Room, an unimposing frame house reputed to be the most exclusive men's club in the United States. They played polo and went yachting on the *Savannah*. Constance occasionally made demands on Martin's time by asking him to lunch with the other ladies, but he enjoyed Savannah's company best.

He was careful never to compliment her on her looks but instead discussed books, music, and art, because those topics seemed to pique Vannah's interest and reveal a glimmer of her former spirit. If encouraged, she could converse intelligently and passionately on a wide variety of subjects, and if she disagreed with him, she let him know it in no uncertain terms. He liked the way her expressive eyes sparkled with enthusiasm when she argued her position, but if she was wrong, she admitted it with good grace. Martin sensed in her a restless intelligence, a yearning to extend herself beyond the confines of her existence as the daughter of a very wealthy man.

Soon, without quite realizing what was happening to him, Martin found that Savannah had taken possession of his very thoughts. He would be sitting in the cool shade of the Reading Room's veranda, half listening to Gerrold Webb and his cronies discussing their latest multimillion-dollar financial deals, and his mind would be filled with images of Savannah at the grand piano, her mind away in some private place as she played a Chopin piece, filling the room with sublime music that moved everyone except her. Or he would be conversing with a dignified, white-haired matron seated next to him at dinner, and he would recall Savannah quietly eating corn on the cob at an evening clambake, never joining in the laughter of those around her as her pensive face stared moodily into the fire.

But he knew that he was falling in love with her the day he found her on the beach.

Vannah sat perched on her rock, watching hungry sea gulls from beneath the wide brim of her straw hat as they careened above in their endless quest for food. She was listening to the roar of the waves as they crested far out to sea and gained momentum as they reached the yellow sands of shore.

A sudden movement down the beach caught her eye, and she turned to see a barefoot man gingerly walking across the hot sands toward her, a man wearing nothing but a pair of tan trousers rolled up to just below the knee. Then he smiled and waved, and she knew it was Martin, so she waved back.

He must have been swimming in the cold sea, for as he drew closer, Vannah could see that he was still wet, the seawater glazing his muscular shoulders, making them ripple and glisten in the afternoon sun. Vannah's gaze followed the *T* pattern of dark, wiry hairs across his chest and down his flat stomach, but her curiosity took her no further than the waistband of his trousers.

She swallowed hard and took several deep breaths, willing herself to resist the blatant masculine perfection of his body, so different from Paul's thin, wiry frame.

When Martin reached her rock, he jumped up, sat down next to her quite unselfconsciously, and proceeded to brush the damp sand off his bare feet.

"I thought I would find you here."

He was sitting so close that his muscular thigh kept brushing against Vannah's arm, causing her pulse to race of its own volition, despite her every intention to remain calm and unmoved. The nearness of him disturbed her, so she shifted her arm just enough to avoid touching, but she could not escape the tangy scent of seawater that clung to his damp skin and hair.

She smiled nervously. "Sometimes I like to come down here to be alone with my thoughts."

"How well I remember."

"Were you swimming just now?"

He nodded, then reclined back on his elbows, stretching out his long, lean body like a panther sunning itself.

"The water was freezing," he said. "Feel how cold I am." And before Vannah could stop him, he sat up, took her hand, and placed it against his forearm, which hadn't been warmed by the sun and was indeed cold to her touch.

Vannah jerked her hand away, ostensibly to anchor down her hat before the sea breeze snatched it away, but in reality she was flustered by the intimacy of Martin's gesture. "You should warm up soon, if you stay in the sun."

They sat in silence for several seconds, then Martin asked, "Do you still draw?"

Thankful for any excuse to take her mind off him, Vannah removed a sketch pad and pencil she had been hiding in her pocket and grinned mischievously. "Of course. My father still doesn't know that I do, but I try to draw whenever I can." Then she told him how Aunt Constance was going to speak to her father about allowing her to study glass design with Louis Comfort Tiffany when she turned twenty-one next year.

Privately he doubted if her father would ever allow it, but he didn't have it in his heart to spoil her illusions.

He reached into the pocket of his trousers and removed a piece of paper—grubby, yellow, and creased with age. Vannah watched in curiosity as he began unfolding it carefully so as not to tear it. Then he handed it to her. "Do you remember this?"

When Vannah saw what it was, she held one hand up to her face to conceal her blush of embarrassment and groaned. "Oh, dear! It's that sketch I did of you the day you left."

She studied it. "But this doesn't even look like you. One can tell I was very young when I did this. I'm so much better at it now." Vannah lifted the cover of her pad and picked up her pencil. "Here. Let me do another for you."

Before Martin could protest, she was studying him carefully, her pencil moving across the paper in sure, rapid strokes. In a matter of minutes she handed it to him. "What do you think?"

The sketch was honest, almost painfully so. This Martin Ash was an older, world-weary man with all of his expectations and dreams indelibly written on his lined, scarred face. There was cynicism touching the corners of his mouth, as well as intelligence and snatches of humor about the eyes.

"You know," he said quietly, "in the first sketch I look so noble and perfect, but in the second one I seem more human." He flashed her a teasing grin. "More of a likable sort of rogue, don't you think?"

Vannah brushed a stray wisp of hair off her face and didn't return his teasing smile, for suddenly she understood herself very well.

"Don't you see? I made that first sketch when I was a child. I saw you as the human embodiment of that portrait of Sir Lancelot hanging in Clairvaux's foyer. But now that

I am grown-up, I see you as a man, with all his faults and virtues."

"More virtues than faults, I hope."

Vannah smiled and shook her head. "Poor Martin. I really made such a fool of myself, didn't I, chasing after you so relentlessly every time you came to Newport? I do apologize for my infatuation."

He sat up, propping himself with one hand as he twisted toward her. Her face, shadowed by the brim of her hat, was a beguiling mixture of innocence and knowing.

"And what are your feelings for me now, Vannah?" he asked softly.

"Feelings for you?" She laughed nervously. "Martin, whatever do you mean?"

"Don't play the innocent with me. You once declared your love for me right on this very beach, remember, the day I was leaving for Wyoming."

Her expression froze in panic and fear before she looked away uneasily. "I was fifteen years old then, merely a child, as you so often reminded me. I'm afraid I have no feelings for you, Martin."

"You said you loved me once, Vannah. Couldn't you try to resurrect those feelings?"

"I told you I still love only Paul Demarest."

"So you won't allow yourself to ever have feelings for another man, is that it?" he asked. "You intend to remain a vestal virgin forever, tending some cold, pure flame to Demarest's memory?"

When Vannah flinched, Martin instantly regretted his harsh, taunting words.

"But why is it that every time I come near you or touch you"—he reached out and ran the backs of his fingers down Vannah's cheek in a sensuous caress before she realized what was happening—"I feel a flame of quite a different sort?"

"Don't you dare touch me!" she gasped in outrage, springing away from him and sliding down the rock so fast, she skinned the palms of her hands.

"Why not?" Martin called down to her. "Are you afraid that I'll prove I'm right?"

Vannah glared up at him, her breath coming in ragged gasps as she shook from the force of her emotions. "And I thought you were different, Martin Ash. But you're just like every other arrogant male I've ever met, so damned sure that no woman can resist you."

Then she turned on her heel and stormed away, Martin's mocking laughter following her.

In the days to follow, Vannah never went out of her way to avoid Martin, for she wanted to prove to both him and herself that the feelings she had once had were nothing more than a childish infatuation.

And she almost succeeded until the day of the storm.

On that day Martin and Constance were drinking lemonade on the terrace and watching ominous, thick black clouds gathering in the west.

Suddenly the staccato drumming of hoofbeats split the air, and both Constance and Martin looked up to see Vannah come charging across the lawn on a lanky dappled-gray stallion with the long stride of a racehorse. Vannah was leaning over his neck, urging him on, the long veil of her riding hat streaming out behind her.

"Oh, my God!" Constance cried, leaping to her feet and clutching at Martin's arm in panic. "She's taken the new hunter. Martin, that half-crazed beast has already injured one of the grooms, and even Gerrold has trouble riding him." She gave a worried glance at the sky. "And it's going to storm any minute. Will you please go after her before she gets killed!"

But Martin was out of his chair and racing across the terrace before the words were out of Constance's mouth.

As soon as a horse could be saddled, Martin was off, galloping in the same general direction that Vannah had taken. At first he was riding blind, for Vannah and her wild hunter were nowhere to be seen. He prayed that he would catch up to her soon, for he didn't like the looks of the weather. The very air was thick with moisture and the scent of an approaching summer storm. Toward his back the sky was a calm, bright blue, with the sun shining, but before him to the west, heavy black clouds were amassing on the horizon and rolling toward land with incredible speed. Off to his left the sea was a sickening gray-green color, and the waves seemed high and choppy, crested by large, frothy whitecaps.

"Damn it! Where in the hell is she?" he muttered between clenched teeth as he drew up his horse on the crest of a hill and stood up in the stirrups so he could scan the area.

And then he spotted her.

Vannah was riding toward the marshes that bordered the sea, and Martin was relieved to note that she was still in the saddle and not lying unconscious in a ditch somewhere. His heart flew to his mouth when he saw Vannah send the animal sailing over a high hedgerow, then he spurred his horse in pursuit down the hill, praying that he could reach her before she killed herself.

He finally caught up with her in a field bordered by hedgerows. Vannah had seen Martin approach, so she halted her horse and waited for him.

Even in his fear for her, Martin couldn't fail to notice what a breathtaking picture Vannah made. Beneath her, the hunter arched his neck and danced in place, but Vannah, seated so tall and erect in her sidesaddle with her hands lightly on the reins, controlled him as effortlessly as if the giant animal were a lapdog on a leash.

"Why did you follow me?" she demanded coldly. She still had not forgiven him for that day on the beach.

"Your aunt sent me after you. There's a storm brewing or hadn't you noticed?"

As if to underscore the truth of his words, a loud clap of thunder split the sky. The sudden and unexpected crack and boom startled the high-spirited hunter, and without warning he screamed again and reared high on his hind legs, his forelegs flailing the air. Vannah, caught off-guard, didn't even have time to struggle to keep her balance. With a surprised cry she was unceremoniously tossed out of the sidesaddle to land with an unladylike grunt and thud on the ground. As soon as her horse realized that he was riderless, he bolted for home before Martin could even snatch at his reins to stop him.

Martin was out of the saddle and kneeling beside Vannah before she even sat up. "Vannah, are you hurt?"

"Only my pride," she muttered, taking Martin's hand so she could struggle to her feet.

"You're sure?" he asked as she stood beside him, for Vannah was all disheveled. Her hat had fallen off, so her hair was beginning to come out of its pins, and sections of it were hanging down around her shoulders in disarray. There was a smudge of dirt on her cheek and bits of marsh grass clinging to the skirt of her habit.

She looked so delectable with her rosy lips parted and bosom heaving that Martin found himself aching to take her in his arms and kiss her.

"Quite sure," Vannah replied, unmindful of the effect she was having on him as she tried to tuck a falling lock of hair back into place without success.

"You could have been killed!" he growled, grasping her by the shoulders and giving her a little shake.

Suddenly Martin could resist her no longer. There, in the middle of an open field, with menacing black storm clouds gathering over the ocean and tall cattails bending to the will of the rising wind, he roughly pulled her into his arms.

Vannah gasped in surprise when her body hit Martin's, and she struggled to batter him with her fists as one of his arms encircled her waist like an iron band and the other pressed against the center of her back.

For one second his smoldering eyes burned into hers, and then, with a low growl of desire, his hot, hungry mouth was against her own. Vannah tried to cry out in protest, but the only sound she managed to utter was an outraged whimper.

Martin's lips were hard and warm, and when the bruising pressure finally eased, Vannah relaxed, thinking that he had gotten what he wanted and was about to release her. Suddenly he startled her by renewing his assault and forcing her lips to part and accept his invading tongue. Totally unprepared for the intimacy of his kiss and the jolt of liquid heat that ignited her, Vannah whimpered again, reared back, and tried to pull away, but Martin seemed to expect that reaction from her and only tightened his hold.

As she felt the tip of his tongue caress her own with slow, sensuous movements, Vannah's tumultuous thoughts mocked her. So you thought you could resist him, they seemed to say. But you can't. You know you can't. . . .

Though Vannah desperately willed her body to defy him, it ignored her and responded to Martin's sure, deft touch. She could feel her nipples rise as her breasts were crushed against his muscular chest, and her hips molded themselves to his instinctively. Her cheeks reddened when she felt his maleness harden against her thigh, but paradoxically, she felt a primitive thrill of power that she had the capacity to arouse a man so. Finally, with a soft sigh of surrender, Vannah stopped struggling.

When Martin felt her yield, he immediately released her and took her upturned face in his hands, savoring the soft, velvety touch of her skin against his rough, callused palms.

He stared deeply into her eyes. "I was right. You do feel something for me after all."

"No!" Vannah cried with a vehement shake of her head. "I love Paul Demarest. I always will. I feel nothing for you. Nothing!"

But she made no attempt to break his hold and flee.

"Your body tells me differently, Vannah," he said gently, "and I'll prove it to you."

Wordlessly he pushed aside a stray lock of hair and began caressing her ear with his lips and warm, sweet breath, raking his teeth against her earlobe until she shuddered, her will no longer her own. Vannah's light, mossy perfume filled his nostrils as he held her face with one hand and began leaving a trail of hot kisses down the slender column of her neck. Then he reached up to cup a breast, letting his thumb tease the hard nipple through the rough twill of her riding habit.

"Martin!" Vannah cried, aghast, as she jerked away to escape the intensity of her own response.

His hand dropped, and he looked down at her with a mocking smile twisting his mouth. "Haven't you ever let your precious Paul fondle your breasts?"

"Never!" She turned away so he wouldn't see her cheeks burning with mortification. It was one thing to discuss such intimate matters with her friends or Lysette but quite another to have a man actually take such liberties with her person.

"It's what men do to women when they make love to

them," he said behind her, his words harsh and brutally frank.

Vannah said nothing, still baffled and shaken by her traitorous response to Martin's touch.

Suddenly the sky darkened ominously as the scudding, black storm clouds swallowed the sun and blanketed the sky. In the distance a fork of lightning stabbed at the sea like a pitchfork. Vannah felt several raindrops patter against her face, cooling her burning cheeks.

Martin squinted and stared up at the horizon. "We should be getting back to Clairvaux before we're caught in a storm. Since we only have one horse, I'm afraid you'll have to ride with me and endure my company."

He went to his horse, grazing placidly a little way away, and led the animal back to where Vannah stood, her body stiff with humiliation as she stared at the ground. Martin swung effortlessly into the saddle and extended his hand to her.

When she didn't take it, he said, "Coming? I wouldn't advise walking all the way back home in a storm. You might be struck by lightning, and then how would I explain myself to your Aunt Constance?"

But Vannah already felt as if she had been struck by lightning of quite a different sort.

She walked up to the horse and waited for Martin to slip his foot from the stirrup so she could mount. She stepped into the iron, grasped his proffered hand, and effortlessly he pulled her up. Once Vannah was seated securely behind him, her arms wrapped around his slender waist, he clucked to his horse and they started off for Clairvaux.

Those few tentative raindrops now gathered momentum and were falling steadily in a wet, gray curtain that turned the path into mud and nearly obliterated it. In just a few minutes Martin's clothing was soaked to the skin, his hair plastered against his head. Behind him he felt Vannah shudder and huddle against him for warmth, resting her cheek against his shoulder to shield her face from the persistent rain. Feeling her soft breasts pressed against him and her arms wrapped so tightly around his waist, he experienced a warmth of quite a different kind, and he had to force himself to concentrate on keeping his horse on the right path.

As the dark silhouette of Clairvaux loomed before them, a vision of Katherine flashed before him, then was gone.

Suddenly the earth beneath their feet seem to tremble from the force of a thunderclap, quickly followed by a blinding explosion of lightning that lit up the sky. Martin yelled to Vannah to hold on tight, then he dug his heels into his horse's ribs and raced the storm the rest of the way.

The violent storm lashed at Newport for the remainder of the afternoon and well into the evening before giving up and blowing out to sea. Soon a bright full moon appeared through the scattering of clouds, and all that was left of the storm was fitful grumblings and growlings of thunder in the distance.

It was almost midnight, and Vannah still couldn't fall asleep, her mind in turmoil. She rose from her bed, padded over to a window, and flung it open, letting the cool, storm-washed air soothe her burning skin and riffle through her flowing hair.

She couldn't stop thinking of Martin and his harsh, possessive caresses on the marsh that afternoon. Her lips still felt bruised and her breast scorched, as though his very touch had branded her for the world to see.

"But I still love Paul!" she protested between clenched teeth, tears of frustration filling her eyes.

With a sigh Vannah turned away from the window and crossed her darkened room. She felt restless and confined, one thought stopping, then several more plowing into it until they all became jumbled together in confusion. She had to go down to the sea tonight, for the ocean was always like a soothing balm to her troubled mind, and she knew the waves would whisper to her, bringing her the answers she sought.

From his own rooms on the other side of the house, Martin stood by an open window and looked out over the shimmering silver sea. He breathed deeply, savoring the cool night air, so clean and fresh, as though the rain had scrubbed it. But even that couldn't clear his head, which was filled with disturbing, persistent thoughts of Vannah.

A sudden movement on the lawn below caught his eye, and as he watched, he saw Vannah's sylphlike form go flitting over the wet grass. With her gossamer-white nightgown catching the breeze and billowing out around her, she looked like a beguiling siren in the pale moonlight, beckoning to him as she floated toward the cliff's edge.

Martin cursed and gripped the windowsill so hard, his fingers hurt, as though he could physically restrain himself from surrendering and going to her. He knew that he should just turn away from the window, return to bed, and forget about the enchantress down by the cliff's edge. He reminded himself over and over that he was a gentleman and an honorable man, and she out of bounds as his host's daughter. And, of course, there was still his conscience plaguing him about Katherine.

But as he watched, Vannah reached the very end of the lawn and turned, seeming to look right up at him, destroying any scruples he might have left. Martin quickly dressed, then whirled on his heel and went storming off into the darkness.

Vannah thought she was alone until she saw a figure leave the darkened mansion and come toward her. She knew at once that it was Martin, and her heart began to hammer against her ribs in terror. Or was it anticipation?

He looked as though he had hastily thrown on his trousers and a white lawn shirt. When he was about ten feet away, he stopped and waited.

Tonight Vannah did look as though she could make a monk think twice about his vows. The moon bathed her in cool white light, bleaching the paleness of her long, flowing hair even further. A fitful breeze caught at her batiste nightgown with greedy fingers, pulling it away from her while at the same time pressing it even closer to her slender form, outlining her full breasts, boyish hips, and long legs.

As he watched, her lovely face mirrored the emotions warring deep within her.

"Why must you always torment me?" she demanded hoarsely, tears of frustration stinging her eyes. "Why can't you just leave me alone?"

Yet she stood her ground and made no attempt to evade him.

"Because you know you don't want me to leave you alone," Martin replied.

Then he walked toward her. "Please, Vannah, don't try to fight me anymore. You were made for love, my darling, and I'll prove it to you if you'll let me."

Martin was standing so close to her, Vannah knew he could have touched her, yet he let his arms remain by his sides. He just looked down at her out of eyes that seemed to reflect the stars overhead, and there was nothing veiled and guarded about them now. She read the desire so blatant in their depths and shivered.

"You're too late, Martin," she said. "When I wanted you, you didn't want me because I was a child. Now I love Paul Demarest. I—"

She placed her palms flat against his hard chest, fully intending to push him away, but suddenly her hands went sliding upward, then her arms were locking around his neck so she could hold him to her while she stood on tiptoe and reached for his mouth.

Martin sucked in his breath and held himself in check, giving Vannah enough time to change her mind. But when her honeyed kisses became deeper and more insistent, he knew he had won.

When they reluctantly parted, he moved just enough away from her so that he could tug open the narrow satin ribbons that held the neckline of her nightgown together. His eyes held hers as his questing fingers slipped beneath the soft, embroidered fabric to find her bare breasts.

At that moment Vannah knew that she was lost. A deep groan betrayed her as Martin cupped a breast in his palm, and Vannah had to lean back against his protective arm encircling her waist, for her legs had suddenly lost the ability to support her. Her eyes half closed in delight as she savored the sensations welling up from deep within her, spreading through her body like some raging fire and cooled only by the night breezes off the ocean.

When Martin took a nipple and gently rolled it between his fingers, Vannah did not pull away indignantly but caught her breath in surprise.

"Martin, you mustn't."

"Oh, but I want to," he murmured, kissing her again to silence her, pulling her even closer against him.

When they parted, he took her face in his hands and gazed at her with infinite tenderness. "I want to make love to you, Vannah, but you must say that you want me."

There was a great roaring in her ears, whether from the ocean or the blood pounding through her brain, Vannah couldn't tell. All she knew was that she wanted him tonight.

Her response was simply, "Petit Clairvaux."

"Not good enough, Vannah. *Say it*! Say you want me!"

She could fight him no longer. With a trembling sigh of surrender Vannah murmured. "I want you, Martin."

She was relieved when Martin swept her up into his arms, because her knees were so weak, she never would have crossed the lawn without collapsing.

When they reached the playhouse, standing so dark and still among the copper beeches rustling softly overhead, Vannah led Martin into the drawing room where he lit a lamp. Then he removed several cushions from the divan, placed them on the floor before the cold fireplace, and turned to her expectantly.

"Undress for me," he said.

Blushing furiously and shivering with nervousness, Vannah nonetheless managed to shrug the nightgown off her shoulders and let it glide softly down to the floor. She resisted the impulse to cross her arms over her breasts in maidenly modesty and held herself proudly before him.

Just staring at the perfection of her form made Martin catch his breath. The feeble lamplight warmed Vannah's ivory body to a soft gold except for the dusky tips of her breasts. The patch between her thighs was as pale and tawny as her hair. He felt the familiar ache of deep wanting start in his groin and take possession of him.

"Now undress me," he commanded thickly.

Shaking with anticipation at the prospect of seeing Martin naked, Vannah walked over to him and tugged his shirt out of his trousers, then slipped her hands beneath the soft fabric, savoring the heat and smoothness of his skin and the hardness of the muscles in his chest and shoulders. After she pushed the shirt off his arms and his torso was bare, she impulsively lowered her head and began kissing and licking him, reveling in the salty taste of his skin, the clean, masculine scent of it.

At the featherlight touch of her lips and tongue, Martin felt like he was going to explode.

"Go lie down," he murmured. "I'll do the rest."

Vannah glided over to the fireplace and reclined against

the cushions, waiting for Martin to come to her. Her heart resumed its reckless pounding even faster when she heard his trousers and drawers rustle to the floor, and then he was standing naked before her.

Vannah tried to keep looking into his eyes, glittering like twin emeralds in the lamplight, but she couldn't. Slowly her gaze traveled down his chest, crisscrossed lightly with dark hairs, to his flat, hard belly, and finally the juncture of his thighs, where his manhood rose rampant from its nest of curls.

Martin just stood there, giving her time to accustom herself to their differences.

He was relieved that Vannah was relaxed enough to grin impishly and say, "I've always wondered what the statues in the Metropolitan Museum had beneath those annoying leaves."

He leered at her. "Are you disappointed?"

"I don't have another standard to judge by, now do I?"

"That's reassuring."

Then he walked toward her with silent, catlike grace. Martin dropped down beside her, reclining on one elbow while he proceeded to smooth the hair away from her face with one hand.

"Your hair is like spun silk," he murmured, burying his face in it, "and it smells like the forest after it rains."

Then his soft, gentle kisses were like a butterfly's touch against her forehead, her eyelids, her cheeks, her mouth. She nestled more closely against him, delighting in wonder at the hardness of his body in contrast to the yielding softness of her own. As his lips nibbled at her chin and throat Martin's free hand cupped and stroked her breasts, causing Vannah to whimper and her nipples to harden as though seeking his touch. But when he lowered his head to flick his tongue against one rosy peak and then the other, Vannah was quite unprepared for the intensity of her own response.

Lysette had warned her that most men enjoyed bestowing such attention on a woman's breasts, but she had neglected to tell Vannah that the effect would be so arousing, so devastating.

"More," she whispered urgently, arching toward him, groaning in pleasure and shock when he began to suckle her.

Vannah gasped and gave herself up to the sheer rapture of it, her fingers entwined in his springy curls in mute encouragement.

Martin raised his head long enough to murmur, "If you wish more, my darling, than you shall have it," and proceeded to love her slowly and thoroughly, as if he were exploring a tropical island he had just discovered, and soon there was not one patch of Vannah's ivory skin that hadn't known the exciting, exquisite touch of his fingertips, lips, or tongue.

Wherever they rested, he left a trail of white-hot flame dancing across her pliant flesh, a flame that burned away the last vestiges of her virginal modesty, leaving a ravenous, mindless hunger in its place.

As her ardor rose, Vannah couldn't seem to get enough of him. She stroked and kneaded his muscular shoulders, trailing down the column of his spine, clutching at his firm buttocks that tightened at her touch. Her questing fingers trailed down his sensitive inner thigh.

When she thought she would finally go mad from the pleasure of his caresses, Vannah cried, "Take me, Martin. Now!"

As he positioned himself above her, carefully balancing his weight on his elbows so he wouldn't crush her, Martin gently parted her unresisting thighs and slowly entered her.

Vannah's eyes flew open in surprise and panic, and she

stiffened, suddenly remembering Lysette's warnings about the pain to come. But Vannah felt only a brief sting, nothing more, and by that time she was beyond caring.

As Martin began to move his hips Vannah thought she was going to die of the pleasure rising within her. She wrapped her legs around him, drawing him even closer to her, his damp skin sticking to hers, the musky scent of arousal filling her nostrils like an enticing perfume. Vannah groaned and writhed in delight, raising her hips to meet Martin's every thrust in an ageless dance of desire.

Suddenly the tempo of his lovemaking gained momentum, as he thrust harder and faster. Vannah felt the heat rise from the very core of her soul to consume her in wave after shuddering wave, and she screamed in ecstasy. Then Martin gave one final thrust, cried out her name, trembled, and sagged against her.

They lay locked together in a tight embrace, damp and panting, then they curled their bodies together and slept.

Chapter Ten

VANNAH FELT LIKE the world's biggest fool.

She and Aunt Constance were sitting on the terrace, just finishing luncheon with Alva Vanderbilt and her daughter, Consuelo. Mrs. Vanderbilt was discussing her plans for the marble mansion currently being constructed for her family farther up Bellevue Avenue, but Vannah's thoughts were not on marble staircases and circular drives. She couldn't stop thinking of the night a week ago that she and Martin Ash had given themselves to each other in her childhood playhouse.

After love's languorous afterglow had worn off and reality had begun to intrude once again, Martin had raised himself up on one elbow and looked down at her with infinite regret in his eyes.

"Damn it, Vannah, I am sorry!" he'd muttered.

"Why? I'm not."

"I don't usually make it a practice to seduce my host's daughter or . . . virgins."

Vannah had chuckled softly and reached up to kiss his chin, rough with stubble. "And I thought you admired me for my intellect."

Her teasing had brought a faint smile to his lips, then he'd become serious once again. "But what are you going to tell your husband on your wedding night when he discovers he's not the first man who has known you?"

Vannah had grown still as a deadening cold suddenly seeped into her bones. She'd almost blurted out, "But you are going to be my husband," then held her tongue before she made an utter fool of herself. Why, Martin had never even told her he loved her, let alone asked her to marry him.

So she'd flippantly replied, "Oh, I shall just tell him that I lost my maidenhead through frequent and vigorous horseback riding."

Martin had laughed, a grumble that shook his chest. "Knowing the way you ride, that's certainly a plausible explanation."

Then they'd risen, dressed, put all the cushions back on the divan, and stole back to the main house before anyone had noticed that they were not in their respective bedchambers.

And after that Martin had virtually ignored her. If they

met at mealtimes, he was scrupulously polite but not especially attentive to her, seeming to prefer her father's company all of a sudden. She and Martin were never alone now.

Vannah was reluctant to admit it, but Martin was acting like a cad who no longer needed to keep up even a pretense of interest now that he had seduced her and gotten what he wanted. She, like countless gullible young girls before her, believed that if she loved a man and slept with him, he would want her in return.

But the cruelest irony of it all was now that he had introduced her to the pleasures of the flesh, her newly awakened body continued to respond to him. Even now, as Vannah watched Martin go cantering along the cliff edge on her father's big gray hunter, she could feel the tips of her breasts tighten and her heart began its irrational pounding, which echoed through her mind like a drumbeat.

"Vannah?"

The sound of Aunt Constance's husky voice impatiently calling her name snapped Vannah out of her daydream like a dash of cold water.

"Yes, Aunt Constance?" she said, finding all three women looking at her rather strangely.

"Consuelo wanted to know if you would like to accompany her to Hammett's Book Shop."

Vannah smiled across the table at the pretty, dark-haired girl, so unlike her strong-willed mother. "I would adore it, Consuelo. It's time I found some new books to read."

Something to take her mind off Martin Ash and his shameful treatment of her.

The two young women excused themselves, rose, and left for town.

Martin Ash halted his horse and watched Vannah and the other girl leave the terrace and go into the house. He knew that his coolness and aloofness were puzzling and painful to Vannah. All he had to do was look into her questioning eyes, filled with hurt and rejection, to know that he was treating her disgracefully. Many were the times when he could endure her suffering no longer and almost reached for her, tender words of apology and explanation on his lips, but he restrained himself with superhuman effort.

He wasn't free to declare himself yet, and it wouldn't be fair to Vannah to raise false expectations. He still needed time to think, time to plan the future, and he couldn't afford the very large distraction Vannah presented. No, he had to do things in his own way, in his own time, and Vannah would just have to understand when the time came.

He touched his heel to his mount's ribs, and the hunter sprang away.

Gerrold Webb stood before his study window, watching the Marquis of Fleet race the gray hunter away from the cliff's edge and toward the marshland.

Why hadn't he thought of it before? he wondered. Fleet would make the perfect son-in-law. True, he was only a marquis, and Gerrold had rather fancied a duke or even a prince in the family, but he would do. Gerrold had to admit that he hadn't been too impressed with the man at first, finding his life rather aimless, first working for his father, then enlisting in the British Army, then off to run a ranch in Wyoming. But now that he had inherited the family estate and title, he was sure to be more stable.

All Gerrold had to do was offer the young man enough, and he would surely agree to the match.

Gerrold rang for Parkins and told the butler that he wanted to see Lord Fleet the second he returned from his ride.

An hour later there came a knock on the study door, and Lord Fleet strode in, still in his riding clothes, his face flushed and his hair tousled from the ride.

"You wished to see me, Webb?"

Gerrold rose and indicated a chair. "Yes, Fleet, I do. I have a business proposition for you that I think you'll find most interesting."

Martin's dark brows rose in curiosity as he seated himself. "What sort of proposition?"

"A marriage proposal, Fleet."

That caught Martin unawares, and he suddenly coughed.

"As you know," Gerrold continued, "my daughter, Savannah, is of marriageable age. She's been 'out' for two seasons already, and it's time she married and settled down. But I don't want her marrying just anybody, Fleet. It's my responsibility as her father to choose a suitable husband for her. Until now I haven't found a man I'd be proud to call my son-in-law."

"I'm flattered, Webb, but what if Vannah doesn't wish to marry me?"

He dismissed his daughter's objections with a brief wave of his hand. "Her feelings are of no consequence, Fleet. This is an arrangement between gentlemen."

"Which is as it should be," Martin said with a smile. Curious as to just how much Webb valued his daughter, he leaned back in his seat and asked, "And Savannah's dowry, should I agree to the match?"

"Half a million dollars," Webb said without hesitation.

Oh, no, Martin thought to himself, she is worth much, much more than that.

When Martin made no comment, Gerrold added, "The amount is more than generous, I can assure you."

Martin still said nothing.

Then Gerrold chuckled. "Look, Fleet, I know you English aristocrats are all in financial trouble. Farming isn't as profitable as it once was, and your grand estates are going to rack and ruin. You need money, my friend, and plenty of it. Good old American dollars."

Although that might have been true for many of Martin's countrymen, it was not true of the Ash family. They had always prospered, thanks to careful management and shrewd investments, and Ashwood was thriving. Even Constance knew that, though it was obvious that her brother-in-law hadn't thought to ask her opinion on the matter. Martin had no need of Gerrold Webb or his money. He could afford to marry Vannah even if she were as poor as a parlor maid. But he wasn't about to tell her father that. Not just yet. He was going to toy with him, like a cat toys with a mouse before killing it.

"And what do you get out of the deal, Webb?"

"The prestige of having a member of the British nobility in my family, that's all."

Martin laced his fingers together and studied his fingertips, pretending to consider Webb's offer. Finally he looked up and said, "Make the settlement three million and you've got yourself a deal."

Even an experienced and astute businessman such as Gerrold couldn't keep the surprise from registering on his face. Why, the audacity of the Englishman to think that his title was worth such an exorbitant amount!

"One million when you marry my daughter and another million on the birth of my first grandson," was Webb's counteroffer.

"I'll accept those terms only if you agree to make the boy one of your heirs," Martin shot back.

Gerrold scowled at that and stroked his mustache as though giving such an offer careful consideration. When he felt that Fleet had squirmed long enough, he rose and held out his hand. "You drive a hard bargain, Ash."

Sold to the highest bidder for two million dollars, Martin thought contemptuously as he shook the other man's hand to seal the deal.

"And there's just one other thing," he added.

"Oh? And what's that?"

"Don't tell Vannah about our, er, arrangement. I want her to think I asked you for her hand of my own volition."

Gerrold smiled slowly. "Don't want her to know she was bought and paid for, eh, Fleet?"

Martin had to resist the impulse to send his fist crashing into his future father-in-law's face. He forced himself to smile and say, "Something like that, Webb."

After they drank a toast to their agreement and Martin left Webb's study, he found himself thinking of Katherine. Why hadn't he told Webb he was already married? He knew the answer at once. He was afraid he'd lose Vannah. Besides, no doubt he was legally divorced by now. No, he decided, Katherine was no longer an obstacle. There was plenty of time to tell Vannah and her family later.

Vannah had just returned from her outing with Consuelo Vanderbilt when Parkins told her that her father wanted to see her right away in his study.

"Yes, Father?" she said when she walked through the door, undoing the blue satin ribbons of her wide-brimmed straw hat and setting it on a nearby table along with her books from Hammett's.

"Sit down, daughter. I have something very important to tell you."

When Vannah was seated, she looked across at him questioningly.

"You're twenty years old and it's time you were married," her father said.

Vannah started. "M-married?"

He nodded. "It's all arranged."

Beads of sweat suddenly rose on her forehead as her vision blurred. "And whom am I marrying, Father?"

He glowered at her, his pale eyes cold as ice. "When I tell you, I don't want to hear one objection from you, daughter, not one word. Am I understood?"

Vannah's heart sank, and she gripped the arms of her chair so hard, she felt like her knuckles were going to break through the skin. "Yes, Father. Just please, tell me who he is."

"Lord Martin Ash, the Marquis of Fleet."

When Vannah's eyes widened and she gave a gasp of surprise, her father glared at her. "You have no objections, I trust?"

Objections? How could she possibly object to marrying the man she loved? Since that night in her playhouse Vannah had known the only man for her had always been Martin. She had appreciated Paul Demarest's attentions since no one else had ever shown her different paths a woman might take in life; no one had ever helped her to be self-reliant. But Martin made her feel like a woman, not a student whose eyes needed opening. She knew her life with Martin would be enriching and satisfying for them both, for despite their differing nationalities, both were of a similar background and would understand more readily each other's hopes and desires.

Vannah felt her spirits soar, and she became giddy with sheer elation. Martin had asked for her hand in marriage. He wanted to marry her! Vannah was so deliriously happy, she could have hugged even her father.

"Well, daughter, don't just sit there. Say something."

Vannah's smile was so wide, she thought her face would crack. "I would be delighted to marry Lord Fleet, Father."

"Hmph. I was certain you'd find something objectionable about the young man." He almost sounded disappointed that she was so amenable to the match.

"I find him quite acceptable, Father. Quite acceptable."

Then he chuckled. "The lad certainly knows how to drive a hard bargain, I will say that for him."

Suddenly a chill of foreboding wrapped itself around Vannah, and she crossed her arms to warm them. "What do you mean, Father?"

"I'm talking about your marriage settlement, of course. I thought I was being most generous offering him half a million for you, but he thought his title was worth more. Finally got me to agree to a dowry of one million now and another million when my first grandson is born. Plus I have to agree to make the boy one of my heirs, can you beat that?"

Vannah's smile died, and she felt sick to her stomach. "So—so Martin agreed to marry me only if you agreed to his terms."

"That's right, daughter. I never suspected—Savannah, where are you going? I'm not finished with you yet."

But she didn't hear him because she was already out the door, her hat and books forgotten.

When she reached her bedchamber, she flung herself on the bed and let the tears finally come. Her shoulders shaking from the violence of her sobs, Vannah kicked and pounded at the coverlet like a child having a tantrum. Finally, all of her fury and disappointment spent at last, she just lay there, moaning softly in agony. She felt as though her heart had been squeezed dry of any love or tenderness, and an empty shell remained.

Martin doesn't love you . . . he only wants the money. Martin doesn't love you . . . he only wants the money. The realization kept running through her tormented mind like a bizarre litany.

She was worth two million dollars to him.

Vannah just lay there, unable to move, and stared at the

ceiling. When she ignored her emotions and concentrated on her mind, everything became so crystal-clear, she wondered how she hadn't seen it before.

Martin was nothing more than a fortune-hunting aristocrat. Oh, when she was a child, she wasn't worthy of his notice, but once she reached a marriageable age, that suddenly changed.

Vannah smiled bitterly to herself. How easy for him to play upon her childhood infatuation for him and use it for his own gain. And she had been so gullible, she had actually thought his attentions were genuine this time.

Vannah sat bolt upright in panic and clutched at her middle. And her seduction . . . Had that been part of his plan as well, to impregnate her and make sure she had to marry him if he failed to make her fall in love with him? She shook her head in distaste, refusing to believe it.

Then Vannah rose to her feet and went into the washroom to splash cold water on her red, swollen eyes. Well, she had a few things to say to Martin Ash. If he thought he had won, he was sadly mistaken.

Later, after telling Parkins to deliver a message for her, Vannah went to Petit Clairvaux to wait for Martin.

When she glanced into the drawing room where she had given herself so freely to him, Vannah felt as if a knife were turning in her heart. She swallowed hard to hold back her tears and hurried upstairs to her studio.

She hadn't been there in years, and to her adult eyes the room that had once seemed so spacious seemed small and confined now. Vannah smiled bitterly. Everything looked so different to a child: rooms seemed larger; people seemed noble and trustworthy.

She strolled idly around, opening the built-in cupboards filled with dusty old toys that should have been packed away years ago and relegated to Clairvaux's attics. When she came to the last cupboard and saw what was inside, a nostalgic smile touched her mouth.

"Mademoiselle Fanchette."

She reached in and took out the French doll, her long dress of ivory Alençon lace now dark yellow with age and her real hair dull and dry.

"Oh, how I wish you really could talk, Fanchette," Vannah mused. "I wonder what advice you would have for me now."

But the doll just stared blankly out of blue glass eyes.

Suddenly Vannah heard the front door open and close. She put the doll away to the accompaniment of footsteps ascending the stairs, and she just had time to walk over to one of the windows before Martin appeared in the doorway.

She tried not to look at him, but she couldn't help herself. Vannah's traitorous heart skipped a beat in response, and forcibly she had to remind herself over and over and over that this devil of a man who had enslaved her emotions was nothing more than an unprincipled fortune hunter.

He looked as though he had just come from the Reading Room in his crisp white linen suit that fit him to perfection. After greeting her Martin casually loosened the knot of his brown silk tie as though he were about to undress and make love to her again. Vannah forced herself to look away and steeled herself not to succumb to him this time.

"How much do you think I'm worth, Martin?" she asked conversationally, looking out the window. Even the sparrows had all gone, and not even their nest remained.

"Worth?" he asked, puzzlement in his deep bass voice.

"Yes. In dollars. Pounds sterling. Francs."

As he crossed the room his footsteps seemed to echo the pounding of her heart. When they stopped, she sensed him standing right behind her.

"A human life can't be measured in monetary terms," he said softly. "And you, Vannah, are a pearl without price. You know that."

She forced herself to turn her head and look at him, trying to fight the hold he had over her, especially when he was looking at her the way he was now, with desire deep in his eyes.

"Oh, do I? It was my understanding that I am worth precisely two million dollars."

Now Martin grew very still and his eyes narrowed. "What do you mean, Vannah?"

Now she stepped away from him, her anger overriding any feelings she had for him. "I mean the price you exacted from my father for my hand in marriage!"

She heard his sharp intake of breath. "Vannah, it is not what it seems."

"And what of your professed love for me, Martin? Is that not what it seems also? And what of the night we spent together downstairs in this very building? Was that also not what it seemed?"

He extended his hand and took a step toward her. "You must believe me when I say that I love you and want you to be my wife."

She whirled away, just out of his reach. "If that is true, why did you bargain with my father for my dowry? First it was a paltry half a million dollars, and then you negotiated for more." Vannah was trembling with rage.

Martin was scowling now, and he reached up to run his fingers along his scar. "I know you're upset, Vannah, but you must give me a chance to explain."

"I'm listening."

"First of all, your father approached me and offered me your hand in marriage for a handsome settlement."

"Oh, so you had no intention of marrying me otherwise."

"For God's sake, Vannah, will you please stop putting

words in my mouth!" When Vannah fell silent, Martin continued in a much calmer voice. "I just want you to know that I had every intention of asking his permission to marry you, but he approached me first."

She stared up at him, her eyes flashing. "If that is true, Martin, why didn't you refuse the money? Why didn't you tell him that you would marry me even if there was no dowry?"

"The reason is quite simple. It gave me great pleasure to best your father at one of his own deals."

Vannah's hopes soared. She wanted desperately to believe Martin, but there was still that nagging doubt in her mind that he was somehow in collusion with her father.

She stubbornly shook her head. "I don't believe you, Martin. I think you planned this entire episode with my father to get what you wanted."

"Vannah!" Her name was a cry of anguish and shock. "I can't believe that you would think such things of me."

He sounded so wounded, so devastated, that for a moment she almost doubted herself. Perhaps she had unfairly judged him, after all. Perhaps he was telling the truth.

Suddenly Martin's face hardened into an angry mask, turning him into a man she didn't know. His words were filled with contempt as he said, "So you think this is all some mercenary plan on my part, do you, Vannah? You think that my loving you was nothing more than a ploy to secure myself a part of your father's fortune?" Now his tone became biting and sarcastic. "Well, my love, if you think so little of me that you could believe such nonsense, then I'm afraid that I didn't know you as well as I thought I did, and you certainly don't know me at all. And, if that's the case, then we have nothing whatsoever to say to each other."

He stood looking down at her with supreme disdain. "You disappoint me greatly, Savannah." And he turned and strode away, stopping at the door only long enough to say, "I wouldn't marry you if you were the last woman on earth."

Then he was gone.

Much to Vannah's surprise, Martin didn't leave Clairvaux, and nothing more was said about their wedding. But they still avoided each other. Vannah took all of her meals on a tray in her rooms, went riding only when she knew that Martin was out with her father, and took to attending boring ladies' luncheons with Aunt Constance.

Many were the times when Vannah almost asked Aunt Constance for her opinion of the entire affair, but her aunt seemed so oblivious to the tension between her niece and their houseguest that Vannah wondered if her father or Martin had even told Constance about her father's offer for Vannah's hand. So she said nothing.

A week passed.

Vannah spent the days alternately consumed by remorse for having doubted Martin and convinced that he loved her only for her father's money. Had she been a fool for making such accusations against him, or a fool for falling in love with him?

Then came the night she received her answer.

The August night was hot and muggy, and a thick fog had rolled in off the ocean, enveloping Newport in an impenetrable gray blanket.

Restless and unable to sleep, Vannah went to her open window, praying for just a little puff of wind to cool her, but there wasn't even enough movement to cause a candle flame to flicker.

Vannah pulled her nightgown away from her hot, sticky body, but it afforded her little relief. Finally she poured some eau de cologne from an Irish crystal bottle into her palm and splashed it on her neck and shoulders, savoring the refreshing coolness as the liquid trickled down between her breasts. Perhaps now she could relax. She extinguished the lamp by her bedside, climbed into bed, and soon fell into a fitful slumber plagued by formless dreams.

Much later the sound of her bedroom door opening caused her to stir, but her brain was still too fogged with sleep to register hurried footsteps crossing the room. Vannah was barely aware of her mattress sagging and creaking as someone got in beside her, but she began to awaken when she felt a weight resting against her upper body. And by the time she felt warm, insistent lips pressed against hers, she was conscious enough to realize that a man was in bed with her.

Her eyes flew open in alarm. Even in the darkness she could tell that the intruder was Martin, just by the taste of his warm, sweet mouth, the feel of his body weighting hers down. Vannah went rigid, then twisted, trying to buck him off, but she soon discovered that she couldn't move because he held her arms above her head, her wrists pinioned to the pillow while most of his weight was resting on one elbow. She was helpless and at his mercy.

When she whimpered and tossed her head from side to side in an attempt to evade his mouth, he released her.

"Just what in heaven's name do you think you're doing, Martin Ash?" she hissed.

She sensed him smile in the darkness. "I am here to talk, and you are going to listen."

Vannah struggled. "Get out of here this—" But she was cut off when Martin kissed her again.

"Keep still," he said.

"Martin, if you don't leave at once, I am going to scream this house down. I am going to—"

Once again he effectively silenced her.

This time, when he raised his head, Vannah said nothing.

"I'm gratified to see that you're going to be sensible

about this." His breath was soft and warm against her face, his hands clasped around her wrists firmly but gently, so as not to hurt. "Now, I'm quite tired of this little game we've been playing with each other, and it's got to stop. We've both been the victims of a painful misunderstanding, Vannah. I know I owe you an explanation for my actions, and by God, you are going to listen to me whether you like it or not. Agreed?"

"Agreed. But reluctantly."

"Reluctantly is better than not at all. Now, if I release you, also reluctantly, there will be no talk of screaming the house down, agreed?"

"Agreed."

"Sensible woman."

As promised, Martin released her wrists and rolled away from her. Perversely Vannah missed his touch, feeling suddenly cold even in the room's steamy heat. She felt the bed creak and spring back as he rose, and she heard him fumbling for matches to light the lamp on her nightstand. There was a scratch, the match flared, and suddenly light filled the room, revealing Martin, fully dressed and staring down at her sardonically. She sat up and covered herself with the top sheet.

He went to the foot of the bed and grasped a carved mahogany bedpost in one hand. "When I told you I loved you and would marry you even if you had no dowry, Vannah, I meant it."

"Then why didn't you tell my father that?" she demanded, drawing up her knees beneath the sheet.

"Because the temptation to beat him at his own game was just too good an opportunity to miss!" Martin said. "I dislike your father almost as much as you do. I think he's cold, unfeeling, pompous—I could go on and on. So, when he called me into his office and offered me your hand in marriage, I couldn't resist pushing him to see just how far he would go to negotiate a marriage settlement."

Martin released the bedpost and ran his hand through his hair. "I wish now that I had told him to keep his money. At least now you wouldn't be so suspicious of my motives." When Vannah said nothing, he went on with, "And you're not entirely blameless, my girl. You accused me of being a fortune hunter, that I seduced you for material gain. . . ." His voice trembled when he said, "I'll have you know that that hurt me terribly, Vannah, and made me quite furious with you. That the woman I loved could even think me capable—"

Vannah moaned. "I—I don't know what to believe anymore, Martin. I'm so confused."

He sat himself down on the edge of the bed and took her hand in his. "You're just going to have to trust me, Vannah. You're just going to have to believe me when I say that I love you and that I never intended to marry you for your father's money. And if you can't, well . . ." He shrugged. "I'll be leaving for England alone at the end of the week."

She pulled her hand away, rose from the opposite side of the bed, and went to stand before the window. She desperately wanted to believe him, yet at the same time a nagging, lingering doubt remained in her mind.

Behind her, she heard Martin rise from the bed, but he didn't make any attempt to approach her. "I want your answer, Vannah," he said flatly, "and I want it before I leave this room." When she didn't respond, he added, "If you let me walk out that door, you'll never see me again."

In the seconds it took her to envision her life without him, a bleak, arid vista stretching out along the endless, lonely years, Vannah came to her decision. "Martin!" she cried, whirling around.

He was already at the door, his hand poised to grasp the

knob, when the urgency in her voice stopped him. She could hear his shaky sigh of relief as his hand fell away and he turned.

Then they were rushing toward each other, and when they met in a crushing embrace, any misunderstandings were swept away by the onslaught of their mutual passion.

Even as Vannah rained kisses down on Martin's face, her hands were attacking him, tearing at his clothes, popping off buttons in her haste. She wanted to feel Martin's hot skin against her own again, be consumed by him.

The lustful look gleaming in Martin's eyes told Vannah that there was not going to be any gentle, patient wooing this time. Even as she sought to rid him of his clothes, his hands were slipping beneath her nightgown for the same purpose, and when the material refused to yield, he simply ripped it from her body.

When they were both free of constraining garments, they clung to each other, their hands roving, stroking, tugging in the bliss of exploration. Finally they managed to stagger over to the bed and came together in a mutual frenzy of desire, quickly exploding in blinding ecstasy that left Vannah shattered.

Finally they parted, falling back on the bed.

"My fierce Martin," Vannah murmured, dropping a kiss in the hollow of his throat.

Still gasping for breath, he raised himself up on one elbow. "I feel like I've been run over by a locomotive."

Vannah giggled. "Me too." Suddenly her face fell, and she grew serious. "I'd like to explain why I was so angry with you, Martin."

"I'm listening."

Vannah was silent while she collected her thoughts. Finally she said, "My father has always tried to control my life. He forbade me to draw, and he forced me to break off a promising relationship with Paul Demarest. So when he told me that you came to him and negotiated my marriage settlement"—she shrugged—"I convinced myself that you and he were conspiring to control me again. He would get a titled son-in-law, you would get two million dollars, and I would be sold to the highest bidder."

Martin reached over to brush her smooth cheek with his thumb. "I don't want you for your father's money, Vannah." Then he gave her a ribald wink. "I want your body."

"So all this time you've been after my virtue, not my intellect." Vannah let her hand rove down his belly until she found what she sought and began arousing him shamelessly. "Well, then, we're even, because I'm not exactly marrying you for your title, Martin Ash."

He fell back, gasping. "Vannah, if you keep doing that, I'm never going to leave. And I must get back to my rooms before someone discovers that I've seduced my fiancée."

She sighed and reluctantly released him.

He kissed her, then rose and dressed. Just as he was leaving, Martin said, "Tomorrow I shall tell your father that I won't accept a dowry for you."

Vannah grinned at him from the bed. "I've had second thoughts, Martin. If Father really wants to sell me, I don't think we should deny him the pleasure of paying. I'm sure we can put two million dollars to good use."

"Savannah Webb, I never dreamed you could be so unscrupulous and devious," he said.

"I'm Gerrold Webb's daughter," she retorted.

Then they said good night, each returning to their beds and their dreams of a rosy, perfect future together.

"I have an announcement to make," Martin said.

Seated by his side with her father and Aunt Constance in the drawing room, Vannah felt light-headed with anticipation. As she bathed and dressed that morning and refrained from throwing herself into Martin's arms at breakfast, she never dreamed that this moment would ever arrive. But it had.

Martin rose, beamed down into Vannah's upturned face, took her hand, and squeezed it. "I have asked Savannah for her hand in marriage, and she has most graciously accepted me."

"Wonderful, lad," her father said, rising as well to shake Martin's hand. Then he came over to Savannah, kissed her on the cheek, and said, "You've got a good man there, daughter."

For once his coldness didn't disturb her. "Oh, I know, Father, I know."

Aunt Constance, with tears flooding her eyes, first hugged Martin, then Vannah. "My dear, you don't know how very happy this makes me." She dabbed at her eyes with her handkerchief. "You must introduce Martin to your mother and tell her the good news."

"There will be plenty of time for that later," Gerrold said. "I think such a momentous occasion calls for a toast."

Moments later a footman bearing a silver tray containing a large bottle of champagne and four crystal glasses set the tray down and departed. Gerrold popped the cork, filled each glass, and made sure everyone had one for the toast. The men remained standing while the ladies stayed seated.

Just as Gerrold raised his glass, there came a frantic knock on the door.

"Who in blazes is that?" he grumbled.

When he bade them come in, a flustered Parkins entered. "Please forgive the intrusion, sir, but—"

"What is it now, Parkins?" Gerrold growled. "Can't you see that we're busy toasting my daughter's betrothal to Lord Fleet?"

Suddenly, to everyone's astonishment, the diminutive

figure of a young woman burst into the room and said, "Marty can't marry your daughter because he's already married to me!"

Everyone froze like wax figures in a tableau for what seemed like an eternity, while the intruder's unbelievable accusation hung in the air like an ax waiting to fall.

Vannah was the first to recover from the shock. She stiffened and glared at the woman out of narrowed eyes. "This is absurd! Parkins, please show this . . . young woman out."

The intruder planted her feet in the rug and belligerently folded her arms across her flat, boyish chest. "I'm not goin' anywhere. Tell 'em, Marty. Tell 'em I'm your wife."

"Fleet, is what this woman is saying true?" Gerrold demanded.

Martin was as pale as paper, and his voice cracked as he said, "I'm afraid so."

Vannah's champagne glass slipped from her stiff, nerveless fingers, but no one seemed to notice that it splashed the delicate skirt of her muslin dress or broke into a thousand shards when it crashed to the floor. She felt as though she had wandered into a nightmare by mistake, and any moment she would awaken from it and the intruder would be gone.

Suddenly Aunt Constance took charge of the situation with practiced ease. "Gerrold . . . Savannah. I think Martin and this young lady need to be alone for a while. Shall we withdraw to the music room?"

After darting a malevolent glance at Martin, Gerrold muttered something under his breath, then said, "Very well. Come along, Savannah."

"No!" she cried, her eyes never leaving Martin's white, pinched face. "I want to stay here and—"

"Savannah, you will come at once!"

She had no choice but to follow. As she walked out of the study between Aunt Constance and her father, like a prisoner being escorted to her own execution, Vannah couldn't resist taking the measure of the woman who claimed to be Martin's wife. She was dressed plainly in a faded blue cotton dress of no particular style, and she wore a little straw hat perched comically on the crown of her head. Physically the woman was merely pretty, not as beautiful as Vannah, with a pert, upturned nose, plain brown eyes, and plain brown hair scraped back in a dowdy bun. But there was something about her, a palpable strength and determination belying her fragile appearance, that sent a shiver of fear racing along Vannah's arms.

The woman assessed Vannah just as coolly, her eyes following the trio out the door. When she and Martin were alone, the woman said, "She's right beautiful, like an angel."

Martin swallowed hard to ease the tightness in his throat. "What are you doing here, Katherine? You were supposed to be divorcing me."

"I came here to tell you I changed m' mind."

"Changed your mind?"

She nodded as she crossed the room, her eyes staring up at the mural painted on the ceiling, then moving down to the huge fireplace of gilt-and-blue Campan marble that took up nearly one wall.

"Fancy-dancy," she said, touching one of the Louis XV chairs upholstered in ivory moire.

Then she was standing before him, reaching no higher than his heart. "I love you, Marty. I never realized just how much till after you left. Why, even Pa he said that I was moonin' around like a calf without its mother. He's the one who told me to go after you if I really wanted you. So I did. I was scared somethin' fierce, 'cause I never been away from Wyoming before, but I had the address of this here place, so I got myself a ticket on a train and came right up here to find you." Katherine's eyes hardened into flint. "And what do I find? My husband fixin' to marry another woman."

Martin clutched at the back of his chair for support. "I told you, Katherine, our marriage is over. We are too different, you and I. You even admitted as much yourself."

"That's before I realized that I can't live without you, Marty." She reached up to touch his cheek, but he recoiled from her and strode over to the window.

"I love Savannah Webb," he said brutally. "I always have. And I'm going to marry her."

"You can't. You're still married to me."

He glared at her. "But not for long."

"I won't give you a divorce, Marty," she said. "I'm your wife all legal and proper. I've decided I want to go with you to England and be Mrs. Marquis of Fleet just like you wanted me to."

"That's the Marchioness of Fleet, Katherine."

"Don't matter what they call me, Marty."

"Well, it matters to me!"

Martin fell silent as he stared out at Clairvaux's tranquil green lawn and the sea beyond, sparkling like a field of sapphires in the sun. Sapphire. The color of Vannah's eyes. He couldn't lose her now, not after all the wasted years, not after what they meant to each other.

He turned back to Katherine. "I want my freedom, Katherine. I want to marry Savannah."

Suddenly Katherine planted her feet squarely on the floor and put her hands on her hips in a stance he had seen often enough. It meant that her mind was made up and not even a tornado could root her from her position.

"Sorry, Marty," she said. "I'm your wife, and your wife I'm goin' to stay."

"I don't want you, Katherine. I'm going to put you on the first train back to Wyoming in the morning."

"Sure you'll be rid of me, but you won't be free 'cause I won't divorce you. And your lady friend don't look like the sort who'd live in sin with you."

"I wouldn't ask her to," Martin said softly, more to himself than to his wife.

They faced each other in silence heavy with hostility, neither giving an inch. Finally he said, "You have so little pride that you would live with a man who doesn't love you?"

She nodded. "Don't have any pride where you're concerned, Marty. Never did. I reckon you've always known that about me."

Martin walked over to her until they were so close, they were almost touching. His tone was low and menacing, uttered between clenched teeth. "I swear to you on your Pa's Bible, Katherine, that if you insist on us living together as husband and wife, I'll make your life a living hell. I'll never touch you, I'll parade my mistresses in front of you, I'll—"

"No, you won't," she said, calmly contradicting him. "You're a good man, Marty Ash, and an honorable one. The best man I ever met, next to Pa." Before he could grasp her wrist and stop her, Katherine reached up and ran her fingertips lightly down his scar. "You forgot how you got this, Marty?" she asked quietly. "You forgot what you owe me?"

He was beaten, and he knew it as surely as he knew that he had lost Vannah forever. His shoulders slumped, and his drawn-out sigh of defeat seemed to fill the drawing room and linger there.

"I hate you." The words were spoken softly, without virulence or rancor, just a simple declaration of fact.

"I know you do, Marty, but I got enough love for the

both of us. And, even if you do hate me, it won't stop you from doin' right by me, and don't the both of us just know it."

And because he knew she spoke the truth, he went to tell Vannah why he could not marry her, after all.

Vannah waited alone in the music room for Martin.

As she endured the hard, straight-backed chair digging into her back and stared out the window at nothing in particular, she was glad to be alone. Her father had been furious at this unexpected turn of events and quite openly condemned Martin's ungentlemanly behavior without even hearing his side of the story. Vannah was grateful to Aunt Constance for intervening and spiriting Gerrold away so that his daughter could have a moment's peace to collect her tattered emotions, her stunned thoughts.

Please God, Vannah prayed, don't let it be true. Please don't let Martin be married to that woman.

Yet he'd admitted that she was his wife. Vannah had heard him.

So many questions kept buzzing around in her brain like a swarm of persistent bees that she couldn't even keep track of them all. Who was that woman? Why did he marry her? Why did he profess to love Vannah if he still loved this woman? Why didn't he ever tell her he already had a wife? Why . . . why . . . why?

There had to be some explanation.

Vannah leaned her head back against the unyielding carved wood of the chair, pressing against it until her scalp hurt and the pain brought tears to her eyes.

Suddenly she heard the door to the music room open and shut softly, heard the familiar tread of Martin's light step as he walked toward her. But she didn't rise and go to him. She sat there with her eyes closed until she sensed him standing before her chair. Then Vannah opened her eyes and wordlessly stared up at him.

Martin looked like a man who had just peered through hell's window. His rugged face mirrored the anguish he must have been feeling, but it was his eyes that frightened Vannah the most. Their smoldering spark, their inner fire, was gone. He was a beaten man, a man without hope.

All this time she had been waiting for him to come to her to reassure her that this was all some dreadful mistake, another misunderstanding. But seeing him torn apart like this, Vannah realized that he needed her strength far more than she needed his reassurance.

"Martin," she murmured, extending her hands to him, "please tell me what this is all about."

He grasped them as if he were a drowning man and she his lifeline, and Vannah was startled to find his fingers as cold as the sea. She rose from her hard chair of penance and led him over to the divan.

When they were seated, Vannah said, "Is that woman your wife?"

He nodded. "Katherine—Katie—Costello and I have been married for the past two years."

Vannah dropped his hands as though they had suddenly caught fire. "Then why did you ask me to marry you, Martin?"

"Because I love you, and because she was supposed to be divorcing me," he said.

Vannah felt bewildered. "Why don't you start at the beginning, Martin? Tell me all about this Katie Costello and why she should have been divorcing you."

He rose from the divan and began pacing back and forth nervously. "Do you remember my telling you how I got my scar?"

Vannah nodded "You said some cattle thieves shot you and left you for dead."

"That's right. What I didn't tell you was that Katherine found me and nursed me back to health." Martin's voice shook with emotion as he said, "I would have died otherwise, Vannah."

"I see."

"She was pretty enough, and I was lonely. You can't imagine what it's like, Vannah, to be cut off from any semblance of civilization for years at a time, never to see a fine painting, never to see a play unless some third-rate provincial traveling company drifts through town, never to hear an orchestra play fine music. I needed companionship, and Katherine was there." He took a deep shuddering breath. "She fancied herself in love with me, so when I asked her to marry me, she accepted.

"We got along, and the time passed tolerably. And then I received word from my family's solicitors in England that my brother and his family had died and that I was the new Marquis of Fleet. Suddenly my fortunes changed overnight. I no longer needed to continue ranching in Wyoming. I had the life I was born to awaiting me in England now, a family estate to care for, the wherewithal to do whatever I pleased."

"And your wife?" Vannah asked quietly.

"Katherine wanted no part of it." Martin's voice was soft with compassion. "You've seen Katherine, Vannah. She belongs to the plains of Wyoming, not the drawing rooms of Mayfair and Sussex, and I think she realized it. When I told her that I was turning the ranch back over to the syndicate and returning to England, she pleaded with me to stay. She always has been afraid of the unknown. I told her that a wife's place is by her husband's side, and if she didn't agree to come with me, our marriage was over." A wry smile dragged down the corners of Martin's mouth. "I think I knew what her answer would be and was half hoping that she would refuse. She did. She said she couldn't imagine living anywhere except Wyoming, and I would just have to go on without her."

Martin sighed dismally and ran his hand through his hair. "When we parted company that last time, she promised me that she would begin divorce proceedings immediately on the grounds that I had deserted her. Since I was planning to visit your family, I gave her this address to forward any pertinent papers."

"Then why is she even here?" Vannah demanded, confused. She just wished Katherine Costello Ash would disappear and never come back.

Martin stood before her, his face a picture of abject misery. "She says she has changed her mind, Vannah. She says she wants to be my wife again and live with me in England."

"She can't!" Vannah cried, springing to her feet. "She gave you up once, Martin, and she just can't have you back every time she feels like it." When Martin made no comment, Vannah was suddenly assailed by fresh doubts. "Unless—unless you want her back, Martin."

With a shake of his head and a groan of consternation, Martin drew her into his arms, clutching her to him. "You are my one true love, Vannah. I think I've loved you from the very first day I saw you when you came marching into your father's study to ask him to allow you to draw. Do you remember that?"

She nodded and smiled through her tears. "How could I ever forget?"

"And even when I was married to Katherine, I think some part of me was still in love with you."

Now Martin took her face in his hands and looked deeply into her eyes. "When I came here and saw what a lovely, intelligent woman you had become, I quite lost my heart to you, Savannah Webb."

Suddenly Vannah became infused with fresh hope. "Then

she must give you a divorce, Martin. She must agree to let you go. You don't love her, you love me. Surely she must realize this."

His hands fell to his sides, and his voice was flat and leaden. "She wants me back, my love, and will not agree to a divorce. Katherine has just informed me that even if I refuse to live as husband and wife, she will not grant me a divorce."

"What are you saying, Martin?"

"I am saying that she will not give me my freedom, and I could not marry you in any case."

Vannah just stood there, silent and numb with shock. Finally she said, "Then we won't marry. I shall be your mistress and go with you to England."

"Vannah, my dear sweet love. Thank you for offering, but I can't allow you to sacrifice yourself so."

"I'm not sacrificing myself. I want to be with you always, Martin, and if that's the only way I can, then so be it."

He shook his head. "You'd be a social outcast, and our children bastards, shunned by all," he said bitterly. "No, I'm sorry, my love, but I can't allow it."

Vannah grew very still. "You—you're going back to her, aren't you." It was a statement, not a question.

Martin just looked at her, his eyes mirroring his pain at long last. He nodded imperceptibly.

"No, Martin, no. You can't mean that. You don't love her, you love me." Vannah backed away from him, her eyes wild with disbelief and terrified of losing him.

In three strides Martin was by her side, but she flew at him, her hands balled into fists as she tried to strike him. "Damn you, Martin Ash!" But he just held her tightly.

"Don't you understand, Vannah?" he murmured against her hair. "I owe Katherine my life. I am honor-bound to go back to her."

Gradually Vannah's sobs subsided into shudders and she was able to look up at him. "I don't give a damn about honor. All I care about is losing you!"

"Do you think I want to leave you, my love?" he asked with heartbreaking tenderness. His eyes roamed over her face as though looking at it for the last time. "I would just as soon cut off my right arm. The thought of never seeing your face again, of never waking in the morning with you lying next to me . . ." He swallowed hard and fought back tears of his own. "You must be brave enough for both of us, my love."

"I don't want to be brave, Martin, I just want you!"

"*Stop it!*" he cried, snapping at last, grasping her by the shoulders and giving her a little shake. "You're tearing me apart! Don't make this any harder for me than it already is!"

Vannah bit her trembling lower lip and tried to control herself. He really was leaving her to go away with another woman. She would never see him again, never hear his voice whisper her name so lovingly in the darkness, never feel him possessing her so completely.

"I'm going to leave with Katherine as soon as we've finished our good-byes, Vannah," Martin said. "There's no point in prolonging our suffering."

Vannah nodded mutely through her tears. "Good-bye, Martin." And she reached for one last kiss, an embrace that she would have to remember for the rest of her life.

He held her so tightly, they seemed as one, and they kissed for the last time, a lingering kiss filled with longing and regret, a chaste kiss that could promise nothing beyond the moment. Vannah closed her eyes, savoring the smooth hardness of his lips and his body clinging to hers.

And then he was gone, leaving her feeling hollow and alone.

"Martin?"

But no one answered.

Chapter Eleven

New York—1894

CONSTANCE WAS VERY WORRIED.

Ever since Vannah's romance with Martin Ash had ended so tragically, she had lost all interest in living. Every day, after Vannah's bath, her maid would ask what she wanted to wear, and she would always listlessly reply, "I don't care, Maeve. Choose something for me." When she was through picking at breakfast, Vannah would sit in the high-backed wing chair in her sitting room and stare out into space for hours. Sometimes she would repeatedly open and close a painted ivory fan until Constance thought she'd go mad from the constant snap, snap, snap.

Vannah never went anywhere or did anything, except float silently through the house like a ghost. Oh, she listened and conversed and occasionally laughed mirthlessly, but it was as though her heart were in exile and never coming back.

Constance had tried everything to lift her dispirited niece out of the doldrums but to no avail. Now she was becoming desperate.

"Vannah," she said one snowy day in January, "I am very worried about you."

Vannah snapped the ivory fan shut and looked up out of eyes that had lost their sparkle long ago. "Don't be, Aunt Constance."

"But I am, my dear. It's been five months since"—she

took a deep breath and steeled herself—"since Martin left, and it's time you accept the fact that he's not coming back. It's over between you, Vannah. Time to get on with your life."

"What life?" Vannah asked bitterly. "I have no life without Martin."

"But you do, my dear. Why, there is a stack of invitations a foot high just waiting for you to answer. You could be so busy, you wouldn't have time to think of Martin Ash."

Now Vannah rose from her chair and went to stand before the window. "You make it sound so easy, Aunt Constance. All I have to do is fill every waking hour with one meaningless activity after another and I'll heal, is that it?"

Constance went to her and put her arm around her. "You will feel better in time, Vannah. I promise. But you have to make the effort."

"I'm not ready, Aunt Constance. I still hurt too much."

"I know, my dear, I know. Martin was a very special man."

Now, for the first time in months, Constance saw tears well up in Vannah's eyes. Her lower lip trembled as she said, "Why did he have to go back to her, Aunt Constance? I would have followed him to China had he asked me to, and he knew it. I didn't care about marriage. I just wanted to be with him for the rest of our lives."

Constance gave her a little shake. "Because Martin Ash is an honorable man. He owed Katherine Costello his life, Vannah, and he repaid that debt the only way he knew how, by giving her what she wanted, by meeting her price." She was silent for a moment while Vannah sniffed noisily into a handkerchief. "And here is something else for you to consider, Vannah, and you're not going to like it." Constance paused so she could frame her question properly. "How would you feel if you were in Katherine Costello's position? Would you give Martin up so easily?"

Vannah didn't answer at first, and Constance could see that the brutally frank question both disturbed her and was making her think. Finally she shook her head imperceptibly and said, "No," in a wee, watery voice.

"I didn't think so. Sometimes it helps to see a situation from the other person's point of view. Always remember that, Vannah."

Still crying, Vannah put her arms around her aunt and hugged her fiercely. "Oh, Aunt Constance, whatever would I do without your wisdom?"

When they parted, Constance took her own handkerchief and wiped Vannah's cheeks as a mother would her child. "Also remember that we can't always have what we want in life, Vannah. We must put our obligations to others before our own desires."

Vannah understood all too well. Her aunt was telling her as kindly as she could that it was her duty to marry whomever her father eventually chose to be her husband.

She sighed heavily and turned her attention back to the snow, which had now tapered off to a few fitful flurries. "I am heartily sick of words such as *duty, honor,* and *obligation,* Aunt Constance."

"They form the cornerstones of our lives."

Yours, perhaps, Vannah thought rebelliously, but not mine.

Too drained to argue with her aunt any longer, Vannah said, "I feel like having lunch downstairs today."

Constance felt both relieved and happy. Vannah had been taking her meals in her room ever since Martin Ash left, and for her to want to eat with the family today was surely a sign that she was beginning to recover.

"Wonderful. I'll have Sapphira make fried chicken and corn bread and—"

"Stop, Aunt Constance!" Vannah laughed. "I'll become as big as a house!"

Constance scowled and gave her niece an appraising glance. "But you need to put some meat on your bones, Vannah. Your clothes just hang on you."

"I'm sure Sapphira's cooking will remedy that soon enough."

As they walked arm in arm out of Vannah's rooms, Constance said, "Your father and I are having dinner with the Vanderbilts tonight. Why don't you come with us? There are just going to be a few people there, not a crowd."

Vannah hesitated and shook her head. "I'm not ready yet, Aunt Constance. Perhaps some other time."

Constance nodded in understanding. "Very well. I don't want to push you into something you're not ready for."

She was just relieved and grateful that Vannah was beginning to return to the land of the living at long last. There would be time enough for her to reenter the social whirl.

Later that evening, while her father and aunt were dressing for dinner, Vannah went to the music room and began playing the piano, just letting her fingers wander over the keys from memory, for her thoughts were not on the sheet of music set before her.

Today, for the first time since that day in August when her whole world seemed to collapse and come to an end, Vannah felt alive again. She had plunged down into deepest despair, hit rock bottom, and now, like a drowning swimmer, was fighting her way to the surface and back to life.

She knew that losing Martin had scarred her forever. There would always be a part of her that would love and mourn for him, but Aunt Constance was right. It was time to get on with her life, to forge ahead and leave the past behind her, where it belonged. But what did the future hold?

Her hands fell still upon the ivory keys.

"That was quite lovely, my dear."

Vannah started and turned in her seat to see Aunt Constance and her father standing in the doorway. Both were dressed to go out for the evening, her father wearing a charcoal-gray topcoat and a white woolen scarf, Aunt Constance looking splendid wrapped in her floor-length Russian sable with diamonds sparkling in her hair.

"There's still time to change your mind and join us, Savannah," her father said.

She smiled. "Thank you, Father, but I'm going to decline. I—I don't feel quite ready to face the world just yet."

He didn't even try to dissuade her, just nodded his head briefly and said, "Very well. Come along, Constance, the carriage is waiting."

Then they bade Vannah good night and disappeared down the hall.

When Vannah heard the front door close, she went upstairs to her sitting room, took out a large sketch pad, a tin of watercolor cakes, and a sable brush from its hiding place in the chest at the foot of her bed, then fetched a container of water from her bathroom. When all her materials were assembled, she sat down and prepared to paint undisturbed.

Meanwhile, inside the Webb carriage, Gerrold suddenly turned to Constance and said, "I think Savannah should come with us tonight."

"But, Gerrold, she said she wasn't ready. She would need time to dress and arrange her hair."

"I'm going to persuade her to change her mind."

Constance, who knew better than to argue with him

when his mind was set on something, just sat back in silence while he tapped on the roof with his cane and told the driver to turn the carriage around in the middle of Fifth Avenue and return home.

When they arrived and went inside, Constance waited in the foyer while Gerrold trotted upstairs to his daughter's room.

He knocked once and called, "Savannah?" Even though he heard her reply, "One moment, please," he impatiently thrust open the door and barged into her sitting room where he found a white-faced, wide-eyed Savannah staring at him in terror while she clutched something to her chest.

At first he couldn't understand the reason for her distress. "Savannah, what is it?" he asked in bewilderment as he walked toward her.

Her guilty expression first warned him, and then he spied the open tin of watercolors on the table beside her chair. It looked so out of place that for a moment its significance eluded him. He looked at Savannah in puzzlement, then back at the tin of paints. And then Gerrold understood all too well.

He felt the blood drain from his face, and he was shaking as he extended his hand and barked, "Give it to me!"

For a moment he thought she was going to refuse, then Savannah reluctantly handed her father what turned out to be a sketch pad. He began flipping through the pages. The first one looked like nothing more than dabs of green paint, but all the other sketches were of Martin Ash. As Gerrold leafed through the pad one thought was uppermost in his mind: His daughter had been drawing for a long, long time.

Now he looked up at her, barely able to contain his fury. "I thought I had forbidden you to draw some time ago, Savannah."

"You did," she replied. Now there was defiance in her eyes and her voice as she said, "But I felt it was most unfair of you, Father, so I did it, anyway."

"Oh, you did, did you?" Gerrold flung the pad down on her chair. "Well, I must say that it comes as a very great shock to me to finally discover that you have been disobeying me all these years, Savannah, that you have been going behind my back."

"What has been the harm in it?" she demanded. "Drawing is such an innocent pastime, it—"

"You disobeyed me!" he bellowed, feeling his face turn scarlet with rage. "And you must have had help because I suspect that this has been going on for years."

Now Savannah looked frightened, but she quickly recovered herself and said, "I had no help. I merely drew whenever and wherever I could. I used pens and the backs of envelopes. I—"

"Oh, no, my girl. You are much too good to have done that. Someone secured you paper and proper supplies, and I want to know who!" But even before Savannah could say a word, he knew. "Constance. It was your aunt all the time, wasn't it?"

Both were so intent on their argument, they failed to hear the light, hurried footsteps in the outside corridor. Suddenly Constance, herself, appeared in the doorway. "Have you persuaded her to join us, Gerrold?" She looked from Vannah's white, frightened face to Gerrold's red, furious one. "Gerrold . . . Vannah? What's wrong?"

He turned to her, his voice silky but edged with steel. "I've just discovered something rather interesting, Constance. It would appear that my daughter has been drawing behind my back for, oh, I would say nigh on to ten years now. And after I expressly forbade her to."

Constance was caught, and she knew it would be pointless to lie. "Gerrold, I can explain."

"Oh, can you now?"

Vannah wailed, "I'm sorry, Aunt Constance, but he just came bursting into my room."

Her father glared at her. "This is my house, and I may burst into as many rooms as I please." Then he turned back to Constance. "Is it true that you've been helping Savannah to disobey me?"

Constance felt a knot of fear begin to form in the pit of her stomach, for she had never felt Gerrold's rage directed at her before. "Yes, I did, Gerrold, but I—"

"Constance, will you please come with me? We have several grave matters to discuss."

And without another word or glance in her direction Gerrold strode out of Vannah's sitting room.

Vannah rushed over to her aunt's side. "What's he going to do, Aunt Constance?"

"Don't worry, Vannah. I'll calm him down."

"Constance, are you coming?" Gerrold bellowed from the hall.

Not wanting to incur his wrath further, Constance gave Vannah a reassuring pat on the arm and hurried after Gerrold. As she followed him in silence down the corridor her mind raced ahead, concocting excuses that would mollify his rage. For if there was one thing Constance had learned about Gerrold in all her years as his mistress, it was that he was a proud man who ruled both his business empire and his home with an iron fist. In Gerrold's eyes, to flout his supreme authority was the worst sin someone could commit. And she had just committed it. Constance knew that she would need all her wits and feminine wiles to extricate herself this time.

Much to her surprise, they did not go downstairs to Gerrold's study but to Constance's own sitting room. Gerrold held the door for her with icy politeness and once they were inside, turned on her.

"I'm waiting, Constance," he said.

She smiled her best soothing smile. "Gerrold, when I first met Vannah, she was such a lonely, shy child, and her one pleasure in life seemed to be art. When you took that away from her, she was inconsolable." She walked over to him and put her hand on his arm, hoping that her touch would calm him once again. But when she felt his arm grow hard and tense beneath her hand and his eyes remain cold, she withdrew it.

Then Constance explained about the daily deportment lessons.

A muscle twitched in Gerrold's jaw, and his scowl deepened. "So you willfully encouraged my daughter to disobey me, to lie, to cheat, to go behind her own father's back!"

"I saw nothing wrong in allowing the poor child such a simple pleasure," Constance replied.

"Simple pleasure!" Gerrold began pacing the sitting room, his rage so strong that it was like a third person there with them. "No wonder the girl entertained thoughts of consorting with rabble like that journalist fellow. No wonder she sulks for six months after being jilted by another man." Now he stopped and faced Constance squarely. "She's turned into a rebellious, disrespectful young woman, and it's all your fault!"

Though seething inside at the injustice of his accusations, Constance willed contrite tears to spring to her eyes. "You're right, of course, Gerrold. Vannah's behavior is entirely my fault, and I'm sorry." She placed her hands on his chest and began caressing him while staring deeply into his eyes. "Can you find it in your heart to ever forgive me?"

Her persuasive touch, the promise in her smoky eyes and parted lips, and the intoxicating scent of her perfume usually coaxed Gerrold out of any mood, no matter how surly or unforgiving. Constance waited for a smile to soften the harsh line of his mouth and the first sparkle of desire to warm his icy eyes. She waited for the laugh of surrender indicating that all was forgiven.

So she gasped in surprise when he grabbed her wrists tightly and flung her away with such force that she reeled back and would have fallen if she hadn't caught at a chair.

"I don't think so, Constance," he said, breathing hard. "Not this time. In fact, I want you to pack your bags and get out."

She stared at him in disbelief and horror. "Gerrold, you don't mean that!"

"I most certainly do. I want you out of this house tonight. And I never want to see you again."

"Gerrold, you—"

"I trusted you!" he screeched. "I took you into my home when those scheming stepchildren of yours drove you out of England. I gave you jewels, furs, Worth gowns . . ." Now his face twisted in torment. "And I loved you more than any woman I have ever loved, and this is how you repay me—with betrayal."

Constance would not humiliate herself further by offering him her body. She stood proud and tall. "And I never did anything in return for those jewels, furs, and Worth gowns, Gerrold? Need I remind you that I have betrayed my own sister by becoming your mistress? That I have raised your daughter as if she were my own? That I have served as your hostess and was responsible for persuading Caroline Astor to accept you? Do all those count for nothing, Gerrold?"

His face remained unmoved by her passionate declaration. All he said was, "I can forgive anything except betrayal, Constance. You have half an hour to pack one bag, and I'll thank you to leave all jewels and the sable coat behind.

When you're ready, James will take you to a hotel or Grand Central Station, whichever you prefer."

"But—but I have nowhere else to go."

"You're resourceful, Constance. I'm sure you'll find another protector," he said with a sneer. "And, in any case, I don't really care what happens to you."

"At least let me say good-bye to Frances and Vannah."

"That won't be necessary. I'll tell them tomorrow that you have gone."

"How are you going to explain my absence to all of our friends? Surely someone will think it odd that I've just moved out without a word to anyone. If the truth be known, there could be a scandal."

"I'll think of something," Gerrold said calmly. "There will be no scandal." Then his voice became hard and menacing. "And it would be to your advantage to go along with whatever story I circulate, Constance."

"Of—of course, Gerrold."

The enormity of her situation finally seeped into Constance's numb brain, and she began shaking. But she refused to panic or to plead for mercy. Instead she said, "Martin Ash was right about you, Gerrold. You are a cold, unfeeling bastard. Do you enjoy making people fear and hate you, especially your own daughter? Well, there is going to come a time when you are going to need Savannah's love and she is not going to have any left for you."

"A half hour, Constance" was all he said before leaving her room and closing the door behind him.

Half an hour later Constance heard the brownstone's front door close behind her forever. She shivered in her woolen coat, so cold after the luxurious warmth of the sable. A dusting of snow covered the empty street, and the air was crisp and cold. James had been given his orders, for he had the carriage door open for her and was standing at attention, his face carefully schooled to reveal nothing.

As Constance reached for her bag he rushed to her aid, murmuring, "Allow me, madam."

She gave him the address of one of her friends as he assisted her into the carriage.

As Constance sat there in the darkness she thought of her future, and even though it looked bleak at the moment, she was optimistic. Hadn't she always landed on her feet before? And she would do so again. Gerrold's snide parting shot about finding another protector flitted through her mind, but she disregarded it. No, she would never do that again.

She started thinking, and by the time she arrived at her friend's house, she had a plan.

When Vannah went down to breakfast the following morning she found only her father in the dining room reading the *Herald* and eating his usual breakfast of ham, eggs, and warm corn bread dripping with honey.

"Where's Aunt Constance?" she asked when she noticed that there was only one other setting of china and silverware on the table instead of the usual two.

"Gone," Gerrold replied without looking up from his newspaper.

"Gone?" Vannah echoed, clutching the high back of her chair. "Where did she go?"

"I don't know, and quite frankly, I don't care. I threw her out last night and told her not to come back. Ever."

Vannah's jaw went slack. "You what?"

"You heard me, unless you've suddenly gone deaf."

"Father, you didn't!"

Now he folded his newspaper and set it beside his plate. When he looked up at Vannah, his expression was one of annoyance. "Daughter, I can do anything I please, and I'll thank you to remember it. Constance betrayed me. I will not tolerate disloyalty from anyone."

Vannah knew that her father would be furious with her, but she could keep her feelings locked away inside no longer. "You threw her out on a cold and snowy night just because she let me draw? How petty and cruel!"

He scowled at her, the cleft between his brows becoming more pronounced. "The issue is not that she allowed you to draw, daughter. The issue is that she countermanded my orders, that she allowed you to draw after I had expressly forbidden it. She was disloyal and she betrayed me."

"Well, so have I," Vannah pointed out. "All these years I have been drawing behind your back as well, Father. Are you going to throw me out too?"

His eyes narrowed. "That's different. You are my daughter, child of my blood."

"But she is your wife's sister. She has been like a mother to me, and she's lived with us for ten years, Father! Surely you could have forgiven her. Surely you could have—"

"I don't wish to discuss it any further, Savannah," he said coldly. "Your aunt will not be coming back. I have already informed your mother. Should anyone ask for her, you will tell them that she chose to leave for her own accord, is that clear?"

Vannah almost lost her temper then, but she restrained herself. Telling her father precisely what she thought of him would not make him relent and take Aunt Constance back. If anything, it would antagonize him further. And if there was one thing Vannah had learned about her father over the years, it was that it was best not to antagonize him.

"Oh, what's the use!" she muttered, whirled on her heel, and went rushing out of the dining room, breakfast forgotten.

When Vannah reached her sitting room, she locked the door and began pacing around the room, twisting her fingers together nervously as her mind reeled from this latest turn of events. Aunt Constance was gone, and she was never coming back. Now there would be no one here to intercede with her father, no one there to comfort her and give her sage advice. Vannah felt as alone and bereft as the day Martin Ash had left her.

But as she continued her pacing Vannah realized two things: her father was a merciless tyrant interested only in having his own way, and she had to escape his domination.

She just had to.

It was as though Constance Travers had never existed.

Vannah awoke one day to find that her aunt's suite had been cleared out and all her belongings packed away and relegated to the attic. When friends came to call, the redoubtable Parkins always informed them that Lady Travers was "not at home." Callers went away mystified, and speculation was soon running rife through New York society that there was more to Constance's departure from the Webb household than appeared on the surface.

Within two weeks of Constance's leaving, members of the Webbs's set took to calling on Vannah herself, hoping to learn the truth, but all went away disappointed as Vannah merely repeated her father's story that Constance had left of her own accord, now that she had raised her niece for her invalid sister. Even *Town Topics* told its eager, curious readers nothing. Gerrold had visited Colonel William d'Alton Mann the day after he had thrown Constance out just to make sure that no breath of scandal ever wafted across the Webb name.

About three weeks after "the incident," as Vannah had taken to calling her aunt's abrupt departure, she was just about to visit the Tiffanys when a boy arrived with a message for her. Vannah tore the envelope open at once and was startled to discover that it was from Aunt Constance.

The note said: "Please call at this address at one o'clock on February 10, and I shall explain everything to you. Love, your aunt."

Within a half hour Vannah was ringing the bell of a charming town house located not far from Central Park. A butler showed her into a tastefully appointed drawing room that smelled of beeswax and hothouse flowers, and two minutes later, none other than Aunt Constance herself walked in, smiling broadly. She looked like a governess in a plain dark blue dress with no ornamentation.

"Aunt Constance!" Vannah cried, throwing herself into her arms and giving her a crushing hug. "I've been so worried about you! You don't know how much I've missed you!" When they parted, Vannah looked around at the drawing room. "Whose house is this and what are you doing here?"

Constance laughed. "My darling niece, bursting with questions. Let me ring for tea and I shall explain everything to you."

After tea was served, Constance told Vannah exactly what had happened between her and Gerrold that night.

Now Vannah looked around again. "So what are you doing in this house?"

"This is the home of Winifred and Jock Grover, my new employers."

Vannah started and her eyes widened. "Employers! Aunt Constance, you haven't hired yourself out as a housekeeper or lady's maid, have you?"

Constance burst out laughing, her eyes filled with mirth. "Good gracious, no! But I have hired myself out to the Grovers as a social adviser."

Vannah had heard of society women who had fallen on hard times who salvaged their dignity by offering to guide brash, newly rich upstarts through New York society's social maze, but she had never dreamed that her own aunt would be reduced to such extremes.

Vannah looked dubious. "Are you sure this is what you want to do, Aunt Constance? I'm sure your friends would let you stay with them for as long as you liked, and I could give you money out of my own allowance."

Constance was shaking her head even before Vannah finished speaking. "No, I wanted to be independent, and this seemed like the best way. Jock Grover is a steel magnate from Cincinnati, Ohio, and he and his wife have been trying to be accepted by New York society for two years now. And I think I can help them—for a generous price, of course. I can show Mrs. Grover how to dress stylishly, how to give a proper dinner party, and how to summer in Newport."

"Well, if this is what you want, Aunt Constance . . ."

"It is. The Grovers are wonderful people and have been kindness itself to me." Constance sipped her tea. "Now, Vannah, tell me how you have been faring through all this."

So, while her aunt listened attentively, Vannah unburdened herself about her fear of her tyrannical father and her fears for her own future.

"I have to get away from him, Aunt Constance. I have to get out of that house before it's too late. I just have to!"

"What about your dream of designing stained glass windows?"

Vannah shrugged ruefully. "I doubt if Father would allow it. I'm sure he plans to marry me off before I'm 21. And without you there as my ally, Aunt Constance . . ."

Constance reached out and patted Vannah reassuringly on the arm. "When the time comes, you will find a way, just as I did."

But Vannah was not so sure.

* * *

Three weeks later Vannah's worst fears were realized.

Her father called her into his study and informed her that he had chosen the man she would marry, no titled European aristocrat this time but an American from their own set, Raymond McGraw. Vannah blanched when she heard the name. Twenty-three-year-old Raymond, for all his good looks and his father's considerable silver fortune, was not considered a "good catch" by any New York society matron, for his love of gambling and fast women were common knowledge. It was rumored that Raymond kept not one but three *petites amies*, and of course there were those stories circulating last year about the real reason one of the McGraw parlor maids had hung herself. The general consensus was that the unlucky woman who married Raymond McGraw was doomed to a life of unhappiness and regret.

Vannah didn't know McGraw except by reputation, yet now, it seemed, she was destined to become his wife whether or not either of them desired it. She knew why, of course. Her father wanted a chunk of the McGraw silver fortune, and Raymond's father wanted the Webb social connections. An even trade in their eyes.

Vannah said nothing when her father made the announcement, but as soon as she was excused, she rushed upstairs, collected examples of her best work, and rushed right over to the Tiffanys'.

There, in his studio, Louis Comfort Tiffany slowly and methodically studied each and every one of Vannah's pieces while she sat on the edge of her chair and twisted her fingers in her lap, nervously awaiting his pronouncement.

Finally, after what seemed like an eternity to Vannah, he sat back and looked at her. "Vannah, I am overwhelmed. These paintings and sketches are excellent."

"Do you really think so?" she cried in elation.

"I wouldn't say so if I didn't mean it."

"It's just that I wasn't sure. I've been drawing in secret for years with only Aunt Constance and . . . one other person to judge the quality of my work. It's difficult to know if one is really good under such circumstances."

"Well, you can put any doubts aside. You are a talented young lady, Vannah." Now he frowned. "I wish you had told me this sooner. All these years you've been coming to my studio and you've never told me that you, yourself, were interested in art?"

"I—I couldn't, Mr. Tiffany," and she proceeded to tell him about her father's decree and its aftermath.

When she was finished, he sighed. "Many people have such foolish notions about art."

Now Vannah moistened her lips and made her request. "Mr. Tiffany, I had a reason for coming here today to show you my drawings." She took a deep breath. "I want to design stained glass windows for you."

His eyes widened in momentary surprise, but he didn't laugh as Vannah feared he might. In fact, he looked quite thoughtful, as though seriously considering her request. Every so often he would pick up one of her paintings and stare at it, then glance back at her as though assessing her determination.

"You realize, of course, that if I did hire you, you wouldn't be designing windows right away. You'd start cutting glass for other designers and assisting them."

"I realize that."

"Well," he said, "you certainly have the artistic skill to be a designer, and as you know, I do employ women at my Corona studio. In fact, one of my best designers is a woman." Now he hesitated. "But what will your family say, Vannah? I'm sure your father has plans for you, and they don't include working for Tiffany and Company."

Vannah smiled. "Leave my father to me, Mr. Tiffany."

He smiled back and extended his hand. "If your father

has no objections to your coming to work for me, then I would be happy to hire you, Vannah."

"Oh, thank you, Mr. Tiffany, thank you!" she cried, pumping his hand. "You've just made a dream come true."

All the way home Vannah's mood swung from elation to uncertainty. Mr. Tiffany would hire her, but there was still her father to contend with, and Vannah knew that he was going to be her greatest obstacle.

Still, Vannah had a plan.

Frances leaned back against her lace-covered pillows with a sigh of defeat. Every day was an uphill battle, and she was so tired of fighting. All she wanted to do was sleep and be left alone.

She closed her eyes. Suddenly she saw herself and Constance as little girls, both wearing identical white organdy dresses as they played on the lawn of their parents' home in New Haven. Their spinster aunt, Lucilla, always bought them identical dresses, even though the Adams sisters were not at all alike, even then.

Frances opened her eyes and the vision vanished. Funny that she should recall long-dead Aunt Lucilla and her identical dresses after all these years. But that's all she remembered these days, fragments of images and memories from her past. She sighed and closed her eyes again, willing another such comforting memory into her mind.

But voices outside her door intruded, and she scowled irritably, wishing them gone. However, the door opened, revealing Edna Ferris.

"I'm sorry to disturb you, Mrs. Webb, but your daughter has requested to see you. I told her that you weren't having one of your good days, but—"

"Tell her I'm not feeling well, Edna," Frances said, closing her eyes again.

Then Savannah's voice boomed out at her from the doorway. "Mother, please! It's very important that I speak to you now. I know you're not feeling well, but I must insist!"

Edna's voice rose in protest. "Miss Webb—!"

"Nurse Ferris! I wish to see my mother now, and—"

"Will the both of you stop it!" Frances grumbled from the bed. "Edna, please leave us. I shall speak to my daughter."

The protective nurse darted Savannah a quick look of disapproval, then left the sickroom, closing the door behind her. Frances looked at her daughter and was surprised to see Savannah walk into the room with what looked like large sheets of paper tucked under one arm. Suddenly another image flashed into Frances's mind, of a large, bright room and a handsome young man holding just such a large sheet of paper. Frances shook her head and the image vanished.

Now Savannah set down her papers, approached the bed, and kissed Frances on the cheek.

"I know you're not feeling well, Mother, but I have something very important to talk to you about, and I hope you'll be able to help me."

"I'm very ill, Savannah. I doubt if I can help you with anything."

"I know that, Mother, but you must try."

"What is it, my angel?"

Vannah drew up a chair and sat down. Since everyone had always left their problems at the door of Frances's sickroom, this was the first time she had ever seen her daughter look troubled, and it was something of a shock. Frances was accustomed to seeing a bright, happy Savannah, not this dispirited creature.

"I don't want to upset you, Mother," Vannah went on, "but I want to go away. I want to leave this house and make a life of my own, just as Aunt Constance is doing. I just can't tolerate Father's tyrannical behavior any longer, and I don't want to marry the man he has chosen for me."

Frances just stared at her daughter. "But if you leave this house, Savannah, where will you go? What will you do?"

Vannah rose and picked up her papers. "I want to design stained glass windows for Louis Comfort Tiffany." Now her face brightened, and the words came tumbling out in an excited rush. "You remember him, Mother. He's the man who designed the window of you and Aunt Constance that is in the parlor downstairs. I went to him today and showed him my paintings, Mother, and he has agreed to hire me."

Frances sat up. "Paintings? What paintings?"

"My paintings, Mother," Vannah replied, setting them atop the bed covers. "With Aunt Constance's help I have been drawing in secret for years."

And while Frances listened, Vannah told her why she had had to paint in secret and the tragic aftermath of her father's accidental discovery of that secret.

As Frances began looking at her daughter's work she thought of Alastair, and tears began forming in her eyes. So their lovely child had inherited his artistic talent as well, and if anything, she was even better than her father. And Gerrold was trying to crush her spirit, to defeat her as he had defeated Frances all those years ago. She felt strength flow through her veins. He may have defeated her, but Frances could not allow him to defeat her daughter. Alastair's daughter.

"So you see, Mother," Vannah went on earnestly, "I have artistic talent. Mr. Tiffany even said so. But I have to find a way to make Father let me go. But you know how he is. His word is law, and if I defy him . . ."

"But what can I do to help you?"

"Reason with him. Perhaps he'll listen to you."

A bitter smile twisted Frances's mouth. Gerrold had never listened to her, never once took her feelings into consideration. No, reasoning would not get Savannah her freedom. But Frances knew something that might if she dared use it. Suddenly she felt dizzy with the power of her knowledge.

"Mother, are you all right?"

Frances nodded, her heart beating so hard, it echoed like thunder throughout her brain. She swallowed hard and moistened her lips.

"Why should Gerrold Webb object to your leaving? You are not his daughter."

The words were spoken so softly that for a moment Vannah thought she had misunderstood them. "What did you say, Mother? I didn't hear you."

"I said, you are not Gerrold Webb's daughter."

Vannah's reaction was swift and instantaneous. "Mother, what are you saying?" She rose and placed her hand over her mother's, which was resting on the top coverlet. "Of course I am Gerrold Webb's daughter. Really, Mother, I think your illness is clouding your mind."

"Don't patronize me!" her mother snapped in a rare show of spirit, and Vannah jerked her hand away. "My mind is as lucid as the day I was born, and I know what I am saying."

Shaking her head in wordless denial, Vannah whirled on her heel and went staggering toward the door when her mother's voice ringing out brought her up short: "Listen to me, Savannah! I can show you how your true parentage will free you of Gerrold Webb forever!"

She was shaking from head to toe, but Vannah forced herself to stop. There would be plenty of time later to think about the ramifications of her mother's startling confession, to wonder about a life that had been a lie. But right now Vannah wanted to hear what her mother had to say. She turned, forced herself to walk back to the bed, and sat down.

"Who—who was my real father?" she asked in a trembling voice.

"His name was Alastair McKechnie," her mother replied, "and he was an artist. I met him shortly after your father—that is to say, my husband, and I returned from our wedding trip to Europe. I was terribly unhappy. I knew that my marriage to Gerrold Webb had been a mistake. And then I met Alastair at the home of a friend— quite an unconventional friend, the sort who invited artists and actors to dinner."

Now Vannah noticed a rare sparkle light her mother's eyes, and even her voice sounded younger, more vibrant. "He wanted to paint my portrait, he said, and I agreed. I knew Gerrold wouldn't approve, so I just didn't tell him. Under the pretext of making morning calls I would go to Alastair's studio."

"Did you love him, Mother?" Vannah asked.

"Oh, yes!" She sighed, blushing like a schoolgirl. "He was so unlike Gerrold. Alastair was loving, warm, witty, gentle, kind . . . All he wanted to do, he said, was please me and make me happy. Gerrold always ordered me about, telling me what to wear, what to do. His favorite saying was that he always knew what was best for me."

Vannah nodded in mute sympathy.

Her mother sighed. "I didn't intend to become Alastair's lover, but under the circumstances, we loved each other too much not to want to give ourselves to each other."

Vannah said, "What happened, Mother? Why aren't you and Alastair together today?"

Frances's faded blue eyes filled with tears. "Gerrold found out about us. He always was so jealous, so suspicious. He had men spying on me and reporting back to him. On the day that I learned I was going to have a child, Alastair and I had planned to run away together. When I arrived at his studio, I found only Gerrold waiting for me."

"Where was my father?" Vannah asked.

"Gone," Frances replied, her lower lip trembling. "Just that morning Gerrold had gone to see him and offered him a huge sum of money to leave the country and never see me again."

"And he took it?" Vannah cried, bolting to her feet. "He sacrificed the woman he loved for Gerrold Webb's money?"

Frances nodded sadly. "He betrayed me. But I can't blame him. We all have our weaknesses, my angel, and I'm sure Gerrold offered him so much money that he would have been a fool to refuse it."

Vannah stormed over to the window, feeling a variety of emotions concerning this Alastair's betrayal.

"Of course, I went back to Gerrold. I had no other choice." Then Frances laughed. "Do you know, he was so arrogant, so sure of his charm, he never once suspected that Alastair and I had been lovers? To this day Gerrold believes that my liaison with Alastair was nothing more than a few innocent trysts, an infatuation never consummated."

Vannah turned. "You mean he's never suspected that I'm another man's child?"

Her mother shook her head. "He's always accepted you as his own. But I know differently. Every time I look at you, my angel, I see another little part of Alastair in you."

Now Vannah understood. "So that's why he forbade me to draw or paint."

"Gerrold is very, very proud. It reminded him of his wife's attraction to another man, an inferior man in his eyes."

Vannah shivered and rubbed her arms for warmth. "Where is my real father now, Mother?"

"Australia, I believe. If he's still alive."

Vannah sighed. "I feel so—so different now, like I'm suddenly somebody else and don't belong here."

Her mother sat up, her voice strong. "You belong here as much as anyone does, Savannah. Gerrold thought of you as his daughter and he raised you as his daughter. Alastair McKechnie helped by conceiving you, that is all. You owe him nothing."

Vannah said, "Why did you decide to tell me about my real father now, Mother? I could have gone through the rest of my life blissfully ignorant of my true parentage."

"You said you wanted your freedom from Gerrold Webb," her mother replied. "Well, I am going to get you that freedom, Savannah. It may be too late for me, but it is not too late for you. I am going to tell you how to turn Gerrold's pride and arrogance against him and to your advantage."

Frances leaned forward. "Listen carefully. Here is what you must do. . . ."

The following morning, after a sleepless night spent tossing and turning, Vannah stood before her father's closed study door and sought the courage to do what had to be done.

She knocked, and when she heard the man she could not help but think of as her father say, "Come in," Vannah took a deep breath to steady her quaking insides and swept into the study.

"I have something of great importance to tell you," she said as she seated herself across from his desk.

Gerrold didn't even glance up from the papers he was reading. "Then be quick about it because I have to leave for a meeting in fifteen minutes."

Vannah opened her mouth to speak and almost lost her nerve. Then she gave herself a little mental shake. If she wanted her freedom, the words must be said.

"I am not going to marry Raymond McGraw. I am going to go to work for the Tiffany Glass and Decorating Company."

Now Gerrold's head came up, and he scowled at her. "What did you say?"

"You heard me." Her knees may have been knocking together, but Vannah felt oddly calm and in control of a confrontation with her father for the first time in her life.

Now Gerrold rose, placed his hands on the desk, and leaned forward so that his face was a mere three feet away from Vannah's. "How dare you speak to your father in that tone of voice!"

"But you are not my father. My real father is Alastair McKechnie, my mother's lover. I am his daughter, not yours."

Once the words were spoken, time seemed to stop in the quiet study. Even the clock on the mantel appeared to cease ticking as Vannah and Gerrold stared at each other. Gerrold looked as though he had just been kicked by a horse.

Finally, with a strangled sound of rage, he reared back. "What are you talking about? Who told you such a monstrous lie?"

"Oh, it's not a lie," Vannah said with a calmness she was far from feeling. "Mother told me so herself, and she should know. Alastair McKechnie was her lover—and my father."

Gerrold breathed heavily through his nose, his nostrils flaring. "Why are you telling me this?"

Now Vannah stood up, placed her hands on the desk, and leaned forward in imitation of him. "I want my freedom. I will not marry Raymond McGraw, and you will not object to my going to work for Mr. Tiffany."

Gerrold's eyes narrowed and he shook his head. "I have raised you as my daughter, and by God, I'll see you married as my daughter!"

Suddenly any sympathy Vannah might have had for him vanished in an instant. Her lip curled in contempt as she backed away from the desk. "You don't care about me at all, do you? All you're concerned about is marrying me into the McGraw silver fortune! Well, I won't be a pawn in your games any longer!"

"And just what do you propose to do about it? You're still not twenty-one and legally my responsibility."

Now the game had begun in deadly earnest. Vannah said, "If you refuse to give me my freedom, I will go to Colonel William d'Alton Mann myself. I'm sure he'd like nothing better than to spread the delectable bit of scandal that Gerrold Webb is not my real father."

"That's blackmail."

"I learned from the master."

Gerrold smiled. "I can pay the colonel whatever it takes to keep such an item from ever seeing print. I've done it before."

Vannah felt her cheeks grow hot. "You think you can buy your way out of anything, don't you? Well, not this time. Even if you manage to buy the colonel's silence, I will make an announcement of my illegitimacy at the engagement party. I will tell everyone I know that I am not your daughter."

"So tell them."

Vannah played her final hand. "You mean that you won't mind Alva Vanderbilt and Caroline Astor knowing that the great Gerrold Webb was cuckolded by a penniless artist? That his wife preferred another man to him?" She laughed then. "I think not."

As she watched, Gerrold's face went from deathly pale to dark scarlet, and he looked at her with such loathing in his pale, cold eyes that for a moment Vannah thought he would round the desk and strangle her with his bare hands. But all he did was say, "I'm going up to see your mother." And he left.

He stayed but a mere ten minutes, and when he emerged, he looked like a man who had just lost every last penny of his fortune.

"All right," he said through tight white lips. "Name your price."

"I don't want money from you. I just want my freedom. And permission to see Mother whenever I please."

"You'll need money to live on. At least let me—"

"I said I don't want money from you, not one red cent. I don't want to owe you anything."

"There will be a scandal."

"You're creative in your own way. You'll think of something to explain my departure."

Then she left without ever saying good-bye to the man who had once been her father. Three bags were already packed and waiting in the foyer. Since she had already said her good-byes to her mother, she left without another word to anyone and went directly to the Tiffanys' to begin her new life.

Chapter Twelve

New York—1894

VANNAH WAS BEGINNING to wonder if she had made the biggest mistake of her life.

In the four months that had passed since she joined the Tiffany Glass and Decorating Company, all she had done, day after interminable day, was practice cutting clear sheets of plain window glass into various shapes. Oh, even she had to admit that she was improving noticeably. Her hand no longer ached from using the glass cutter, an instrument resembling a pen with a block containing a cutting diamond called a "spark" at one end. And she had learned to listen to the glass as she cut it. If it made a decided scratch, Vannah knew that the cut would be a poor one, but if she heard a discernible ripping sound, the glass would break smooth and clean.

After the piece of glass was cut, Vannah had to free it from the main sheet. Straight cuts could simply be broken off, but curved cuts caused Vannah much consternation. This process involved tapping the back of the section with the block of the diamond cutter. Just the right amount of pressure had to be used, not too much and not too little, otherwise the glass would break off into useless, jagged pieces. Vannah had lost count of all the pieces she had ruined when she first began.

But now she was becoming impatient and bored.

It had all seemed so exciting that cold day in February

when she had left Gerrold Webb's house forever to pursue her dream. She had stayed with the Tiffanys just until she could get herself settled in an all-female boarding house within walking distance of the Tiffany Furnaces in Corona, the small Long Island town where they were located. At first Vannah feared reprisals against the Tiffanys for their part in her escape, but much to her relief, Gerrold Webb did nothing.

And she would never forget her first day at work, when she felt like she was on the threshold of an exciting adventure.

Mr. Tiffany, himself, had escorted her on a tour of the studios and furnaces, which, to Vannah's astonishment, were larger than she had ever imagined and divided into different departments. There was a glass shop, where glaziers were assembling windows, and a mosaic shop for the creation of mosaic crosses for churches and architectural friezes. There was even a woodworking shop where special frames for the windows were made.

But of special interest to Vannah was the design department, where men and several women designers sat at long tables scattered with watercolor sketches of window designs or full-size paper patterns Vannah later learned were called "cartoons." How she hungered to be one of the designers' number, yet she realized that there was much she had to learn before that day ever arrived.

But, as she sat at her table, tapping out yet another meaningless piece of glass, Vannah wondered if that day would ever come.

She sighed.

"What's the matter, Vannah?" the brown-haired girl sitting next to her asked. "You sound a bit discouraged."

"I am, Prudence. I would like to do something else besides cut glass all day."

The heavy-set young woman seated at a table in front of

Vannah's turned in her chair and glared out of beady eyes. "So would we all, Miss Webb, but no one here expects to become a designer overnight."

"Oh, leave her alone, Jessie," Prudence retorted. "If you spent more time worrying about your own affairs instead of minding everyone else's, perhaps you'd be a designer yourself today."

Grumbling to herself, Jessie turned around and continued cutting glass.

"Thank you, Prudence," Vannah muttered under her breath.

Her friend leaned over and whispered, "Don't you pay Jessie any mind. Before you came, she submitted some watercolor sketches to Mr. Tiffany and asked to join the design department. But he said she wasn't ready."

"That explains her hostility toward me," Vannah said.

Vannah's spirits plummeted even lower. Not only was she bored, she knew that many of the other young women in her department resented her. They were all graduates of art schools in America and Europe, and many of them had been cutting glass for years. And suddenly Miss Savannah Webb had come into their midst, a wealthy debutante with no formal art training whatsoever, a personal friend of Mr. Tiffany's who was being escorted around the studios as if she were the Queen of England. Who could blame anyone for dismissing her as a dilettante?

Vannah clenched her teeth in determination. Well, she would just have to work harder than anyone here to prove that she deserved to be taken seriously.

She picked up her cutter and went back to work.

The following day was the alternate Saturday Vannah didn't have to work, and she rose early, for Aunt Constance had just returned from Europe with her employers and was coming to visit.

Today, as every morning, Vannah heated her own bathwater on the kitchen stove, hauled it upstairs herself, and poured it into a large, white-enameled pan that sat on the floor. As she stepped into the water and began soaping her body with harsh white soap, she yearned for the luxury of a long, leisurely soak in a real bathtub with scented water up to her chin and a large, fragrant cake of glycerin soap to perfume her skin. At least it wasn't winter. Bathing this way in winter was worse than torture.

"Well, my girl, you wanted your freedom, and this is one of the prices you must pay," she reminded herself as she rinsed, shivered, and scrubbed herself dry with a thin, scratchy towel that left red marks on her white skin.

She smiled in triumph as she slipped into her fine lawn camisole and pantaloons, all trimmed with delicate embroidery and so soft after the harsh towel. She may have had to leave all her beautiful Worth gowns behind, but at least she had kept her frilly, expensive underclothes to make her feel pampered and feminine.

After dressing in the long dark skirt and crisp white blouse that had become her uniform, Vannah went downstairs, ate breakfast with her landlady and the three other boarders, then went back to her room to read some dog-eared copies of an English art magazine called *The Studio*, which Prudence had loaned her.

About two hours later there came a knock on Vannah's door, and when she opened it, there stood her aunt.

"Aunt Constance!" Vannah cried, flinging herself into the other woman's arms for a breathless, crushing hug. "How wonderful to see you!"

When they parted, Constance said, "And how wonderful it is to see you, Vannah. You don't know how I've missed you!"

"Come in, come in." Vannah drew her inside, adding, "Well, what do you think of my new living quarters?"

Constance looked around, taking in the narrow iron bed painted white, the battered chest of drawers with several pulls missing, the blue wallpaper so faded that the design was indiscernible. "It's . . . rather spartan, don't you think?"

Vannah laughed. "You needn't be so kind. After what I've been accustomed to, it's like living in a jail cell. But at least it's clean, very cheap, and close to where I work. And all the other boarders are women also, so I don't have to fear being molested by some strange man."

Constance wrinkled her nose in distaste. "And you really don't mind living this way?"

"When my alternative was marrying Raymond McGraw against my will and tolerating Father's tyranny, yes, I don't mind living this way," Vannah declared stoutly, and meant it.

"It's just that you've always been used to luxury, Vannah," Constance was saying. "You've always had servants to tend to your every want and need, fine food, fine clothes. You've never had to worry about money."

Vannah nodded. "You're right, Aunt Constance. I have been pampered and sheltered. But now I'm learning to do for myself. I do miss having Maeve arrange my hair, but I've found that I can put it up in a simple Psyche knot myself. I also miss having my own horse to ride and a carriage at my beck and call, but," Vannah added with a shrug, "I have my freedom. That's very important to me."

"Perhaps you should have taken some money from Gerrold," Constance said.

Vannah shook her head vehemently. "No! I may have blackmailed him into giving me my freedom, but I wasn't about to take any money."

Constance sighed. "Well, as long as you're happy, Vannah . . ."

"I am, Aunt Constance."

"Truly?"

"Truly. Please don't feel sorry for me or think that I've come down in the world."

Constance sighed. "Well, if you insist . . . Now, I have a special treat for you. Since you are free for the entire weekend, the Grovers have invited you to spend it with us."

"Oh, Aunt Constance, I couldn't impose."

"Nonsense. You mustn't offend them by refusing. They are wonderful people, Vannah. You'll like them, I promise." Constance arched one brow. "Unless, of course, you fear that you'll be corrupted by exposure to luxury once again."

Vannah laughed. "Don't be silly. Just let me pack a few things and I'll be right with you."

When they were seated in the Grovers' large, comfortable carriage, Vannah said, "And how was Europe, Aunt Constance?"

"Just wonderful," she replied, her smoky eyes sparkling. "I got Mrs. Grover completely outfitted at Worth's. Poor Winifred wanted to buy all of the latest fashions, but I warned her that she mustn't be the first to wear a new style if she wants to be accepted in society."

"Good advice," Vannah murmured. She looked out the window at passing houses, and her voice had a faraway yearning to it as she said, "And did you get a chance to visit England while you were there?"

"No, Vannah, I'm afraid not," Constance replied.

Vannah was silent for a moment. "And will you be going to Newport next month?"

Constance shook her head. "The Grovers spent last summer—or part of last summer, I should say—in Newport, and it was an unmitigated disaster. They rented a mansion and began giving parties. People can be so cruel. Everyone regarded them as interlopers and no one came. Mr. Grover wasn't invited to join the Reading Room or the Casino

Club, and one day poor Winifred and the children were turned away from Bailey's Beach. Can you imagine the humiliation? They returned to New York before July was even over. I've advised them to avoid Newport like the plague until they're sure of acceptance there."

Vannah made a soft sound of sympathy for the Grovers. In all the years she and her family had summered in Newport, she had taken acceptance for granted. But she found herself wondering how she would fare now if she ever returned there. Would people still receive her in their homes now that she was a bohemian artist?

"Well, perhaps someone like Alva Vanderbilt will take them up."

"That would be my fondest wish," Constance said with a sigh.

"So, if they are not going to Newport, where will your employers be spending the summer?" Vannah asked.

Constance smiled and patted her hand. "They've taken a house right here on Long Island, so I'll be able to visit you frequently."

"Oh, Aunt Constance, that's wonderful!"

Constance looked at her niece. "Have you seen Frances lately?"

Vannah's face clouded. "I try to see her as often as I can, but usually she's too sick to have visitors. And if I try to stay, she sends me away. She knows I can't stand to be in the same house as Gerrold. So I write her letters."

Constance just shook her head.

Vannah sighed. "I wish she could have come with me."

"She couldn't, Vannah. You understand why, don't you?"

"She said it was too late for her."

"First of all, Gerrold never would have allowed it. Too many people would have asked too many questions, and a scandal would have resulted. Also, you can barely support yourself, my girl. How would you support an invalid mother as well?"

"I understand."

But at least Vannah had escaped, and she resolved to remain free so her mother's sacrifice wouldn't be in vain.

Vannah's weekend with the Grovers was like a journey back into the past. Once again she luxuriated in hot, scented bathwater up to her chin and slept in embroidered sheets of fine French percale, so smooth and silky against her skin. She ate delectable meals prepared by the Grovers' French chef and served on translucent bone china and eaten with sterling silver utensils. She drank fine wine from sparkling crystal goblets. But she especially enjoyed horseback riding in Central Park, even though several people she had once known snubbed her as they went riding or driving past.

Vannah adored her host and hostess. Jock Grover was a bluff, down-to-earth man who usually said what was on his mind and said it so all could hear. It was obvious that he worshiped his beautiful, dark-eyed wife, Winifred. Vannah found her to be so charming, warm, and unaffected that she wondered why New York society was so reluctant to accept them. Their two children, Robert and Amy, were obviously so doted upon by both parents that Vannah couldn't help feel a little envious of them.

By the time Sunday afternoon rolled around, both she and the Grovers had taken each other to their hearts, and she regretted leaving such an open, bighearted family.

But she longed to get back to work. This was her life now, a life she was determined to make successful.

As the summer slipped away and fall began, Vannah was still practicing cutting window glass. But then came the day she had longed for, the day that told her she had not made the biggest mistake of her life.

One morning in early October Vannah was concentrating so hard on the task before her that she failed to notice that the women's glass department had gotten unusually quiet.

Suddenly a voice said, "Miss Savannah Webb?"

She looked up to see Agnes Northrop, who, along with Frederick Wilson and Edward Peck Sperry, was one of Tiffany's best designers.

"Yes, Miss Northrop?"

The woman smiled. "Will you please follow me? I need some assistance with a window."

Vannah's hand flew to her heart in startled surprise. "Me?"

"Yes, if you are Savannah Webb."

"I am, I am," Vannah babbled, unable to believe her good fortune. She rose excitedly, ignored Jessie's glare of envy, and just had time to smile at Prudence before she was falling in step with Miss Northrop.

"I don't understand," Vannah said as they walked along. "What is it you want me to do?"

"Mr. Tiffany has told us that he thinks you display enough artistic talent to become a designer. But, before you can become one, you have to know a great deal about the construction of a stained glass window. So, from now on you shall assist me."

Vannah could hardly contain her excitement. "What will my duties be?"

"First you will cut glass for my window. Then, when Mr. Tiffany feels you're ready, you'll design a window yourself."

When they reached Miss Northrop's table in the design department, she leafed through several sketches and pulled one out. "The window we shall work on first is a small portrait window."

She handed the watercolor sketch to Vannah, who studied it with keen interest. The subject was a pretty young woman with a soft, sweet smile, only her head and shoulders visible in the drawing. Surrounding her was a border of blue morning glories.

"Since we work primarily with architects," Miss Northrop explained, "our designs must be approved by them, their patrons, and Mr. Tiffany himself. We do everything in our power to please them, and if that means submitting several designs, so be it."

Tiffany's desire to satisfy his customers was well known, and it was one of the main reasons he was so successful. If a customer preferred to have a painting copied into glass, that's what he got. There were even teams of technicians who would travel anywhere in the world to install a finished window for a customer.

First Miss Northrop showed Vannah the portrait window's full-size cartoon, then they went to select glass from the thousands of numbered sheets stored in the cellar. That done, they returned to the design department where Miss Northrop cut up the cartoon and positioned the pieces on a clear glass easel on which black lead lines were drawn. The easel was then positioned before a window so light would illuminate it from behind.

Satisfied, Miss Northrop said, "Now, let's cut glass and I'll show you how a stained glass window is made."

And for the next week Vannah did just that. Miss Northrop would give Vannah a number, and she would run to the cellars and retrieve the corresponding sheet of glass. Then she would hold it up to the light, and Miss Northrop would study it and tell Vannah which part of the glass she wished to use. The pieces of the cartoon then became paper patterns, showing Vannah which shapes to cut. When the individual piece was cut and any rough edges smoothed, it was adhered to the easel with a dollop of beeswax.

Finally, when the subject's features were painted on glass and fired, all of the pieces of the puzzle finally came together on the glass easel. With the light shining through the true beauty of the glass was revealed.

"It's—it's beautiful!" Vannah gasped in awe, standing back to admire what she had helped to create.

"Oh, we're not done yet," Miss Northrop said briskly. "Now it goes to the glazier to be set in the lead cames and then to the cementer's table."

Finally the window was finished. All of the other designers came by to inspect it and offer their congratulations to both Miss Northrop and Vannah. Even Mr. Tiffany himself came by to see their handiwork.

"A fine piece of work, Miss Northrop," he said, his eyes sparkling. "And you, too, Miss Webb. You did very well on your first assignment."

"Thank you, sir," Vannah said.

But in truth Vannah felt that she had played only a very small part in the creation of the window. All she had done was cut the glass to Miss Northrop's exacting specifications. Until she had seen a designer at work, she had never really understood the high degree of skill necessary to create a window.

In the weeks to follow, Vannah became Miss Northrop's rapt pupil. She listened carefully and watched intently, eager to learn. When she had a free moment, she would observe the other designers at work or go down into the cellars to familiarize herself with the glass itself.

As she removed sheet after sheet from its slot to study it, Vannah was amazed at the innumerable shades of glass, both clear, opalescent, and iridescent. Her favorite was the mottled glass with its vibrant two-color combinations.

She soon became a familiar sight at the furnaces themselves, though the heat and odor of chemicals kept her from lingering too long. And while the glassblowers were fascinating as they created Mr. Tiffany's newest invention of Favrile glass, Vannah was more interested in the men making window glass.

Vannah would watch in awe as a glassworker, wearing thick asbestos gloves and holding tongs, began to make drapery glass. First he would throw molten glass onto an iron table, then begin molding and working it as a baker would knead dough, shaping and twisting it until it fell into folds. When finished in many colors and various degrees of translucencies, drapery glass would be used for the figures' vestments in religious windows.

On other occasions the glassmakers would scatter irregular bits of glass on the iron table, then pour molten glass on top of it. After the mass was rolled and cooled, it became what was known as fractured glass.

Each time Vannah saw glass being made, she tried to think of the ways in which she could use such glass in her own windows.

She was so absorbed in her new world that she seldom thought of the one she had left. But soon it was Christmas, and that former world intruded once again.

Before Vannah went to the Grovers', where she had been invited to spend the Christmas holidays along with Aunt Constance, she stopped at the Webb brownstone to see her mother and wish her a Merry Christmas. Except for a balsam wreath on the door, the house was dark and inhospitable, and with Frances so weak and tired, it was a brief, sad visit that upset Vannah.

In sharp contrast, the moment Vannah walked into the Grovers' house, she was suddenly enveloped in a palpable warmth that had nothing to do with the huge fire snapping cheerfully away. She saw it in the radiant smile of welcome from Winifred Grover and her two children, Robert and Amy, heard it in Jock Grover's boisterous, hearty laugh, felt it in Aunt Constance's hug. Even the maids and footmen coming in and out of the room had warm smiles and wishes of "Merry Christmas, miss" for their guest.

The evening passed much too quickly for Vannah. The towering, fragrant spruce tree swallowing up one corner of the parlor was decorated too soon and the splendid dinner consumed too quickly. Before anyone knew it, Robert and Amy were nodding off and had to be taken up to bed. That left just the four adults, who set about exchanging gifts.

The Grovers were delighted with the watercolor sketches Vannah had made of the children, and she protested that the blouses they had given her were much too extravagant. Still, Vannah was delighted with them and with the warm nightgowns and cakes of scented glycerin soap from Aunt Constance.

By the time Vannah, herself, went upstairs to bed, she knew she had spent the most memorable Christmas Eve of her life. All it needed was Martin Ash to be perfect.

Later that night, long after both children and adults were tucked away in their beds, Vannah was still wide-awake.

After several unsuccessful attempts to fall asleep she rose, wrapped the comforter from the bed around her, and curled up in the high-backed wing chair. The only source of light in the darkened room was the orange glow emanating from the coals in the grate.

Vannah hated the vast, endless emptiness of the night. Its total stillness and absence of activity afforded her too much time to think. She liked to fill her waking hours by working herself long and hard at the studio, then, when she returned to Mrs. O'Neill's boardinghouse, occupy her mind with reading or still more designing. Sleep came easily then, and there was not a second in the day to spare for Martin Ash.

But on nights like tonight, when sleep wouldn't come, he haunted her until she could think of nothing else.

Suddenly his face materialized out of the darkness and flickered before her eyes.

"No!" Vannah cried, burrowing deeper beneath the coverlet as though she could find refuge there. But no matter how tightly she screwed her eyes shut, his face refused to go away. She could clearly see his scarred cheek, the eyes bright and glittering like emeralds, imprisoning her will again, sapping her strength to resist.

Her head lolled back and her lips parted. "Martin!" The tortured whispering of his name echoed through the quiet room as though it could summon him out of another woman's arms and across the sea to her.

When Vannah opened her eyes, he was there in the room with her, smiling, drawing her into his arms again. She felt enveloped by the heat rising from him as she pressed herself shamelessly against him, felt his warm, sweet mouth devouring hers rapaciously, and she groaned in response. The room teetered and spun out of control, bright orange embers dancing behind her eyes as her desire rose to meet his. Martin's kisses fell like fiery snowflakes against her forehead, eyelids, cheeks, and throat, each branding her. She tossed her head from side to side as though seeking to escape him, but even as her fingers rushed to unbutton the buttons down the front of her flannel nightgown, she knew that there was no escape. When his lips grazed the tops of her breasts, Vannah arched toward him with a cry of anticipation and expectation.

Suddenly the relentless chiming of a clock shook Vannah out of her dreamlike state.

"Martin?" she cried out eagerly.

But as she dazedly looked around the room she realized that it was empty. She was alone. There was no one in the room with her.

Vannah sat there, her coverlet slipping down to the floor, an aching loss growing in her heart.

"A dream," she muttered in bitter disappointment as she buttoned up her nightgown. "It was only a stupid dream."

The clock had chimed the midnight hour. Christmas Day found Vannah sobbing as though her heart were being broken all over again.

Chapter Thirteen

New York—1895

THE FOLLOWING APRIL, Vannah was cutting a section of mottled glass when Miss Northrop suddenly looked over at her and said, "I think it's time."

"Time for what, Miss Northrop?"

"Why, time for you to try your hand at designing a window, Savannah."

Vannah started, sending her cutter skittering off course with a grating screech of protest. She looked up at the other woman with an expression of disbelief. "Me? Design a window? Do you mean it, Miss Northrop?"

She smiled. "I wouldn't have said it if I didn't mean it. No, during the months you've been assisting me, I've been watching you carefully, Savannah. We've all been watching you carefully. And we all agree that you work hard, learn quickly, and seem to have a true understanding of glass."

Vannah flushed with pleasure. "Thank you, Miss Northrop."

"I am to meet with some people this afternoon about a design for a church window," she said. "I'd like you to accompany me."

After meeting with several church elders to determine their needs, Vannah returned to her department to work on her first design. She wasn't surprised when both Miss Northrop and Mr. Tiffany rejected her depiction of the Christ child, but she was when they rejected her second design two days later, for Vannah had poured her soul into the sketch of St. Peter guarding the gates of Heaven. However, panic didn't set in until Mr. Tiffany rejected a third design featuring several angels, and he called her into his office.

Vannah tried not to cry when she closed the door behind her and turned to face him. "I know I'm a failure as a designer and that I'm to be dismissed."

Tiffany smiled gently. "Now, Savannah, wherever did you get the idea that you were going to be dismissed?"

"But—but this is the third design you've rejected."

He indicated a seat for her. "I merely called you here to offer a suggestion, to guide you in another direction."

Vannah could have slid off her chair in relief. Her career wasn't over. She said a mental prayer of thanks.

"Quite frankly your Biblical figures are less than inspiring, but the landscape in the foreground and background is excellent," he said. "I would suggest that you do a design for a landscape window instead."

Vannah wrinkled her brow in puzzlement. "But the other designers have told me that many church officials prefer scenes from the Scriptures rather than secular themes."

Tiffany's blue eyes twinkled. "Then you must make your landscape window full of deep religious symbolism. Go through your Bible, Savannah. I'm sure you'll find suitable inspiration there. Remember, infinite, endless labor makes the masterpiece."

That evening, back at the boardinghouse, she did just that and worked until past midnight on yet another design that finally won Tiffany's enthusiastic approval the next day. And when the church elders expressed their dismay that her design wasn't a Biblical figure window, Vannah solemnly explained that her lush landscape of flowers and trees was entitled "The Earth is the Lord's and the Fullness thereof." They went away pleased and satisfied.

Her design accepted, Vannah suddenly found herself in charge. Since she would be selecting the glass this time, she needed someone to cut for her, so she chose Prudence. They worked together under the careful guidance and watchful eye of Miss Northrop, who, Vannah was pleased to note, only disagreed with her choice of glass three times during the building of the window.

Finally Vannah's first window was done.

All the other designers gathered around to admire it and offer their congratulations, and as Vannah stood before it, admiring the way the strong light illuminated each piece of glass like a jewel, she knew a satisfaction she had never known. This is what she had been born to do: create windows of beauty.

In the weeks to come, Vannah was given more windows to design, several portrait windows, and two rather large memorial landscape windows. By the time the summer ended, she was accorded full designer status, with an increase in salary and greater responsibilities.

Yet Vannah's artistic triumph was to be overshadowed by unexpected tragedy.

One morning in September, just an hour after Vannah arrived at work, she was startled to see none other than Aunt Constance come rushing into the design department.

Just one look at her aunt's white, pinched face told Vannah that something was dreadfully wrong.

She rose to her feet and, without a word of greeting, said, "Something has happened to Mother."

Constance closed her eyes and nodded. "She's dying, Vannah. I just received word from Gerrold an hour ago, and I came as fast as I could. She wants to see us before—before . . ." She couldn't finish.

Vannah just stood there in a daze while the rest of the room fell silent. Her mother was dying. At the moment they were nothing more than words without meaning. Later she would feel the pain behind that simple sentence, but right now she could feel nothing at all.

She told Prudence to tell Mr. Tiffany her reason for leaving so abruptly, then she and Aunt Constance hurried to catch the train.

They said little to each other on the way over, but by the time they arrived at the Webb brownstone, the reality of the situation had finally penetrated Vannah's numbed brain, and she was trying to steel herself for the upcoming ordeal.

As soon as Constance and Vannah arrived, they went upstairs to Frances's suite. Vannah barely glanced at Gerrold and Nurse Ferris as she went sailing past them in the sitting room. But when Vannah saw her mother lying on her narrow bed in the darkened room, she broke down.

"Mother?" she said through her tears as she took the cold, skeletal hand in her own. "It's Vannah."

Frances was so wasted away, she was as small and fragile as a child. But her eyes still held a bright spark of life.

She turned her head slowly and smiled with great effort. "Savannah, my angel. You came."

"Of course I came, Mother." She reached out and gently stroked her mother's dry cheek. "Nothing could keep me away. You know that." When Frances fought to speak, Vannah said, "Please, Mother, don't try to talk. Save your strength."

The smile faded, and she clutched at Vannah's hand. "There is no time. There are things I must know before I die."

"Mother, you're not going to die. You're—"

"Was it worth it?" she demanded, straining to raise her head from the pillow but failing and falling back. "I must know, Savannah. Please."

Vannah swallowed hard to keep her voice from trembling. "Yes, Mother, it was. You know I am a designer for Mr. Tiffany now, and you should see the beautiful stained glass windows I create. You would be so proud of me!"

Frances smiled wanly and sighed. "Then it was worth telling my secret to help you escape. I never escaped. Didn't have the courage. I just . . . retreated from life. Too painful. Hid myself away. Now it's too late. What a waste."

Suddenly the fire seemed to dim in Frances's eyes, and she rallied against it. "Never retreat, my angel. Don't make my mistakes." She spoke softly, slowly, as if each word were an obstacle she had to overcome.

Vannah was crying harder now, the tears streaming down her face. "I won't, Mother. I promise."

"You mustn't weep for me." With the last of her strength Frances raised her hand to touch Vannah's wet cheek with her fingertips. "My little angel," she whispered before her hand fell away.

"Perhaps one day in the spring, when you're better, I can take you to the Tiffany Studios and show you how I make a window. Would you like that, Mother?" When Vannah looked down, she saw that her mother's eyes were closed and her expression one of peace. Since she was sleeping, Vannah patted her hand, kissed her on the cheek, and tiptoed out into the sitting room.

"She's just dozing," Vannah announced to those assembled. "Aunt Constance, perhaps you can see her when she wakes up."

Nurse Ferris and Gerrold Webb exchanged looks, then went into the bedroom, only to emerge just seconds later.

"Frances is dead," Gerrold said.

Vannah shook her head and ignored the pitying looks. "Mother is only sleeping. And when she is better, I'm going to take her for a tour of the Tiffany Studios so she can see how I make stained glass windows."

Aunt Constance came forward and took her in her arms. "I'm so, so sorry, Savannah."

Vannah pushed her away. "What is there to be sorry for? I told you, Mother is just sleeping." She looked from her aunt to Gerrold and finally to Nurse Ferris. "She can't be dead," she wailed in disbelief. "Mother can't be dead!"

Now she flung herself in her aunt's arms and vented her deep grief.

Much later, after Vannah had had a chance to compose herself, she was sitting in the downstairs parlor, staring at the portrait window of her mother and aunt when Gerrold came into the room.

As she watched him out of the corner of her eye she realized that they had been estranged for nearly a year and a half. Then she turned her head to look at him, to study him to see if he had changed. She was somewhat dismayed to discover that he hadn't. If anything, he looked more vigorous, leaner, his face newly bronzed by a season of bright Newport sun. She had hoped that his treatment of her and Aunt Constance would somehow appear on his face as lines of bitterness, but there were none.

"Savannah?" he said.

She rose and turned to face him, wondering what she would see in the depths of his pale, cold eyes. Pain? Sorrow? Remorse? But all she saw was wariness and reserve.

"Yes?" she said.

"If you wish to remain here until after the funeral, a guest room will be readied for you."

"That is most generous of you," she said with more sarcasm that she had intended, "but I shall be staying with Aunt Constance."

"As you wish," he said, turning to leave. He obviously did not want to remain in her presence any longer than necessary. Her next words brought him up short.

"Did you ever really love my mother, Gerrold?"

He turned. "As difficult as this may be for you to believe, Savannah, I did love Frances once. Before she betrayed me."

"Oh, yes, I had forgotten," Vannah muttered savagely. "You see everyone in relation to what they do for you or to you." She rounded the settee and approached him. "And what about what you do to others, Gerrold, or doesn't that matter?" Vannah was trembling so hard, she found it difficult to speak. "You cruel, inhuman monster . . . I'll never forgive you for what you did to Mother. Never!"

She lunged at him then, with fists upraised, but he was ready for her and merely caught her wrists before she could strike him and deflected the blow.

"You're hysterical, Savannah," he hissed. "This house is in mourning, and if you can't conduct yourself with the proper respect and decorum, then kindly leave."

And he whirled on his heel and left before she could gather her strength to strike again.

Vannah returned to the boardinghouse immediately after the funeral three days later.

She loathed the hypocrisy of standing and sitting by Gerrold's side during the wake and in church for the funeral services, everyone pretending that they were a loving family. The only way Vannah came through the trying ordeal was to remember her mother's dying words to her: never to retreat from life. Somehow, just the fact that Vannah had escaped from Gerrold and was doing what she wanted was living proof that her mother hadn't died in vain. She comforted herself with that thought as mourner after faceless mourner passed before her with soft words of sympathy.

Finally it was over, and she was on the next train back to the Tiffany Studios where she plunged into her work with renewed vigor, despite Mr. Tiffany's advice to take as much time off as was necessary. But Vannah felt that her work was a tribute to her mother as well, and she strove to perfect her craft.

Then, one day several weeks later, Vannah received quite a different legacy from her late mother.

When she returned to the boardinghouse, weary after an especially long and tiring day, Vannah was surprised to find a visitor waiting to speak with her.

As she walked into Mrs. O'Neill's front parlor, a small, dapper gentleman with spectacles and thinning dark hair jumped to his feet and said dubiously, "Might you be Miss Savannah Webb?"

"Yes, I am Savannah Webb."

His brown eyes flicked over her, and he seemed surprised by her in some way. "My name is Peabody, Nathaniel Peabody, of Hawthorn, Hawthorn, and Peabody."

She recognized the name as belonging to the law firm handling all of Gerrold Webb's legal matters.

"Mr. Peabody . . . how do you do?" And she extended her hand. "To what do I owe the pleasure of your visit?"

He stared at her outstretched hand, started, then shook it. "I'm here on business, Miss Webb."

Vannah's smile died, and she stiffened. "What business could Gerrold Webb possibly have with me, Mr. Peabody?"

"Oh, this has nothing to do with your father, Miss

Webb," the young man said apologetically as he rummaged through his valise. "I'm here concerning the estate of your late mother, Mrs. Frances Glessing Adams Webb."

Vannah stared at him in astonishment. "My late mother's estate? Mr. Peabody, my mother was an invalid for some twenty years. Everything she has belongs to her husband."

Mr. Peabody pushed his spectacles back onto the bridge of his nose. "As much as I detest arguing with a lady, Miss Webb, especially one as"—he blushed—"lovely as yourself, I must tell you that you are wrong."

When he looked longingly at the divan he had just vacated, Vannah realized that she had been keeping him standing, so she indicated the divan for him and seated herself across from him.

"It appears that when your mother was first married, she received a gift of several thousand dollars from a maiden aunt living in Boston. Your father, being a wealthy man, let her keep the money. She, in turn, deposited it with a banker friend, who, over the years, had invested it for her."

Mr. Peabody sat back. "Well, over the years, this small account was forgotten and continued to grow. Your mother left a will with her friend that in the event of her death the money was to go to her daughter, Savannah."

Vannah raised her brows. "I never knew my mother even had a will."

"Neither did your father," Mr. Peabody said. "He was most surprised when it came to light, as were we all."

"And just how much is my inheritance worth, Mr. Peabody?"

"Approximately thirteen thousand dollars, Miss Webb."

Vannah sat up straight, as though someone had suddenly slapped her between the shoulder blades.

"Thirteen thousand dollars? Are you quite sure, Mr. Peabody?"

He grinned. "Quite sure, Miss Webb."

Vannah rose and placed her hands up to her burning cheeks. "That's—that's quite a fortune, Mr. Peabody."

"Well, compared with your father's holdings, it's not quite a fortune, but—"

"Oh, it is quite a fortune to me, Mr. Peabody," Vannah said.

Her mind was whirling so fast, she felt a little dizzy. Thirteen thousand dollars! Whatever would she, a stained glass window designer, do with all that money? Well, there would be time enough to decide what to do with it. Right now all Vannah could think about was her mother.

She may have been an invalid, her world bounded by four walls and medicine bottles, but Frances Webb had had enough presence of mind to think of the future for her daughter. And she had outwitted her husband in the end.

Vannah smiled at Mr. Peabody. "Tell me, sir, what was Gerrold's—my father's—reaction when he learned of this?"

"Quite frankly he embarrassed us all by flying into a proper rage. I was quite surprised by his behavior. He claimed that the will was invalid, but we found it perfectly legal and in order."

So Frances had had the last laugh after all.

Vannah smiled and asked Mr. Peabody to stay for supper, but the flustered young man declined. When he left to return to New York, Vannah went upstairs to write Aunt Constance a note telling her of her good fortune.

Vannah wasn't looking forward to Christmas this year.

It would be her first Christmas since her mother's death, and all she really wanted to do was spend it alone, in the boardinghouse. But both Aunt Constance and Winifred Grover insisted that she spend the holidays with them as she had last year. This year one of Winifred's distant English cousins, Basil Edgewood, a journalist who had come to America to write his impressions for his newspaper, would be there.

A journalist, just like Paul Demarest. . . .

At least Vannah was going to be able to afford proper Christmas gifts for everyone this year, so on the Saturday before Christmas she withdrew a bit of her inheritance and went shopping, something she hadn't done since leaving Gerrold's house. She also went to a dressmaker and had a simple black velvet dress made, since she was still in mourning for her mother.

So when she stepped down from the hansom cab on Christmas Eve, she was laden down with gifts.

As soon as she entered the foyer, Robert and Amy appeared, their young faces alight with pleasure as they escorted their "Aunt Vannah" into the parlor. This time, she noticed, there were two other guests for the Christmas festivities: a very tall, very thin gentleman with a thick mane of white hair who looked to be in his early or middle fifties; and a young man Vannah assumed to be the English cousin, Basil Edgewood. Both men rose upon her entrance, as did her host.

"Ah, here's our Savannah now," Jock Grover said in his hearty, booming voice, coming over to give her an avuncular kiss on the cheek and to wish her a Merry Christmas.

"And what is this?" Winifred protested with a stern look at the bag Savannah carried.

"Gifts," Vannah replied, "real gifts this year, because your family has been so wonderful to me."

"Savannah, you shouldn't have."

"Yes, Winifred, and no arguments, please. Why don't you introduce me to your guests?"

Winifred drew Vannah over to the white-haired gentleman who couldn't take his eyes off Aunt Constance and said, "Savannah Webb, I'd like you to meet Mr. Frederick du Winter. Frederick is from Virginia."

"Savannah is the niece I was telling you about," Constance said, looking up at him with reciprocated interest.

"Miss Webb," he said with a faint Southern drawl as he bowed over her hand. "It's an honor to meet you."

"How do you do, Mr. du Winter?" she said. "The pleasure is mine."

"And this charming rogue," Winifred said as they turned, "is my cousin, Basil Edgewood. I must warn you, Vannah, that this young man is quite irreverent and incorrigible. He's been keeping us in high spirits ever since he arrived."

As Vannah came face-to-face with the Englishman she felt a brief stab of disappointment, for she half expected another journalist to be like Paul Demarest, half wild, his eyes alight with the fever of idealism. Mr. Edgewood looked quite tame by comparison, slight of build and very pale with huge, merry brown eyes and straight, light brown hair that dipped over one eye.

"I'm afraid Cousin Winifred maligns me, fair lady," he murmured as he bowed over her hand.

Hearing an English accent brought Martin Ash so forcefully to mind that for a moment Vannah was speechless. But Basil Edgewood was so unlike Martin that no comparisons came to mind. "It's a pleasure to meet you, Mr. Edgewood."

He wiggled his brows up and down in a comical manner. "Dear, dear, that will never do. You must call me Basil, like the herb. Everyone does."

There was something so jovial, so unselfconscious, in the young man's manner that Vannah was not offended by his informality.

Winifred just shook her head. "Didn't I tell you that he was irreverent?"

"If I am to call you Basil, then you must call me Savannah."

"Odd name, that," he commented with a smile, his eyes twinkling mischievously. "Why did your parents name you after a treeless grassy plain?" Then the brows shot up.

Vannah burst out laughing. "They didn't. They named me after a city in the state of Georgia, my father's birthplace."

The mystery of Vannah's name solved, Basil then said, "I understand from Cousin Winifred that you are an artist." He turned to look at the watercolor sketches of Robert and Amy that Winifred had framed and hung on the parlor wall. "Those are excellent," Basil said, quite serious this time.

"Why, thank you, Basil, but I'm far from an artist. I design stained glass windows for the Tiffany Studios."

He reached up to push back that stray lock of hair that kept falling into his eyes. "Stained glass windows? The kind one sees in those great medieval cathedrals?"

"And private homes, colleges, and libraries . . . many buildings, really," Vannah explained as she took a glass of champagne one of the footmen was serving.

"How fascinating!" he declared as they sat down on the divan together.

"And you are a journalist?" Vannah asked, sipping her champagne.

He nodded. "I'm here in New York on a special assignment from my newspaper, the *Chronicle*. I'm to write my impressions of America for English readers—in my own inimitable style, of course, laced with great insight and wit."

Vannah laughed, for the pretentious words were uttered in such a humorous way that they ceased to be offensive.

"And do you intend to travel around the country?"

"Perhaps later." Then he smiled, a charming display of

large white teeth. "But right now I think there is enough here in New York to interest such a droll fellow as myself."

Vannah smiled in agreement. "New York is infinitely fascinating."

"Perhaps you could show me the city, fair lady, since Cousin Winifred tells me that you have lived here all your life."

"I'm afraid the only times I am free, Basil, are every other Saturday and every Sunday. I'm a working girl, you see."

"I would greatly appreciate any time you could spare me."

Then Vannah asked him about his life in England, and Basil Edgewood told her of his childhood growing up near the marshes of Kent and of how his father had been a country squire.

As Vannah listened to him alternate between moods of deep seriousness and high mirth, she found herself relaxing in a man's presence for the first time in months. There were similarities in their backgrounds that struck a responsive chord in her. Although Basil was from a family that was not as wealthy as Vannah's, he had rebelled against his father at a very early age, for he wanted to be a journalist more than a country squire, "forever chasing a pack of bloodthirsty hounds over fences."

Then it was time to decorate the Christmas tree, and by the time dinner was served, Vannah felt that she had known Basil for years.

Finally the ladies retired for a few moments while the gentlemen remained at the table to enjoy their port and cigars. Winifred went upstairs to check on the children, leaving Aunt Constance and Vannah alone in the drawing room.

Constance said, "You seem to have found yourself an admirer tonight, my dear."

"As did you," Vannah retorted good-naturedly. "I didn't see Mr. du Winter leave your side for the entire evening. He's spellbound."

Aunt Constance colored prettily. "He is rather a distinguished man, isn't he?"

"And he seems quite taken with you, Aunt Constance."

"And I am quite taken with him," she admitted. She fanned herself with her hand. "This is madness, Vannah! I am a middle-aged woman of forty-seven years, and here I am, acting like a schoolgirl in the first throes of love."

Vannah gave her aunt a long, assessing look. Her aunt may have been middle-aged, but she was still quite attractive. Her figure hadn't yet become fleshy, even though her light brown hair was beginning to reveal a smattering of silver, and there were new lines in her face. In addition, Constance had a sparkle about her that many women half her age lacked, a quality the French called *joie de vivre*.

Now Aunt Constance turned the tables. "And what of Basil Edgewood, Vannah? The poor young man couldn't take his eyes off you."

"He is such a charming, comical young man," she admitted. "I can't remember when I last laughed so hard." Then her face clouded and she rose. "But I'm not ready for a romance, Aunt Constance. I don't know if I ever shall be."

"It's still Martin, isn't it?"

She nodded, her voice filled with pain. "Lord, it's over two years since we parted, and I still can't forget him. I've tried filling my life with work, but sometimes, when there's nothing to do, especially at night, I find myself thinking of him, wishing we were together again."

Constance rose and put her arm around Vannah's shoulders. "But you've got to start living again, my dear. Or do you fully intend to remain nothing more than a spinster who designs stained glass windows?"

Vannah shrugged. "I don't know. I look at Robert and Amy and think how wonderful it would be to have children of my own someday, but one needs a husband to do that."

"Well, a woman needs to let a man know that she's receptive to him, too, you know. I've watched you, Vannah. Sometimes you retreat within yourself and put up walls where no one can reach you. A man might get the wrong impression and think you're only interested in your work, with no room for him."

Vannah suddenly felt upset with herself. "Do I really do that, Aunt Constance?"

She nodded. "Give yourself a chance, Vannah. Perhaps you'll meet someone who will make you forget Martin Ash."

Suddenly the men returned to the parlor, and Vannah caught Basil Edgewood's eye. He smiled.

"Perhaps I shall, Aunt Constance," Vannah said.

After Christmas, Vannah returned to Corona, and Basil Edgewood receded into the background as she resumed the work she loved. Oh, he was always there whenever Vannah spent a free Sunday visiting Aunt Constance at the Grovers' and was always most pleasant to her, saying outrageous things to make her laugh. While Vannah enjoyed Basil's pleasant, undemanding company, he never stirred her passions the way Martin Ash had. She was content to lose herself in her work.

With every passing week Vannah's proficiency in glass grew. Everyone agreed that she had a natural affinity for the medium. And all her years of painting landscapes from Aunt Constance's terrace and vases of flowers made her especially skilled at designing landscape and floral windows that were much in demand.

Soon Vannah was designing windows for libraries, colleges, private yachts, railroad cars, and private homes. These secular windows were her favorites. When Vannah was called upon to design a window for someone's town house, she often visited their country home for inspiration. Then she would translate the customer's favorite view into a landscape window, so all he or she had to do was look at the window to be transported back to their country estate. Such themes were immensely popular with rich patrons.

One day in the middle of May, Mr. Tiffany called her into his office.

"Your father was just here," he said.

Vannah felt herself go pale. "He didn't want you to dismiss me, did he?"

Tiffany smiled gently and shook his head. "No, Savannah, nothing like that. He was here on business."

"Business? What kind of business?"

"He wants to commission not one, but several memorial windows to your late mother."

Vannah gave him a suspicious look. "He does? You'll forgive me if I seem a bit skeptical, Mr. Tiffany, but that doesn't sound like Gerrold Webb at all."

He shrugged. "Well, whatever his motives, the commission would be a most lucrative one. He wants one done for a church in New Haven where your mother's family comes from, I understand, another for Columbia College, and a third for his summer residence in Newport."

Vannah did some quick addition in her head. The total cost of three such windows would amount to about ten thousand dollars. Mr. Tiffany was an astute businessman, and Vannah could see that he wanted this commission very badly.

"I'm sure I don't need to tell you that I have no influence whatsoever with my father," she said.

Tiffany smiled. "I wasn't about to ask you to use any influence with him. I called you in here to ask if you would like to submit some designs for these windows. After all, Frances Webb was your mother. What could be a more fitting tribute to her than to have her own daughter design the memorial windows?"

Vannah smiled even as her eyes misted over with tears. "Thank you. I'd like that very much."

"Well, off with you now and get to work."

When Vannah returned to the boardinghouse that evening, she knew just what her designs would be, and after supper, she took her watercolors and began working.

The following day she submitted her designs to Tiffany.

As he studied them a slow smile of satisfaction illuminated his face, and he kept nodding. When he was through, he set them down and said, "These are outstanding, Savannah. I think they are the best you've ever done."

She beamed. "Since my mother was an invalid who never went out of doors, except to travel between New York and Newport twice a year, I thought it would be most fitting to have the memorial windows depict scenes she never saw." Vannah indicated the topmost design. "This shows the sea as seen from the terrace at Clairvaux, and this"—she took the one beneath it—"is a landscape using a grove of copper beeches on the estate, and the third is a portrait window bordered by lilies."

Tiffany nodded. "Excellent. I'm sure your father will be pleased."

However, a week later, a somber-faced Tiffany called Vannah into his office once again to tell her that Gerrold Webb had not liked any of the designs submitted and had taken his most lucrative commission to a rival firm. Vannah would not be making her mother's memorial windows, after all.

"He did it on purpose, Aunt Constance!" Vannah cried when her aunt came to visit her that Saturday afternoon.

She paced around her room at the boardinghouse, barely

able to contain her rage. "He had no intention whatsoever of letting me or anyone else at Tiffany's design those windows. He just wanted me to get all fired up with enthusiasm, then he pulled the rug right from under me."

"That does sound like something Gerrold would do," Constance agreed with a shake of her head.

"And it's his way of denigrating my abilities."

"What do you care what Gerrold Webb thinks of your work, Vannah?" Constance pointed out. "You know you're good. Mr. Tiffany certainly knows that you're one of his best designers."

Vannah felt the anger suddenly leave her. "You're right, of course. Gerrold is just playing games with me. I shouldn't give him the satisfaction of letting him upset me so."

"That's the spirit." Then her aunt glanced at the small watch pinned to her dress and said, "Well, I must be going. Frederick is taking me to the theater tonight."

"Sounds serious, Aunt Constance," Vannah teased.

"Could be," she agreed amiably.

Before she left, Constance added, "By the way, I would advise you to stay home tomorrow. I think Basil has a surprise for you."

"For me?"

Constance nodded. "I promised him I wouldn't tell you what it was."

As Vannah watched the carriage drive off she stood at the gate until it was out of sight. Then she went back into the boardinghouse and wondered just what kind of surprise Basil Edgewood had planned.

The next morning, after Vannah returned from church, she found a one-horse carriage parked outside the boardinghouse, and when she went inside, she heard whoops of laughter coming from the parlor. There she saw the usually dour Mrs. O'Neill laughing so hard at something Basil had said that she had to wipe her eyes with the corner of her apron.

"Ah, there she is now," he said, jumping to his feet. "Good morning, fair lady. Are you ready?"

"Good morning, Basil. Am I ready for what?" she asked in bewilderment.

"Well, it's such a warm, beautiful spring day outside, I thought you'd like to go on a picnic," he replied, his merry eyes glowing. "Cousin Winifred's peerless cook has prepared a basket of delicacies, I have rented a horse and carriage for the day, and I thought we could ride out to some quiet country field with a babbling brook nearby to chill the wine."

Although Vannah was still feeling angry and depressed about her loss of Gerrold's commission, she nonetheless found Basil's enthusiasm and high spirits contagious. She smiled back at him. "I would love to go on a picnic with you."

They drove out into the countryside, but Basil rejected site after site. "I am searching for the perfect savannah to go with your unusual name," he told her with a straight face.

Finally he found what he considered to be the perfect spot: a high, grassy hill topped with a tall, leafy tree.

"But this isn't a proper savannah," Vannah protested. "Isn't a savannah supposed to be flat and treeless?"

"Let's not quibble, fair lady. Our savannah shall be allowed a tree or two," he replied as he tethered their horse to a hedge by the side of the road. "From now on this spot will forever be known as Savannah's Savannah."

"Clown," Vannah muttered with a shake of her head.

Then Basil and she trudged up the steep slope to the top of the hill. While she spread out the crisp white linen tablecloth, he secured a bottle of wine with twine and gently lowered it into a nearby stream to be chilled. When he rejoined Vannah, who was sitting back against the wide tree trunk, he took off his coat and hat, pulled off his tie, and rolled up his sleeves.

"I do so like being comfortable on a picnic, fair lady," he declared with a broad smile as he sat down next to her.

Vannah sighed. "It is a perfect day for it—warm, without a cloud in the sky, and just a hint of a breeze." She closed her eyes and breathed deeply. "Even the air smells differently in the spring."

"It certainly does," he agreed. "It smells of new grass, budding flowers, freshness, life"—Basil wrinkled his nose—"and, unfortunately, cows."

Vannah laughed.

Even though she was still in mourning for her mother and wore a somber black skirt and blouse today, she refused to feel morbid on such a bright, lovely day and in the company of the delightful Basil.

"Thank you for asking me along," she said.

Basil turned his head slightly so he could look at her, and his bantering mood had vanished. "Constance told me about what your father did to you, and I thought a picnic would be just the thing to lift you out of the doldrums."

Vannah was genuinely touched. "Why, thank you, Basil. What a sweet thing for you to do."

"Didn't I tell you I was a sweet, considerate person?" he teased. Then he became serious again. "I know how I would feel if someone took away the work that I love."

Vannah pulled up a dandelion and began plucking at it. "It was Gerrold Webb's way of telling me that he doesn't think highly of my artistic capabilities."

"Well, he's wrong," Basil said vehemently. "You design beautiful windows, Savannah, and you're a great artist."

Vannah felt herself coloring slightly. "I don't know how great an artist I am, Basil, but I will say in all modesty that I do design beautiful windows." Suddenly she turned to him and said, "Tell me about your work, Basil. What have you been writing about for your English readers?"

He pushed back the stubborn lock of hair and reached for his coat so he could take out several pieces of folded paper.

"I thought you'd never ask." He handed them to Vannah. "Tell me what you think, and don't be afraid to be brutally frank."

Then she unfolded them and began reading Basil's article about an elderly East Side doctor who had dedicated his life to providing medical care to the poor.

When she finished, she said, "Basil, that is the most moving article I've ever read. You've captured the doctor's personality and his selfless dedication, yet you haven't made him sound like some martyr. This is wonderful, Basil. I had no idea that you were so talented."

She fully expected him to grin and tell her that of course he was talented, but all he said was, "There are many things you don't know about me, Savannah."

Vannah sensed another mood change at once. Gone was the lighthearted, carefree young man of a short time ago. Basil was becoming much too serious, and Vannah wasn't ready for it.

She rose nervously. "I'm famished, aren't you? Why don't you get the wine while I set out lunch?"

Vannah and Basil were relatively silent while they ate cold chicken, lobster salad, and crusty chunks of bread. But by the time they were ready for a simple dessert of cheese and purple grapes, the wine and the perfect spring day had conspired to soothe Vannah and take away any reservations she might have had about Basil Edgewood.

She began telling him about what it was like to grow up surrounded by all the comforts and conveniences that great wealth could provide and yet still be lonely. Once she started, Basil seemed so attentive and sympathetic that

Vannah's tongue took flight and she couldn't stop herself. She found herself speaking of Paul Demarest and how her father had come between them, and she told Basil about her deep love for Martin Ash and how it had led to heartbreak.

When she was through, Basil removed a handkerchief from his coat pocket and gently began dabbing at the tears Vannah didn't even know she had shed.

"I'm—I'm sorry," Vannah murmured. "I don't know what came over me."

"I wish I were half as lucky as this Ash fellow," he said softly, leaning toward her until his face was just inches from her own.

Vannah was mesmerized by the soulful look of longing in Basil's dark eyes, and she felt drawn to him, unable to pull away. His ardent gaze went from her eyes, down to her mouth, and up to her eyes again, as if imploring her to allow him to kiss her. And suddenly Vannah wanted him to. Her eyelids drooped, and she reached out to him blindly, giving Basil all the encouragement he needed.

His first kiss was brief and tentative, a mere brushing of his lips against hers, and when it was over, Vannah was surprised to feel keen disappointment.

"Kiss me again," she whispered.

He smiled. "With pleasure, fair lady."

As he gathered her into his arms and his mouth sought hers, Vannah felt a great healing warmth encompassing her. It had been so long since a man had held her in his arms, she had almost forgotten how sublime it could be.

But as Basil's kisses became more insistent, his moist lips parting beneath her own in invitation, Vannah suddenly became afraid of the unexpected whirlwind of passion she had unleashed within herself. With a cry of fear and protest she jerked away from him, scrambling to her feet before Basil knew what was happening.

"Savannah, what's worng?" he demanded in a bewildered voice. "Have I offended you in some way?"

She crossed her arms and stared down at the grass. "It's too soon for me, Basil."

Now he rose and came up behind her. "I understand."

Vannah turned her head and stared at him. "You—you do?"

He nodded, his merry brown eyes soft with sympathy.

Vannah gave a shaky laugh of relief. "Thank you, Basil. I was afraid you wouldn't."

"I will always understand you more than you understand yourself, fair lady. Come, the picnic's over and reality intrudes. Let us pack our basket and be on our way."

As spring slipped into summer Vannah did see as much as she could of Basil. He was always patient and understanding, never attempting to take liberties or demanding of Vannah more than she could give. Soon she found herself actually looking forward to his visits.

The summer of 1895 was a summer Vannah would always remember as a summer of changes. In July, Gerrold Webb married the wealthy widow of a steel magnate in a wedding that was the talk of New York society and achieved his heart's desire of having a palatial residence on New York City's exclusive Millionaires' Row. The brownstone on Thirty-fourth Street was sold.

Soon after, Aunt Constance announced that she would be marrying Frederick du Winter in August and moving to Virginia with him once they returned from a wedding trip to California. While she had reservations about leaving her niece, Vannah assured her that she was capable of taking care of herself.

But, a month after Aunt Constance's wedding and departure, forces were hard at work to rob Vannah of the very independence she had worked so hard to achieve.

Chapter Fourteen

DAHLIA DAVENPORT WEBB FROWNED at her new husband across the breakfast table.

"I wish you had let me invite your daughter to our wedding."

Gerrold poured thick honey on his corn bread and smiled indulgently. "Your kindness and thoughtfulness overwhelm me, dear Dahlia, but I'm afraid Savannah never would have come. As I've told you, she blames me for everything that has gone wrong in her life—losing the man she loved, her mother's death . . ." He shrugged. "And all I've ever done was to try to guide her, but she's always resented it. We've been estranged for years."

Dahlia shook her head sadly as she tried to ignore the platter piled high with freshly baked sweet rolls. She and Claude, her late first husband, hadn't been blessed with children of their own, and now that Dahlia was married to Gerrold Webb, she had been looking forward to welcoming his daughter into their home.

"That's very sad, Gerrold," she said.

"I quite agree, but it's not my fault. Savannah is a very stubborn and headstrong young lady."

Succumbing to a third roll, Dahlia decided to broach the subject of a plan she had been considering for several weeks now.

"I think it would be splendid if we could be a real

family," she said. "Why don't you invite Savannah to come live with us?" She glanced around the cavernous dining room of her sprawling Fifth Avenue mansion, the house poor Claude hadn't lived to see completed. "We certainly have more than enough room."

Gerrold stared, his corn bread poised halfway between the plate and his open mouth. "You can't be serious."

"Oh, but I am," she replied sweetly. "I am Savannah's stepmother now, and while I know I could never take her real mother's place, perhaps we could get along and even become friends."

"My daughter will never agree to it." He wrinkled his nose. "She chooses to wallow in poverty as an artist."

"But perhaps if you were to ask her nicely . . ."

Gerrold's cold eyes warmed as he stared at her thoughtfully. "You really want this badly, don't you?"

"I do." Dahlia ran a fingertip along the rim of her plate. "I was an only child born to two only children. I had no aunts, no uncles, no cousins, no brothers, no sisters—no family whatsoever, except for my parents. And when I was married, even a child of my own was denied to me."

Her pale gray eyes held a steely glint of determination as she said, "Families should be together, not apart because of silly misunderstandings."

Gerrold reached across the table and clasped his wife's hand tightly in his. "I am truly touched that you would want my daughter to live with us. You are a warm, generous woman, Dahlia. It's one of the many reasons why I married you."

Dahlia loved Gerrold, but she was not a fool. She knew the only reason he had married her was because of Claude's vast fortune and her considerable social connections.

Now Gerrold looked doubtful. "I don't know . . ."

Smiling, Dahlia rose and went around the table to stand

behind her husband's chair. Caressing his shoulders lightly, she murmured, "Please, Gerrold? Do this for me?"

He caught one hand and brought its palm to his lips. "You know you're the best thing that has ever happened to me and I can deny you nothing. If you wish Savannah to live with us, I shall think of something to persuade her."

Vannah knew something was wrong the moment she walked into Tiffany's office. He looked very somber, and the usual spirited sparkle in his eyes was gone.

Once Vannah was seated, he picked up a scrap of glass off his desk and played with it before saying, "Your father came to see me last week."

Vannah sat up even straighter, on guard now. "Oh? And may I ask what he wanted?"

Tiffany gave her a level look. "He wanted me to dismiss you."

Vannah's blood ran cold. "And what did you tell him?"

"I told him the truth, that you were one of my best designers and I had no intention of dismissing you."

Vannah sighed in relief, but Mr. Tiffany's next words brought her up short. "He told me that would be most unwise, and the following day, three commissions were withdrawn, including the Vandermeer memorial window."

"And you think my father is somehow responsible?"

Tiffany threw the piece of glass down on his desk. "I'm afraid so, Savannah. Even though your father made no threat against me, I think he is using his influence with his friends to withdraw these commissions just as he did with your mother's memorial windows. What else could it possibly be, especially since his new wife is Emily Vandermeer's closest friend?"

Vannah tried to fight the rising tide of panic. Tiffany had personally courted Emily Vandermeer for six months to convince her that no other studio could possibly do justice to the window she planned to commission in her late husband's memory. It was a particularly lucrative commission and, if executed to Tiffany's plans, would result in the most expensive window the studio had ever created.

"We've already lost over twenty thousand dollars in commissions, Savannah," Tiffany said.

Vannah knew that no designer, however skilled, was worth such a loss of income to the company. She tried to control the trembling in her voice as she rose and said, "I shall speak to my father about this."

"I hope you can make him listen to reason. Otherwise . . ." He shrugged apologetically.

Otherwise he would be forced to dismiss her, and the career Vannah had worked so hard for would be over, and Gerrold Webb would have won.

Vannah went to call on him the following Sunday afternoon.

On this warm September day Fifth Avenue was crowded with people who had come to participate in the popular pastime of gaping at all the splendid mansions that lined "Millionaires' Row," the two miles running from Fifty-ninth Street all the way up to Ninetieth.

As Vannah disembarked from the Grovers' carriage and looked up at Gerrold's new Seventy-third Street residence for the first time, she just shook her head. So, he had gotten his heart's desire at long last, a mansion alongside the likes of the Astors, Goulds, and Whitneys. What did it matter if it had been built by his wife's first husband? It was Gerrold Webb's now.

A butler answered the door, and when Vannah told him who she was, he showed her to a grand drawing room.

While Vannah waited for Gerrold she glanced around at the tasteful decorating done in the Louis XIV style. She could tell that the graceful furnishings and exquisite bibelots were from Europe and very old, but then, Gerrold's new wife, Dahlia Davenport, was known throughout New York society for her exceptional taste.

Vannah was admiring a gold ormolu clock when the drawing-room doors suddenly opened to admit Gerrold Webb and a big, robust woman nearly six feet tall who must have been his wife.

Vannah fought to control her shock and surprise. Not only was Dahlia Davenport as plain as pudding, she was obviously older than her husband by a good five years. Jowls were beginning to form near her chin, and her hair had already turned iron-gray.

He obviously married her for her money was Vannah's first thought.

"Savannah," Gerrold said as he closed the doors behind him. "Dahlia was just saying how much she wanted to meet you, and you appear. What a stroke of luck."

For a moment Vannah was taken aback, for there was something different about Gerrold today. He didn't glare at her for once, or bark at her in his customary fashion. In fact, he actually seemed pleased to see her and was proudly introducing her to his new wife.

"What a pleasure it is to meet you at long last, Savannah," Dahlia said with a gracious smile as she sailed across the drawing room and took Vannah's hand.

All of Vannah's best intentions to be cool to Gerrold's second wife dissipated the moment she heard Dahlia's soft, warm voice and looked into her kind gray eyes. There was just something so sincere, so likable about the woman that disarmed Vannah. Dahlia appeared quite self-assured, yet as eager to please as a puppy. Vannah found her initial reservations vanishing.

"How do you do?" she murmured politely.

But she was not about to allow a mere good mood to

distract her. She faced Gerrold squarely. "I have something of great importance to discuss with you."

"Dahlia, my dear," he said, "would you be so kind as to excuse us?"

Vannah piped up with, "Oh, I think Mrs. Davenport would be very interested in what I have to say."

Dahlia shook her head. "I have several urgent matters that need attending to. If you'll both excuse me . . . Savannah, I'm sure I'll be seeing you before you go."

Then she smiled graciously and glided out of the drawing room with Gerrold's eyes following her departure.

When Vannah and Gerrold were alone, she said, "I won't waste any of your valuable time, Gerrold. Is it true that you asked Tiffany to dismiss me?"

Instead of answering her question immediately, he asked, "What do you think of Dahlia?"

Vannah was momentarily taken aback. "Why . . . she seems pleasant enough."

"Pleasant?" His face softened, and a smile played about his mouth. "She is the most wonderful woman I've ever known."

"Gerrold," Vannah said tartly. "I didn't come her to discuss Dahlia. I asked, is it true—"

"I didn't ask. I *told* him to dismiss you."

Vannah felt her face grow warm. "And when he refused, you used your influence to have several commissions withdrawn from his company."

Gerrold shrugged. "I merely informed several good friends that Tiffany's windows were much too expensive and they could do much better by buying their windows elsewhere. I certainly can't be blamed if they chose to withdraw their commissions."

"Why are you doing this, Gerrold?" Vannah asked, fighting to control her rising temper. "What do you want from me?"

"You've had your little fling at living the bohemian life of an artist, Savannah," he replied. "Now it's time for you to come to your senses and return to the loving bosom of your family."

"I have no family," she retorted. "And, unless you've so quickly forgotten, you are not my real father, Gerrold."

She saw something like anger leap into his pale eyes, then it was gone. "Oh, but I am. At least, that's the way the world sees me. And, unless you've so quickly forgotten, daughter, my name is on your baptismal certificate, and I, not Alastair McKechnie, raised you."

"I'm warning you, Gerrold. If you try to make me do anything against my will, I shall tell the world of my true parentage."

He chuckled. "Oh, I think I can squash any such rumors, Savannah. After all, your mother is not here to contradict anything I say, now is she?"

Vannah was so furious, she was speechless.

"And besides," he went on smoothly, "my sweet, generous Dahlia wants you to come live here with us. She thinks a daughter belongs with her father."

"Until, of course, she can be married off to the likes of a Raymond McGraw," Vannah retorted.

Gerrold shrugged apologetically. "But once Tiffany dismisses you, where will you go?" When Vannah didn't answer, he said, "And he will dismiss you, never fear. You see, Louis Comfort Tiffany is just as ruthless a businessman as I am, in his own way."

Vannah made a scoffing sound.

"Oh, but he is, daughter. Have you ever heard of John LaFarge?"

"Of course I have. He used to be one of Mr. Tiffany's chief rivals."

Gerrold nodded. "And did you know that he also developed a method for creating opalescent glass at about the same time that Tiffany did? But did you also know that Tiffany talked him out of patenting it with the promise that they would work together, perhaps even form a partnership? Then Tiffany, who had been developing his own method of creating such glass, filed his patent and left LaFarge out in the cold." His smile was smug. "In plain English, your paragon cheated him, Savannah."

"You're lying."

"Oh, no. And if the man has no scruples about stealing another man's invention, he's not going to lose any commissions just to keep one of his designers."

Vannah felt herself go cold all over because she knew he spoke the truth.

"So," Gerrold said, "when can we expect you to join our family?"

"After what you did to my mother, I—"

"Stop it!" Gerrold snapped. "Did you ever once consider what it must have been like for me, Savannah, to be married to a woman who purposely shut herself away from the world?"

"She wouldn't have shut herself away if you hadn't been such a tyrant!" Vannah cried.

"Oh, yes, everything is always my fault. Frances was never to blame." Gerrold's voice was laced with bitterness.

"Well, it's true. Then to remarry when she wasn't even cold in her grave . . ."

His face drained of all color. "I'll have you know that marrying Dahlia was the best thing that's ever happened to me. She is everything your mother never was—warm, understanding, unselfish."

"And what of Aunt Constance?" Vannah shot back. "After serving as your mistress for all those years you just—"

"Threw her out into the cold without a penny to her name? Don't go putting that woman on a pedestal as well.

She never did anything for anyone in her life without expecting to get something in return. I kept my part of our bargain, but she betrayed me."

"I refuse to listen to your lies any longer," Vannah said, turned on her heel, and started striding toward the door. She had almost reached it when she felt Gerrold's hand on her arm, restraining her.

"You've never ever been fair to me, Savannah, and you know it. You won't even try to understand me," he said.

"What is there to understand?" she replied, without turning her head to look at him. "If someone doesn't give you what you want, you use your money and your power to bend them to your will. You haven't changed, Gerrold. Not one bit."

Then Vannah shook off his hand and went storming out of the house.

Several minutes later Dahlia reappeared in the drawing room to find her husband standing near a window, peering out at the street from behind a curtain, an expression of consternation on his face.

"What happened, Gerrold?" she said softly as she went to him. "I was just coming down the stairs when I saw Savannah go running out of here. I called to her, but she wouldn't stop." Dahlia took a deep breath and frowned in puzzlement. "Whatever did you say to upset her so?"

At first her husband seemed reluctant to tell her, but Dahlia finally wheedled the whole story out of him.

"Oh, Gerrold, you didn't . . ." she groaned when he was through.

He glowered at her for the first time in their marriage. "When I want your opinion, Dahlia, I shall ask for it. I know how to best handle my daughter."

Without waiting for her reply he bowed stiffly and was gone.

When she was alone again, Dahlia sighed. Her new

husband had much to learn about love, compassion, and forgiveness, but she had all the patience and determination in the world to teach him. By the time she was through with him, Gerrold Webb would be a changed man.

Her thoughts were in such turmoil that Vannah couldn't bear to face the Grovers just yet, so she ordered the driver to ride around Central Park until she could gather her wits about her.

She knew that her career with Tiffany was over. Gerrold had seen to that. But as Vannah sat in the solitude of the carriage, she tried to think of alternatives, and several presented themselves.

Tiffany's studios may have been the largest, the most innovative, and the most well known, but there were several other fine studios in the New York area alone. And with Vannah's impressive credentials she was sure to be hired by any one of his rivals.

Until Gerrold Webb and his friends began withdrawing commissions from them as well. And if someone like Tiffany feared losing window commissions, what would the proprietor of a smaller studio do?

Or Vannah could open her own studio. She still had her small inheritance from her mother, and she was sure that someone like Jock Grover might be willing to make an investment and back her.

But, once again, Vannah was assailed by fresh doubts. Any studio, even her own, couldn't exist without the patronage of the wealthy. And Gerrold Webb was sure to see that she didn't receive many commissions.

Vannah rested her head back against the squabs and tried to fight the tears of frustration that threatened to fall. She felt as though she were lost in a boxwood maze. No matter where she turned, the exit was blocked.

Needing fresh air to clear her head, Vannah ordered the

driver to stop, and she got out to go for a walk along one of the park's many tree-lined pathways.

Just as she started down one she heard a familiar voice call her name, and when she turned, she saw Basil hurrying toward her, his open frock coat flapping in the breeze.

"Basil, whatever are you doing here?" she asked as he joined her.

He was panting from exertion. "I've been following you . . . ever since you left Cousin Winifred's."

"Following me? But why?"

"I was worried about you, silly goose."

Vannah was deeply moved. "There was no need."

"But of course there was!" he cried in exasperation. "You're a friend, Vannah. I . . . care a great deal about you."

As she looked into Basil's soulful eyes Vannah read more than simple caring there. She turned and started strolling down the path. "Thank you for your concern, Basil."

He fell in step beside her. "So, what did your scurvy knave of a father have to say for himself?"

As they walked, Vannah told Basil everything that had transpired between herself and Gerrold Webb.

Finally, when she finished, Basil was furious. "There must be a way to stop him from destroying your career, Vannah! He can't be allowed to get away with this."

She sighed. "My father is a man of considerable power and influence, Basil, and since his marriage to Dahlia Davenport, he has acquired even more."

Basil tossed his hair out of his eye. "Perhaps I should challenge the scurvy knave to a duel right here in Central Park." Then he wielded an imaginary sword, thrusting and parrying at the air.

He looked so comical that Vannah couldn't help laughing. "Clown. You'd only be arrested and sent to prison, and it would accomplish nothing. But thank you for your gallant gesture. What's so frustrating is that my father's intimidation is very subtle and sly," Vannah said. "He knows everyone in New York society, and I'm sure that if he hears that one of his friends is going to commission a window from Tiffany, he urges him to go elsewhere."

"But can't you take some kind of legal action against him?" Basil asked.

"How could I possibly prove that he is sabotaging me?"

"That's true."

"So you see," she added dismally, "he has me boxed into a corner."

Basil shook his head. "How such a contemptible beast could sire such a sweet and gentle creature as yourself is beyond my comprehension."

Vannah almost blurted out that the reason for it was because the contemptible beast was not, in fact, her real father, but she held her tongue. Only she and Aunt Constance knew her mother's secret.

Instead she said, "Oh, I must admit that he appears to have mellowed a bit. He genuinely seems to adore Dahlia, his wife."

"But obviously he hasn't mellowed enough to leave you alone."

Vannah shook her head as she caught at a passing branch. "Unfortunately not."

Basil stopped and looked at her. "So what are you going to do, fair lady?"

She shrugged. "I really haven't decided, Basil. I still have most of the money that my mother left to me when she died. Perhaps I shall just live off that for a while."

"And give up designing windows?" he asked incredulously.

"I really don't know." Then Vannah turned to see the

carriage waiting patiently at the beginning of the path. "I think we should be getting back to the Grovers'. I have plans to make."

Basil looked like he was about to say something, and she looked at him inquiringly. But all he did was draw her arm through his and walk back to the carriage with her.

The following Monday was one of the saddest days of Vannah's life.

The moment Tiffany arrived at the studios, she went to him and explained she had to leave before any more commissions were withdrawn on her account. He seemed both sad and relieved, offering to assist her in finding a position with another studio or to otherwise help in any way he could. Vannah thanked him and said all she wanted were the cartoons from several of her most acclaimed window designs.

After gathering her materials she said her good-byes to the other designers and Prudence as quickly as possible, to avoid breaking down, then returned to Mrs. O'Neill's to pack her things.

No sooner had Vannah packed one bag than Mrs. O'Neill came up to tell her that Basil was waiting for her downstairs in the parlor.

"Why, Basil," she greeted him with a smile as she extended her hands, "this is a surprise."

"A pleasant one, I hope," he replied.

"Of course. But, since we just saw each other yesterday—"

"You're wondering why I came all the way out here today."

Vannah nodded.

"I've come to take you to Savannah's Savannah," he said, "because I have something very important to ask you."

Vannah was still puzzled by his behavior, but she replied, "All right."

As they rode out to their favorite picnic spot Vannah noticed that Basil seemed serious and lost in thought, so she made no attempt to engage him in conversation. She waited until they arrived before turning to him and saying, "Now, what do you have to ask me, Basil?"

He sat down on the grass beside her and took her hand. "I find myself in a rather unusual situation."

"Oh? And what is that?"

"I am a journalist. Words are my stock-in-trade. Yet, in this particular instance, I find that those very words fail me."

"That must be a first," Vannah teased, trying to cajole him out of his somber mood.

"Now, now, fair lady, this is one of those rare times when I am trying to be serious, so would you please pay attention?"

She composed her face and matched her mood to his.

Now he dropped her hand to rise and lean against the tree trunk. "You don't know how often I've rehearsed just what I want to say to you, and yet, now that we are together, I find myself as uncertain and shy as a schoolboy."

Vannah rose to join him. "Then why don't you just come right out and say whatever it is you have to say to me?"

He stared down at the ground. "Because I'm afraid that you won't take me seriously. I am afraid you'll refuse."

"You'll never know until you ask."

Basil turned and looked deeply into her eyes. "Will you marry me, Savannah Webb?"

His declaration was so unexpected that Vannah actually took a step back in surprise. "Why, Basil . . . I—I don't know what to say."

"A simple yes or no would do nicely."

"Ah, but it's not that simple, Basil," she replied.

He studied her, his dark eyes both grave and yearning. "You must know that I love you, Vannah, and have for some time now. We're two of a kind, Vannah. We're both talented people who love life, and we shouldn't waste it." He sighed. "You can't shut yourself away forever."

Had she been shutting herself away emotionally, she wondered, just as her mother had shut herself away physically?

Vannah said, "I've come to care for you a great deal in the last few months, Basil. You understand me and you make me laugh. But I'm not sure that caring is the same as loving."

"I'm not asking that you love me, Vannah—at least, not right away." His sudden smile was disarming. "I'm arrogant enough to think that I'm such a charming, lovable fellow that you will one day come to love me as much as I love you."

She couldn't help but smile. "Dear Basil . . . I'm not quite sure I deserve you."

"Oh, no. It is I who don't deserve you, fair lady." Then he reached for her hand and held it tightly. "We could be so good together, Vannah, so good for each other. Once we were married, we could go to England to live. I could write, and you could design stained glass windows. I'm sure that there are many studios there that would hire you. And you'd be free of your father."

That caught Vannah's attention. "I had never thought of that."

Basil said, "Oh, I'm not suggesting that you marry me merely to get away from your tyrannical father. But wouldn't it be splendid? Life would be one grand adventure after another."

Privately Vannah agreed. Then she said, "There is something you should know, Basil, before you offer me marriage."

"And what is that?"

Vannah could not meet his steadfast gaze. "Martin Ash and I . . . we were lovers, you see. So you would not be the first man I have known."

"And you would not be the first woman I have known," he replied. Suddenly Basil reached out to take her face between his palms. "But I would be the last, and that's all that matters to me. Do you understand?"

Vannah nodded. "It would make a great difference to some men. But then, I think you know that you are a most unusual man, Basil Edgewood."

He dropped his hands, moved away from her, and said in mock affront, "How could you think me anything less?"

Vannah laughed. "Clown."

"About some things," he agreed, "but not about loving you with all my heart and soul."

Vannah turned serious once again. "I don't know, Basil. I must have time to consider your proposal."

"Take all the time you need, my love. But I feel I must warn you that my series of articles is complete and my editor wants me to return to England as soon as possible."

To Vannah's surprise, something like dismay flooded through her. The thought of being without the lighthearted young Englishman made her feel quite dejected.

"Ah, do I detect tears of sorrow in those bright blue eyes of yours, my fair lady? Perhaps there is hope for my suit."

"Perhaps," Vannah replied lightly.

"Do you really mean it?"

She nodded. "I will seriously consider your proposal, Basil, and tell you my answer when I go to the Grovers' on Wednesday."

His face brightened. "Thank you, fair one, thank you."

"No promises," she warned him.

"I am forewarned." Then he grinned. "Am I not allowed one brief sweet kiss, fair lady?"

He slipped one arm around her waist and gently drew her to him until their bodies were just lightly touching. Then he cupped his free hand against Vannah's cheek and bent his head to kiss her. His warm, smooth lips touched hers, lingered for several seconds, then pulled away, slowly and reluctantly. It was a brief kiss, more to seal a bargain than to arouse passions.

Then he stroked her cheek with his thumb as his brown eyes stared lovingly into hers. "I won't demand what you're not ready to give, Savannah."

"Thank you, Basil, for being so considerate."

The clown reappeared. "Usually, after one of my kisses, women swoon at my feet and beg me to marry them."

Vannah laughed. "You impossible man. You shall have to wait until Wednesday to see if I swoon at your feet and beg you to marry me."

He sighed. "If I must, fair lady, then so be it."

Wednesday morning found Vannah seated in a hansom cab parked before her old home on Thirty-fourth Street, visiting it for the last time. The brownstone looked the same, even though a new family lived there now, and Vannah was assailed by memories, not all of them unpleasant.

Finally, when she had made peace with her past and her mother's suffering, she told the driver to drive on. Basil was waiting for her answer.

Soon the hansom was pulling up before the Grovers' house. Before Vannah even had a chance to step down, the front door flew open, and Basil himself came charging down the steps at breakneck speed.

"Well, fair lady?" he asked eagerly, his dark eyes filled with hope as he opened the door and extended his hand to help her alight. "Are you going to swoon at my feet and beg me to marry you?"

"Well, Clown, I refuse to swoon at any man's feet, but will you please marry me?"

He let out a great whoop of joy that startled the poor cabby's horse, but before the animal could bolt, Basil grabbed Vannah by the waist and swung her down onto the sidewalk where he promptly enfolded her in his arms and gave her a hug that crushed the breath out of her.

"Savannah Webb, you have made me the happiest man in all of Creation!" Basil cried when they parted. Then he turned and hollered, "Attention everyone! Miss Savannah Webb has just begged me to marry her!"

"Basil!" Vannah exclaimed, glancing around nervously. "The neighbors will think me most improper."

"Oh, who cares what those scurvy knaves think? I'm the happiest man in the world today, and I want the whole world to know it."

"Will you settle for the Grovers?"

"For now at any rate," he replied as he paid the cabbie, who was eyeing him as though he had just escaped from a lunatic asylum.

Then Basil and Vannah walked hand in hand into the house.

As they were walking through the foyer he said, "Before we tell Cousin Winifred our news, there's something I've got to talk to you about, Vannah."

She looked at him in dismay. "Oh, dear. You sound so serious, Basil."

"It's very important," he assured her as he drew her into the vacant library. After he closed the door behind them he turned to her and said, quite solemnly, "Are you sure you want to marry me, Vannah?"

She took his hands. "Yes, Basil, quite sure. I've stayed up several nights thinking about it long and hard, and I am honored that you asked me to marry you, and I'm also honored to accept."

His voice was soft and grave. "And what about Martin Ash? Can you finally lay that ghost to rest?"

Vannah tightened her hold on his hands and faced him squarely. "Martin is part of my past, Basil. Oh, I'll never forget him, and I'm sure a part of me will always love him, but I've finally accepted the fact that we just weren't destined to be together. His honor compelled him to return to his wife. I can't spend the rest of my life mourning him. I've got to start living again, and I choose to start with you."

Basil closed his eyes and sighed deeply with relief, then drew her hands up to his lips. "My fair, fair lady."

"Come," Vannah said, her eyes shining with happiness, "let us tell the Grovers our news, then make plans for our wedding day."

Basil grinned, bent his head for a quick kiss, then led Vannah out of the library.

One week later Savannah Webb became Mrs. Basil Edgewood.

Torrential rains were falling on Vannah's wedding night, but she was too nervous to notice the incessant drumming of raindrops against the windows.

Just that morning she and Basil had been married in a quiet, simple civil ceremony with only the Grovers in attendance. Vannah had wanted to wait until Aunt Constance and Frederick returned from California so they could be present on this happy occasion, but Basil gently reminded her that he was due back in England and had no time to spare. Gerrold Webb was not told of Vannah's marriage, and no announcement was placed in the newspapers. The last thing that Vannah needed was Gerrold's interference on this of all days.

After the ceremony and an elaborate wedding luncheon Vannah and Basil proceeded to the Grovers' sprawling house on Long Island, which overlooked picturesque Oyster Bay, where they could spend a few days alone together before leaving for England. They had a chance to stroll around the well-kept grounds before a sudden shower drove them indoors, then they had a light supper and retired to their rooms.

Now, as Vannah sat before her mirror, brushing her long, pale hair with a silver-backed brush as she waited for her bridegroom to come to her, she felt the first stirrings of apprehension. How would lovemaking be with Basil? she wondered. Her reflection gave her a wry smile. Well, she would soon find out.

She looked around her bedchamber, a large, spacious room done in the warm, muted shades of yellow and ivory that Winifred favored. In the dim light of the solitary lamp on the nightstand, it looked shadowed and restful. The mahogany bed on the other side of the room was a large half-tester affair featuring elaborately carved cupids, doves, and roses on the headboard, the kind of bed Vannah had always dreamed of sharing with her husband on their wedding night. Yet when she thought of the simple bed of cushions before the fireplace in Petit Clairvaux . . .

Vannah rose and paced the room, twisting the narrow gold band on her finger. This was to have been the beginning of a wonderful life with Martin, and here she was, married to another.

"You must forget about Martin," she chided herself. "You must! It isn't fair to Basil."

Suddenly the connecting door to their suites opened, and Basil stood framed in the doorway. Vannah could tell that he wore nothing beneath the green paisley dressing gown belted loosely around his waist, and suddenly she felt as awkward and shy as a virgin around him. With Martin she had felt no such misgivings, only an eagerness to give herself to him freely and without shame, to please him.

"You look so beautiful, fair lady," Basil murmured as he walked into the room, his dark gaze roving over her hungrily. There was nothing of the clown about him tonight. In fact, he looked like a complete stranger.

Vannah smiled and resisted the impulse to take a step backward for every step he took toward her. "And you look so very handsome, Basil."

When they were facing each other, almost touching, Basil reached up and began running his fingertips lightly from her temples down her cheeks, all the while saying, "You don't know how long I've waited for this moment, Vannah."

His gentle touch and soft voice soothed her, and she closed her eyes, savoring the gooseflesh that was starting to ripple across her skin in a sensual tide. Basil's fingers traced a path down her throat, caressed her beating pulse, then slipped beneath the fabric of her ivory satin dressing gown, pushing it off her shoulders until it came free and fell to the floor in a soft rustle.

Vannah's eyes flew open when she felt cool air against her bare skin, and she longed for Basil to take her in his arms and warm her, but all he did was grasp her hand, then take a step back. As his bold, penetrating gaze studied her naked form dispassionately, Vannah felt like a slave being purchased for a sultan's harem and she felt demeaned. Before she could voice her objection, Basil suddenly jerked her hand, and she went stumbling against him with a startled cry. Then, with an exultant laugh, he swung her into his arms and strode over to the bed, where he dropped her as though she were a sack of potatoes.

Just as she was about to protest in annoyance, Basil reached for her hand and kissed it. "You've made me the happiest man in the world, fair lady, and I hope you will be just as pleased with me tonight."

When he said such endearments, her heart melted. "I'm sure I will, Basil. Just come to me, please?"

Without another word he turned out the light in spite of Vannah's protestations, so she heard him remove his dressing gown and felt him slip into bed beside her.

As Vannah took her husband into her arms, she tried to kiss him, but he had already buried his face between her breasts, fondling and suckling with wild abandon until Vannah's senses danced with such intense pleasure that all of her misgivings and fears vanished. But as his caresses grew more vigorous and ardent, her pleasure soon gave way to physical discomfort.

"Basil, please be a little more gentle," she murmured to his shadow. "You're hurting me."

"Can't help it," he muttered thickly into her neck. "Can't control myself."

Her husband took her then. All Vannah was conscious of was his sweating, straining body above hers, groaning and thrusting. The next thing she knew, Basil shuddered, then went rolling off her toward his side of the bed, panting and muttering, "Wonderful, fair lady . . . wonderful."

She stared at his back for a few seconds, then placed an encouraging hand on his shoulder. "Basil?"

He shrugged her off with a curt "So sleepy now . . ."

With tears of disappointment stinging her eyes Vannah was thankful for the blessed, welcome darkness.

As she lay there in silence, listening to Basil breathe deeply in sleep, she felt used and cheated. Every inch of her aroused body ached for fulfillment, yet she knew that the ecstasy she craved would not be forthcoming, at least not tonight. She tried to convince herself that it didn't matter. There was more to marriage than carnal desires. Vannah loved her husband, and in time she was confident that she could show him how to please her just as she had apparently pleased him tonight.

She rolled over to the opposite side of the bed, as far away from her oblivious bridegroom as she could go.

Vannah squeezed her eyes shut and refused to consider the unthinkable. Her traitorous thoughts flew back to the night at Petit Clairvaux, when Vannah had given herself to Martin and he had so patiently tutored her in the art of physical love between a man and a woman. Had she been a fool to believe that all men were so considerate of a woman's pleasure?

Martin had been so tender, holding her, hugging her, kissing her, prolonging their sweet intimacy far into the night. He seemed to take great delight in awakening her to all the sensual pleasure her body was capable of experiencing and showing her how to please him in return. Basil, on the other hand . . .

Instantly Vannah felt ashamed of herself for thinking such disloyal thoughts of her own husband.

You mustn't judge Basil by one night, she warned herself again as she reached down to cover herself with a sheet.

But what if all the nights to come were just like this one?

The only sounds in the darkened room were the steady hiss of raindrops pelting against the windows and Vannah's sigh of desperation.

Chapter Fifteen

London—1896

VANNAH TRUDGED UP the steep front steps of the small, terraced house she shared with Basil and fought back bitter tears of frustration and disappointment. Today, as she had done virtually every day since arriving in London four months ago, Vannah tucked her heavy portfolio of window designs under her arm, endured one dark, crowded omnibus after another, and went from architectural firm to design studio looking for employment. And today, as on all the preceding days, no one wanted to hire her to design stained glass windows. It had been one crushing rejection after another. Finally, tiring of all the pitying looks and regretful voices, she gave up her search three hours earlier than usual and came home.

As Vannah walked in the door, set down the portfolio, and hung her coat up on a rack, Rosie, the young maid-of-all-work Basil had hired to do the cleaning and the cooking, came into the foyer.

" 'Afternoon, ma'am," she greeted Vannah as she wiped her red hands in her apron and curtsied. "Any luck today?"

"No, Rosie," Vannah replied with a defeated sigh, "I'm afraid not."

The maid's round face fell. "I'm sorry to hear it, that I am. But you do look like you're fit fair to drop, Mrs. Edgewood. May I get you a nice hot cup of tea and a slice of lardy cake just out of the oven?"

"That sounds heavenly, Rosie. Where is Mr. Edgewood? Has he gone out?" Vannah asked.

The maid shook her head. "No, ma'am, that he hasn't. He's in the parlor."

Having been well schooled in hiding her true feelings from the servants, Vannah waited until Rosie had gone back to the kitchen before she let displeasure register on her face. While she had been tramping around London until her feet hurt and her back ached, enduring more discouragement and rejection than a person could bear, her husband had been sitting home.

She took a minute to make her expression pleasant before walking into the tiny parlor, but the sight that greeted her eyes did nothing to improve her disagreeable mood.

Basil, dressed informally in shirt and trousers since this morning, was lounging in his favorite chair, his stocking feet resting up on the ottoman as he read a newspaper by the bright light of the window. He looked as though he hadn't moved all day.

When he saw her come into the room, he smiled and rose to give her a peck on the cheek. "Hallo, fair lady. You're home from your travels early today."

Vannah forced herself to smile. "My head was splitting and my feet were aching, so I decided to give up and come home."

Basil returned to his seat. "Well, at least it's not winter anymore."

When Vannah recalled all the bitterly cold, snowy days she had endured in her quest to find work while her husband remained in their warm, dry, terraced house, reading the newspaper and sipping hot tea . . . She banished the thought from her mind at once and sat down with a grateful sigh.

"Yes," she agreed, "at least it's no longer winter."

Just at that moment Rosie appeared carrying a large tray laden down with a plain brown crockery teapot, two cups, napkins, and a plate piled high with slices of warm lardy cake. Once the maid set the tray down on a small table, Vannah dismissed her and began pouring.

"Tea?" she asked Basil, who was immersed in his newspaper once again.

"No, thank you," he murmured. Then he folded up the paper and gave her one of his engaging smiles. "So, no luck today, I take it?"

Vannah shook her head as she took her cup of tea and several slices of cake back to her chair. "No, I'm afraid not, and I'm quite discouraged, Basil."

"Well, don't be. I'm sure the scurvy knaves wouldn't know true talent if they walked into it."

Vannah smiled at his compliment. "I'm afraid my problems may run deeper than that. First of all, some architects and studios are prejudiced against women designers. Tiffany hired them, but many here won't. In fact, just today an architect told me quite bluntly that he wouldn't work with a woman. When he looked at my cartoons, he conceded that my designs were excellent, but he insisted that he just wouldn't be comfortable working with a woman."

Vannah sipped her tea, then added, "The proprietor of one studio told me that he was reluctant to hire me because I am an American."

Basil scowled. "What does that have to do with your abilities?"

"A great deal. You see, English and European stained glass windows use different types of glass. I think they're afraid I can't adapt."

While Vannah explained that English stained glass artisans relied more heavily on paint and enamels than their American counterparts, she watched Basil carefully for the signs of boredom that he usually displayed whenever she tried to discuss her craft with him. He didn't disappoint her. Soon he began staring dreamily out the window and stroking his temple with his middle finger.

She finished the rest of her lardy cake, then said, "And what did you do with your day today, my dear?"

He smiled. "Oh, the usual . . ."

Sleep until noon, eat the hearty luncheon that Rosie prepared daily, sit and read the newspaper until Vannah came home.

Vannah fought to control her temper, but her fingers tightened around her teacup. "I thought you were going to visit several newspapers today to see if anyone would hire you on a permanent basis."

"I didn't get around to it. Tomorrow, fair lady," was his blithe reply.

Vannah's resentment came boiling to the surface. She rose, closed the drawing room door so Rosie wouldn't hear what she was about to say, and turned to confront her husband.

"Basil," she began, her cheeks flushed with anger, "ever since we arrived in England you've promised me that you're going to find another job on a newspaper."

"And I will," he assured her, rising.

"When?" she demanded. "We've been here four months, and not once have you gone out in search of another position!"

Now he glowered back at her, his handsome face sullen and all humor gone from his voice and manner. "I refuse to have my own wife shouting at me. Kindly lower your voice, Mrs. Edgewood." He always referred to Vannah as "Mrs. Edgewood" when he was angry with her.

"How do you think I feel," she went on, "to rise at the crack of dawn every day and go trudging all over this huge, unfamiliar city in all kinds of weather, looking for work, only to come home exhausted and find you sitting here doing nothing?"

"I do not sit here all day doing nothing," he retorted. "I study the newspapers for ideas that can lead to stories of my own, something I can present to an editor as evidence of my talent."

Before Vannah could stop herself, she blurted out, "Do you, Basil? I wonder."

He stared at her in icy silence for a few seconds, then his lip curled contemptuously. "Well, thank you very much for your unwavering faith in me, Mrs. Edgewood." He rose and strode toward the door.

Vannah was overcome with remorse and said apologetically, "Please don't go, Basil. I didn't know what I was saying. I'm just exhausted, that's all."

He stopped and glared at her. "I'm going out for a breath of fresh air, Mrs. Edgewood. I don't expect to be back in time for dinner." He opened the door. "In fact, I don't know when I'll be back."

"Basil—"

But he had already slammed the drawing room door after him, and Vannah could hear his quick, angry footsteps in the foyer as he headed for the front door. When she heard that slam after Basil as well, she turned and walked back into the parlor.

Vannah returned to her chair, seated herself, and let great tears of helplessness fall silently. Then, when she could cry no more, she began to reflect upon everything that had happened since her marriage to Basil Edgewood.

The first disappointment had occurred on her wedding night, when Basil didn't live up to her expectations as a lover, but the second didn't occur until they reached England. While they were staying in a hotel until they could find a suitable place to live, Basil revealed to Vannah that he wasn't a salaried employee of the *Chronicle* as he had led everyone in New York to believe. Oh, the *Chronicle* had paid his passage to America, but once he was there, he was paid for each individual article he sent back, leading to a rather sporadic income.

While Vannah had been most upset with him for not telling her the truth right away, she quickly forgave him when he assured her that it was only a matter of time before some editor realized what a great writer he was and hired him on a permanent basis. And, in the meantime, they had the money that Vannah's mother had left her to live on.

So they rented a small, terraced house situated between a print shop and a confection factory in the Clerkenwell section of London, and with Rosie assuming all household duties, Vannah was free to search for design work.

After one week of having doors closed in her face, Vannah realized that her dream of working in England was not going to be easy to fulfill.

At first she didn't mind the interminable omnibus rides through the great, sprawling city and suburbs to hunt down architects who might use her services or to call upon the other designers Mr. Tiffany had recommended. But as the winter days grew shorter and cold rain and snow froze her feet and hands, Vannah quickly lost her enthusiasm.

Suddenly there came a knock on the drawing room door, and when Vannah said, "Come in," Rosie appeared.

After bobbing a curtsy she said, "Mrs. Edgewood, if I prepare supper early tonight, may I go home early?"

"Of course," she replied. "And, Rosie, Mr. Edgewood will not be dining with me tonight, so just make enough for me if you would."

The maid curtsied again and left her mistress alone.

Basil didn't return home until eleven o'clock that night. Vannah, who had been sitting up in bed waiting for him since nine o'clock, put aside the book she had been reading and sat up expectantly, listening for the familiar sound of his footsteps on the stairs. In a few moments Basil was standing in the doorway.

"I'm sorry," she said softly from the bed.

"Apology accepted," he said with a forgiving smile.

"I don't ever want us to argue again."

"Neither do I, fair lady."

That resolved, Vannah put her hand to her mouth to stifle a yawn. "You must forgive me, but I'm so tired, I could sleep for a month." She turned off the light by her bed. "Good night, Basil."

However, her husband had other plans.

Suddenly, just as Vannah was drifting off to sleep, she felt the bed sag and creak as Basil got in beside her.

"I need you so much tonight, fair lady," he whispered into her ear, struggling to hike her nightgown up to her chin.

"Basil, please. I'm too tired," Vannah grumbled.

"But you're never too tired for this, are you?" He began stroking and squeezing her breasts, teasing the erect nipples with his thumbs until Vannah whimpered in surrender and turned to him. She sensed him grinning down at her. "I thought not."

As Vannah felt the first ripples of pleasure stirring deep within her, she prayed that it would be different tonight, but as Basil continued to maul her breasts, she realized with a sinking heart that it was going to be the same unless she took the initiative. Emboldened by weariness and frustration, Vannah suddenly grasped Basil's hands and held them in her own.

"Please, Basil," she whispered seductively, her face inches from his own, "let me show you what pleases me tonight." And she guided one of his hands down toward her triangle of golden curls. "Let me teach you."

Without warning he jerked his hand away, grasped the

startled Vannah by the shoulders, and threw his whole weight against her, forcing her down against the pillows.

"Slattern!" he shrieked, his fingers biting into her painfully. "Don't you ever do that again, do you hear me? I'm a decent man and I won't tolerate any whorish behavior from my own wife!"

Vannah just stared up at him numbly, unable to resist or explain herself. She didn't even utter a word of protest when Basil fell on her to satisfy himself. When it was over, with merciful quickness, Vannah rolled away from him and willed herself to sleep.

The following day, Basil returned to being the delightful, amusing young man who had so charmed Vannah in New York City, and she wondered if she had imagined the furious, indignant husband who had rebuffed her advances the previous night.

She was cool and reserved toward him at breakfast, but he didn't seem to notice as he urged her to forget about scouring the city for work today and to join him in the festivities he was planning to celebrate the arrival of March. Soon Basil teased and cajoled Vannah out of her black mood, and she was soon laughing at his verbal antics.

First they went to the British Museum and spent the morning looking at all the exhibits, then they had a rather extravagant lunch in a fine restaurant. When they were through, they splurged on a hansom cab to Hyde Park.

Once there, Vannah concentrated on enjoying Basil's high-spirited, lighthearted mood. Even as she slipped her arm through her husband's and stood on the Serpentine Bridge, laughing with him and staring out over the water, Vannah couldn't know that she was experiencing one of the final tranquil moments in her life with Basil Edgewood.

The following morning after breakfast, when Vannah prepared for her usual ordeal of looking for employment,

Basil surprised her by ordering her to remain home for the entire day while he went out to make the rounds of various London newspaper offices.

Since today was Rosie's day off, Vannah had the house to herself and an entire day to do whatever she wished. So she got out her watercolors and spent the morning painting a Newport landscape from memory.

Around noon there came a knock on the front door. Vannah almost called out for Rosie to answer it, remembered that the maid wasn't here today, and went to answer it herself.

As Vannah swung the door open and saw who was standing there, her breath left her body in a great gasp of astonishment. She couldn't have uttered a word if her life depended on it.

Beloved emerald eyes burned into hers, and a deep, resonant voice said, "Hallo, Vannah."

"M-Martin" was all she could manage to say as she stepped back a pace.

Time slowed, then stopped. The house, the street, the world ceased to exist.

Vannah couldn't tear her eyes away from the tall, familiar figure standing on her front steps. As she greedily devoured every detail of his appearance, vivid memories of the two nights of bliss they had shared came flashing back to torment her: the clean, fresh scent of his hair; the puckered surface of his scar against her lips; and, as always, the look in those compelling, enigmatic green eyes as they peered into her heart and read the secret desires written there.

That remote piece of her mind still capable of rational thought kept urging her to send Martin away now, before it was too late, but Vannah was helpless against him.

From far away she heard herself say, "Won't you come

in?" as she swung the door open wider in invitation and stepped back into the foyer.

Without saying a word Martin entered her house and closed the door after him. His handsome face was an impassive mask, but Vannah noticed his hands shaking imperceptibly as he set his gray felt Homburg on a peg and stripped off his black calfskin gloves, followed by his gray overcoat.

Then he turned to her.

"Vannah . . ." Martin began. "Dear God, I—" But his voice broke, and all he could do was stare at her helplessly.

Too much time had passed for him to be gentle with her. His deep love and all-consuming desire had been too long denied. With a groan he extended his arms to her.

Mindlessly Vannah went to him, conscious only of the fact that Martin was here with her now and that he wanted her as much as she wanted him.

As they came together Vannah felt as though she were being hurled against a stone wall, her soft, pliant body yielding to his superior strength. Then that strength was encompassing her, so warm and comforting, as Martin wrapped his arms around her in a crushing hug.

His kiss was not tender. From the first bruising touch of his lips against hers, Vannah felt her senses snap to life one by one, and she responded willingly, hungrily, opening her mouth so he could kiss her as deeply and intimately as he wished. Martin's mouth tasted sweet and familiar, and Vannah abandoned herself to the dizzying sensations his touch released.

Finally they parted breathlessly, only to have Martin begin kissing her forehead, her temples, her eyelids, her cheeks, all the while murmuring, "Thought I lost you forever, my Vannah . . . Dear God, how I missed you, my love! Never let you go again . . . I promise."

The rational part of her intellect warned her that he was

making promises he couldn't possibly keep under the circumstances, but she ignored it. The only reality was the warmth of Martin's breath against her face, the hardness of his cheek against hers, the strong, steady beating of his heart. Martin was here with her now. Nothing else mattered.

Without warning he stopped kissing her and stared deeply into her eyes. "I want to make love to you, Vannah," he said, his voice trembling. Then he looked at the staircase. "I'm assuming your bedroom is up there?"

The bedroom . . . Suddenly a picture of her and Basil in bed together cut across Vannah's mind like a razor. The spell was shattered, swept away by cold reality.

She moved away from Martin, seeking to distance herself from him physically as well as emotionally. "I—I can't, Martin." Vannah twisted her wedding ring. "I'm married now, you see."

"I know."

Vannah's eyes widened in astonishment. "You know? But—but how?"

"Constance told me."

"Aunt Constance? But—but what were you doing in America?"

Martin took a great, shuddering breath, and his eyes were shadowed with pain. When he spoke, Vannah heard a grim, self-mocking quality to his voice that she had never heard there before.

"I went there to find you, to ask you to marry me again. Katherine left me, Vannah. After three years she couldn't tolerate England and she couldn't tolerate my cold indifference any longer. The day she left me to return to her father in Wyoming, I filed for divorce, then caught the first available ship to New York."

Vannah felt the blood drain from her face so fast, the floor came rushing up to meet her. The next thing she knew, Martin's arm was around her waist and he was leading her over to a chair in the parlor.

"Are you all right?" he asked quietly as she sat down.

Vannah pressed her cold hands to her cheeks and nodded, but in reality she wanted to scream and go on screaming until she couldn't scream anymore.

Martin was no longer married to Katherine Costello. He was free, but now Vannah was not. She fancied that she could hear the Fates laughing at her, taunting her.

She watched as Martin crossed the parlor to the bottle of brandy on the sideboard and poured some into a glass.

"Why didn't you send me a cable?" she cried. "Why didn't you tell me that you were no longer married?"

Why did you allow me to marry Basil Edgewood?

Martin smiled wryly. "For the most foolish of reasons. I wanted to surprise you. I wanted to suddenly appear at the foot of the stairs the way I did at Clairvaux when I returned from Wyoming. I wanted to see the expression on your face when I asked you to marry me all over again."

Now his face clouded as he took the glass of brandy and handed it to her. "But when I arrived in New York City, I found that your mother had died and the house you used to live in sold. I'm sorry about your mother, Vannah."

Vannah nodded as she sipped the brandy and coughed as the liquid seared her throat. "Thank you. Gerrold remarried. He lives in a fine French château on Millionaires' Row now."

"So I soon discovered," Martin replied, going over to the window that faced the print shop. "When I went to call on him, I discovered that many things had changed in my absence."

"He told you about Aunt Constance and me?"

Martin nodded somberly. "When I saw your father, he hadn't learned that you were married, only that you had left the Tiffany Glass and Design Company. So I went to

Virginia to see Constance, and she told me all about your true parentage. It must have been a great shock to you, Vannah."

Vannah sighed. "It was, but at least I was able to use it to escape Gerrold and fulfill my dream of designing stained glass windows."

"I know," Martin replied. "I've seen some of them."

"You have?" Surprise and pleasure filled Vannah's voice as she set her glass down and rose. "Where? Which ones?"

"Oh, there was one in a church in New York City and another in a Brooklyn church. Then there were windows in several private homes that I wanted to see. Sometime I'll have to tell you what I had to do to see those."

Suddenly Martin shook his head in wonder, and his eyes shone with pride as he looked at her. "They are beautiful windows, Vannah. When I looked at them, I was quite overcome to think that the woman I loved created such works of beauty. You have every right to be proud of your accomplishments, my dear."

It was too much for Vannah to bear. She could fight his passion but not his admiration and respect. She burst into tears and turned away from him.

Martin was beside her in a second, a comforting hand on her arm. "Vannah, love, what is wrong?"

She shrank away from his disconcerting touch and wiped her eyes with the back of her hand. "It's too late for us. Don't you understand? I am another man's wife, Martin."

A muscle twitched in his lean jaw. "That can be easily remedied."

"What do you mean?"

"You can divorce Basil Edgewood and marry me."

For one wild, heady moment Vannah's spirit soared. Martin's solution was so simple. Divorces were relatively easy to obtain nowadays, and there was no stigma attached to being a divorced woman. She could simply explain to

Basil that she was sorry for any pain she had caused him, but the man she had always loved with all her heart was now free, and she was going to marry him.

But Vannah couldn't. No matter how much she might want Martin, she just couldn't coldly discard Basil as though he were a plaything she had suddenly outgrown. He was a human being with feelings, and he loved and needed her. Vannah was honor-bound to remain his wife, just as Martin had been honor-bound to remain Katherine's husband.

Vannah knew what she had to do. She looked Martin squarely in the eye and said the one and only thing that would make him accept her marriage and leave her alone: "But I love my husband, Martin. I don't wish to divorce him."

His eyes narrowed into slits. "I don't believe you."

"You may disbelieve me, if you wish, but it's true." She shrugged helplessly. "I thought you were lost to me forever. Basil helped me through a particularly difficult period of my life, and I fell in love with him. What else can I say?"

"You can tell me the truth, Vannah." He moved closer toward her, caressing her with his eyes only. "You love me as much as I love you, dearest. I can see it in the way you look at me." Martin grinned wickedly. "That kiss you gave me in the foyer a while ago was not the kiss of a woman in love with her husband."

Vannah crossed her arms to erect a physical barrier between them. "I was startled to see you after all this time, that's all."

Martin shook his head, a sardonic smile twisting his mouth. "Trying to resist me again, Vannah, my love? I seem to remember that you once put up a valiant struggle in Newport, but it didn't work then, and it won't work now."

She moved away from him, fearful of losing the last shreds of her resolve if he remained. "I think you had better leave, Martin. And I also think it would be best if we never see each other again."

"You know I can't agree to that."

"You must!" she cried in desperation.

Martin sighed deeply and just regarded her solemnly for the longest time. His eyes were veiled again, for he had withdrawn into himself, deliberately concealing his true feelings from Vannah.

Finally he held up his hands in surrender. "All right, Vannah, you win. If you insist that you love your husband and don't wish to divorce him, I won't try to come between you. But I would like to remain your friend and become a friend to your husband. Will you at least allow me that privilege?"

When she gave him a wary, skeptical look, Martin added, "In all modesty, I am a man of some influence in certain circles. If you ever need anything—"

"Basil and I will do just fine without anyone's help," Vannah retorted.

Martin walked over to the table and looked at the sketch Vannah had been doing. He smiled. "This is Petit Clairvaux in the grove of copper beeches, isn't it?" When Vannah nodded, he said, "I thought so. I assume you'll be designing windows here?"

Vannah's face fell, and she muttered, "I would love to, if I can ever find someone to hire me."

Before she could stop herself, she told Martin all about her frustrating months of trying to find work.

He listened intently and sympathetically, then said, "I move in rather artistic circles these days and number many artists among my friends. Let me see what I can do to help."

Vannah felt the stirrings of hope for the first time since

arriving in London. "Oh, Martin, do you really think you could find me such a position?"

"I can try."

"I'd be forever in your debt."

"I know." His gaze scorched her as he looked her up and down. "And I would expect to be repaid."

Vannah swallowed hard. "How?"

His face was as innocent as a choirboy's. "You could design a window for Ashwood."

Vannah laughed shakily. Suddenly the tension between them seemed to vanish, and she felt more at ease in his company. "How did you ever become involved with artists?"

Martin grinned. "Offer me tea and I'll tell you."

Later, as they sat together drinking tea and eating the last of the lardy cake, Martin told Vannah about his many and varied enterprises.

"But the one I'm most involved in is my publishing company," he said, handing Vannah his card. "We publish everything from the wildly successful romances of the Baroness Minska to more scholarly works."

Vannah studied the card with its brown ash-tree symbol and the words *Ashwood Press* printed in bold, black letters. "Do you still live at Ashwood?"

Martin shook his head as he dabbed at his lips with a napkin. "Very rarely now. After the solitude of life on the range I prefer the excitement and bustle of London."

"You seem to have found your place in the world at long last, Martin. I couldn't be happier for you," she said.

"I do have almost everything I want," he said, giving her a significant look. "Almost everything."

Vannah rose to conceal her nervousness and started clearing their plates away. "Well, as Aunt Constance always used to tell me, one can't have everything in life."

Martin said nothing, just rubbed his scar thoughtfully.

Later, when it was time for her guest to leave, Vannah

showed Martin to the door. Much to her relief, he didn't try to force any intimacies upon her but was politeness itself.

"Please remember, Vannah," he said as he put on his hat, "if you ever need anything, anything at all, call on me."

"Thank you, Martin. I shall."

She watched him climb into his carriage and wave to her, then she closed the door and went back inside.

As Martin rode back to his office he rubbed his scar and thought of Vannah. He had thought of no one else during those seemingly endless years during which he had had to endure Katherine. He leaned his head back and closed his eyes. But that was all behind him now.

Martin recalled his deep devastation when he had finally tracked Constance Travers to her new home in Virginia, only to be told that Vannah had married someone else just several months ago and was now living in London. On the return ocean voyage Martin Ash promised himself that he would not allow the Fates to snatch Vannah from him a second time. He would find a way to win her back, husband or no.

His expression softened. She was still as beautiful as he remembered with her wide blue eyes so quick to sparkle with humor and intelligence and her ready smile. He thought of her seated across from him while they had tea, the light from the window playing on her golden hair and warming her delicate ivory skin. Suddenly he was overcome with love for her.

But he knew that he would have to move very, very carefully if he wanted to win her back. Vannah was as proud and honorable as any ten men Martin had ever known. When she had told him that she would not divorce her husband, Martin knew that she meant it. He also knew that she would never see him again if she suspected him of trying to destroy her marriage just so he could have her.

He intended to do just that. Despite Vannah's protestations that she loved her husband, Martin wasn't so sure. Perhaps it was a certain look that came into her eyes when she spoke of him, but Martin sensed that she wasn't happy with this Basil Edgewood of hers. He didn't know why, but he intended to find out and exploit it for his own gain.

Anger consumed him when he thought of Vannah in such humble surroundings as a terraced house in Clerkenwell. She belonged in a Mayfair town house or a country estate like Ashwood, but obviously her husband couldn't provide those for her. And, judging from the plain white blouse and black skirt Vannah wore, he couldn't provide her with the fine clothes she deserved as well.

Already an impression of Basil Edgewood was beginning to form in Martin's mind, and he didn't like it. But there was nothing he could do about it just yet.

"But one day you shall be mine again, Vannah," he promised himself.

It was dark before Basil returned home that evening.

Even though Vannah was watching from the parlor window, she resisted the urge to meet him at the door and pounce on him, demanding to know if he had had any success today. When he came storming into the parlor, his face twisted into a mask of anger, she was glad she hadn't.

He looked at her quietly reading and snarled, "Before you say one word, Mrs. Edgewood . . . no, I did not find myself gainful employment today. I must have walked a thousand miles and had a hundred doors slammed in my face."

Vannah put her book down and went to him, placing her hands gently on his shoulders. "I'm so sorry, darling. I know it can be very frustrating, but one just has to keep looking."

He pushed her hands away and glared at her. "You are really unbelievable, Mrs. Edgewood, do you know that? I've just experienced the most humiliating day of my life, and all you can do is stand there and tell me I've got to endure more of the same tomorrow."

Vannah felt her temper flare, but she suppressed it and tried to be conciliatory. "I'm sorry, Basil, but the only way you're going to find a position is to go look for one."

He stalked over to the sideboard, poured himself a generous glass of brandy, and tossed it down in one gulp. "Those scurvy knaves wouldn't know a good writer if one fell on them from out of the sky. I don't know why I waste my time bothering with the likes of them."

Vannah knew that there was no reasoning with him when he was in one of these black moods. So she said, "I think the pot pie that Rosie left for our supper is almost ready. If you'll excuse me, I'll go into the kitchen to check."

No sooner had Vannah lifted the fragrant pie out of the oven and set it on a cast-iron trivet than Basil came in. "What's this?" he demanded, shoving something under her nose.

Vannah started when she saw Martin's card. She had forgotten that she had left it on the table in the parlor, and Basil must have found it.

"Oh, that . . ." she said nonchalantly, turning to the cupboards to hide her guilty face. "Martin Ash came to call this afternoon. Aunt Constance must have given him my address." She stood on tiptoes to reach some plates. "He's involved in some publishing venture or other and left that card."

"You know *the* Martin Ash, of Ashwood Press?" Basil asked incredulously.

Vannah turned, plates in hand. "I told you before we were married, Basil. Martin Ash and I . . ." The memory was so fresh, she couldn't finish and instead made a great pretext of setting the table.

Suddenly Basil let out a great whoop, grabbed Vannah, and started dancing around the kitchen with her in tow.

"Basil," Vannah said, stumbling after him, "whatever is the matter? Have you taken leave of your senses?"

He released her and laughed. "I can't believe my good fortune, fair lady. My wife was once enamored of Martin Ash, one of the most successful and influential publishers in England."

"I'm sorry, Basil. I don't understand. What was between Martin and myself has long been over. He was just paying a social call today."

Basil grabbed her arms. "Honestly, fair lady, sometimes you can be so—so thick. Don't you realize what this means to me?"

She shook her head.

"A golden opportunity! Why should I waste my time scribbling for some newspaper that doesn't appreciate my talent when I can be writing books for Ashwood Press? You did tell him your husband was a writer when he came to call, didn't you?"

"I—I don't believe I mentioned it."

For one brief moment anger flitted across his face, then he said, very sarcastically, "Why, thank you for your ceaseless support, Mrs. Edgewood." Then he brightened at once. "No matter. You can invite him to dine with us one evening and I'll approach him with an idea I've had for some time now for a novel. I take it you're still on good terms. I'm sure he'll agree, if only for your sake."

Vannah twisted her wedding ring. "Basil, I just wouldn't feel comfortable asking such a favor of Martin Ash." It was one thing to allow him to help her find a position but quite another for him to help her husband as well.

He glared at her, his dark eyes so cold, Vannah shivered in the warm kitchen. "You are refusing to do this, Mrs. Edgewood? My own wife is refusing to help me?"

"It's not that I don't want to help you, Basil. You know there's nothing I wouldn't do for you. But I'm just afraid that if I ask this favor of Martin, he's going to want something in return." Vannah looked at him helplessly. "He still loves me, Basil. I could tell when he came today."

"But you don't love him, do you, Mrs. Edgewood?"

"Of course not!" was Vannah's indignant reply. "You know I don't."

Basil sighed. "I'm not asking you to prostitute yourself to Martin Ash for my benefit, Vannah. All I'm asking is that you invite him to dinner so I can approach him about my novel." Now he walked over to her and began stroking her cheek with the backs of his fingers. "That's not too much to ask, is it?"

She knew that if she refused, she would never know a moment's peace. "No," Vannah replied quietly, "I suppose not."

Basil grinned, then kissed her on the forehead. "Oh, thank you, fair lady, thank you! Now, what's for dinner? I'm starved."

Later that night, after Vannah was certain that Basil was sound asleep, she rose and went downstairs to the parlor.

"Dear God," she whispered to herself in the darkness, "what am I going to do?"

Just seeing Martin today brought home quite forcefully the fact that she had never stopped loving him in spite of her marriage to Basil. And Martin knew it. That's what made the situation so very tense and volatile.

She rose and went to the window, opening the curtains

so that the light from a street lamp flooded into the room. The street was quiet, in marked contrast to the tumultuous emotions warring within her.

Vannah knew that the only way she could possibly save her marriage was to keep herself far away from temptation, far away from Martin Ash. He hadn't been boasting when he insisted that Vannah couldn't resist him. She never had been strong enough to withstand the magnetic force of his personality and she knew it.

How could she make Basil understand that he was throwing her to the lions by insisting that she use her past relationship with Martin to further his own career?

With a sigh she closed the curtains and went back upstairs to bed.

Chapter Sixteen

THE FOLLOWING MORNING Vannah was just about to leave for her rounds when a man calling himself Lord Fleet's driver appeared at the door, handed her an envelope, and told her that he would wait for a reply.

Vannah scowled as she stood in the foyer, reading Martin's message. It said: "I have a business proposition to discuss with you. If interested, my driver will convey you to my offices. Martin."

She hesitated, wondering what to do. Vannah knew she should discuss any such proposition with Basil, but he was still sleeping. Besides, Martin's cryptic note had aroused her curiosity.

"Rosie," she said to the maid, "when Mr. Edgewood wakes up, will you please tell him that I am going to the offices of Ashwood Press and don't know when I shall return?"

"Yes, ma'am, that I will."

Vannah thanked her, put on her wrap, and left.

The moment she arrived at the gracious Queen Anne structure of red brick, Vannah was shown upstairs to Martin's office, a large, oak-paneled room that smelled faintly of paper, leather bindings, and tobacco. The moment Vannah appeared in the doorway, Martin rose from behind a long, glass-topped desk and crossed the room in his bold stride, a warm smile of welcome lighting his face.

"Vannah," he said, "I'm delighted to see you here."

In his brown tweed jacket Martin looked more like a country squire than a prominent publisher, but even his casual attire couldn't put Vannah completely at her ease. When he offered to take her wrap and his hands rested lightly on her shoulders for just an instant, she felt her heart quicken of its own accord.

She turned and smiled to hide her nervousness. "Your note was so intriguing, how could I resist?"

"Splendid. Do sit down and make yourself comfortable."

To her dismay he indicated the divan rather than one of the two chairs across from his desk, but she seated herself and folded her hands demurely in her lap.

As Martin watched her wedge herself into one corner of the divan, her body rigid and tense, he wondered if she were afraid of him or of herself.

"Would you like a cup of tea?" he asked as he walked over to the Spode tea service on a small table near his desk. "It's my special blend. Quite delicious."

"No—no thank you," Vannah replied. "Now, Martin, just what is this business proposition you have to discuss with me?"

So, Martin thought with amusement as he poured himself a cup, she wants to get right to the point, then escape from me as quickly as she can.

"Well," he began as he crossed the room and seated himself at the opposite end of the divan, "when I returned home last night, I realized that I have the perfect opportunity for you to establish yourself as a stained glass designer in England."

Vannah leaned forward expectantly. "How?"

"I am having a house built for myself in St. John's Wood, and I would like to commission you to design the windows for it."

The room was silent except for the faint clink of Martin's teacup as he set it back in its saucer.

Vannah stared at him, searching his face for any hint of deception, for she suspected that this offer was nothing more then a ruse to continuously bring them together.

She twisted her wedding ring. "Why, Martin? Why, out of all the stained glass artisans in London, do you want me to design your windows?"

"Because you are one of the best, if not *the* best," he replied smoothly, without hesitation. "I've seen your windows in America, remember, so I'm not buying a pig in a poke."

Vannah rose to stand behind the divan, her hands clutching at its back until her knuckles turned white. "And that's your only reason?"

"No," Martin replied, setting his teacup down. "I must confess that I have another." Then he rose to face her. "I want to help a friend who was once so very dear to me." *And who will be again.*

Vannah slowly let out the breath she had been holding. "And that's all?"

A smile played about Martin's mouth. "Don't tell me

you suspect me of having an ulterior motive for offering you this commission."

"Knowing you as I do, the thought had crossed my mind," she replied dryly.

His hearty burst of laughter filled the room. "I assure you, Vannah, my motives are of the noblest." Then he grew serious. "Of course, I expect to be closely involved. This is to be my London home, after all. I will approve all designs, and I expect you to keep me apprised of your progress. I am assuming, of course, that your husband will have no objection?"

"My husband will not object," she said.

"Splendid." Martin began pacing around the room like a nervous jungle cat, his hands jammed into his pockets, his brow furrowed in concentration. "My house was designed by Watson Greene, one of our finest new architects, and when it's completed, I'm going to invite artists, architects, and critics to see it. Watson's buildings always generate excitement in any case. And once word gets around that a newcomer named Savannah Webb—"

"Edgewood."

"Savannah Edgewood, student and employee of Louis Comfort Tiffany, designed the windows . . ." Martin shrugged expressively.

Suddenly Vannah felt the first stirrings of excitement at the prospect of doing what she loved best. She had no idea of how she looked right at that very moment, her eyes sparkling, her soft smile lighting her entire face and making it glow radiantly, but Martin did. He thought his heart would burst with all the love he felt for her, and the need to enfold her in his arms tenderly was almost more than he could stand. But he held back for both their sakes. At least, for now, he would have to content himself with the knowledge that he was helping her.

"Thank you, Martin," she said simply.

"Don't thank me just yet. Watson still has to approve of you, and he can be a bear. He's a perfectionist and an iconoclast. He always likes to do things his own way, and he's not going to take kindly to my choosing someone to design the windows."

"Do—do you think that will present a problem?"

He shook his head. "Once he meets you and sees your designs, I don't think so. As a matter of fact, why don't you and your husband come to dinner this Saturday? I've invited Watson and one of my authors, and I know they would like to meet you."

Vannah's face fell in dismay. "I—we couldn't."

"Well, we can make it next Monday evening, then."

"I—I don't think so, Martin."

His smile was wry. "Your husband doesn't wish you to socialize with old lovers, is that it?"

"No, it's not that. As a matter of fact, Basil has an idea for a novel that he would like to discuss with you."

"Fine, then. We can discuss it when you come to dinner."

Vannah blushed furiously and forced the words out. "I can't, Martin. I have nothing to wear."

Martin almost laughed in relief, then composed himself, for he knew that a woman's lack of suitable attire for such a formal occasion was no laughing matter and not to be taken lightly.

Vannah stared at the floor to avoid looking at Martin. "When I left Gerrold's home, I left my Worth gowns behind. And with both Basil and myself trying so desperately to find work . . ." She couldn't bring herself to tell Martin the shameful truth that she hadn't enough money to buy a new dress.

But she didn't need to say anything. Martin was perceptive enough to guess. And as he watched her standing there, fighting back tears of humiliation, he mentally cursed her husband for reducing her to such a state.

Whirling on his heel so Vannah would not see the rage that darkened his face, Martin went to his desk, scribbled something, then rose and handed it to Vannah. "This is to retain you to design my windows."

Vannah lifted her head proudly, eyes blazing. "I cannot accept money from you, Martin. I don't want your charity."

"Charity, is it? And I thought I was hiring you to make windows. Unless, of course, you're proposing to do the work at no charge? That's very generous of you, Savannah," he said, taunting her, "but it's hardly the way to conduct business, my dear. Mr. Tiffany wouldn't approve."

Vannah opened her mouth to say something, then changed her mind, for she knew that he had outfoxed her this time. "Very well, Martin. I shall accept your retainer."

"Good," he said with a grin as he extended his hand to seal their agreement.

As Vannah placed her hand in his, Martin gripped it hard and possessively, but she remained steadfast and did not pull away.

Then Martin said, "Now you have no excuse not to attend dinner on Saturday night. I'm sure my secretary can suggest the names of several dressmakers, and my driver will take you wherever you want to go, then home again."

"Martin, I—"

"Do not argue with me, Vannah. You should know by now that it is pointless."

"Thank you, Martin," Vannah said, lightly resting her hand on his arm for a brief second before turning to leave. "You are a true friend."

And I intend to be much more than that, my dear, he thought. Much more.

"I shall send my carriage for you at six o'clock Saturday evening," he said.

"We'll be ready," Vannah replied just before hurrying out the door, relieved to be free of him at last.

* * *

Martin's town house was located in Upper Brook Street, just a short distance from Grosvenor Square, and when Basil disembarked from Lord Fleet's carriage that Saturday evening, he stared up at the imposing Georgian building enviously.

"Most impressive, fair lady," he murmured to Vannah as he offered her his arm. "Must have been in the family for a century or more."

Vannah was too nervous to notice. She was not worried about her appearance, for with her innate sense of style, she knew that she looked her best in an evening gown of shimmering blue silk cut low enough across her breasts to cause Basil to whistle in admiration when he first saw it. Rosie had even managed to put up Vannah's hair into some semblance of style so she could have walked into Mrs. Astor's ballroom and not been out of place.

She was worried about how her husband and her former lover would get along.

When she had first told Basil of her visit to Martin's office, his dinner invitation, and the commission, she was relieved that he was so pleased. Vannah had feared that he might be jealous, but Basil actually seemed to be looking forward to the evening, primarily because he would have a chance to discuss his proposed novel with Martin.

Now Basil patted her hand as they walked up the steps to the front door. "Just think, fair lady. Once Ash publishes my book and it becomes a success, we'll be able to live in luxury like this."

"Oh, I think it takes more than one book to make your fortune, Basil," Vannah said.

Suddenly he threw her hand off his arm and said petulantly, "There you go again, Mrs. Edgewood, always doubting my abilities."

"Basil, I am not doubting your abilities. I'm merely

asking you to be a little realistic, that's all." As he rang the bell she added, "Let's not argue, shall we?"

Martin's butler answered the door, and once Basil told him who they were, he graciously relieved Vannah of the designs she carried and requested that they follow him to the drawing room where Lord Fleet was waiting.

As soon as the butler announced the Edgewoods, Martin rose and crossed the room toward his guests. Vannah looked breathtakingly beautiful tonight in a blue gown that intensified the color of her eyes, and Martin had to force himself to conceal his frank admiration.

"Vannah, you look especially lovely this evening," he said, bowing over her hand. Then he turned at once to her husband, and the two men regarded each other in curiosity, each sizing up the other.

Martin didn't like what he saw. While good-looking in a pale, poetic way that had been all the fashion ten years ago, Basil Edgewood's eyes were greedy and his mouth petulant.

"Basil," Vannah was saying, "I'd like to present Martin Ash, the Marquis of Fleet. Martin, this is Basil Edgewood, my husband."

"Edgewood," Martin said, extending his hand. "You're a lucky man."

Edgewood grinned in triumph as he shook hands. "And don't I know it, Fleet."

"Well," Martin said, "why don't you come into the drawing room and meet one of my other guests?"

For the first time Vannah noticed another man standing over by the Sheraton sofa, and her mouth felt dry with apprehension. This tall, large man with the wide shoulders and barrel chest was doubtlessly Watson Greene, the architect Vannah would have to impress in order to design the windows for Martin's new house.

As the three of them crossed the room toward him,

Vannah felt two eyes as black as soot sweep over her, appraising her as though she were a piece of furniture. She met his gaze squarely with a frank appraisal of her own.

"Watson Greene," Martin said, "I'd like you to meet Mr. and Mrs. Basil Edgewood. Vannah and Basil, this is Watson Greene, one of the best—"

"The best, Martin," the man interrupted.

Martin grinned. "Pardon me, Watson. The best architect in England today."

"Pleasure to meet you, Greene," Basil said, shaking hands.

When the man turned his full attention on Vannah, she had to admit that he was quite dashing, with wide swaths of silver flaring out from his temples through blue-black hair.

"And this must be Savannah," he murmured, taking her hand and bowing over it extravagantly while his eyes remained at the level of her breasts.

"The best stained glass window designer in England," she replied with a smile.

Watson Greene jerked up to attention, and there was no hint of an answering smile on lips, almost hidden within his grizzled black beard. His look was glacial and penetrating, and for one horrible moment Vannah saw her glorious career flying right out of the window.

Suddenly the architect bellowed, "Yes, yes, *yes*! I like you, girl. If your designs are just as spirited as you are, then I shall allow you to design the windows of my house."

Martin laughed and shook his head. "Watson, my friend, you are quite outrageous."

"Where are your designs, girl?" Watson said, rubbing his hands together in relish and looking around the drawing room like a hound on the scent. "I must see them at once. Immediately. Now."

While Vannah went to retrieve the designs the butler

had left on a nearby table, a footman walked in bearing several glasses of champagne on a silver tray.

"Champagne, Edgewood?" Martin said.

"Don't mind if I do," Basil replied, taking the proffered glass.

With Watson and Vannah absorbed in her designs, Martin turned his attentions to Basil and indicated that he should be seated.

"So, Vannah tells me that you're a writer."

"A journalist," he replied.

"I take it you haven't had any luck finding a suitable position."

Basil leaned forward and shook his head. "Most of the scurvy knaves running newspapers in this city just don't appreciate true talent."

Martin tried not to choke on his champagne. "Where have you looked for work? I know the editors of several newspapers, and perhaps I could arrange for one of them to see you and evaluate your work."

"Don't trouble yourself, Fleet," Basil said. "I've been considering a change. I think writing a novel would be more my line. More creative."

Basil leaned back in his chair and surveyed the elegant Regency drawing room with frank appreciation and envy. "My wife said you'd be willing to help me, Fleet, seeing as how you were once so . . . close."

Martin nodded, trying to stifle his growing dislike of the man. "I am always seeking to publish new talent, Edgewood. I'd be very interested in hearing what type of book you plan to write."

"It's an adventure tale, similar to the kind Rider Haggard writes, and—"

Basil was interrupted by a great, "Yes, yes, *yes!*" from Watson Greene, who came striding across the room toward them with Vannah's cartoons in hand.

"Have you seen these, Ash?" he asked, while staring at Vannah in blatant admiration. "They are sheer poetry. The girl is a genius. For an American, of course."

Vannah grinned. "Oh, no, Mr. Greene, not a genius, merely the best stained glass window designer in England."

The architect roared with laughter, his barrel chest shaking. "Edgewood, I've quite fallen in love with your wife and must have her; otherwise, I shall never design another building as long as I live." Then he kissed Vannah's hand with a resounding smack and rolled his eyes in rapture.

When Martin glanced at Basil to see how he was taking the architect's outrageous teasing, he was somehow not surprised to see the other man's face darken ominously.

He intervened quickly, placing a hand on Basil's arm and murmuring, "You must excuse Watson. He's only jesting with you. I can assure you that he's quite harmless."

Basil's smile was forced. "I realize that, Fleet. Now, about my book—"

But Basil was interrupted once again by the butler announcing the arrival of the last dinner guest, the Baroness Minska.

The baroness came sweeping into the drawing room as though she fully expected a fanfare of trumpets to herald her arrival. She looked like a Tartar princess in a dramatic black robe all embroidered with peacock feathers worked in various metallic threads of blue and gold.

Martin rose and went to meet her, hands extended and a warm smile on his face. "Sophia, you look magnificent." He brought both of her hands to his lips and kissed them.

As the baroness smiled and leaned toward Martin with an easy familiarity, Vannah was startled to feel something strangely akin to jealousy stiffen her back.

Then Watson leaned over and whispered in her ear, "Our Polish authoress."

Vannah stared at the other woman's jet-black hair, worn

loose and wild about her shoulders. "I thought all Poles were fair," she murmured to Watson.

"It's our Sophie's dark Turkish blood," he replied with a wicked glint in his eye.

Now Martin was escorting her over to their little group for introductions, and Vannah had a better opportunity to study her. The baroness was of average height, and striking rather than beautiful with a strong, square face and prominent Slavic cheekbones. She was flamboyant in both dress and manner, the kind of woman who both demanded and commanded attention wherever she went.

When the baroness came to Vannah, her tilted hazel eyes narrowed speculatively, like a tigress sizing up its prey, but Vannah met the intimidating gaze squarely.

"Baroness . . ." she murmured, nodding her head to acknowledge the introduction.

"Mrs. Edgewood," the baroness replied in a sultry voice with just a trace of a French accent. "Dear Martin has told me so much about you."

Before Vannah could respond to such an ambiguous remark, Watson came to her rescue. "Yes, the marquis raved so much about your beauty and your talent that poor Sophie here has been green with envy. Isn't that true, Sophie?" he added innocently.

The tiger's eyes flashed as the baroness gathered herself up, the very picture of icy hauteur. "The Baroness Minska envies no woman."

"You missed your true calling, Sophie," Watson said. "You should have been an actress with your flair for the dramatic."

"Peasant!" she snapped.

But Watson was unflappable. "Now, now, Sophie. If you're not pleasant to me, these good people will get the impression that you don't like me. And we know that's not true."

She whirled on Martin. "Pah! I don't know why you allow this insufferable man into your home! All he does is ridicule and torment me."

Vannah could see that Martin was trying to keep from laughing as he addressed Watson. "Do you think we could have a truce at least for tonight?"

Watson gave an exaggerated sigh and rolled his eyes. "If you insist . . ."

The baroness's smile was smug and triumphant as she took the glass of champagne Martin offered, then promptly seated herself on the sofa and invited Martin to sit beside her.

Once everyone was seated, Vannah asked, "What types of books do you write, Baroness?"

"Books about men and women," she replied with a grandiose sweep of her arm. "Romantic books that touch a woman's heart and soul. Books about love."

Vannah thought she heard Watson stifle a cough of surprise, but she couldn't be sure. She said politely, "They sound wonderful."

"They are," the baroness replied.

"The critics would—and often do—disagree with you, my dear," Watson said, lifting his champagne glass to her in a parody of a toast.

The baroness's eyes narrowed. "Pah! What do those imbeciles know? I seek only to please those thousands who read and enjoy my books."

Martin patted her hand. "And you do, Sophia." Then he addressed Vannah and Basil. "The baroness is my firm's best-selling author."

As Vannah watched the baroness beam up at Martin, she found herself hoping that there was nothing more to their relationship than that of author and publisher.

Suddenly the butler appeared and announced that dinner was ready, so Vannah went to her husband's side while the baroness possessively claimed Martin as her dinner partner. Watson was left to go into dinner alone, and he trailed behind, hands in his pockets, whistling softly to himself.

As their procession made their way toward the dining room, Vannah looked up at Basil and whispered, "You haven't said two words all evening. Aren't you enjoying yourself?"

"Of course I am," he replied, but Vannah could tell from his sulky expression that he was not.

She sighed. Well, she was enjoying herself even if her husband wasn't, and she refused to let him spoil the evening for her.

Dinner reminded Vannah of the formal ones served at the Webbs', course after course of fine, rich food eaten at a long mahogany table set with the finest heirloom china, crystal, and silverware. But any resemblance ended there. Topics of conversation were not restricted to the usual bland ones of food, wine, horses, and European travel, especially with such strong personalities as Watson Greene and the Baroness Minska sitting at the table. Ideas about art and creativity were bounced around and kept in play like a tennis ball during a frenzied match, and Vannah felt herself responding with her own opinions as well.

Sometimes Watson would disagree with the baroness and forget himself, wagging a fork or spoon to make his point, and she would retaliate by uttering an angry stream of Polish that no one else could understand. Then Martin would have to intervene and placate them.

But Vannah hadn't felt so mentally stimulated since she had worked with Louis Comfort Tiffany, and she was sorry when the evening came to an end and it was time to leave.

Vannah sat back against the squabs in Martin's carriage and declared, "I can't remember when I've had such a pleasant evening."

"Well, I'm glad you did, Mrs. Edgewood," Basil grumbled, "because I surely didn't."

Vannah, who had reveled in the stimulating company and was still in high spirits, just sighed with exaggerated patience. "I'm sorry to hear that, Basil."

He crossed his arms. "Can you imagine owning a townhouse in Mayfair and having another built in St. John's Wood just because you want a building in a different style? Must be wonderful to be so wealthy."

When Vannah made no comment, Basil went on with, "I can't say that I was very impressed with your friend, Lord Fleet. He seems quite full of himself, don't you think?"

"Martin is dynamic, but I wouldn't say he's full of himself."

"Of course you wouldn't. After all, the man was once your lover. And the way he was staring at you all night, it looks to me like he'd like to resume your relationship."

Vannah clenched her teeth together to help contain her anger. "Need I remind you that you were the one who encouraged me to cultivate a friendship with him? I warned you that he still might harbor deep feelings for me, but you insisted that he could be helpful to us."

"Everything is always my fault, isn't it, Mrs. Edgewood?" Basil snapped petulantly before ensconcing himself in a corner of the carriage and wrapping himself in a cocoon of cold silence.

They were almost home when Vannah finally relented, as always, and made the first overtures to mend the tense situation.

"Did you have a chance to speak to Martin about your novel?" she asked.

"Yes, until that overdressed Minska woman interrupted us with her grand entrance."

"And did Martin like your idea?"

"He said he was interested and that I'm to write a proposal for him. If he accepts it, he'll advance me some money to live on while I complete the book."

"Why, Basil, that's wonderful! I'm so happy for you."

He unwound himself from his tight little ball and came over to sit beside Vannah. She could see him smile by the light of the carriage lamps.

"Literary fame and fortune is just around the corner for me, fair lady," he said softly into her ear. "Once my book is published, we'll have a grand house of our own in Mayfair and rub elbows with the finest people."

Vannah opened her mouth to warn him once more about having unreasonable expectations, but when she recalled what had happened the last time, she said nothing. Basil would not thank her for her candor.

"We are going to be wealthy, fair lady," he murmured, reaching for her in the darkness.

She felt his fingers grope beneath her evening cape until he found a breast to knead and squeeze. Vannah gasped, more in discomfort than arousal, and had to restrain herself from pushing Basil's hand away in annoyance.

"Basil, the driver will hear us. Besides, we're almost home."

The hand fell away. "I can wait," he said.

When they arrived, Basil insisted on undressing Vannah himself, then he fell upon her like a rutting stag and bedded her in his usual clumsy fashion, ignoring her feeble protests that she needed time to take her usual steps to prevent conception. Her pleas fell on deaf ears.

Yet in spite of her fears that she would become pregnant, Vannah found that she was so preoccupied with Martin that for the first time in her marriage, she knew ecstasy in her husband's arms, and it startled her with its intensity.

As she stared at the ceiling Vannah knew only too well that her long-denied body had responded to mental images of Martin, not the physical reality of her husband. She had felt Martin's hard length moving within her, heard Martin's low growl of pleasure, tasted Martin's sweet mouth against her own, not Basil's. Vannah closed her eyes to the sensual images dancing across her brain, enticing her again, but she couldn't close her mind to Martin no matter how hard she tried.

She had been a fool to think that she could forget such a masterful, dynamic man so easily, even though she was married to another. Martin still exerted a power over her that pulled her toward him inexorably, a power she couldn't deny. And here she was valiantly trying to pretend that they were just friends. She should have known that once Martin Ash became a woman's lover, they could never be just friends again.

And Vannah's torment was just beginning. Bright and early Monday morning, she was scheduled to meet with both Watson and Martin to study the plans of the house in detail and determine what types of windows Martin wanted. She would be in the same room with him, hear his deep bass voice, feel those enigmatic green eyes on her whenever she happened to glance in his direction.

Vannah wanted to run to a place where Martin couldn't find her, a place where she and Basil could have a chance for some sort of life together, free of Martin's disturbing influence. But she knew deep in her heart that no matter where she ran, Martin would always find her.

She closed her eyes and finally slept, but all her dreams were of Martin.

Vannah came rushing into the house, her face flushed with excitement and her arms laden with back issues of *The Studio*, which Watson had ordered her to study.

"Basil?" she called out as she set the magazines down on the table in the parlor and removed her hat.

Rosie appeared in the doorway, wiping her hands in her apron. "Mr. Edgewood isn't home, ma'am, and that's a fact."

Vannah tried to hide her disappointment. "Oh? Did he say where he was going and when he would return?"

"No, ma'am."

"Thank you, Rosie. That will be all."

After the maid returned to the kitchen to prepare supper, Vannah seated herself by the window and began reading, hungry to know all about the artistic trends in England and Europe. She didn't stop until several hours later when Basil, himself, appeared in the doorway.

He sniffed the air. "Something smells good. I wonder what Rosie is cooking for dinner?"

Vannah smiled, put her magazine aside, and went to give her husband a welcoming kiss on the cheek. "Where have you been all day, my dear? I came home just bursting to tell you all about my meeting with Martin and Watson and you weren't here."

"Sorry, fair lady, but I went out to get some inspiration for my novel. You're not the only talented one in this family, you know," he said lightly, kissing her cheek in return.

"That's wonderful, Basil. Martin asked me when you were going to have your ideas on paper to show him."

"Oh, probably by the end of the week."

Vannah took his hand. "Come. Let me tell you all about my meeting today. You should see the splendid house Watson has designed for Martin. He showed me sketches of it and the plans, and—"

Basil balked. "Can we talk later, fair lady? I've had an exhausting day, and I'd like to take a nap before dinner."

Vannah dropped his hand and tried to hide her disappointment. "Pardon me for being so thoughtless, Basil. Of course we can talk after dinner. You just get your rest."

But after dinner Basil said he had just gotten a flash of inspiration for his novel and just had to put it down on paper before he lost it. Apologizing profusely and begging Vannah to understand, he locked himself away in his own bedroom and didn't come out for the rest of the evening.

As Vannah sat alone in the parlor, Watson's list of windows and their dimensions before her, she thought less about designs than about her own husband's apparent disinterest in her work. Back in New York, when he had been courting her, Basil had seemed so proud of her and so encouraging.

To Basil's credit, the following morning he did ask Vannah all about her meeting and seemed to listen with interest as she described the house Watson had designed and the number of windows she would be expected to make.

But somehow it was not the same, and Vannah didn't feel offended when Basil excused himself before she had even finished speaking and locked himself in his bedroom to write.

She told herself it didn't matter, but in her heart of hearts she knew that it was beginning to matter a great deal.

Chapter Seventeen

A WEEK LATER VANNAH was working on her window designs in the parlor when Basil came bursting in with a huge grin on his face.

"I'm on my way to fame and fortune!" he whooped,

raising his arms above his head in triumph. "Fleet approved my proposed novel."

"That's wonderful, dear," Vannah murmured absently as she continued to sketch, hurrying to put her idea on paper while it was still fresh in her mind.

Suddenly Basil snatched the paper away and held it behind his back. "There," he said spitefully. "Now perhaps I can have your undivided attention, Mrs. Edgewood."

"Basil, please!" Vannah cried in annoyance. "I've been working on that design all day and—"

He flung the sketch back at her in a fit of pique. "Fine. If your sketch is more important to you than what your own husband has to say . . ." And he turned and started storming out of the parlor.

"Wait, Basil!" Vannah pleaded as she jumped to her feet and went after him, the sketch forgotten. When she caught up with him at the door, she grasped his arm to restrain him. "I'm sorry, darling. I just become so absorbed in what I'm doing that I tend to shut out the world."

"You're forgiven," he said tightly, "but in the future, when I speak to you, I expect you to stop whatever you are doing and pay attention to me."

"Of course, Basil."

"A good wife always obeys her husband."

All Vannah said was, "I'm so pleased that Martin approved of your proposed novel, Basil."

"That's not all he did," Basil said, reaching into his pocket. "He gave me quite a sizable advance as well. We're rich, fair lady, rich!"

And he grabbed Vannah around the waist and whirled her around the parlor.

When he stopped, laughing and out of breath, he said, "We must go out and celebrate. I think we should have dinner at the Savoy, then go to the theater."

Vannah hesitated. She still had one last design to complete, and she was scheduled to meet with Martin and Watson tomorrow morning to show them what she had accomplished. She was sure that Watson, if not Martin, would dismiss her as a frivolous dabbler rather than the professional she was if she arrived with her assignment incomplete. Yet, if she spent the rest of the evening out celebrating with Basil, there would be no time to finish the final design unless she worked late into the night.

She put her hand on Basil's arm. "Don't you think we should be a bit cautious with our money now? Even though we both received generous advances from Martin, we still have to be frugal."

"I never thought I'd see the day when Gerrold Webb's daughter talked of frugality. You always had all the money you ever wanted."

"Yes, but you're not a millionaire like Gerrold Webb," Vannah pointed out. She took a deep breath to steady herself, for she decided that now was the time to tell her husband the truth about her parentage. "And Gerrold Webb isn't my real father."

And, before Basil could say another word, Vannah quickly told him about her mother's affair with Alastair McKechnie.

"Why didn't you tell me this sooner, Mrs. Edgewood?" Basil demanded quietly.

Vannah raised her head. "Does it make any difference who my real father is?"

"Of course not! I just thought a husband and wife aren't supposed to have any secrets from each other."

"I didn't think it was important."

"I agree," Basil said lightly. "Now I want to celebrate. Why don't you wear that blue dress you wore to Fleet's dinner party?"

"I'll have to," Vannah replied wryly. "It's the only evening dress I have."

"Well, buy another," Basil said as he turned to go upstairs. "A man wants his wife to be a credit to him," he added, sounding suspiciously like Gerrold Webb.

When she was alone, Vannah walked over to the table and put her drawings away with a sigh. She could tell that it was going to be a long, long night.

The following morning a yawning, bleary-eyed Vannah arrived for the meeting promptly at nine o'clock, her designs complete and in hand, to find only Martin there.

After they exchanged greetings she looked around in dismay. "Where is Watson?"

Martin grinned. "Our esteemed architect sent word that he would be a little late this morning. Knowing Watson as I do, I would attribute it to a night of carousing in the company of certain women of his acquaintance."

"I know how he must feel," Vannah said, smothering a yawn as she peeled off her gray chamois gloves and removed her feathered hat. "Basil and I did a little carousing ourselves, to celebrate the launching of his new career as a novelist." She gave Martin a heartfelt smile. "Thank you for accepting his proposal."

Martin walked over to the tea service and began pouring. "What's there to thank me for? I read his ideas and felt they have merit, so I bought it. Of course, it remains to be seen if he can write the book, but since he is a journalist, I don't foresee any problems in that area."

Vannah took the proffered cup and sat down on the divan. "I'm sure Basil's work will be a credit to Ashwood Press."

He seated himself across from her so he wouldn't have to endure the maddening nearness of her, but the teasing scent of her perfume was severely testing his self-control. "Do you suppose I could have a look at your designs before Watson arrives?"

Vannah's eyes, shadowed from lack of sleep, lit up at once. "Of course. I'm eager to show them to you and see what you think."

They set their teacups down and started over to Martin's desk where Vannah had left the designs. As Martin walked behind her he noticed that she had neglected to fasten the top two buttons of her dress.

"Hold one moment and don't turn around," he said.

Vannah stopped. "What is it?"

"Two buttons came undone."

"Oh, dear . . ." she murmured, blushing as she reached her free hand up behind her neck to fasten them.

"Allow me," Martin said.

Before Vannah could protest, he reached up and deftly fastened them, his fingers brushing the nape of her neck. Brief as his touch was, it sent gooseflesh dancing along Vannah's arms, and she had to fight hard against the urge to lean back against him.

"There," Martin said. "Now you're fully dressed."

"Thank you," Vannah said, trying not to blush again. "It's rather difficult managing all the buttons without a ladies' maid."

"Oh, I'll have you know that I make an admirable ladies' maid."

She ignored the innuendo in his voice and proceeded to the desk.

"And I'll have you know that I stayed up half the night just to finish these designs," she said.

Martin's face was the mirror of his concern. "You shouldn't jeopardize your health just for my windows."

"Don't worry about me. I'm none the worse for wear."

"Oh, but I do worry about you. Constantly."

"There is no need," she replied, trying to keep the lightness in her voice, though it was difficult to ignore the disquieting look in Martin's eyes.

Vannah hurriedly turned back to her designs, showing him the simple ones featuring Watson's favorite motifs of a crescent moon and stars for the mullioned windows upstairs, then progressed to the more elaborate ones for important rooms such as the drawing room and foyer. She watched Martin's face carefully as she showed him each design, and she turned pink with pleasure and gratification when she saw the excitement light up his green eyes.

"Vannah," he said, shaking his head in wonder, "these are beautiful. You have outdone yourself."

"Do you really like them, Martin?"

"Like them?" He stared at her as though she were daft. "Someone would have to be a fool not to hire you to design windows for them."

She smiled. "But I have saved the best for last," and she took out the final sketch and set it before him. "As you are well aware, your main foyer has a vaulted ceiling, and there are four long windows high over the front door. I would suggest one female figure representing each of the four seasons."

Vannah held her breath as Martin took the sketch and studied it, his brow furrowed. When he didn't say a word for what seemed like hours, she said, "Each figure is set against the same landscape that changes with the season. The flowers that make up the border also change appropriately. So spring is a blonde woman with apple blossoms, summer is a brown-haired woman with roses, autumn a titian-haired beauty with chrysanthemums, and winter a black-haired woman standing in a snow-covered landscape without any flowers at all in the border."

When Martin still made no comment after her explanation, Vannah moistened her dry lips and added nervously, "Of course, if you don't like it, I can design something else."

"Oh, no," he said softly, shaking his head, "these are

the windows I want, and if Watson doesn't approve, he can just go to hell."

At that moment Vannah experienced the special bond of closeness that can blossom between two people when they realize that they share the same hopes and dreams. Martin understood her work and appreciated it.

He looked at her. "May I make one suggestion?"

"Of course."

"Would you paint each of the women with your face?"

Vannah's smile froze, and she took a step back. "Do you really think my husband would ever allow such a thing, Martin?" she asked, her voice ragged and angry.

"Of course not. Please forgive me for even suggesting it. I just thought that it would generate excitement among the critics to have you as both model and designer for the windows."

"If anything, they would dismiss me as nothing more than a vain, conceited woman," she replied, "plastering her likeness everywhere."

Martin gave her a long, level look. "Anyone who knows you could never think such a thing."

Vannah sensed that they were moving on to dangerous ground again. She said, "I have a better idea. Why don't I give each of the Four Seasons the baroness's face? That would certainly cause speculation among the critics."

A smile played about Martin's mouth. "Now why would I want that?"

"Don't you . . . ?" Vannah floundered. "Aren't you. . . ?"

"Lovers?" Martin shook his head. "Sophia is doing her damnedest to convince the world we are, but you are the only woman I have ever loved and still love, Vannah. You know that."

She turned away, not trusting herself to remain detached when he used that silky, seductive tone of voice. "Martin, don't. Please don't say such things."

He rounded the desk until he stood before her. "Don't say what's in my heart, what I'm feeling for you this very moment? You ask the impossible of me, Vannah."

She stared at the carpet, afraid that if she looked up at him, he would read what was in her heart as well. "As I've told you before, Martin, it's too late for us. I'm married to someone else."

"You may be married to Basil Edgewood, my love, but your heart and soul belong to me, and mine to you. They always have and they always will. Don't shake your head and try to deny it, because I can see it in your eyes every time you look at me."

He caught her hand, and before she could pull away, he slipped it beneath the lapels of his morning coat and held it to his heart.

With her hand captured between Martin's strong fingers and the hard muscles of his chest, Vannah was his prisoner, unable to move. She glared at him defiantly, willing him to release her.

But he didn't. He just smiled with infuriating confidence. "Do you know what I was thinking as I fastened your buttons a few moments ago? How much I would like to unfasten all the rest of them, one by one, and . . ."

Vannah closed her mind to the picture he was painting and clenched her teeth together. "If you did, Martin Ash, I would tear up these designs right before your very eyes and never speak to you again."

His lids drooped, hooding his eyes. "Is that a threat, my beautiful Savannah, or a challenge?"

And because she doubted her own ability to carry out such a threat, Vannah did pull away to break the alluring spell of intimacy Martin was beginning to weave around her. No sooner did she move away from him than the door suddenly swung open to reveal Watson in a plaid Inverness cape and a dramatic, black, wide-brimmed hat.

"Good morning, good morning, good morning," he sang as he came charging into the room like a bull on the loose, oblivious to the tension that hung in the air.

He pitched his greatcoat onto the divan but left his hat on and headed straight for the desk. "Now, let's see what the greatest stained glass window designer in all of England has done for us."

As he leaned over the desk and started examining her sketches, Vannah tried to explain them, but Watson silenced her with an impatient wave of his hand. His scrutiny seemed to take hours, and by the time he straightened up, Vannah was so jittery, she felt ready to jump out of her skin.

"Yes, yes, *yes!*" he suddenly bellowed. "The girl's a genius, Ash, and I'm going to be considered even more of a genius for discovering her. These are perfect. Just what I had in mind."

Vannah let out the breath she had been holding and smiled shakily.

"I'll have you know, Watson," Martin said, "that I was going to have these windows made with or without your approval."

"Oh, were you now?"

Martin nodded.

"Now, when can you have the cartoons finished?" Watson demanded of Vannah.

"In two or three weeks," she replied.

Watson's head bobbed in approval. "I've made arrangements for you to work at the Swallow and Swan Glass Studios. They have all the materials you'll need to make the windows."

Vannah could barely hold back her tears of happiness. She clasped her hands together in childlike glee. "I'm going to be making windows again! I feel as though I'm dreaming!"

"You're not," Watson assured her, his black eyes twinkling. "Once you prove yourself, once people see what you can do, there should be many other commissions for you besides mine."

Vannah looked from Watson to Martin. "Thank you both from the bottom of my heart," she said softly.

"No thanks needed," Martin replied.

"Don't just stand there blubbering with gratitude," Watson said, admonishing her with a wave of his hands. "Shoo! Off with you! Get to work!"

The following day, Vannah began work at the Swallow and Swan Glass Studios.

She knew she was regarded as something of a curiosity, being both a woman and an American, but her sunny disposition and gentle nature soon won her many friends. And once these skeptical men saw how well she knew her craft, she won their grudging respect and admiration as well.

As Vannah had feared, the selection of glass she would have to work with was rather limited. There was no mottled glass, no drapery glass, and very little opalescent glass, which was inferior quality. She would have to rely more on paint and enamels, something that Tiffany had always disdained.

But, being the artist she was, she regarded it as a challenge. She fully intended to make these windows as beautiful as any she had made for Tiffany. They would be different but just as powerful in another way.

One week after she began going to the studio, Vannah happened to be sketching at home, in the parlor, when she heard the door creak open slowly.

Without taking her eyes off her work she said, "Yes, Rosie, what is it?"

"Fallen on hard times, have we, princess?"

PASSION'S FORTUNE 393

Vannah started, causing her brush to jump out of control and land in the middle of her painting. But she didn't give her ruined effort a second thought as she whirled around to stare at the man standing in the parlor doorway.

"Paul? Paul Demarest?"

He inclined his head. "The same."

But Vannah wouldn't have recognized him otherwise, for this Paul Demarest was a vastly changed man. He was still so thin, a good wind would blow him over, and he had let his beard grow back, longer and more defiant than ever. Yet his black hawk's eyes were now dull and bloodshot, and there was an air of bitter disillusionment about him. Paul Demarest looked like a tired, defeated man.

Vannah smiled nervously, not knowing quite what to say to him after all this time, after all that had happened between them. "Please forgive my atrocious manners. Do sit down and I'll have my maid bring us tea."

"Don't trouble yourself. I won't be staying long."

"Then why did you come here, Paul?" she asked softly. "And what are you doing in London? You are the last person I would have expected to see here."

"I live here now," he replied. "I'm a writer for an English newspaper."

While Vannah listened, he quickly told her how he had returned to New York but soon tired of the city, how he moved to England for fresh challenges.

"And I have tracked you down for two reasons, princess." Paul took a deep breath and watched Vannah closely. "First I came to warn you about your husband, Basil Edgewood."

Vannah gaped at him. "What—what do you mean?"

He ran his hand through his beard and groaned. "It's common knowledge in journalistic circles that he's a fortune hunter, Vannah. He married you for your money. And before you choose to disbelieve me, remember that we journalists are a close fraternity. One hears things about other reporters. And I've heard—"

"I don't wish to listen to any filthy lies about my husband!" Vannah drew herself up to her full height, the very picture of disdain.

"Damn it, Vannah, you must know that I would never lie to you, especially about something like this. When I learned that you were married to Basil Edgewood, an English journalist, I checked his background. He's a talented writer, but he can't hold down a position because he has a higher opinion of his abilities than anyone else. And he's lived off other women. He's—"

"Get out! Leave this instant or I'll throw you out myself!"

He shrugged and turned to go. "Suit yourself, but don't say no one warned you." Then he stopped at the door and looked back. "One other small matter . . ."

"Yes?"

He swallowed hard, and a look of desperation twisted his face. "Why did you send me away, Vannah? Why did you destroy me?"

Vannah took a deep breath to steady her quaking insides, then told him how Gerrold Webb threatened to destroy Paul's family if she didn't agree to break off their relationship.

Paul kept nodding, as though he had known it all along, and his eyes were unnaturally bright. "And I was so quick to believe the worst of you. I guess I'll have to live with that for the rest of my life, now won't I?"

Vannah said nothing.

"Good-bye, princess."

"Good-bye, Paul."

Long after Paul left, Vannah sat in the parlor, alone with her thoughts. Paul had been lying about Basil, of course. He just wanted to hurt her in return for destroying him when she was eighteen. Basil a womanizer . . . She shook her head at the absurdity of it. She wasn't even going to dignify Paul's lies by confronting her husband with such an accusation.

Vannah rose and tried to salvage her painting.

One Saturday morning Basil, who usually spent the better part of the day locked away writing in his room, came down to the parlor, a stack of papers in his hands, and demanded that Vannah recopy what he had just finished writing.

Vannah just stared at him in shock for a moment, unable to comprehend what he was asking of her. Finally she said, "Basil, I don't have time to recopy your manuscript. I thought I would go to the studio today to start work on the Four Seasons windows."

His face was set in the stubborn, angry mask she knew so well. "But it's Saturday, Mrs. Edgewood."

"I often go in on Saturday, you know that."

"Well, you can stay home just this once."

Vannah was so angry, she was beginning to tremble. "I'm sorry, Basil, I won't do it. I've told you, I have work of my own to do."

His fury matched her own. "A fine wife you are, Mrs. Edgewood, unwilling to help your own husband. When I married you, I never dreamed that you could be so selfish and inconsiderate of my feelings."

"And I never dreamed that you could be so unreasonable!" she retorted.

He shook his head pityingly. "You always have to have everything your own way, don't you? You're still a spoiled little rich girl masquerading as an adult."

His words stung and wounded her, but all she said was, "I refuse to exchange insults with you, Basil."

"Oh, can't tolerate the truth, can you, Mrs. Edgewood?" he sneered.

Vannah coldly turned her back on him and started for the door.

"Don't you turn your back on me when I'm speaking to you!" Basil snarled, grasping her shoulder and jerking her around to face him.

Vannah cried out in pain and alarm as she felt Basil's fingers cruelly digging into her shoulder. But even when she faced him, staring into his wide, furious eyes, he wouldn't release her and just squeezed harder.

"I told you once before that I expect obedience from you, Mrs. Edgewood," he said between clenched teeth, his voice low and deadly. "I am going upstairs now to write. When I come down, I expect to see this manuscript recopied."

Then he flung her away contemptuously so that she staggered and fell against the opposite wall. Basil said, "I would do as I'm told if I were you."

Then he turned and climbed the stairs.

When he reached his own room, Basil slammed the door shut and growled, "Bitch!"

Then he leaned against it, breathing heavily through his nose, thinking of all the little annoying ways he could punish his wife for daring to disobey him. Finally he walked over to a bureau, unlocked the top drawer, and fumbled around way in the back until he found what he sought.

Then Basil began the ritual that had become so sacred to him as the Sunday church service so sacred to his mother. He opened the leather case almost reverentially, took out the small glass bottle of clear liquid, and watched with rapt fascination as it slowly filled the hypodermic needle.

Then he rolled up his sleeve, noting the marks already there in the crook of his arm. And his naive, unsuspecting wife wondered why he always made love in the dark. . . .

He felt the prick of the needle and waited. Soon the ensuing euphoria would make him think that he was the greatest writer in the world.

For the longest time after Basil disappeared up the stairs, Vannah stood propped up against the wall, unable to accept or comprehend her husband's cruel treatment.

He didn't mean it, she thought as she finally rubbed her sore, bruised shoulder and went into the parlor. I made him angry at me, and he lost his temper.

Vannah crossed her arms to comfort herself and slowly began walking around the parlor to calm herself and decide what to do. It would be so easy for her to give in to Basil's unreasonable demands once again, as she usually did, but something in her resisted being so compliant, especially when she felt so strongly that she was in the right.

"My work is just as important as his!" she said defiantly.

But she knew that Basil didn't see it that way and never would. To him a man's work always took precedence over a woman's. That was just the way of the world, as Vannah well knew.

Her frustration and anger were just so overwhelming, Vannah felt great, uncontrollable sobs rack her body, and the hot tears rolled unchecked down her cheeks.

"I will not give in to him this time!" she swore passionately. "I will not!"

Suddenly there came a knock at the door, and Rosie appeared. "Mr. Ash to see you, ma'am."

Vannah whirled around and frantically began wiping her cheeks with the back of her hand. Martin must not see her in such an agitated state. "Tell him I'll be with him in a moment, Rosie."

"Yes, ma'am, that I will." And the maid disappeared.

When Vannah was certain that her cheeks were dry, she

took several deep breaths to compose herself and went to receive Martin.

He knew something was wrong the moment she appeared in the parlor doorway. Perhaps it was the false heartiness of her greeting that betrayed her or perhaps the tears still clinging to her thick lashes, making her eyes look too bright.

"Why, Martin, what a pleasant surprise," she said, and Martin thought he detected a slight tremor in her voice.

"I just thought I'd call to see how both you and your husband were progressing on your respective projects."

"Basil's locked himself in his room to write," she replied, preceding him into the parlor.

As soon as Martin had the door closed securely behind him, he said, "What's wrong, Vannah?"

She turned to him, fighting valiantly to look innocent. "Why—why, nothing at all. What makes you think that?"

"Because I can tell that you've just been crying," he replied flatly. "And I want to know why."

"It—it's nothing, Martin, really," she said, turning away from him.

"Vannah—" he began, reaching out to place a hand on her shoulder.

Suddenly, to Martin's surprise and chagrin, she uttered a strangled whimper of pain, and he jerked his hand back.

"Is something the matter with your shoulder?" he demanded, moving so that he faced her. "Did you hurt yourself?"

Suddenly a thought so repugnant came to mind that Martin's face twisted savagely and he snarled, "Or did someone else hurt you?"

"Martin!" Vannah cried. "Basil would never hurt me. I was reaching for a hat on my closet shelf and strained my shoulder this morning, that's all. I'll be fine."

He suspected her of lying to protect her husband, but he

knew that he would just upset her further by pressing the issue. "But that's not why you were crying, is it?"

Vannah shook her head and proceeded to tell Martin that Basil wanted her to recopy his manuscript. He listened attentively and soon solved that problem by offering to have one of the firm's secretaries transcribe the manuscript using a typewriter.

Vannah felt as though the world had been lifted from her shoulders. "Oh, Martin, that would be wonderful. Then I wouldn't have to take time away from my own work to do Basil's."

"Exactly. Besides, the typewriter is much more legible than human handwriting." Then he smiled. "Any more problems I can solve for you today?"

Vannah thought of Basil, but she just shook her head. "No, Martin. You've just solved them all."

Privately he doubted it, but he just wished her good day and took his leave before he succumbed to temptation and strangled Basil Edgewood.

When Basil came downstairs for dinner, it was with a sheepish expression on his face and apologies on his lips. He said he was sorry for being so angry with her that morning, but she did, after all, disobey him.

Vannah accepted his apologies graciously, if a trifle coolly, and told him about Martin's visit and what had ensued. Later Basil said he was exhausted and went straight to bed in his own room, leaving Vannah not disappointed but relieved.

As she sat before her vanity table, slowly brushing her hair with a silver-backed brush, her eyes kept straying to the vivid, purplish bruises on her shoulder, each one so stark against her white flesh where Basil had gripped her so punishingly. The only time she had ever been physically injured by a man in such a way was the one time Gerrold had struck her in the face.

Now, her own husband, the man she loved and trusted, had physically hurt her.

When Vannah thought of Martin's visit that afternoon, she felt fresh tears sting her eyes. His deep, abiding tenderness and concern for her had nearly been her undoing.

As he stood there in her parlor, so tall and invincible as the Sir Lancelot of her childhood fantasies, all she had wanted to do was surrender, to flee to the strength and shelter of his arms and never let him go again. And, judging from the look of primitive savagery that had twisted his face when he thought that Basil had hurt her, Vannah knew he would fight the world for her.

But once again, honor had won out over desire.

As Vannah gingerly touched one of the round marks left by each of Basil's fingers and winced at the pain, she found herself recalling Paul Demarest's surprising visit and his accusations against Basil. Perhaps there was some substance to them after all.

Even if there weren't, Basil's crude and callous treatment of her today had altered the love Vannah had once felt for him. And even if she couldn't bear to admit it to herself, she would never quite feel the same way about her husband again.

The following Monday morning, Vannah had to consult with Watson, so she took an omnibus to his house, a rambling, whitewashed edifice near the Thames River in the Chelsea section of London.

The first few times she had called on him, she was a little ill at ease, for the man did have something of a reputation as a rowdy and a womanizer. But, as Vannah came to know him better, she treasured Watson Greene as a dear friend.

After their creative consultations Watson would sit at his drafting table and talk about his impoverished youth in a

Yorkshire slum, sharing a room with five brothers and sisters. Vannah's heart went out to him when he confessed that he designed such spacious houses because his own as a child had been so small and cramped with no privacy whatsoever. She in turn told him of growing up in not one, but two, houses, each with more rooms than a child could count. Yet, in spite of such differences, their dedication to their respective crafts forged a bond between them.

On that particular day Watson surprised her by saying, "Would you be offended if suddenly I were to turn serious on you, my beautiful genius?"

Vannah looked at him and smiled. How could she take him seriously when he was once again wearing his wide-brimmed hat indoors, "to keep my brain warm and to prevent my creativity from escaping up into the atmosphere"?

"Well, now, that depends on how serious you intend to become, Watson."

"I want to talk about my good friend, the marquis."

"Martin? What about him?"

"He's out of his mind in love with you."

Vannah swallowed hard and folded her hands primly in her lap. "You're treading on dangerous ground, Watson," she said quietly.

He left his drafting table to walk over to the whiskey decanter and poured himself a glass. "That's my nature, Vannah, treading on dangerous ground. But, in the time we've been working together, I've gotten to know you pretty well. I like you," he said with a wolfish grin as he raised his glass to her and drank it down. "And there's not many women I truly like. Oh, most any woman will do to warm my bed if she's not ugly or toothless, but there are precious few of your sex that I honestly like, and you're one of them."

"I'm truly flattered, Watson."

"And so you should be, girl!" Then he leaned back

against a chest, stroked his grizzly beard, and got a faraway look in his soot-black eyes. "I remember when I first met the marquis several years ago. Do you know what was the first thought that popped into my head?"

"No. What?"

"I said to myself, 'Now there is a troubled, unhappy man if ever I saw one.' And then I met his wife and I knew why."

Vannah raised her brows. "You knew Katherine?"

He nodded. "Cowboy Katie. That's what everyone called her behind her back because she was a little too rough around the edges for a marchioness." Watson chuckled. "I don't think London was quite prepared for the likes of Cowboy Katie. Myself, I felt sorry for her. All she wanted was for the marquis to love her, but of course, he couldn't because he loved you. Oh, he was attentive to her in a distant sort of way, but one could sense that his heart wasn't in it. There was always this air of detachment about him, as though the real Martin Ash were somewhere else and this husk of a man was taking his place."

"Poor Martin," Vannah murmured.

"But you should have seen him the day she left him. The marquis was a changed man, a veritable Lazarus rising from the dead. All he could talk about was you, girl, and how you were going to be together at last."

Vannah sighed. "I suppose we were never destined to be together."

Watson took off his hat and set it on a table next to her. "Would the best stained glass window designer in all of England mind answering a hypothetical question for me?"

"Of course."

"If there ever came a day when you didn't love your husband, would you leave him for the marquis?"

Without hesitation Vannah shook her head.

"And may I ask why not?"

"Honor. Loyalty. When I married Basil, I promised to love, honor, and obey him for better or for worse. Lord knows my own parents never honored their marriage vows. My mother took a lover who betrayed her, and my father had his string of mistresses. I just promised myself that I would never be like them, that's all."

"Noble sentiments, those. But passion can be like a raging river, Vannah," Watson warned her, "overwhelming us, sweeping away sanity, reason, and the best of intentions."

"How well I know that. But at least I can try to do what's right and good, to think of Basil's needs instead of my own." Vannah laughed self-consciously. "I hope that doesn't sound too pompous and self-righteous."

Watson grinned back. "Just a little, girl." Suddenly he reached for Vannah's hand and drew it to his lips. "Now I know why so many men have lost their hearts to you, including your humble servant, the best architect in the world."

Vannah reached for his hat and placed it on his head at a rakish angle. "Your brain is getting cold again, my friend. Time to get back to work. Time for both of us to get back to work."

"Yes, yes, *yes!*" Watson bellowed with a grin as he showed her to the door and summoned a hansom cab to take her back to Clerkenwell.

Three months later, in the beginning of June, the windows were finally ready.

Once they were installed, Martin's house was ready for occupancy, and he invited Vannah to tour it before the grand opening just a week away.

On the day she was supposed to go, Vannah awoke feeling a little queasy, but she attributed it to simple indigestion that would soon pass. So she quickly washed and dressed and, by the time Martin called for her, was ready.

When they arrived at St. John's Wood, a neighborhood just beyond Baker Street and Regent's Park, and Martin assisted her down from the carriage, Vannah was a bit dismayed. All she saw was a very high garden wall of brick and a row of even taller linden trees behind it. From the street Martin's house could not be seen.

"It's very private and secluded," Martin conceded as he unlocked the garden gate, "but that appeals to me. That and the people who live here. They're mostly writers, artists, actors, singers, and a retired Army officer or two."

"And now one peer of the realm," Vannah said as she stepped through the gate.

"No, one publisher," he replied.

Now Vannah could see the house through the linden trees, and she stopped and stared in admiration. "Oh, Martin . . ."

The sketches that Watson had shown her couldn't have prepared Vannah for the simplicity and elegance of the house itself. Built on long, clean horizontal lines except for the three tall chimneys, it was made of plain white roughcast rather than the red brick and gray stone of many London houses Vannah had seen. The long, narrow, mullioned windows on the ground and first floors were set in groups of two, three, or four.

Vannah had to stop and admire it. "It's very different, Martin, very modern. Most of the buildings in Newport were copies of other styles, either French châteaux or English manor houses, but this style is rather unique."

Martin smiled down at her. "Unlike many of his peers, Watson doesn't like to restrict himself to building materials indigenous to the area where the house is to be built. Whether he's designing a house for Devon or London, he prefers the white roughcast for its clean, spare look."

"Well, I think it's very striking."

As they started down the narrow flagstone path Vannah said, "What name have you chosen for your house?"

"I haven't decided on one yet," he replied evasively.

Actually Martin had decided months ago to call his house Petit Clairvaux after Vannah's Newport playhouse where they had shared their first night of blissful passion, but he wanted to make sure she was his before he did that.

"Wait until you see the interior," he said excitedly as he unlocked the front door. "I think you'll find it quite surprising."

When Vannah stepped into the foyer, with its dramatic, vaulted ceiling and saw the Four Seasons windows in their proper setting at long last, illuminated by the sunlight streaming in, she gasped in delight.

"Oh, Martin . . ." was all she could say.

Just seeing her face aglow with pleasure and pride made him want to take her into his arms and hug her, but he knew that she would misinterpret his gesture, so he jammed his hands into his pockets and restrained himself.

"They're all I hoped for and more," he said.

Vannah stepped back a few paces and frowned in concentration as she studied them. "If I had made these in Tiffany's studios, they would have been even better."

"Different, perhaps, but better?" Martin shook his head. "I doubt it."

"Thank you, Martin, for having such faith in me."

"And why shouldn't I?" He grinned. "After all, aren't you the best stained glass window designer in all of England?"

Vannah laughed.

Then Martin said, "But in order to do your windows justice, they have to be seen in their proper light. So I'm going to schedule my gala for late in the afternoon, so my guests will be able to fully appreciate your windows. Since the house faces west, the afternoon and evening light will be just perfect."

"I had been wondering how anyone could appreciate them at night," Vannah confessed. "But you, Martin, have thought of everything."

Not everything, he said to himself. I haven't yet thought of a way to make you leave your husband and come to me.

He said, "Come. Let me show you the rest of the house. I think you'll find it just as surprising as the exterior."

And that Vannah did. If the exterior of the house was a masterpiece of simplicity, the interior was just the opposite, a decorative feast for the eyes. Thick, lush Oriental carpets in shades of wine covered the floors, and instead of the rather plain stick furniture favored by "arts and crafts" architects, the furniture in Martin's house was imaginatively carved with sensuous, sweeping whiplash curves.

"Martin!" Vannah exclaimed, kneeling to examine a breakfront more closely. "Wherever did you find such beautiful furniture? I've never seen anything like it anywhere."

"I bought it at a wonderful shop in Paris by the name of L'Art Nouveau. Its proprietor, Monsieur Bing, has assembled all the best practitioners of the new style on the continent."

Vannah frowned. "Monsieur Bing . . . Didn't he sell Oriental merchandise at one time? I recall visiting his shop once when I was at finishing school in France."

"He's the very same." Martin chuckled. "Watson and I had several ideological differences of opinion concerning the interior decoration of my house. He has no use for the Continental style, including this furniture, but I like it, and since it is my house . . ."

Vannah rose to her feet. She could just imagine a clash of wills between too such forceful personalities as Martin and Watson, and she was glad she hadn't been there to witness it.

She looked around the room. "I can see you won."

"I like having my own way," Martin said pointedly. Before Vannah could comment, he turned abruptly and said, "Come. Let me show you the rest of the house. Did I tell you I had it wired for electricity? The lighting will be electric rather than gas."

As they strolled through the house Martin was glad to see that Vannah approved, for he vowed that one day soon this house would be hers as well.

Chapter Eighteen

MARTIN'S CARRIAGE CALLED for Vannah and Basil promptly at three o'clock on June twenty-sixth, a bright and warm Friday afternoon. As Vannah settled back against the leather squabs she was especially pleased that the weather had cooperated, for a sunny day would display her windows to their best advantage.

When Basil climbed in and sat across from her, Vannah smiled at him. "You look very handsome today, Basil."

And he did in his black evening attire with the white shirtfront drawing out the color in his pale complexion.

Basil pulled off one white glove to brush a lock of hair off his forehead and grumbled, "Now, I don't want you to leave my side all evening."

Vannah sighed in ill-disguised annoyance. "Please, Basil. I am one of the guests of honor and am expected to converse with Martin's other guests. And need I remind you that this isn't entirely a social affair for me. Hopefully I'll meet some people who will be interested in commissioning me to design windows."

Basil just crossed his arms and stared moodily out the window.

To smooth his ruffled feathers Vannah added, "Besides, I'm sure there will be many people there to whom you will want to talk. I know Martin has invited other writers as well."

Not only was Martin expecting writers to attend, he had invited other artists, actors, actresses, playwrights. . . . The guest list he had shown to Vannah had included some of the best creative talent in London, if not the world. Her head spun when she thought that the likes of Aubrey Beardsley, the illustrator, and Ellen Terry, the actress, would be attending a gala where she, Savannah Webb Edgewood, would be one of the guests of honor.

But Basil didn't seem impressed. "By other writers are you referring to that untalented Minska woman?"

"Yes, I'm sure the baroness will be there, but Martin has invited other writers as well. I'm sure you'll find an enthusiastic audience."

"I doubt it, but I shall try," he declared loftily.

"That's all I ask, Basil."

Now he stared at her with a critical eye. "I'm not sure I approve of that gown you're wearing, either. Isn't it a bit too daring?"

Vannah had to admit that her gown was quite daring and unusual. Made of soft peach-colored silk that draped in flattering folds down her slender, uncorseted figure, the gown was pulled tightly across her back, then gathered from a bib of elaborate embroidery across her breasts so it tumbled loosely to the floor. It had no sleeves to speak of, just several loops of thin satin cord giving the illusion that they supported the entire dress. The short train was embroidered with the same crescent moon and stars motif she had employed in Martin's windows.

"Perhaps it is a bit daring," Vannah conceded, "but I'm sure no other woman will be wearing a gown like it. Tonight is my night, and I wanted to stand out in a roomful of beautiful women."

"You don't need a gown to do that, fair lady," Basil said.

"Thank you, but I'm afraid you're prejudiced."

He grinned. "I'll be the very envy of every man there tonight."

"Tonight will be a triumph for both of us," Vannah said.

As the carriage rolled through the noisy, crowded streets of London toward the tranquillity of St. John's Wood, Vannah could not know that before the evening was out, fate would once again betray her so cruelly, bringing changes in her life she never could have foreseen.

"Where is she?" Martin muttered irritably as he paced up and down the foyer. "Vannah should have been here by now."

"Patience, my friend," Watson admonished, "patience. The lady and—need I remind you?—her husband will be here shortly."

Martin rubbed his scar nervously. "I wish I could forget that Basil Edgewood even existed."

Watson, who seemed oblivious to the fact that his favorite wide-brimmed hat looked quite out of place worn with a formal dinner jacket and tie, rested one hand on his friend's shoulder. "My dear Ash, why do you torment yourself so over this woman? Not that she isn't a splendid creature worthy of such a grand obsession. One glance out of those eyes of hers . . ." He rolled his eyes toward the ceiling in an exaggerated expression of bliss. "But, my friend, she will not leave her husband, no matter how much she loves you."

Martin said, "I will never understand how a woman who fought so hard to free herself from her father's tyranny could allow herself to become trapped in such a marriage."

Watson dropped his hand and shrugged. "Women can be the most inconsistent of creatures. I gave up trying to understand them when I was about seven."

"Well, one day she'll come to her senses, and I'll be waiting."

Watson sighed. "Thank God I have more sense than to fall in love."

Martin grinned. "You're just envious because I saw Vannah first."

Watson opened his mouth as if to deny it, then he looked as though he had just had a revelation. "I daresay you're right. With a woman like that by my side to inspire me, what buildings I could create!"

Martin clapped him on the back. "You see? Even a confirmed bachelor such as yourself is not immune to her."

Just then the two men were interrupted by Mrs. MacGregor, the Scottish housekeeper, who informed Martin that everything was ready for the two hundred guests they expected to tour the house and partake of an elaborate buffet supper before the evening was out.

Watson's bushy black brows rose. "Two hundred guests? Ash, you must be mad! I know the house is large, but two hundred people wandering through these rooms? There won't be enough air to breathe! We'll all die!"

"Oh, I don't expect everyone all at once, Watson," Martin assured him. "People will be arriving late and drifting in and out."

"It's unfortunate that poor Wilde is still in prison,"

Watson mused. "He would have made an entertaining addition tonight."

Martin nodded as he glanced at the clock again. "And if Whistler's wife hadn't died just last month, I would have liked Vannah to meet him as well."

Suddenly the bell rang, and since he was expecting Vannah to arrive before any of the other guests, Martin answered the door himself rather than waiting for the butler.

The sight that greeted his eyes left him speechless.

Vannah had never looked lovelier or more radiant than she did today. As she greeted the two men and stepped into the foyer the material of her gown rippled around her elusively, first clinging to her long legs, then briefly shifting the emphasis to her slender hips before concealing her entire body. Vannah apparently didn't notice that one of the satin loops had slipped seductively off her shoulder, but Martin did, and he had to resist the impulse to reach out and slide it back up.

Suddenly he had a flash of comprehension. "Your dress . . . you had it copied from a Mucha poster, didn't you?"

A smile of delight lit up Vannah's face. "I thought you'd recognize it."

"Mucha?" Basil piped up. "Who is this Mucha?"

Without taking his eyes off Vannah Martin replied, "He designs theater posters for Sarah Bernhardt," then reached for Vannah's hand. "And it does you justice."

She blushed prettily. "Thank you, Martin. And both you and Watson look quite distinguished this evening. The hat is an especially debonair touch," she added dryly, addressing Watson.

He swept off his hat with a flourish that would shame a cavalier as he let his gaze rove boldly over Vannah's figure. "If my hat offends thee, I shall pluck it off."

"Watson Greene, you are the most outrageous man I have ever met," she said with a laugh.

Martin finally realized that he had to take his eyes off Vannah long enough to say something to her husband, who was glaring sullenly at the three of them.

"Edgewood," he said, extending his hand, "I'm glad you could attend the festivities this evening."

"Now, you didn't think I'd let my wife come alone, do you, Fleet?" he asked as he shook Martin's hand.

"Of course not," Martin replied.

Now Vannah said, "Basil, turn around and look over the door." When he did so, she asked, "What do you think of the Four Seasons?"

Basil just stood there, staring up at the windows. "Fair lady, I am speechless. They are beautiful. You have surpassed yourself." Then he leaned over to give Vannah a proprietary kiss on the cheek. "Congratulations, darling. All of London will be flocking to our door to have you design their windows."

Vannah was somewhat surprised, for Basil had never really shown an interest in her work except as a means of earning them money.

Suddenly Watson said to Basil, "Why don't you come with me and I'll show you the rest of the house? I'd be very interested in hearing your opinions of it as well."

And before Basil could say another word, Watson was leading him off by the arm to the accompaniment of a lecture on the principles of "arts and crafts" architecture.

Soon the first guests began arriving, and Vannah was so busy being introduced to people and remembering all their names that she had scant time to think of Basil at all. As she stood in the foyer with Martin on her right and Watson on her left, listening to one person after another exclaim over the Four Seasons and compliment her lavishly on her talent, Vannah felt a heady mixture of pride, elation, and happiness.

Even the dramatic entrance of the Baroness Minska could not bring Vannah's soaring spirits back down to earth. The baroness wore another of the exotic flowing robes she favored, this one of vivid red poppies embroidered on a contrasting background of midnight blue. But what really made her stand out was her gleaming gold headdress encrusted with jewels. Vannah had no doubt that each of the emeralds, rubies, sapphires, and pearls was genuine and quite valuable.

The baroness smiled brightly and stood on tiptoes to give Martin a kiss on the cheek, but when she came to Vannah, her smile died and those tilted hazel eyes raked her from the top of her upswept hair to the hem of her gown.

"Aren't you afraid of catching cold, my dear?" the baroness said with a patronizing sniff.

Vannah in turn scrutinized the other woman's attire just as mercilessly. "Did Martin fail to tell you that this wasn't a costume ball? You are impersonating the Empress Theodosia this evening, I take it?"

Since she wasn't expecting a retort from Vannah, the baroness just gaped at her in disbelief. Before she could recover herself and unsheathe her claws, Watson grabbed her arm and said, "Ah, my dear Sophie, I've been waiting for you to make your grand entrance," and he whisked her away from Vannah.

"Well done," Martin murmured with an appreciative chuckle.

Later, as the sun went down and the new electric lights were turned on, some guests left and still others arrived, keeping Vannah so busy that she had no time to check on Basil despite her best intentions. She hoped he was enjoying himself as much as she was.

Suddenly Watson materialized out of nowhere.

"Well, girl," he said with a wolfish grin, "I would say that you are the toast of the London art world tonight."

"I've had many compliments on my windows," she said, her face flushed with pleasure.

"I'm not talking about compliments, girl! I'm talking about cold, hard commissions. Four people I'm designing houses for have asked me if you would be willing to design the windows. And at least another seven want you to design windows for their existing houses."

"Watson, you're not just teasing me, are you?"

His face was the very picture of seriousness. "I never jest about work, girl, or filthy lucre. You should know that by now." As he stroked his beard a crafty gleam appeared in his eyes. "If I were a shrewd businessman, I'd sign you to an exclusive contract. Then you'd design windows only for my buildings."

Vannah regarded him skeptically. "I think I should discuss such an arrangement with Martin before I agree to it."

"Girl, how can you be so suspecting of my motives when I'm such a likable, upright fellow?"

"I've come to know you too well, Watson Greene," Vannah replied dryly.

"Smart girl," he said. Then he glanced over the many people crowded almost shoulder-to-shoulder in the drawing room. "Where has the baroness gone? It's time that I tormented her further."

And with a curt nod Watson wandered away.

Suddenly the heat, the noise, and the champagne Vannah had been drinking all seemed to overwhelm her at once. She felt strangely light-headed, and she knew that if she didn't get some fresh air at once, she would either faint or become very ill. Quietly and without being noticed, she slipped off to the kitchen and then out the back door into the garden.

The moment she shut the door behind her, all noise ceased. As the cool air caressed her bare shoulders Vannah breathed deeply, letting the scents of flowers and freshly turned earth clear her brain. Then she took a turn through Martin's garden.

Vannah hadn't been outside for more than five minutes when she sensed that she was not alone. She turned as quickly as she dared and came face-to-face with Martin himself.

The sun had set long ago, and the last bit of twilight was rapidly fading into night. Yet Vannah could still discern his features by what little light was left.

"I—I came out here for a bit of fresh air," she explained.

"So did I."

"It's a wonderful party."

"Your presence makes it wonderful."

Vannah knew she shouldn't remain with Martin alone in the garden at night, when any one of his guests could glance out the window, see them together, and speculate. But it was so quiet out here, so pleasant, she couldn't bring herself to excuse herself and return to the safety of the light and noise inside.

So she just stood there in the darkness, one bare arm nearly brushing the sleeve of Martin's dinner jacket as she desperately searched her clouded mind for something innocuous to say.

Suddenly she saw the shadow that was Martin reach up, and she felt his fingertips softly brush her temple, then trail down her cheek and jaw in a tender caress of desire. Vannah knew she should have pulled away, whirled on her heel, and escaped back to the safety of the other guests before Martin could go any further. But she could not. It was as though they were the only two people left in the world, the only two people who mattered.

"Please don't run from me," he begged. "Not this time."

The moment Vannah felt his warm mouth on hers, testing and exploring, she realized that she was too weak to resist him any longer. When his hungry kiss deepened and his body pressed possessively against hers, demanding a response, Vannah drew him to her with a soft moan of surrender. She savored the arousing touch of his fingers against the smooth, bare flesh of her upper back, stroking, caressing, stirring the slumbering passion within her as only he could.

Soon he reluctantly tore his mouth from hers and trailed fiery kisses down the slender column of her neck, the rising heat of her skin releasing the delicious scent of her perfume into the night air.

"Oh, Martin . . ." Vannah moaned as she felt him push aside the satin loops of her gown so he could kiss her rounded shoulder.

"I know you still want me, Vannah," he growled against her warm flesh. "And it's about time you admitted it to yourself."

Then, as if to assert his complete mastery of her, Martin cupped her breast possessively until the nipple grew taut against his palm through the thin silk. He smiled in satisfaction when Vannah groaned, her lips parted enticingly, and he became so reckless with desire, he wanted to love her right here, in his garden, where any number of people could just wander outside and discover them. But sanity reasserted itself just in time.

With superhuman effort he stepped away, one hand supporting her around the waist lest she misinterpret his action as rejection.

"Stay with me, Savannah," he whispered in the twilight, his voice persuasive and urgent. "Leave your husband and stay with me. Tonight. Forever."

Then he released her only to take her face in his hands so he could gaze deeply into her eyes. "I love you, Vannah.

I want you. You must know that we belong together. Say you will stay with me. Say it!"

Vannah's lips parted, and she was on the verge of responding when the spell was broken by Watson's voice booming out at them through the darkness: "I say, Ash, you haven't seen Vannah anywhere, have you? Cecilia Hargreaves from *The Studio* wants to speak to her."

Vannah jerked to attention, and Martin's hands fell to his sides. He swore softly under his breath as Vannah glided away from him without answering his question.

"Yes, Watson," he replied wearily, "Vannah is here with me."

The architect came lumbering at them, only to stop a few feet away. Martin could tell at once that Watson had seen too much.

"Sorry" was all he said.

Vannah smiled at him, her beautiful face illuminated by the light from the windows as she drew her arm through Watson's. "That's quite all right. Now, who is this Cecilia Hargreaves, and why does she want to speak to me?"

Vannah didn't look back at Martin as Watson returned her to the land of the sane and the rational. It wasn't until she was back among the talking, laughing throng that she realized she hadn't given Martin any answer at all.

Cecilia Hargreaves was a pleasant young woman with a mane of coppery curly hair, and Vannah warmed to her at once when they were introduced.

"I am very impressed with your windows, Mrs. Edgewood, and I would like to write an article about you and your work for an upcoming issue of *The Studio*, if you would be willing," she said.

"Yes, yes, *yes*!" Watson exclaimed. "Of course she would be willing. When would you like to interview her?"

Vannah shook her head. "Thank you for your enthusiasm, Watson, but I can speak for myself, you know."

"Of course you can, my girl."

But before Vannah and Miss Hargreaves could discuss an appropriate time and place for the interview, Basil, his pale face flushed, interrupted them. "Vannah," he began, plucking at her arm, "I would like to speak to you for a moment."

"Please, Basil, I'm speaking to Miss Hargreaves," Vannah said sharply. "If you will wait one moment . . ."

"Oh, and I suppose this Miss Hargreaves is more important than your own husband?" he muttered petulantly, increasing his grip on her arm.

"Basil, please!" Vannah snapped, fearing that he had had too much champagne.

"I want to go home this instant," he said. "I am having a miserable time and don't want to stay a moment longer."

Vannah glanced around nervously and was embarrassed to find people staring at them, for Basil's voice had carried and attracted attention. She smiled apologetically at Miss Hargreaves, who was regarding Basil as though he were some vagrant who had just wandered in off the street. "Will you please excuse me, Miss Hargreaves?" Then Vannah turned to Basil, her anger rising dangerously. "Can we go somewhere more private to discuss this?"

Basil's eyes narrowed maliciously, and he turned a furious shade of red. "There is nothing to discuss, Mrs. Edgewood!" he cried, his voice booming throughout the drawing room. "I want to go home right this minute, and you will accompany me!"

Conversation dwindled and came to an abrupt halt as people continued to stare, then resumed again as the guests tried to pretend that they were not witnessing a private domestic quarrel between the guest of honor and her husband.

Vannah felt her cheeks burn with mortification. "Basil, please!" she hissed. "Don't make a scene."

"If I have to make a scene to get my wife's attention, then I shall! I told you that I want to leave right now!"

"Well, I don't!" Vannah retorted. "I'm enjoying myself."

Suddenly Martin appeared out of nowhere. "Is something the matter?"

"I wish to leave," Basil said bluntly. "I would appreciate it if you would send your carriage around, Fleet, to take us home."

"But surely you don't want to leave before dinner, Edgewood," Martin said smoothly, trying to take him aside. "The evening is still young. Some of my guests haven't even arrived."

Basil scowled as he shook off Martin's hand. "I don't care. I want to leave right this minute."

"Then why don't you go home alone?" Martin suggested. "I'll have my carriage return Vannah later."

"I'm not leaving without my wife, Fleet," Basil said menacingly.

"But she can't leave just yet," Martin insisted. "She's the guest of honor. Miss Hargreaves wants to interview her for *The Studio*."

"I don't care if the Queen of Sheba wants to interview her!" Basil shrieked, totally out of control now. "We're leaving. Now!"

A muscle twitched in Martin's jaw, and Vannah knew that if they had been alone, without all these people gaping, he would have struck Basil. But, as it was, Martin only glanced at Vannah and raised his brows in mute question.

The last thing that Vannah wanted was a fistfight or an unpleasant scene, so she raised her head proudly and squared her shoulders. "Would you be so kind as to have your carriage brought around, Martin? If Basil wishes to leave now, then we shall."

"As you wish," Martin said, but Vannah could see that he was most displeased.

She said good-byes to no one as she marched through the drawing room ahead of Basil. Vannah was so humiliated, all she wanted to do was get her husband out of Martin's house before he caused any more unpleasantness.

When they reached the front door, Martin took her hand in his and looked at her pointedly. "Remember what we discussed earlier."

"I shall consider your offer most carefully," Vannah replied as though Basil weren't there. "Good night, Martin. Please extend my regrets to everyone."

And the Edgewoods left.

Once they were seated inside the carriage and on their way home, Basil said, "What a boring gathering full of boring people!"

Vannah looked out the window at nothing in particular and made no response.

"Do you think anyone there was interested in what I had to say? No! All the other writers just wanted to talk about their latest book. None of them were interested in mine because I haven't been published yet."

As Vannah sat there in stiff, angry silence, listening to Basil's childish tirade, she realized that she could no longer endure being married to him for one more day, despite her best intentions. He was petty, selfish, and cruel, and she began to wonder what she had ever seen in him.

Then she recalled Martin's fervent embrace in the garden, his plea that she leave her husband and come to him, and she felt a warm knot of pleasure begin to grow in her heart. She loved Martin and wanted him. They belonged together. Vannah now realized that she had been deluding herself to think that her marriage to Basil had destroyed the all-consuming love she had for Martin. If anything, it had intensified it.

So, when the carriage came to a stop in front of their

house and Basil handed her down, Vannah told Martin's driver to wait.

"Why do you want him to wait?" Basil grumbled.

"Step into the parlor and I'll tell you," Vannah replied as she preceded him up the front steps.

Once there, Vannah whirled on Basil, her face white with anger. "I'm leaving you, Basil."

He stared at her. "What did you say?"

"You heard me. I said I'm leaving you. I don't wish to remain married to you a moment longer."

Basil scoffed, "What nonsense is this? You're just miffed at me because I made you leave Fleet's party early." He loosened his tie and reached for her. "Come, let's go to bed. You'll be yourself in the morning."

"No!" Vannah shouted, pushing his outstretched hand away with a violence that surprised her. "I am not going to bed with you now or ever again, Basil. I said I am leaving you, and I mean it."

He stopped and grew very still. Vannah could see his face set into a cold, hard mask of anger, and she sensed that he wanted to strike her, to hurt her physically for daring to defy him. But as much as she feared Basil's violent streak that could erupt at any moment, she knew she had to resist and fight for herself.

"You don't know what you're saying, Vannah," he said.

"Oh, I most certainly do!" she retorted, standing her ground and balling her hands into fists to keep them from trembling. "I have endured your petty jealousies and your abuse for the last time, Basil."

As Vannah watched, all the anger drained out of his face, to be replaced by a soulful look of genuine hurt and a glimmer of fear. "How can you accuse me of such things, Vannah? I love you!"

"Love me?" She shook her head. "You don't love me, Basil, if you ever did. You love only yourself."

"What about your marriage vows, Mrs. Edgewood?" he said stiffly. "Have you so quickly forgotten them?"

Vannah took a deep breath to stop the trembling in her limbs. "I do regret having to break them, but I'm afraid I no longer feel married to you, Basil. Life with you has become a living hell for me, and I refuse to endure it for a moment longer."

Suddenly Basil became wild-eyed and grim. "This is all Martin Ash's doing, isn't it? He's poisoned your mind against me."

Vannah shook her head. "No, Basil. The decision to leave you is mine alone. Martin had nothing to do with it."

"Liar!" he shrieked. "You're going to him. That's why you asked the driver to wait. You've probably been fornicating with him behind my back for months!"

She glared at him, refusing to cower before his mounting fury. "I wish we had," she retorted. "But, no, I've been faithful to you, Basil, despite what you may think to the contrary."

"You're nothing but a liar and a slattern. A lying whore!"

She saw him pull his arm back, and Vannah knew that he was going to strike her, but she was too quick for him, darting back just out of range as he swung at her with such force, he would have broken her jaw if his blow had connected. As Vannah backed up against a table her questing fingers found a heavy metal candlestick, and she gripped it with both hands, wielding it like a club.

"You have threatened me for the last time, Basil," she said, her voice soft but edged with steel.

He started toward her, saw the candlestick, and stopped in his tracks.

"If you try to hurt me again, I will hurt you back," she warned. "I will fight you, Basil."

Her opposition seemed to take the wind out of his sails,

and he just stood there, repeatedly running one hand through his disheveled hair. "I'm sorry. I—I didn't want to strike you, Vannah. It's just that the thought of losing you makes me crazy." He looked at her with sad, soulful eyes. "Please don't leave me. I'll have nothing left."

"I'm sorry, Basil. It's just too late."

"Vannah, please!" he begged. "Take pity on me. Give me just one more chance to prove myself to you. I promise I'll change."

She thought of Martin and hardened her heart against the pathetic wretch standing before her so humbly. "I'm going upstairs to my bedroom to pack a few things. And you had better not try to stop me, Basil, or so help me God, you'll live to regret it."

Then Vannah turned on her heel and resolutely left the parlor for her bedroom.

As she quickly climbed the stairs she heard Basil's plaintive wail of, "Vannah, please don't leave me!"

I did it, she thought as she reached the top of the stairs. Soon Martin and I will be together again, and this nightmare will be over.

But the nightmare was just beginning. Without warning Vannah couldn't catch her breath. She felt weak and light-headed, and the upstairs foyer suddenly seemed to veer off to the left and go sliding into a yawning, dark void. She screamed Martin's name once in stark terror before disappearing into a yawning, black chasm and nothingness.

Chapter Nineteen

WHEN VANNAH OPENED her eyes, her first thought was that Basil had followed her up the stairs and struck her from behind. She started in panic and tried to sit up, but insistent hands pushed her back.

"Hush, Vannah," a soothing voice said.

As her eyes focused and she became aware of her surroundings, she saw Basil's worried, concerned face floating above hers.

"What happened?" she demanded. "Where am I?"

"You fainted," he replied, tenderly placing a cold compress across her forehead.

Oh, my God! she thought with rising terror. He's gone mad and locked me away somewhere so I'll never escape him. I'll never see Martin again.

"You're in your bedroom," he said. "I've sent the Browning boy next door for the doctor. He should be here shortly to examine you and find out why you fainted the way you did."

As Vannah turned her head and looked around she realized with relief that Basil had spoken the truth. She was indeed in her own bedroom, not locked away in the attic like some demented relative.

She took a deep breath and tried to sit up, but the dizziness assailed her once again, and she had to lie back down.

"I wouldn't try that if I were you," Basil said, rising.

"But I have to go now. Martin's carriage is waiting."

Something like malicious pleasure flickered in Basil's eyes, then was gone so quickly that Vannah thought she had imagined it. "I sent him on his way. You're in no condition to go anywhere at the moment."

"I am leaving you, Basil," Vannah insisted. "As soon as the doctor pronounces me fit . . ."

"As you wish," he said with uncharacteristic compliance, bowed, and left her.

He returned moments later with Dr. Chetwynd, who lived at the end of the street, then left again so the doctor could examine Vannah privately.

When the doctor finished an examination that Vannah thought more extensive than necessary, she anxiously asked him, "Well, Dr. Chetwynd, what is wrong with me? What caused me to faint like that?"

He smiled down at her brightly. "It is my great pleasure to inform you that you are going to become a mother, Mrs. Edgewood."

Vannah just stared at him in shock and disbelief. "But— but that's not possible!"

"And why not? You're married. Most married couples have babies sooner or later. It's perfectly natural."

"But I don't want a baby!" Vannah cried.

The doctor's kind face turned stern. "Every woman wants a baby, Mrs. Edgewood. God has blessed you with new life. You must accept it gratefully." He wagged his finger at her like a concerned uncle. "Now, let's not hear any more talk about not wanting this child."

Vannah put her head back against the pillows and let the tears come. She was pregnant with Basil's child! How could she possibly go to Martin now?

"What's this, what's this?" Dr. Chetwynd said. "Tears

on such a happy occasion, Mrs. Edgewood? Most women are overjoyed when I tell them the news."

Not wanting another lecture from the doctor, Vannah managed a tremulous smile. "They're merely tears of joy, Dr. Chetwynd."

He grinned from ear to ear as he put the rest of his instruments back into his black bag. "And that is as it should be, Mrs. Edgewood. We're all part of God's great plan, you know."

God's great plan, Vannah thought bitterly. More like God's supreme jest on me.

"You're young and you're in excellent health, Mrs. Edgewood," the doctor went on, "so I foresee no problems with your pregnancy. I fully expect you to visit me regularly."

Then he went on to explain what she could expect during the months ahead as her pregnancy progressed, but Vannah listened only halfheartedly, replying, "Yes, Dr. Chetwynd," every once in a while.

Finally, when he had finished and was preparing to leave, Vannah couldn't bring herself to thank him for coming and bringing her such devastating news, so all she did was wish him a dispirited "Good evening."

He gave her one last puzzled glance, then wished her good evening as well and left.

Vannah managed to rise from her bed and go to the window. Her upswept hair was coming out of its pins and tumbling down around her shoulders in disarray, and several of the gown's satin loops had slipped down her upper arms. She knew she looked as dreadful as she felt, but she didn't care. She had been bested by the tiny, helpless adversary growing within her, an adversary she couldn't possibly fight.

"Damn, damn, damn!" she cried in helpless rage, pounding her fist against the windowsill.

When she heard the bedroom door open, she knew it

was Basil, and she turned to face him, fully expecting him to gloat and mock her. But he didn't. He stood in the middle of the room, a strange mixture of wonder and joy on his face.

"Dr. Chetwynd told me," he said softly.

Vannah nodded numbly, crossed her arms, and turned her attention back to the window.

"Are you still going to leave me?" he asked.

"How can I?" she replied in bitter resignation. "I can't expect Martin to accept another man's child."

"No, I suppose not." Basil was silent for a moment. "Then you're not going to leave me after all?"

Vannah had thought of leaving Basil, anyway, but where would she go? Back to Gerrold Webb? To Aunt Constance and her husband? She knew in her heart that she couldn't burden any of them with her problems.

Basil drew closer, though he didn't attempt to touch her. "Give me another chance, Vannah, please? You're going to have my child. I'll be a good father to it if you'll just give me another chance." He hung his head. "I know I haven't been the best of husbands to you, and I know some of your accusations about me are well deserved. But I can change, Vannah! Surely I deserve a chance to prove to you that I can."

"Leave me alone, Basil. I have to think."

He nodded wordlessly and left her.

When she was alone, Vannah undressed, taking great care to avoid looking at her body for the telltale changes Dr. Chetwynd had told her about. She slipped her nightgown over her head and put on a dressing gown, then sat before her mirror to brush out her hair. When it flowed down past her shoulders in a silken, golden mane, she crossed the room like a sleepwalker and went downstairs to tell Basil her decision.

She found him pacing around the parlor, and when he

saw her standing in the doorway in her dressing gown, a look of hope lit up his features.

"I will stay with you, Basil," she said, her voice flat and devoid of emotion, "but only for the sake of our child." For the first time in months Vannah thought of Alastair McKechnie, the father she had never known, and added, "He, or she, deserves to know its true father."

With tears streaming down his face Basil rushed up to her and grabbed one of her hands. "Thank you, Vannah, thank you!"

She pulled away, disgusted by his touch. "But you must also realize that our marriage will now be in name only, Basil. I don't love you the way I once did, and can't bring myself to share a bed with you ever again."

"I understand," he said.

Vannah nodded wordlessly, turned, and went back upstairs, her once proud head bowed in resignation, her soul empty and bleak.

When the slow, measured footsteps died and the house was silent once again, Basil smiled to himself. Whether Vannah knew it or not, she was in his power now. Even though she detested him, Basil didn't care. This baby was going to be Gerrold Webb's first grandchild, and if it was a son, he would be Basil Edgewood's ticket to more wealth than he had ever dreamed possible.

And he had never dreamed that a simple visit to Cousin Winifred in America would result in such a splendid catch as Savannah Webb, the daughter of a millionaire. When he first met her, he knew he didn't stand a chance with such a woman, but her aversion to men of her own class had evidently worked in Basil's favor. After that it was so easy to woo and win her.

He made sure the front door was locked, then extinguished the gaslight in the parlor. As he trotted up the dark staircase he chuckled to himself. Oh, he would play the game by Vannah's rules, at least for a little while. But soon he could drop his act of the contrite, humble husband and be in control again.

When he reached his own bedroom, Basil decided that such a victory deserved a little celebration. He locked his door, then listened to make sure that Vannah was not still awake. When he heard nothing, he went to begin the ritual.

First the cocaine, then Zoe. Both were his dark little secrets, and both were exacting mistresses. One stimulated his mind; both stimulated his body. Zoe was the rare whore who actually enjoyed his little diversions, but she expected to be paid and paid well. And Basil was always most generous, especially with his wife's earnings.

Soon his cares ceased to exist, and he was soaring high above the earth in a chariot made of blinding golden sunlight, and the gods spoke to him.

Then he went to Zoe.

The following day was Saturday, so Vannah had the hansom cab take her directly to Martin's house rather than to his office.

As she trudged up the flagstone path she wanted to cry but couldn't. She had cried so much last night, there were no tears left inside. Only a dull ache seemed to exist in the place where her heart had been.

Vannah rang the bell, Ivers admitted her, and she went to the drawing room to wait for Martin.

As she seated herself at one of the long, built-in window seats that overlooked the garden, Vannah's thoughts raced back years ago to the day Martin had broken her heart by telling her that he was returning to Katherine. Now their situations were reversed. Now she was going to have to break his heart.

"Vannah?"

At the sound of her name she turned and rose slowly, regretfully, and looked at the man she loved for what she feared would be the last time.

Martin's tall, commanding figure dominated the room, causing a lump to form in Vannah's throat. He looked as though he had dressed quickly, for he wore no waistcoat and morning coat, just a white shirt left unbuttoned at the neck and stuffed into his trousers. Once again his air of devastating masculinity and power threatened to sway Vannah from her purpose.

He strode across the room toward her, his rugged, handsome face alight with pleasure and triumph. "I knew you would come to me," he said, reaching for her.

She almost succumbed yet again but forced herself to remember her reason for coming today.

Vannah stepped back and blurted out, "I can't leave Basil, Martin. I'm going to have his child."

Martin stopped and stared at her. "What did you say?"

"I'm with child, Martin. Basil's child."

The words hung in the air between them, separating them more heartlessly than time, Katherine, or Basil ever could.

When Vannah saw the pain and incredulity written on Martin's face, she realized that she had destroyed him as she had once destroyed Paul Demarest.

"Dear God, Martin!" she cried, the tears coming at last. "Don't look at me like that!"

He turned without saying a word to her and went out into the garden where only last night he had held her in his arms and told her how much he loved her. Standing there with his hands by his sides and his feet spread apart, Martin was oblivious to the warm sun beating down on his head and shoulders and the sweet trill of a small brown bird perched on his high garden wall. All he could think about was the sad-eyed woman standing in his drawing room.

Vannah was going to bear another man's child.

Even as part of him vehemently denied the truth of her words, another part of him realized that he had lost her forever. A child would shackle her to Edgewood as surely and solidly as iron manacles. And the child's welfare would always take precedence over her own wants and desires because Vannah was the kind of woman who would think of her children before she thought of herself.

Martin groaned and closed his eyes, almost wishing that Katherine had let him die that day he had been ambushed so he would have been spared the exquisite torture of losing Vannah in this cruel, ironic way. He had only cried twice in his adult life, but he felt like crying now, a great outpouring of rage and anguish that would wash away the pain, leaving him cleansed and whole again.

But he couldn't. He had to decide what to do about Vannah, and as he walked back to the house with a heavy heart, he realized that it was the hardest decision he had ever had to make.

When he saw her sitting there, staring out the window, her blue eyes filled with sorrow and her ivory cheeks glazed with fresh tears, he felt such an outpouring of love for her that he almost veered from the path he had chosen. Yet he knew that if he did, he would never know a moment's peace again.

He watched her sense his presence, and she turned at once, her eyes seeking his. Then she rose very slowly, as though already encumbered by the child in her womb, and came toward him.

"I'm sorry, Martin," Vannah said, dabbing at her cheeks with a handkerchief.

"No sorrier than I. When did you learn that you—you are—"

"Last night, when Basil and I returned home."

"I see." *Get on with it, you coward!* he thought.

Martin took a deep breath to steady himself for yet another painful ordeal he was going to subject her to. "Vannah, you know that I will always love you, but under the circumstances, I think it would be best if we never saw each other again."

Then he turned away, afraid to see the stricken look on her face, knowing that it would unman him and hating himself even more for his cowardice.

"Of course I'll continue to work with Edgewood on his novel, and you're welcome to work with Watson as much as you like. But I'm afraid that there is nothing left between us, Vannah."

Martin sighed and closed his eyes, waiting for her to rail at him and call him every loathsome name he deserved to be called, but she said nothing.

"Please, Vannah, say something to me. Anything!"

Silence.

"Damn it, Vannah!" he cried, turning around to face her at last. "I couldn't bear to—"

The room was empty. She had gone. All that was left of her was an almost imperceptible trace of her perfume.

Martin stood there in silence, then softly said to no one, "I couldn't bear to be in the same room with you, knowing that I can never have you."

In the months to come, a resigned Vannah gradually learned acceptance.

The Monday after the disastrous party, Vannah went to Watson's office, explained her situation to him, that she would no longer be seeing Martin socially or otherwise. She expressed the hope that even though she had lost Martin's friendship, she and Watson would still enjoy a profitable relationship as architect and window designer.

Watson kept her so busy during the summer months and into September that Vannah had precious little time to think about her pregnancy, which suited her just fine. Work occupied her mind, so she didn't have time to think about being sick every morning and exhausted every afternoon. As her belly seemed to grow rounder with each passing day, she dreaded the time when her condition could no longer be concealed and she would not be allowed admittance into the Swallow and Swan Studios to supervise the construction of her windows.

She reached that point at the end of September and reluctantly agreed to give up designing windows until after her confinement. Soon Vannah found herself with too much time on her hands, too much time to think. So she filled her days by reading and writing letter after letter to Aunt Constance, who was overjoyed by her news and promised to visit her niece soon. But there were days when Vannah's thoughts got the best of her and she would grow contemplative and often melancholy.

She would think of her own mother, pregnant with one man's child, having to endure marriage to another. The similarity of their situations was not lost on Vannah. But at least Basil was keeping to his part of their bargain and making a concerted effort to change. He was always quite solicitous of her health, spent most of his day writing his novel, and never attempted to touch her. He was kindness itself.

Still, Vannah was obsessed with thoughts of Martin.

One chilly, blustery day in mid-November, when Basil was delivering another chapter of his novel to Martin's office, Vannah had an unexpected visitor.

"Watson!" she cried in delight when Rosie showed him into the parlor.

"Now, now, now," he said, admonishing her as he refused Rosie's offer to relieve him of his hat. "Don't you dare rise on my account." Then he kissed her on the top of her head. "You look positively radiant, girl."

"How can anyone who looks like a big, waddling elephant possibly be radiant?" she grumbled. "I wear potato sacks masquerading as dresses, and as for my toes . . . I haven't seen them in so long, I've quite forgotten how many I have. Is it eight or ten?"

Watson laughed as he eased his large frame into the seat across from her. "Well, if you don't want to be radiant, how about ripe, like a succulent peach?" And he gave Vannah a lascivious wink.

Vannah blushed and burst out laughing. "Oh, Watson, what a terribly improper thing to say to a lady who's breeding."

"Yes, isn't it? But then, I've never been one for the proprieties."

After Vannah finished laughing, she suddenly grew serious. "I'm about to break my own rule, Watson."

"You want to know how the marquis has been faring," he replied.

Vannah nodded as she wrapped her shawl more closely around her.

"Shall I be honest with you, girl?"

"You're always honest with me, Watson."

"The man is in agony, Vannah. Sheer agony. He's back to being the kind of man who was married to Cowboy Katie."

Vannah just shook her head sadly.

"When he lost you for the second time, he lost his heart as well. Oh, he makes a brave show of it, working himself into an early grave, then flitting about London with a different woman on his arm every night."

At this unexpected bit of news Vannah felt a stab of jealousy and winced.

Watson leaned forward. "Are you all right?"

"It—it's nothing. The baby kicked, that's all."

Watson chuckled as he stroked his grizzly beard. "The marquis even bought himself a motorcar, of all things."

"A motorcar!" Vannah exclaimed.

Watson nodded. "He keeps the noisy contraption at Ashwood and goes driving it around the estate every weekend if the weather cooperates. He's even invited me to ride in it, but I refuse."

"You should be more adventurous. You might even enjoy it. They say the motorcar will replace the horse one day."

The architect shrugged. "Oh, I don't doubt that it will. One can't stop progress, after all. But the marquis can go driving by himself. Besides, he always invites our Sophie to come along."

Vannah's smile died at the mention of the baroness.

"Our Sophie thinks that the marquis is going to ask her to marry him any day now."

Vannah tried to hide her dismay and failed. "Oh, Watson, he wouldn't!"

"He's got more sense than to do that, girl." Then he grew serious. "You're the only woman he's ever loved. And he still needs you for a friend, whether or not the bloody fool realizes it."

Vannah rested her head against the back of her chair and stared up at the ceiling. "Oh, you mustn't blame him for not wanting to have anything to do with me, Watson. I certainly don't." She shook her head. "You didn't see his face when I told him I was going to have Basil's baby. He did the only thing he could have, under the circumstances."

Watson's bushy brows came down in a scowl. "A gentleman doesn't desert his friends in time of need, and I told him so!"

"Dear Watson . . . how could you expect a man to see the woman he loves like this"— she placed her hands on her protruding middle for emphasis—"bearing another man's child?" When he didn't answer, Vannah sighed deeply as she was beset by deep melancholy. "We were just never meant to be together, Watson."

"Perhaps not now," he replied, "but someday . . ."

"You're such an optimist, my friend."

"Perhaps I am," he replied.

Sunday, December twentieth, was a day Vannah would long remember.

She awoke with a dull, persistent backache but thought nothing of it as she watched Basil leave for the train station. Some obscure relative of his had died, and he was going down to Kent for several days for the funeral. Since her child was due to arrive in another week, Vannah was remaining at home.

After Basil left, Vannah dressed herself and went lumbering about the kitchen, preparing her breakfast. As she looked out the window she saw that a light snow had fallen overnight, and she hoped it would last until Christmas.

Christmas . . .

Sitting alone at the kitchen table while she nibbled at her toast, Vannah thought of Christmases past in New York City when she was growing up and how this one seemed bleak and dreary by comparison. She realized that it had more to do with her own barren emotional state than the fact that her home boasted not even a single spray of holly to celebrate Christmas. Oh, Basil had suggested that they get a tree, but Vannah couldn't muster the enthusiasm.

Suddenly the door bell rang. Since it was Rosie's day off, Vannah hoisted herself out of her chair and waddled off to answer it. When she opened the door, she saw that her caller was none other than Martin.

As she stared up at him Vannah noticed that Martin's

eyes had lost their smoldering core and now looked haunted and lifeless in their deep, shadowed sockets. His face was thinner and haggard now, the corners of his mouth dragged down.

He hung his head and toyed with his hat. "I won't blame you if you slam the door in my face."

"Don't be a fool, Martin Ash," she said, stepping aside so he could enter.

His deep voice sounded so wonderful to Vannah's ears as he said, "Watson said you didn't have a Christmas tree, so I brought one for you."

As he turned and signaled to someone, Vannah looked into the street beyond. She could see a wagon parked behind Martin's carriage, and in it was a small, but full, fir tree about as tall as Martin.

"Go inside, Vannah," he said, "before you catch your death out here."

She stepped way back into the foyer and watched as the servant brought the tree inside, set it against the wall, then tipped his hat to Vannah and left.

"It's good to see you again, Martin," she said as she watched him remove his black broadcloth overcoat and hang it and his hat on the coatrack. "I've missed your friendship."

A muscle twitched in his jaw as he quickly stripped off his gloves. "Dear God," he said with a heartfelt sigh, "no matter how hard I try, I can't seem to stay away from you, Vannah."

She extended her hands to him. "I understand why you felt you had to, Martin. I don't blame you, under the circumstances."

Martin bowed his head in shame, and his voice shook with deep emotion. "I owe you an apology, Vannah. I just came to tell you that I'm sorry for treating you so shabbily the day after the party. I was so harsh and cruel to you. You didn't deserve it."

As his cold, trembling fingers grasped hers, Vannah felt Martin's strength flow into her, so warm and encouraging. She locked her fingers with his and held on, unwilling to part from him just yet.

"I shouldn't have come," he said. "I know our situation is hopeless, but I couldn't stay away a moment longer, Vannah. I don't care if you are married." He glanced down at her outthrust middle. "I don't care if you're going to have another man's child. I just had to see you, had to hear your voice."

"Dear God, I feel the same way," she replied, shivering.

Then he drew her to him and held her as close as he could. Vannah sighed contentedly as she snuggled against him, her head against his shoulder.

"Are you being well taken care of, Vannah?" he asked. "Is there anything you need?"

I need you, Martin.

"Dr. Chetwynd says I'm young and healthy and should have no difficulty bearing healthy children."

Martin's voice was relieved as he said, "I've been so worried about you. You don't know . . ."

She smiled up at him. "Why don't we go into the parlor? We have much to talk about."

They spent the next hour just sitting together and talking like two old friends, then Martin turned his attentions to the Christmas tree. But the tree never got decorated. Just as Martin finished standing it near the window facing the street, Vannah felt a sharp pain that took her breath away.

"Vannah, what's wrong?" Martin demanded.

"I'm . . . wet," she replied, her cheeks flaming with embarrassment. "Martin, I think my baby is about to be born."

He turned deathly pale but was at her side in an instant, effortlessly, sweeping her into his arms despite her misshapen body. "Let's get you up to bed, then you can tell me where I can find this Dr. Chetwynd of yours."

The only time Martin left Vannah's side was to send his driver to fetch Dr. Chetwynd, who was attending another birth and couldn't come to Vannah for nearly half a day. Martin stayed by her bedside as promised, sponging her face with a mixture of cool water and vinegar, rubbing her lower back to ease the ache, and talking to her incessantly in a low, soothing voice. And when the pains became so great that Vannah screamed and thrashed about to escape them, Martin made her grasp his hands as tightly as she could and look deeply into his eyes.

As hour after interminable hour passed, Martin's unfaltering gaze, encouraging words, and soothing touch enabled Vannah to rise beyond the pain and the fear. He was her anchor, her lodestar. Even when the doctor finally came and the birth was imminent, Martin was never farther than an outstretched arm away. And when it was over at long last, Martin was the one who told a jubilant Vannah that she had just given birth to a son.

Later, smoothing the matted hair away from Vannah's white, exhausted face as she took her well-earned rest, Martin murmured, "Your son has just one tiny imperfection, my love. He's not mine."

He fell asleep in a chair by her bed, his hand lightly clasping hers.

Chapter Twenty

London—1897

"MAY I SPEAK WITH YOU, Mrs. Edgewood, ma'am?" Rosie said, standing in the doorway of Vannah's bedroom, her round face worried.

"Of course," Vannah replied absently, not taking her eyes off two-month-old Lewis Alastair Edgewood sleeping so peacefully in his crib.

He had to be the most beautiful, most perfect baby in the world, Vannah decided with fierce maternal pride as she reached out to gently stroke his small head covered with soft brown down. True, he bore more of a resemblance to his father, but at least he had his mother's large blue eyes and her quick smile, though he was noticeably toothless.

Now she reluctantly turned her attention to the maid, still standing in the middle of the room. "Lewis has just been fed, so he should sleep for hours now," she said, setting down the bottle of liquid baby food. "I think we can go downstairs without disturbing him."

When the two women were in the parlor, Vannah said, "Now, Rosie, what is it you wish to discuss with me?"

"It's all the bills, ma'am," the maid replied, her head bowed in embarrassment.

"Bills? What bills?"

"The bills what hasn't been paid yet. Why, just this morning, Mr. Philpott, the butcher, refused to sell me any more meat until his bill is paid, and I fear that the greengrocer is going to be next, and that's a fact."

Vannah scowled. "There must be some mistake. Mr. Edgewood should have paid those bills weeks ago."

Now Rosie looked panic-stricken. "And that's not all, ma'am. Oh," she wailed, twisting her apron in distress, "I feel so terrible having to tell you this, Mrs. Edgewood, but I haven't been paid since Master Lewis was born."

"You mean to tell me that Mr. Edgewood hasn't paid you your wages for two months?" Vannah felt herself turn white with shock.

Rosie nodded and swallowed hard. "Yes, ma'am, that he hasn't. And with Master Lewis here now, I do twice the work I used to do."

"I know you do. I don't know what I would have done without you," Vannah said, patting her on the shoulder. "You have been a treasure, Rosie, and if anything, you deserve an increase in your wages."

"I spoke to Mr. Edgewood, ma'am, and explained that I have my poor sick mother to support, as well as two younger sisters. He promised that I would get paid soon, but that was a month ago."

"You'll be paid, Rosie. I promise."

"And, ma'am? Would you also promise me you won't tell Mr. Edgewood that I told tales? He'd be frightfully angry with me, and that's a fact."

"I won't tell him you told," she said with a grim smile.

Rosie looked around relieved as she bobbed a curtsy and returned to her duties in the kitchen.

When she was alone, Vannah walked slowly around the parlor, trying to assimilate what the maid had just told her. Even though Basil handled the finances, Vannah knew that they should have had enough money to keep out of debt, what with the small inheritance from her mother. In addition, Martin's advances to both of them had been more than generous, and Vannah's other commissions for windows last summer had enabled them to live comfortably. Or so she had thought.

"I can't understand it," she said to herself. "Where is the money going?"

Well, Basil was due home any minute now and she would soon find out.

Vannah didn't have long to wait. Several minutes later her husband came into the parlor, his arms laden with packages.

"Wait until you see what I bought for my boy," he said excitedly, crossing the room to set the parcels on the table. Before Vannah could say a word, he ripped one open. "Here we have a rattle . . . and a spinning top . . . and a ball."

"Basil, he's too young for a spinning top or a ball."

"He'll be old enough one day," Basil said with a shrug. "And here we have a wooden horse on wheels." He set the toy on the floor and proceeded to pull it across the room. "I know my boy will just love playing with this horse when he's older."

"And may I ask where you got the money for all these wonderful things?"

Basil stopped. "These are for our son, Vannah. Surely you don't begrudge me a few shillings to spend on our son."

"You know I would never begrudge the baby anything, Basil, but unfortunately, Mr. Philpott, the butcher, will not be as understanding."

He stared at her. "What are you talking about?"

"I received a call from Mr. Philpott this morning," she said. "He was very angry. He told me that he's not going to sell us any more meat unless we pay our bill, which I understand is considerable."

Basil shrugged as if the matter were of scant concern.

"Tradespeople should wait for their money. The scurvy knaves should be privileged to serve the likes of us. And if old Philpott doesn't like it, there are other butchers in this city. Send Rosie to one of them."

Vannah bit her lower lip to contain her anger. "And speaking of Rosie, don't you think we should increase her wages? After all, since little Lewis arrived, she has been serving as a nursemaid in addition to her many other duties."

"I disagree," Basil said flatly. "I think we pay Rosie too much as it is."

"Basil, we appear to be running out of money."

He smiled disarmingly. "Don't worry your pretty little head about money, fair lady. Just be a good mother to our son."

"Basil!" Vannah cried angrily, stamping her foot to get his attention. "I want to know what has happened to all of our money." When he looked like he wasn't going to answer her, she said, "Basil, if you don't tell me what happened to the money right this instant, I am going to take the baby, leave this house, and you will never see either of us again!"

She saw raw fear in his eyes then. "You wouldn't keep my son from me, Vannah. You couldn't be that cruel."

"I mean it, Basil."

He bowed his head. "All right, all right. I made some bad investments and I lost it all."

"Oh, dear God." Vannah eased herself into a nearby chair before her legs collapsed beneath her.

"I did it for Lewis," he said, flinging himself down beside her chair, his eyes imploring her to understand and forgive. "I—I thought that if I doubled our money, we would move out of this neighborhood and into a larger house, something in the country, so Lewis could have a pony when he's older. But I lost everything."

"Basil, how could you!"

He rose now and looked down at her. "Can you blame a man for wanting a better life for his son?"

Despite her disappointment and anger, Vannah could understand why he had done it, though she could not forgive him for being so foolhardy and irresponsible. She, too, would have done anything for her baby.

Her anger melted away. "No, Basil, I can't blame you for that. But you mustn't take such risks like that again. What are we going to do for money in the interim?"

"My book will be published soon, and then we'll never have to worry about money again. And, until then, I'm going to try to find another job on a newspaper."

"I can always go back to designing windows for Watson Greene," Vannah mused.

Basil's face clouded. "But what about Lewis? A mother's place is with her child."

"Do you think I want to leave my baby in the care of someone else?" she snapped. "But I have no other choice, at least until you find work. We have to have a roof over our heads, Basil. We have to eat."

"Perhaps Fleet could—"

"Don't even suggest it." Vannah rose, annoyed with Basil once again. "I will not humiliate myself by asking Martin for money."

"I wasn't even going to suggest it," Basil said hurriedly to calm her. "I was going to say that perhaps he could give me another advance or at least publish my book sooner."

That mollified her somewhat. "Well, perhaps I could speak to him about it."

"For Lewis's sake."

As Vannah watched her husband go up the stairs, whistling as though he hadn't a care in the world, she wondered what else he would expect her to do for Lewis's sake. Then she chided herself for being so suspicious of his every motive, dressed warmly against the February chill gripping London, and left for Martin's office.

Martin knew that he would have to tell her sooner or later, but he would willingly endure torture by red Indians on the warpath in order to spare Vannah such a crushing blow. Still, she was strong, stronger than many men he knew.

He sighed as he went to a window and looked down at the hansoms and growlers clopping beneath his window, debating what to do. Should he break the unpleasant news to Edgewood first, or should he tell them together? Either way was most distasteful to him.

Just then, there came a knock on the door, and his secretary peered in. "Mrs. Edgewood to see you, sir."

"Send her in, Clara."

Martin had seen Vannah only once since the birth of her baby, that day he stopped by to deliver his gifts to the new arrival, a crib and a silver cup engraved with Lewis's name and the date of his birth. It had torn him up inside to see Vannah sitting there, cradling another man's child in her arms, while Edgewood just smirked and gloated possessively by her side. But Martin endured and bided his time, for he was a very patient man.

Now, as Vannah glided into his office, Martin felt his breath and his heart begin to quicken simultaneously. Though she wore a plain blue redingote, she was a vision, her pale hair put up beneath a perky felt fedora and her ivory cheeks buffed to a ruddy glow by the cold weather. If anything, motherhood had made her even more beautiful and desirable, giving her features a newly rounded softness. He longed to whisk her away to St. John's Wood and keep her there for all eternity.

He realized that he had been staring too long without greeting her, so he smiled and crossed the room. "Vannah, what a pleasant surprise. But what are you doing out and about on such a cold day? You've just had a baby, remember."

She smiled as he took her wrap, revealing a pale blue dress with a wasp waist to display her restored figure and leg-o'-mutton sleeves. "Martin, I'm fully recovered, and I'm as healthy as a horse. You needn't worry."

But he did worry about her. He worried a great deal, especially how she would bear up under what he had to tell her today.

Suddenly her smile died. "Martin, is something troubling you?"

His smile was forced as he said, "What makes you say that?"

"My friend," she began, slipping her arm companionably through his, "we have shared too much for me not to know when something is troubling you."

As they walked arm in arm over to the divan, he said, "The woman I love more than life itself is living with another man and refuses to leave him. What could possibly be troubling me, I ask you?"

"Martin . . ." she said, admonishing him.

He raised his hands in surrender. "I know. You must stay with Basil for Lewis's sake."

"A father should be able to see his own son, Martin," she replied. "As I've told you before, I never knew my true father, and I don't want Lewis to go through life not knowing his."

"But the price is just too high, Vannah! Must you sacrifice yourself?"

A look of resignation flitted across her face, and she stared down at the floor. "Children often require great sacrifices of their parents."

He regarded her with a mocking smile twisting his mouth, then reached out to run his fingertips down her velvet cheek. "You won't stay with him forever, you know," he said softly, "even for Lewis's sake. There will come a day—"

"Martin, please," she said, averting her head and seating herself on the divan.

He said nothing, just turned and went to pour her a cup of tea, though he would have preferred something stronger right at that moment.

Behind him he heard Vannah say, "Besides, Basil has changed."

He turned his head to gaze at her in patent disbelief. "Oh?"

"Don't be so cynical, Martin. Basil has changed in many ways, and it's all Lewis's doing, I think. He positively dotes on that baby." Vannah shook her head in wonder. "He never loses his temper or acts childishly now. Why, he'll spend hours just rocking Lewis in his cradle and crooning to him. I'll wake up to feed the baby in the middle of the night, and there will be Basil, just staring at him. I've never seen such a loving, devoted father."

The hint of admiration in her voice took Martin aback. Was this some new ploy of Edgewood's, designed to ensnare Vannah's sympathies, to bind her to him so that she could never escape? He had to disillusion her and quickly.

"Vannah," he began solemnly as he handed her the teacup, "there's something I've got to tell you, and it's not going to be pleasant."

She set the cup down with a trembling hand. "Why, what is it, Martin?"

"I'm afraid that the manuscript Basil submitted is unpublishable."

Vannah looked at him in disbelief. "What are you saying, Martin? I don't understand."

He sat down beside her and took her hands in his. "I'm saying that Basil's book will not be published. It's not very well written and is actually rambling and incoherent in many places."

"Oh, dear..."

"It's so bad, Vannah, that even editing won't salvage it. I'm sorry."

She tried to hold back her tears but failed. "It's not your fault, Martin."

"Thank you for saying that, Vannah," he murmured, squeezing her hands. "I was afraid that you'd think I'm deliberately refusing to publish Basil's novel just because we're"—he smiled wryly—"not the best of friends."

"Don't be absurd, Martin," she scoffed. "I know you too well to believe that you could be so—so petty."

"But Basil will not be as charitable," he pointed out. "You, of all people, know how he is. He has nothing but scorn for those who don't appreciate his talent. He will claim he has written a masterpiece but that out of spite, I will not publish it."

As much as she hated to admit it, Vannah knew that he spoke the truth.

"Would you like to read it yourself?" Martin offered. He indicated a stack of papers on his desk. "It's right over there."

She shook her head, then said, "How long have you known?"

"Since shortly after Lewis was born." He looked away and released her hands, though he felt curiously empty. "I couldn't see the point in upsetting you at such a happy time. But I'm afraid I couldn't postpone telling you any longer. Once again, I don't know what else to say, except that I'm sorry."

Vannah rose now, her brain spinning. Not only had Basil squandered away what little money they had, they now had to find a way of repaying the advance Martin had given them for the completion of the book.

"We will, of course, repay the advance," she said, raising her head proudly.

"No!" was Martin's emphatic reply as he jumped to his feet.

Vannah could tell by the determined expression on his face and the warning glint in his green eyes that he would brook no arguments from her. But she had to try.

"Martin, I can't possibly allow you to—"

"Don't argue with me, Vannah. I expect nothing. You owe me nothing."

His generosity touched her so, she couldn't control herself any longer. Vannah suddenly burst into tears. Martin was at her side in an instant, a comforting arm around her shoulders as he led her back to the divan.

"I know this has been a great disappointment for you," he began, "but—"

"It's not that," Vannah interrupted as she reached for a handkerchief, despising herself for her weakness. But she had to talk to someone, so while Martin listened, Vannah poured out her heart about Basil's imprudent investments and how they were now on the verge of destitution.

Martin looked appalled. "Vannah, if you need money—"

"No!" she cried vehemently. "It's Basil's responsibility to provide for his family, not yours."

"Don't be so damned stubborn!" he said in exasperation. "What are you going to live on?"

"I'm on my way to see Watson," she replied. "I hope that he'll want to retain the services of the best stained glass window designer in England once again."

"I have no doubt that he will."

"I'm counting on it." Then Vannah rose. "Well, I must be on my way. When do you intend to break the news to Basil?"

"If you'll tell him to come to my office tomorrow morning, I'll do it then."

* * *

The following day, when Basil learned that he would not be gaining fame and fortune as an author, he returned home in the blackest of moods.

"My book is a masterpiece!" he screeched. "Ash won't publish it because he's envious of me. He's just doing this out of spite."

Vannah refused to listen to his childish rantings and ravings and went upstairs to spend as much precious time as she could with her son. Tomorrow she would return to her work.

And Watson kept her very busy.

At first Basil insisted that Vannah turn over all of her own earnings to him, but after many a heated argument that usually ended with her threats to take the baby and leave, he reluctantly agreed that she should manage the finances from now on. In a few weeks Vannah earned enough money to pay off the worst of their debts and, two months later, was able to give Rosie a well-deserved increase in wages.

Even though Basil grumbled that it was demeaning for a man to receive an allowance from his wife—and such a small one at that—he was not above accepting it. And although he claimed to be seeking employment, he had no success, though he often spoke mysteriously of "his ship coming in."

Then came the day when Vannah finally learned the startling significance of that cryptic statement.

One unusually warm April afternoon, Vannah returned home early from the Swallow and Swan Studios to find a strange man and woman in her parlor, cooing over her baby's cradle and Rosie nowhere to be found.

"Leave my baby alone!" she cried from the doorway.

Suddenly the intruders turned to face her, and Vannah gasped in surprise.

"Gerrold? Dahlia?" She looked from one to the other. "What on earth are you doing here?"

As Gerrold walked toward her she could see that he had changed even more than the last time they had spoken. Those changes went beyond the extra weight he had added around his once flat middle and the threads of silver streaking his wavy gold hair. The eyes that Vannah remembered as being so icy and implacable were now actually filled with warmth. Gerrold Webb seemed almost benevolent now.

"Savannah," he said, "you look more beautiful than ever."

Much to her surprise, he kissed her on the cheek.

Now Dahlia swept forward in a rustle of ivory lace, hands extended, a wide smile on her face. "I hope you don't mind us barging in on you uninvited, Savannah," she said, "but we were on our way to the Riviera, anyway, so . . ."

Vannah couldn't believe the change in her stepmother, either. Dahlia was now almost half the size of the woman Vannah remembered, and in her lace-covered dress and huge, flowered hat, she looked almost pretty.

Gerrold said, "We just had to see our grandson."

When Vannah opened her mouth to protest, he raised his hand in anticipation of her next remark. "I know you're going to say that Lewis isn't really my grandson, aren't you?"

Vannah turned away. "Well, it is the truth."

"Daughter," Gerrold said, taking her arm and leading her to the divan, "it's time we had a heart-to-heart talk and mended some fences."

When all three were seated, he said, "It takes more than blood kinship to make a parent. To put it crudely, all

Alastair McKechnie did was contribute his seed. I was the one who fed you, clothed you, put a roof over your head. I was more of a father to you than your real father ever was, and I hope you'll realize it someday."

Before Vannah could reply, he rose and paced the room. "I admit that in many ways I wasn't a good father. I was disappointed because I didn't have a son. I was always too gruff with you, too impatient. When one gets older, one has time to reflect on one's mistakes." He looked at her, his eyes imploring her for understanding and forgiveness.

Vannah didn't reply right away. She sat there dredging up every injustice Gerrold had ever done to her mother, her Aunt Constance, and herself. And when she had the list firmly in hand, she mentally tore it up and relegated it to the past where it belonged.

She sighed, rose, and took his hands in hers. "I haven't been blameless, either, Father. I have always been headstrong and stubborn."

"That you have, my girl," Gerrold said with a chuckle as he drew her to him for a hug. When he released her, he said, "But at least we both have enough sense to let bygones be bygones."

She nodded. "Let's leave all our differences in the past, where they belong."

"Agreed."

Dahlia beamed at them, her pale gray eyes shining brightly. "You two have just made me the happiest woman in the world."

When Vannah heard Lewis stir fussily in his crib, she said, "Why don't you become better acquainted with your grandson while I find my maid and have her bring us some tea?"

Later, while drinking tea and catching up on all the gossip from New York, Vannah said, "Who told you about Lewis? Aunt Constance?"

Gerrold shook his head. "I haven't heard from Constance in years, and deservedly so. No, I received a letter from your husband telling me of the baby's birth and inviting me to come to England for a visit."

Vannah's smile died, and she grew very still. She set her teacup down carefully and folded her hands to keep them from shaking. "Basil wrote to you?"

Gerrold nodded.

"He never said a word to me." Vannah rose now, angry and upset. "Not one word!"

The tension in the room communicated itself to Lewis, who suddenly burst out into loud wailing. Dahlia was on her feet in an instant, lifted the baby into her arms, and rocked him back and forth until he stopped crying and settled down once again.

When the crisis was over, the baby soothed and back in his crib, Gerrold finally spoke. "Savannah, I have something to say to you, and I'm afraid you're not going to like it."

"I know what you're going to say, Father." She took a deep breath and verbalized what she had been afraid to admit, even to herself. "You think Basil married me for my fortune—your fortune, to be precise."

He glanced at his wife. "I'm afraid so, daughter. If he knew we were estranged, why did he feel compelled to write to me about your child?"

When he saw Vannah's bleak expression, Gerrold said gently, "Savannah, fortune hunters are a fact of life for people like us. That's why we tend to marry our daughters to other wealthy men. I tried to make you understand that principle when you were young, but you wouldn't listen."

She smiled bitterly. "And I thought Basil loved me for myself."

"An heiress is never loved for herself," Gerrold replied.

"How well we both know that, don't we, dear?" Dahlia said sweetly, with a pointed look at her husband.

Vannah was surprised to see a flush of embarrassment creep up on her father's face. "I may have married you for Claude's fortune, Dahlia, but I soon fell in love with you, as you know very well."

"Yes, dear, I do." And she kissed him on the cheek.

Vannah rose and went to Lewis's crib again, where he lay sleeping peacefully, oblivious to the turmoil raging through his mother's mind and heart.

Suddenly Gerrold said, "Why don't you and Lewis come back to New York with me, Savannah?" He looked around the humble, sparsely furnished parlor in distaste. "You don't want to raise your child in a place like this."

"Oh, yes!" Dahlia said, her face shining excitedly. "Please come. We could be a family."

Vannah thought of Martin and replied, without hesitation, "I can't."

"Why not?" Gerrold demanded, rising. "I know you and Dahlia would get along famously. And, after your divorce from Edgewood came through—"

"You would find me a more suitable husband."

He looked chagrined. "I would not meddle, Savannah. Not this time. I promise."

"I would see that he didn't," Dahlia added.

"It's not that. If I returned to New York with you, I would only be running away. I have to resolve my problems myself. Whether I decide to remain with Basil for the sake of our child or leave him, the choice must be mine and mine alone."

Gerrold opened his mouth as if to protest, caught his wife's warning look, then changed his mind and smiled. "You must forgive me, Savannah, but I can't quite accept the fact that you're a grown woman now. You don't need your old father anymore."

She went to him and put her arms around him. "That's not true. I think I've come to realize that I will always need you. But there are certain decisions that only I can make."

Then he said, "If you won't agree to return with us, at least let me give you money." When he saw Vannah's mutinous expression, he added, "For Lewis's sake."

But she was adamant. "Thank you for your generosity, Father, but I must refuse. Basil and I will support our son without any help from anyone."

"And that is how it should be," Dahlia said with finality, rising. "Well, Gerrold, I think we should be on our way. As much as I could spend all day with Lewis, we have a boat to catch."

As they said their good-byes Vannah took her stepmother aside and whispered, "Whatever have you done to Gerrold, Dahlia? He's a changed man."

She sighed. "I just taught him the meaning of love, Savannah, that's all. Oh, it was a long, hard battle, because your father is used to getting his own way. But then, so am I." And she gave Vannah a conspiratorial smile.

At the door Gerrold stopped to say, "Well, if you ever need anything in the future . . ."

"You will be the first person I ask."

But she had no intention of accepting money from him, and she wondered how this news would sit with Basil.

He came home just an hour after Gerrold and Dahlia departed and, after giving Vannah a short greeting, went straight to Lewis's crib and began crooning to him. "Did Lewis miss his papa? Handsome boy . . ."

"Oh, I don't think Lewis missed his papa very much this afternoon," Vannah said, "because he had other visitors today."

"And who were they?" Basil asked without looking up from his son.

"His grandparents."

Basil froze, then rose slowly. "Gerrold Webb was here?"

Vannah nodded. "About an hour ago. You can imagine my surprise when I walked through the door and discovered them here with Lewis, since, to the best of my knowledge, they didn't even know the baby existed."

Basil looked as guilty as a hound caught in the henhouse.

"Why didn't you tell me you had written to my stepfather, Basil?" Vannah asked.

He swallowed hard. "I thought he had a right to know."

"And was that your only reason?"

"Why, fair lady, what other reason could I possibly have?"

"I don't know. You tell me."

He shrugged. "A man has a right to know his own grandson, hasn't he?"

"But you knew that Gerrold and I were estranged, yet you took it upon yourself to inform him of Lewis's birth without my knowledge. Why, Basil?" When he didn't answer, she added, "Could it be because you wanted money from him?"

Basil's eyes narrowed, and his expression became sulky. "All right, I admit it," he sputtered angrily. "I wrote to Gerrold Webb in the hopes that he would give us some sort of an allowance. But I didn't do it for myself. I did it for Lewis. Our son, Vannah!"

She felt herself turn cold inside.

Basil swept a contemptuous hand around the parlor. "Do you really want our son to grow up in a shabby six-room terraced house in Clerkenwell? I don't. And if Webb has the means to see to it that our son has all the best life has to offer, than I say he should provide it."

"Any why shouldn't you be the one to provide all the best life has to offer?"

"I would have, if the great Lord Fleet had deigned to publish my novel," he cried.

"Oh, yes, someone else is always to blame for your failings, Basil, never yourself."

"Well, thank you very much for your overwhelming support, Mrs. Edgewood," he muttered sarcastically. "I should have known better than to expect a little sympathy from my own wife."

Suddenly Lewis began crying, and when Vannah went to him, Basil added maliciously, "Now look what you've done. You've upset the baby."

And he went storming upstairs to his own room where he remained for the rest of the evening.

After feeding Lewis and putting him to bed, a troubled Vannah went down to the parlor to be alone with her conflicting thoughts. Her visit from Gerrold and Dahlia this afternoon had been most illuminating, leaving her feeling like the world's biggest fool. Paul Demarest had tried to warn her, but she wouldn't listen. Basil had married her for her money. He had pretended to love her for herself, when all the time he was just after Gerrold Webb's money.

The next morning at breakfast, a bleary-eyed Basil said less than two words to her as he drank his coffee in sullen silence.

Though Vannah was still annoyed with him, she forced herself to say, "I forgot to tell you this yesterday, Basil, but tomorrow Watson and I are traveling by train up to Colchester to consult with a client. I shall probably have to stay there overnight."

Before Basil could utter a word of protest, Vannah rose and went to give last-minute instructions to Rosie before leaving for Watson's office.

* * *

Nothing further was said about Vannah's trip to Colchester, and she left for the train station bright and early the following morning. Luckily for Vannah, the client was affable and easy to please, so she and Watson were able to conclude their business much sooner than expected and even catch a late-afternoon train back to London.

It was ten o'clock at night when Vannah returned home in the middle of a cold downpour, eager to hold little Lewis in her arms once again, for she had missed him terribly. As soon as she ran up the steps she turned and waved to Watson in the hansom, then unlocked the door and went inside.

The first sound that met her ears was the baby's high-pitched wail of distress.

"Basil?" Vannah shouted, stripping off her sodden ulster while she glanced into the lit parlor for any sign of her husband.

When no one answered, she dashed up the stairs calling for Rosie, but not even the maid appeared. By the time Vannah reached her own bedroom, her heart was pounding wildly from both exertion and panic. She knew the way to Lewis's crib without even having to turn on the gaslight, and she raced to the crying baby and scooped him up in her arms to comfort him.

"There, there now," she crooned, rocking him and drying his tears.

The baby was sobbing so hard, his little body could barely catch a breath, but gradually his mother's warmth and soothing voice calmed him down, and his sobs subsided into hiccups, giving Vannah a chance to turn on the light.

"Why, you're soaking wet, sweetheart," she said, setting him down on the bed so she could change him quickly.

As Vannah worked, she called out Basil's name again,

but only the silence responded, and by the time she was finished, the terrifying truth had dawned upon her: the baby had been neglected for perhaps hours.

"Oh, dear God!" she swore, picking up Lewis and rushing to Basil's bedroom.

The door was open and light was streaming out into the darkened upstairs hall.

"Basil!" she cried angrily. "Why in heaven's name did you leave the baby—" She stopped without finishing her sentence.

The sight that greeted her eyes made her gasp in horror and clutch the baby to her so tightly that he whimpered in protest. Basil's room looked as though a hurricane had gone tearing through it. Clothes were tossed around everywhere—hanging out of open drawers, piled on the bed, scattered around the floor willy-nilly.

As Vannah stepped inside she first feared for Basil's safety. Had thieves broken into their house, rifled through their bureau drawers, then spirited Basil away when he surprised them? But if that were the case, why had only Basil's bedroom been searched? And what had happened to their maid?

Vannah scowled in puzzlement as she slowly picked her way through the disarray, searching for some explanation. She soon found it, though it was not what she expected.

On Basil's bed was an open leather case. Inside was a hypodermic needle.

At first Vannah wondered if Basil had been keeping some illness from her, but when she found a small empty bottle labeled COCAINE nearby, she knew the truth at last.

"Oh, dear God!" she muttered in horror.

Was this what Paul Demarest had been trying to tell her, that Vannah's husband was a drug addict?

Vannah knew what she had to do. Within minutes she

went running out of the darkened house with Basil's leather case in the pocket of her ulster and her baby clutched in her arms.

Luckily for Vannah, Martin's butler hadn't yet locked the front gate for the night, and after paying the cabdriver, she ran inside.

As she hurried past the tall linden trees swaying and sighing in the wind and down the slick flagstone path, she whispered to Lewis, "Hush, sweetheart. We're almost there."

Martin's house was in total darkness, and for one moment, Vannah feared that he had gone out for the evening. But she pressed on, and when she reached the door, she kept ringing the bell as if her life depended on it.

Within minutes a welcoming light came on in the foyer, illuminating the Four Seasons windows high above, and the door swung open to reveal Ivers, who didn't seem at all pleased to find a wet, bedraggled young woman with a baby in her arms on his doorstep.

"It's very late to be calling, isn't it, miss?" he asked in lofty, disgruntled tones.

"Ivers, don't you recognize me? It's Mrs. Edgewood," she replied, wiping raindrops from her face as she brushed past him into the warm, dry foyer. "I'm sure Lord Fleet will receive me."

Now Ivers became most deferential. "I beg your pardon, madam. I'm sorry for not recognizing you at once. Do come in. May I take your wrap?"

"No, thank you. Just summon Lord Fleet and Mrs. MacGregor as quickly as you can," she replied as Lewis began to wriggle and fret in her arms.

"Very good, madam."

While Vannah waited for Martin she looked around the foyer and felt tears of relief sting her eyes. Even Lewis seemed to realize that they had reached a safe haven at last and settled down with a sigh and a gurgle of contentment.

The moment Martin came hurrying down the stairs into the foyer and saw Vannah wet and shivering like a half-drowned kitten, he knew why she had come, and his heart leapt to his throat in anticipation.

She looked up at him, her lovely face resolute and triumphant. "I've left him," she announced, as though both Ivers and Mrs. MacGregor were not present.

He didn't dare to hope, but he had to ask, "Forever?"

"Forever."

Now he turned to his housekeeper, a plump, motherly woman with two chins and a head full of tightly wound, curling papers. "Mrs. Mack, will you see to it that Master Lewis is well taken care of?"

"You just give the wee bairn to me, Mrs. Edgewood," she said with a smile as she reached for the baby.

"I'm afraid I didn't have time to take any of his things with me," Vannah apologized, checking him one last time.

"Don't you worry, Mrs. Edgewood. One of our neighbors just had a wee bairn of her own, and I'm sure she won't mind lending me all the necessities." Once she had the baby's head cradled against her soft, ample bosom, the housekeeper turned and addressed Martin. "And shall I prepare a guest room for Mrs. Edgewood, sir?"

"That won't be necessary, Mrs. Mack," he replied, his gaze daring Vannah to dispute him. "Once you get the baby settled, kindly bring up a hot supper for Mrs. Edgewood. Some of the excellent lamb we had for dinner, hot soup, and a bottle of wine will do very nicely."

"Very good, sir," the housekeeper replied, as though her master's sharing of his bedroom with a woman was a common occurrence, then she and the butler wished them good night, and left them alone.

For the longest time Vannah just stood there, staring at

Martin's tall figure, which seemed to fill the foyer with both reassurance and strength. She noticed that he was wearing a hunter-green dressing gown over his clothes, and she became acutely aware of the lean, long-limbed body.

Vannah flung herself into his outstretched arms, clinging to him desperately while she quivered like a hunted animal.

"Oh, Martin . . ." she cried, hugging him fiercely. "It's been such a nightmare."

"Hush, my love. It's over now," he murmured, stroking her wet, tangled hair. "You are with me now, and you'll never have to see Edgewood again." Then he gently put her away from him. "Come, let's get you out of these wet clothes, and then you can tell me what made you decide to leave him."

Suddenly Vannah was shaking so badly, she couldn't move, so Martin just swung her effortlessly into his arms and carried her upstairs to his spacious bedroom at the end of the hall. A small electric lamp on the bedside table provided barely enough light, leaving much of the room in shadow.

Once inside, Martin set Vannah down before the fireplace that had a hot coal fire going to ward off the persistent chill in the air and removed her wet ulster.

Just as Vannah was about to reach up behind her to undo the buttons of her dress, Martin came up behind her and whispered, "Didn't I once tell you that I make an admirable ladies' maid? Do nothing, my darling. Allow me to wait on you, to tend to your every need tonight."

So Vannah's arms fell meekly to her sides, and she entrusted herself to his care.

While he undressed her with the apparent clinical detachment of a physician, in reality Martin was hard-pressed to control his burning desires for her. His gaze devoured the long curve of her back, her firm, round flanks, and the backs of her long legs. By the rosy light of the lamp she seemed to be carved from lustrous white marble. But he swallowed hard and held himself in check, for Vannah's bruised and battered spirit needed more attention than her body at the moment.

When Vannah stepped out of her clothes, Martin took off his own dressing gown and made her put it on. The sleeves came down to her fingertips and the hem trailed on the floor, but the moment she slipped into it, her shivering stopped. The silk garment was still warm from the heat of Martin's own body and smelled faintly of his musky, masculine scent. He seemed to envelop her senses, and she sighed in contentment.

"Sit by the fire," he commanded, gathering cushions for her to recline on, and Vannah obeyed as though she had no will of her own.

He left and returned minutes later dressed only in another robe and now bearing several plush towels that smelled of dried lavender. While Vannah stared into the glowing coals with glazed, heartsick eyes, Martin removed her water-stained shoes and stockings, then gently began drying her cold, wet feet.

"Feel better?"

Vannah nodded without looking at him.

Then Martin began massaging her toes and the soles of her feet with his strong, warm fingers, slowly kneading and rubbing the life back into them. Vannah closed her eyes and purred in contentment as they lost their stiffness and became supple again.

"Thank you," she murmured, reaching out her hand to touch his face as though to reassure herself that he was real and she was not dreaming.

He smiled. "Ah, but there's more."

Martin positioned himself behind her and drew her

against him so he could dry her hair with the other towel. He left her side only once, to answer a knock at the door, and returned bearing a supper tray.

"You must be famished," he said, setting it down on the floor.

Vannah nodded and began eating greedily while Martin poured himself a glass of wine.

"Do you feel like telling me what happened tonight?" he asked, his eyes as dark and glittering as green glass in the firelight.

So, in between doing justice to the hot barley soup and tender spring lamb that Mrs. MacGregor had prepared, Vannah told Martin about returning home and finding the house deserted, with the baby left alone and screaming in his crib.

She set down her fork as a great shudder passed through her body, making her teeth click together. "If I hadn't come home when I did . . . something appalling could have happened to my baby, Martin, and Basil would have been responsible."

And that had been the final blow that had propelled her into his arms at long last. Martin knew that Vannah wouldn't have left Basil for her own sake, but she would to protect her child.

Martin reached out and cupped her cheek lovingly, relieved that her eyes had lost that dazed, defeated look. "It's all over, Vannah," he said quietly and with great conviction. "Lewis will be safe here, with us. No one will ever harm him again."

"But there's more," she added, her voice troubled as she rose and went to the ulster. Vannah fumbled through the pockets, took out a leather case, and handed it to Martin. "I found this in Basil's bedroom."

When Martin saw what was inside, he felt a mixture of rage and revulsion well up in his throat. "What's it for?"

he said savagely, through clenched teeth. "Opium? Morphine?"

"A drug called cocaine, I think," Vannah replied, resuming her place by the fireside.

Martin just shook his head as he closed the leather case with a fierce snap and set it aside. "I have heard a little about the insidious effects of cocaine. You're well rid of him, Vannah. Basil Edgewood is like a sinking ship. You either stay aboard and be pulled down with him or leave and save yourself."

"I did love him once, a long time ago, when I thought I had lost you. But I was wrong about Basil, so very wrong."

Now Martin looked deep into her eyes and said, "You will stay with me this time?"

Vannah nodded, suddenly twisting off her wedding ring and flinging it into the fire. "I will be your mistress for as long as you want me."

"You will be my mistress only until your divorce from Basil becomes final," he said sternly. "Then you'll become my wife."

A teasing smile played about her mouth. "Are you asking me, or ordering me, to marry you?"

"Begging you," he replied, taking her free hand and kissing the backs of her fingers. "And if you refuse, I shall have no other recourse but to abduct you, lock you in the Ashwood attics, and make love to you until you see the wisdom of accepting my proposal."

Vannah took Martin's wineglass and set it out of the way. Then she propped herself up on one elbow and turned to him. "I don't think you need the Ashwood attics for that," she murmured from behind a golden veil of hair.

Her voice was so husky and inviting that Martin caught his breath. "You're sure, Vannah?"

She unbelted her robe and let it fall away from her body. "As sure as I was at Clairvaux."

Then, much to Martin's surprise and delight, Vannah pushed her weight against one of his shoulders until he was lying on his back, then she pinned him down with her own body and began kissing him in earnest. He lay there passively, savoring the exciting pressure of her soft lips against his own. When her tiny, pointed tongue demanded entrance, he gave himself up to her willingly, letting her explore and discover to her heart's content. Then she pulled away, only to shower the lightest of kisses on his face, down his chin, and into the hollow at the base of his throat. The tantalizing scent of perfume and damp hair filled his nostrils, reminding him of other nights when he had held her in his arms.

When he reached for her, Vannah stayed his hand. "No," she whispered. "You must allow me to make love to you this time. Imagine that I have bound you hand and foot and you are helpless to refuse me. My slave."

As Martin closed his eyes and fell back unresisting, he didn't know whether the pounding in his ears was the sound of the rain lashing against the roof or the beat of his own heart.

Now Vannah unbelted his robe and opened it, pushing the material aside until his entire body was exposed, yet Martin felt only a delicious warmth, especially when he peered up at her through half-closed lids and saw the unbridled desire in her eyes as they greedily roved over his naked body.

Then she began the most delicious assault on Martin's senses that he had ever experienced at a woman's hands. Sometimes her touch was delicate and teasing as she trailed her fingers slowly down his stomach or up his sensitive inner thigh. Other times it was just rough enough to make him gasp aloud with surprise and pleasure. He could sense her watching him closely for his reactions to her ardent caresses, and those that pleased him were repeated in a dozen obliging ways.

When he felt her kisses searing his rigid sex, Martin's eyes flew open. "Good Lord, Savannah!"

Vannah stopped only long enough to chuckle lasciviously and murmur, "Do I shock you?" before continuing shamelessly.

He tried to say that she merely delighted him with her boldness and inventiveness but finally abandoned the attempt and succumbed to the mounting wave of rapture steadily building within him.

Suddenly Vannah eased herself onto him with a sharp gasp of anticipation. She fit him perfectly, like a scabbard to a sword, and when she began rocking so sensuously, Martin could remain passive no longer and matched her rhythm, occasionally reaching up to fondle her full breasts until she made little mewling sounds of passion deep in her throat.

Then Martin was truly enslaved by his overwhelming need to reach the pinnacle of ecstasy with her. As his desire crested in a rush, the room seemed to explode into bright fragments of color, like the bits and pieces in a kaleidoscope, and he cried out Vannah's name again and again when he felt the voluptuous spasms overtake her as well.

With a scream she collapsed on top of him, and they lay locked in each other's arms, entwined as one, their mutual hunger finally appeased.

Later, as Vannah lay curled against her lover, her head pillowed against his muscular shoulder, she said, "This is only the third time I've ever made love with a man."

Martin stirred enough to turn and stare at her incredulously. "You mean your own husband never— Then how do you explain Lewis?"

Vannah giggled at that, then became somber once again. "Basil came to my bed, but only to satisfy his own desires. He never made love to me the way you do, Martin."

He stroked her damp, tangled hair and held her tightly. "My poor, poor darling. That must have been hell for you."

"It was. To have known such bliss in your arms and then experience someone like Basil . . ."

Martin rose and extended his hand to her. "Well, we shall just have to make up for lost time, now won't we?"

They left the cool, dying fire for the cozy warmth of Martin's bed. There he made love to Vannah throughout most of the night, until all memory of Basil Edgewood was burned from her body in the cleansing fires of Martin's love.

Chapter Twenty-One

THE FOLLOWING MORNING, Vannah stirred out of a sound sleep to become aware of a man's heavy leg thrown across her body possessively so she couldn't escape. At first she panicked, feeling that Basil had crept into her room and forced his unwelcome attentions on her, but as she became more cognizant of her surroundings, the fear vanished along with last night's storm.

The moment she saw the sun streaming in through the leaded windows she had designed, she knew that she was in Martin's bedroom. When she turned and saw his dark head lying next to hers on the pillow, his face as calm and reposed as a sleeping child's, she felt such an overwhelming rush of love, she thought she would burst from it.

Suddenly all of the events of last night came rushing back to her with the crushing force of a tidal wave, causing Vannah to tremble and snuggle closer to Martin for protection. When she had fled with Lewis to seek refuge with Martin, Vannah hadn't even considered what would happen when Basil returned to their dark, empty house and found their son missing from his crib. But she didn't care. As far as Vannah was concerned, Basil had forfeited all claims to their son when he placed Lewis's life in danger.

"Good morning."

Vannah turned to find Martin's green eyes open and watching her.

"Good morning," she replied with a lazy smile as she ran her fingers through his tousled curls. "Did you sleep well?"

"After the way you wore me out last night? I should hope so, vixen."

Vannah smiled wickedly and she continued her explorations down his strong, corded neck and across the wiry hairs of his chest. "How would you say I compared to all of your other women, the ones you kept company with after breaking off with me?"

His look was one of chagrin. "Who told you?"

"Ah! You don't like being found out, do you? It was Watson, who else?"

A look of annoyance passed across Martin's face. "Ah, yes, who else but Watson?" Then he gave Vannah a long, level look. "Judging from that dangerous glint in your lovely blue eyes, you're furious with me, aren't you?"

She raised herself up on one elbow. "Not furious. Jealous. Just the thought of another woman sharing your bed, pleasing you more than I . . ."

"Then I must explain something to you." Martin took Vannah's hand and held it against his chest. "After you told me that you were expecting Basil's child, I went out of my mind. Imagine my feelings of hopelessness, of frustration. To be so close to winning you again, and then losing you . . ." He shrugged helplessly. "I just wanted to cut you out of my life the way a surgeon amputates a diseased limb. So I tried to replace you with someone else. I failed."

"I'm glad, Martin," she said with heartfelt relief. "I couldn't bear to lose you to another woman, especially the Baroness Minska."

"I'll have you know that I never slept with Sophia. We have a professional relationship, nothing more. And as for the others . . ." He reached for Vannah and held her tightly, burying his face in her soft, fragrant hair. "They may have shared my bed, but none of them ever won my heart, my love."

Suddenly Vannah sat bolt upright. "Goodness! I'd almost forgotten about Lewis. I haven't heard him crying for his breakfast this morning."

"I'm assuming that's because the incomparable Mrs. Mack is clucking over him like a mother hen. She's a wonder with babies, you know. She can make them do anything."

Vannah looked around the room in alarm. "And where are my clothes? Martin, I took nothing with me when I left Basil. I have nothing to wear!"

"Don't distress yourself. I'm sure Mrs. Mack whisked them away to be laundered and dried." Now he leered at her. "You'll just have to remain naked in my bedroom, my love, or perhaps we can construct a Roman toga out of one of these sheets." Martin sat up and pushed her hair aside so he could nuzzle the warm nape of her neck. "I think you'd look quite delectable wrapped in nothing more than a sheet."

"Martin, be serious for a moment! I can't very well run around naked."

"As you wish," he grumbled, flinging the sheet back and rising. "I shall put on my dressing gown and investigate the Case of the Disappearing Clothes."

But when Vannah saw him standing there, as sleek and virile as a stallion, she felt her desire for him suddenly reawaken with a jolt. Before Martin could take one step away from the bed, she caught at his hand to stop him.

"I think my clothes can wait," she murmured, lying back against the pillows and flinging aside the concealing sheet.

He let his eyes devour her ivory nakedness, then, with a lusty chuckle, rejoined her on the bed.

As Martin had suspected, the efficient Mrs. Mack had spirited away Vannah's wet and dirty clothes to the laundry, so, after Vannah bathed, dressed, and looked in on a quiet, contented Lewis, she joined Martin downstairs for luncheon, since it was already one o'clock in the afternoon.

As they finished a collation of cold meats, cheese, and fruit, Ivers said, "Begging your pardon, Your Lordship, but early this morning Mr. Basil Edgewood came to the front gate demanding to see you."

Vannah's food turned to sawdust in her mouth, and she felt suddenly cold all over.

"And what did you tell him, Ivers?" Martin asked.

"Just that you had not yet risen. I told him to call again at two o'clock, if that is convenient, sir."

"Yes, that is fine, Ivers."

"Very good, sir. Will there be anything else?"

"No, Ivers. That will be all."

When the butler left the room, Martin saw Vannah's stricken, fearful expression, and quickly reached out to grasp her hand. "You have nothing to fear, my love. He can't force you to go back with him, and he can't take Lewis away from you."

"I—I really don't want to see him again."

"I will be right by your side, Vannah. We will face Basil together."

As she looked across the table at him, his jaw set in a resolute line and his eyes shining at the prospect of doing battle for her, Vannah suddenly felt all her fears vanish. Together she and Martin were invincible.

She smiled and returned the pressure of his fingers. "My Sir Lancelot . . ."

Martin shook his head. "I rather doubt that a woman who defies her father to follow her own road needs someone to rescue her like a knight of old."

"Perhaps I don't need rescuing, Martin, but I do still need you."

"And I hope you will never stop needing me."

As Vannah looked at him with adoration she suddenly had a revelation and shook her head in wonder.

Martin, so attuned to her every mood, said, "What is it?"

"I've just realized that you are the only man who has ever loved me for myself."

He grinned and winked at her. "And your body. And your artistic talent, of course."

"Martin, be serious." When she had his attention again, Vannah said, "Basil loved me for Gerrold's fortune, and Paul loved me because he thought he could save me from the corrupting influences of wealth." Now she smiled. "But you, Martin, have always just loved me for what I am."

He reached out across the table and squeezed her hand. "And I always shall. Now let's get ready to face Basil, shall we?"

Even with Martin by her side, Vannah still dreaded their upcoming confrontation with her husband.

Promptly at two o'clock Basil called again and was shown to the drawing room.

Vannah, who had been pacing nervously, stopped when she heard Basil's footsteps approaching and went right to Martin's side. He slipped his arm around her waist, gave her an encouraging smile, and dropped a light kiss on her forehead.

"What a touching little scene." Basil sneered, bursting into the room before Ivers could even announce him.

"Edgewood," Martin said, greeting him coolly and signaling the butler to leave them.

When Basil stared at her out of malevolent, dark eyes, Vannah returned his look with a cold, contemptuous glare of her own but said nothing.

"What in the hell are you doing here, Mrs. Edgewood, and what have you done with my son?" Basil demanded.

"I've left you, Basil," she replied calmly, "and I've taken Lewis with me."

Basil just regarded her with a look of sheer stupefaction. "Left me? What nonsense is this? And where is my son?"

"You heard me, Basil. I said I've left you. I no longer can bear being married to you." Vannah glanced over at Martin and smiled, then turned her attention back to Basil. "Lewis and I will be staying here with Martin from now on. And I'm going to divorce you as soon as possible."

Basil reached up to angrily sweep a lock of hair out of his eyes, and his nostrils were distended like a overexerted racehorse. "You don't mean any of it, Vannah. You can't!"

"I do mean every word of it, Basil," she said. "I'm not returning to Clerkenwell with you."

Now Basil turned his wrath on Martin. "You planned to steal my wife from me all along, didn't you, Fleet?" He waved his hand contemptuously at the drawing room windows. "All of this design business . . . it was just a ploy to be alone with my wife, wasn't it?"

"I'm sorry, Edgewood, but you'll have to take the blame for losing Vannah," Martin replied smoothly. "If you had been more considerate, more loving, she would still be with you."

Basil was silent for a few moments as he let their words sink in. Finally he said to Vannah, "So now you're discarding a life of respectability to become this scurvy knave's whore."

Vannah felt Martin start, and she put out a hand to restrain him. "I love Martin, Basil, and I'm going to stay with him. You can call me any name you like, but it will not alter the fact that I am not going back to you."

Once he saw that anger and sarcasm would not get him what he wanted, Basil made a play for Vannah's sympathies.

"Please, fair lady," he begged piteously. "Please give me another chance. I promise I'll change. I promise to be a good husband to you."

"Basil, I've given you one too many chances already."

"But my son, Vannah!" Basil's voice was shrill with desperation. "You said a son deserves to know his own father. Are you going to go back on your word and keep me away from my boy?"

Martin sensed Vannah start to tremble by his side, and for one terrible instant he feared that her husband's pleas would undermine her resistance and she would capitulate.

But when Vannah said, "How dare you try to use Lewis to your own advantage," Martin realized that she was shaking in anger.

Now Vannah rounded on Basil. "If you truly cared so much about your son, why did you leave him alone last night? You left a four-month-old baby alone, damn you! He could have strangled himself or choked to death! I came home on the early train last night to find our house deserted and poor Lewis wailing his lungs out. Where were you, Basil?"

"I—I had to go out," he muttered. "Damn it, Vannah, I only left him for half an hour."

"Did you go out to be with one of your women, Basil? Or"—she reached into the pocket of her dress, took out the leather case, and showed it to him—"because you needed more of your cocaine?"

Basil's face turned a pasty shade of white. "Where—how did you know?"

"You're a drug addict, aren't you, Edgewood?" Martin accused.

Basil regarded them with a contemptuous curl of his lip. "I don't expect two petty, conventional minds like yours to understand. I am not addicted to cocaine. I can stop taking it at any time. I just choose not to, that's all, because it stimulates my mind and frees me to create."

"Judging by the novel you submitted to me," Martin said, "I would say that it failed."

Basil glared at Vannah, his lip curled in a sneer. "And as for other women . . . why shouldn't I? You never understood what I needed from a woman."

Vannah thought of all the endless nights she had endured Basil's shame and abuse in their marriage bed, and she felt like clawing his eyes out. But she put her hands behind her back and restrained herself.

"And I don't care to listen to your excuses, Basil," Vannah added curtly. "You're not fit to be a father to my child."

"Vannah, please! You mustn't take my son away from me. You mustn't!"

Martin took a step forward. "Edgewood, we've had enough. I think it's about time you left."

"Not until I see my son."

Vannah looked at Martin and shook her head.

Suddenly Basil's face twisted and he screamed, "I will have my son!" before bolting out of the drawing room.

Martin raced after him with a terrified Vannah not far behind. They caught up to Basil in the foyer, just as he was about to charge up the staircase. He only managed to climb up four steps when Martin reached up with his long arm, grasped Basil by the back of his coattails, and pulled. With a strangled cry Basil lost his balance and fell backward, collapsing in a heap at the foot of the stairs.

"I want you out, Edgewood." Martin snarled as he towered above Basil's still form. "Now!"

Without warning a panting Basil managed to spring into a crouching position and hurl himself at Martin's legs. While Vannah watched in horror, Martin went down like a felled oak, and Basil leapt on top of him, his hands seeking a stranglehold on Martin's neck.

Martin managed to clutch at Basil's wrists to relieve the crushing pressure against his windpipe, but as he fought against the burning pain in his lungs, he knew that he had to find some way to break the stranglehold. He heard Vannah scream, then she was attacking Basil herself, twining her fingers in his hair and pulling with all her might. Basil screeched in pain, then released Martin long enough to shove Vannah and send her flying against the opposite wall.

The extra few seconds was all the time Martin needed.

While Basil's attention was focused on Vannah, Martin made his move. His fist shot up, dealing his adversary a glancing blow on the jaw. Then Martin lunged and knocked Basil away.

Vannah, who had the wind knocked out of her when she hit the wall so hard, could only watch the fight in a mixture of horror and fascination. She knew she should call out for Ivers or one of the other men to come to their master's aid, but she didn't have the strength. Besides, although she abhorred seeing two men battering each other so violently, she realized that Martin needed to fight Basil to satisfy some primitive male instinct older than time.

The stillness of the foyer was broken with grunts and groans of exertion as the two men rolled together on the floor in a violent embrace. When they pulled apart and staggered to their feet, Vannah was elated to see that Martin looked the less worse for wear, with only a skinned cheekbone. Basil, on the other hand, had a thin line of blood trickling out of the corner of his mouth, and he could barely stand.

"What's it to be, Edgewood?" Martin said in a rasping voice. "Are you going to leave while you can still walk, or am I going to dump you, unconscious, outside my gate?"

"I . . . want . . . my son," Basil said out of the other corner of his mouth, then took a swing at Martin.

Martin blocked the blow with his left arm and delivered a jab of his own. Vannah cringed at the sickening crack of bone striking bone. Then Basil's head snapped back, and he collapsed on the floor like a rag doll drained of sawdust.

Martin stared down at his vanquished adversary, then turned to Vannah. "Are you all right?"

She nodded and ran to him. "More to the point, are you?"

Still breathing hard from exertion, he managed to nod.

Vannah took his hand and examined his skinned knuckles, then looked up at his face. "Oh, Martin . . ." she murmured in dismay, gingerly touching his cheek.

"If you think I look bad, you should see the other fellow," Martin replied with a grin.

Suddenly Ivers appeared, glanced at Basil, and wrinkled his nose as if there were an offensive odor permeating the air. "Shall I remove Mr. Edgewood from the premises, sir?"

"Please do, Ivers, and get one of the other men to help you."

"Very good, sir."

A footman appeared out of nowhere, and he and Ivers each took an arm and began dragging Basil away.

When they were alone, Martin took Vannah in his arms and crushed her to him. "It's over, my love. You'll never have to see Basil Edgewood again."

Vannah shook her head. "I can't believe that I'm finally, truly free."

"Only until you marry me."

She locked her arms behind his neck and smiled up at the face she had loved ever since she was eleven years old. "And that, my love, is the best freedom of all."

One sunny afternoon in May of the following year, the tranquillity of St. John's Wood was suddenly shattered by the wheezing, sputtering, and chugging of a motorcar as it rolled up in front of Martin Ash's house and came to a shuddering, smoky halt.

The driver, his identity concealed by a long dust coat, cap, and goggles, stepped down, then walked around to the other side to assist his passenger, who was similarly attired.

"My dear Lady Fleet," he said with a smile as he lifted his goggles and extended his arms to her.

"My dear husband," Vannah replied, removing her protective hood and goggles, then allowing Martin to swing her down.

She gave a shaky sigh of relief. "Motorcars! I thought half the horses we passed were going to bolt right down the street and kill someone." Then she smiled at him. "Now, what is this other surprise you have for me? I thought a harrowing drive to our wedding in your motorcar was quite enough of a surprise for one day."

"Dying of curiosity, are you?" he said with a teasing grin.

"Quite frankly, yes."

As they walked arm and arm up to the front gate, Martin said, "I hope you will be pleased with it."

"Martin, you have given me far too much already."

Suddenly Vannah noticed something that had never been there before, a shiny brass plaque bolted into the stone. It was engraved with the words *Petit Clairvaux*.

She felt her eyes fill with sentimental tears. "Oh, Martin . . ."

"You once asked me what I was going to name my house," he said. "I couldn't think of a better one than where we first loved each other. But at the time you still belonged to another man, and I didn't want to remind you of what we had once shared. However, now that we are finally together . . ."

Vannah smiled and shook her head, scarcely daring to hope that fortune was smiling at them. The painful past was behind her, and there was only the future, bright, glowing, and filled with hope, stretching out before her like a wide, endless sea.

"Martin, will we always be just as happy as we are today?" Vannah asked, hugging him fiercely, scarcely daring to hope.

He grinned. "No one can foretell the future, but to quote Watson Greene, the best architect in the world, 'Yes, yes, *yes!*' "

Then he opened the gate for her, and together they strolled up the flagstone path.

About the Author

Leslie O'Grady was born and raised in Connecticut, where she lives with her husband, Michael. A graduate of Central Connecticut State University, she worked as a public-relations writer for a television station and a hospital before retiring to write fiction full-time. When not writing, Ms. O'Grady enjoys movies, museums, and collecting books about nineteenth-century England and Art Nouveau, which provided the inspiration for *Passion's Fortune*. She is the author of several romantic suspense novels. *Passion's Fortune* is her first historical romance.